MORE COOL
SCHOOL STORIES

RED FOX

A Red Fox Book

Published by Random House Children's Books
20 Vauxhall Bridge Road, London SW1V 2SA

A division of Random House UK Ltd
London Melbourne Sydney Auckland
Johannesburg and agencies throughout the world

Runners first published in Great Britain 1995
simultaneously by The Bodley Head Children's Books
and Red Fox
Text copyright © Sue Robinson 1995

Graphicat first published in Great Britain 1991
by Julia MacRae
Text copyright © Marilyn Watts 1991

The Present Takers
first published in Great Britain by
The Bodley Head Children's Books 1983
Magnet Books 1985
Red Fox edition 1994
Text copyright © Aidan Chambers 1983

This Red Fox anthology first published 1999

Phototypeset by Intype London Ltd
Printed and bound in Norway by Ait Trondheim AS

RANDOM HOUSE UK Limited Reg. No. 954009

ISBN 0 09 940023 5

CONTENTS

RUNNERS

Susan Gates

CHAPTER ONE

Five, four, three, two, one: *Brringgg!* The bell for first break hasn't finished ringing before I'm off, like a runner from the blocks. I'm out that classroom, halfway down the corridor before the others have started packing up their books. The teacher's yelling: 'Hey! Wait a minute!' But I don't stop. I've got things to do. And besides, it's only Mad Maxwell, the geography teacher who has riots in his classroom and sticks his maps on the ceiling so people can't nick them or do graffiti on them. Gives you a crick in the neck staring up every time you want to check where the Nile delta is, or Montreal.

I'm zooming along corridors now. There are people stampeding out of classrooms so I go into evasive mode, ducking past year eleven hulks, dodging clumps of baby-faced kids from year seven. No one is surprised. They're used to me speeding here, there and everywhere. Some even shout: 'Hiya Sparrow!' But they don't expect an answer. They know I'm on important business. And I'm always pushed for time.

The school timetable flashes up inside my head like my mind is a computer screen. I know where everybody in the school is supposed to be at any time of day. Just ask me. You want to know where Nicky is now? Easy. He's down the gym, getting changed after basketball.

I exit the school timetable and my mind punches in a plan of the school building. My plan shows every staircase, every corridor, every toilet block. It shows you how to get down into the basement or up on to the roof. I'm working it out now – the shortest route to Nicky, in the changing rooms. And all this time, remember, I'm running, always running.

I change direction so fast my trainers squeal on the floor like car tyres. It'll be quicker going by the fire escape. Ten minutes into break-time and still three messages to go. Things are getting hectic. I've got to think seriously about taking on some help.

Now I'm skidding to a stop outside the boys' changing rooms. Whiffs of sweaty feet and cheesy trainers come through the open door. But I can't go in. Girls aren't allowed in there.

'Is Nicky there? It's Sparrow. Got a message for him.'

He comes to the door towelling his hair. He's been in the shower. Nicky's probably the best looking boy in the entire school. 'Hello Sparrow,' he says. My legs go mushy. But even though he's looking at me, he's not really seeing me. He's only interested in what I'm giving him – a tightly folded piece of pale green paper. It's from his girlfriend, Heather: five feet eight tall, long blonde hair, long

tanned legs, looks like a model. You know the type.
I hate her guts.

"Suppose you've read this?' he says, grinning
down at me. Nicky always talks to me like I'm a
child. Water-drops from his hair sprinkle my white
shirt.

I shrug: 'How should I know what it says.'

"'Cos you've read it. You always read the messages.
You know more about what's going on than anybody
else in the school. So just tell me, OK?' He throws
the paper away, flicking it over his shoulder like it
was a piece of rubbish.

'OK.' I'm jogging on the spot now, revving up,
because in five seconds' time I've got to blast off
down that corridor. 'It says: "See you outside
Safeway, eight o'clock. Luv ya, Hev." I mean, she
can't spell, can she? She's not too bright.'

It's one of my rules that I never, ever hang around
to comment on messages. But somehow, this time,
I can't help myself.

Nicky laughs and aims a punch in my direction.
'Cheeky little brat!'

Check my watch. Two minutes behind schedule.
'Any reply?'

'Tell her I'm too busy tonight. Tell her I got
other things to do.'

'What?' I'm so surprised I stop running. What's
going on? Nicky and Heather are the school's best
known, most serious couple. They've been together
six months.

'You heard.' He digs in his pocket and hands me

the money. That's ten pence — what I charge for delivering your message, anywhere in the school. Discretion assured. Swiftness assured.

I break another of my rules: 'It's free to you, Nicky.' Everybody knows that I never, ever, take messages for free. I don't give credit either. But this is different. This is one message it'll be a pleasure to deliver.

He doesn't thank me. Never expected him to.

On the move again. Clattering up the fire escape juggling timetables and maps inside my head.

I know where Lexie is. He's feeding his face by the chocolate machine, the one outside the science block, because Lexie's class has got double science next. Lexie is a sad case: a man-mountain, fourteen stone of jiggling fat. He's exactly where I thought he'd be, tearing the wrapping off a Mars Bar. Breathless, I dash up: 'Message for you Lexie! This kid says he's going to beat you up after school. Only problem is — he doesn't know where to start.'

I stretch my arms wide and stagger round like someone wrestling with a giant blubber-monster. I'm good at acting. But if you want acting with your message it'll cost you ten pence extra.

'Who sent the message, Sparrow?' someone calls out.

I shrug and look mysterious. 'That's for you to find out.'

I'll take anonymous messages. I'll take any messages, anywhere in the school — long as you've got the money. You want to arrange a meeting; send a love letter; challenge someone to a fight? I'll take your message for you. You don't even have to move out of your chair. You don't have to write it down if you don't want to. I'll remember it. And if I can't, I'll write it on my hand in red biro. When business gets really hectic there are messages scrawled all the way up my arm.

Sometimes the messages are just a word. Sometimes they're like novels, pages and pages of tiny cramped-up writing. Swots print out their messages on word processors. Retards grunt them at me. Long as you pay me, I don't care. But my favourites are when people keep replying to each other. Like this, for instance:

'Claire, were you flirting with Stevie on the bus?'

'No I wasn't we were just talking.'

'Well he's mine keep your hands off.'

'You stuck-up bitch I'll talk to anyone I like.'

'You're a slag, Claire, everybody says so.'

'No I'm not you cow.'

'Yes you are what's those love bites on your neck then?'

'Haven't got no love bites.'

'Yes you have . . .'

I love quarrels like these. They earn me lots of money. Sometimes I'm carrying insults backwards and forwards for months. Even years . . .

The chocolate machine crowd is still hooting with laughter. Lexie looks confused. Then he starts laughing too. But, just before that, pain was flickering in his eyes. I saw it.

11

Nothing to do with me. Not my responsibility. That's another of my rules. I'm just the Runner, doing what I'm told. But as I pound along with my last message, Lexie's face slides into my mind, scrambling up the school plan.

'Not your problem . . .' I'm panting now, jogging up three flights of stairs. Business is booming. I'm going to have to take on extra help. I list all the good runners in the school, crossing each one off in my mind: 'Not him; he's a cretin. Not her; she's a rich bitch − doesn't need the money. Not her; she's a bigmouth − she'd tell everybody's secrets.'

I know lots of secrets. If you only knew what I know . . .

The last delivery is easy. It's an earring. An earring that some girl dropped at some other girl's house when she was sleeping over. I drag it out of my pocket as I run. Wouldn't be seen dead in it myself. It's a gold banana.

I don't just carry pieces of paper. I take all sorts of things round the school: money, that people owe to people; swaps, of clothes and computer games. The Runner keeps the school alive and humming. She's right there at the centre of every row, every rumour. The Runner knows everything that's going on.

'Oh, thanks, Sparrow,' the girl says when she gets her earring back. 'Thought I'd lost it!' She's a dork − just the type to wear a piece of fruit in her ear.

Brringg! End of break. I'm supposed to be in

Music. But the earring girl yanks my arm just as I'm zooming off. 'Wait a minute, Sparrow.'

I grit my teeth. She's only in year seven. She's got a cheek to call me Sparrow. 'Well? I'm in a hurry.'

She pulls a blue fluffy bunny from her bag. 'Sophie in 7R left this at my house when she was sleeping over. Can you give it back?'

'Money?' I rasp at her. Only Nicky gets his messages for free. Only Nicky's allowed to be rude to me. Dorks have to be polite.

She fumbles in a pink plastic purse that's got a rash of red beads on it. It's shaped like a strawberry.

'Come on, come on!'

I grab the money and the blue bunny, stuff them in my pocket, and I'm off, bombing at top speed through empty corridors. Everyone's in lessons now. But I've calculated for that. Mrs Frink, the music teacher, will still be in the staff room stubbing out her third cigarette. She's always five minutes late after morning break. When you do my job, it pays to be observant, know the habits of the teachers.

Even though I'm cutting it very fine, something I see out of the window makes me skid to a halt.

'Wow!'

There's a boy out there, on the running track. He's got big flappy shorts and white legs, thin as bones. But he's the best runner I've ever seen. Better than me even. He's running like a wolf, with long easy loping strides that are eating up the track. He's got style. But then he stops. And he's just another

13

skinny kid wrapping his arms around himself, shivering in the wind. I can't believe that I've just seen him run like that.

'Who *is* that kid?' Never seen him before. He must be new. I don't like not knowing. I pride myself on knowing everything that's going on.

No time to find out. There's Mrs Frink, the music teacher, plodding in her big leather sandals down the corridor. Accelerate to warp speed! I hurtle past her, crashing through the door as she's reaching out her hand to open it. She blinks and looks around in a dazed sort of way. Don't think she even saw me. I moved so fast that I was just a blur. Just a whooshing noise in her ears.

The messages are stacking up for lunch break. There's the fluffy bunny from banana earring. And Nicky's message of course – I'm looking forward to delivering that. But, for now, I slide into my seat and shut my brain down. Lessons are the time when I relax . . .

CHAPTER TWO

Keep your head down, keep a low profile, blend in with the walls – that's my rule for surviving lessons. If you're lucky, teachers won't even learn your name. Mrs Frink drones on and on about some mouldy music writer who's been dead two hundred years. She's asking questions. But I never answer. I don't even lift my head. Never make eye contact with teachers – that's another of my rules. It only encourages them. Makes them think you're interested or something. But I only come alive outside of lessons. That's when all the important things are happening.

When I started at this school, three years ago, I was a sad case. Scared of the crowds, of getting lost, scared of not finding the toilets in time. You'd see me cringing round the place, keeping close to walls. I didn't belong in any group. I was an outsider. Until, one day, this happened:

Two girls, two of the popular people, were standing next to me in the dinner queue. They were carrying on this private conversation as if I was invisible. It was impossible not to listen . . .

'Well, tell him then, tell him that you're not going out with him tonight.'

'I'm not going to tell him. It's too embarrassing. You go and tell him for me. *Please*. You're my best friend, aren't you?'

'What! He's at basketball practice. That's miles away! By the time I get back here there'll be no cheeseburgers left. I'll tell him for you later.'

'No! I want you to tell him *right now*.' She stamped her foot on the ground. 'Or I might change my mind. And then it'll be your fault.'

'I'll tell him.'

Don't know why I said it. I don't usually do crazy things like that. They looked down at me as if I was some kind of irritating insect, pestering them.

'What did you say?'

I nearly lost my nerve: 'I'm a real good runner. I was really good at running in junior school.' It's true. In junior school I was famous for my fast running. 'You tell me his name. And I'll go and tell him. Be there and back before you get to the till. Honest.'

They laughed. They seemed to find it amusing. But I was deadly serious. 'Go on,' I begged them, 'let me take your message for you.' It was really important to me to take that message, to show them how fast I could run.

One of them shrugged. 'OK then.' She told me his name. 'Just tell him,' she said, 'that it's all over between us. But we can still be friends. Love Vicky.' And she reached out her hand for a banana, saw a tiny speck of black on it, and put it back.

I took off, running faster than I've ever run before. I knew even then that it was some kind of a trial, a chance to belong, to be where things were happening, instead of on the outside looking in.

When I got back their eyes nearly popped out of their heads. They were amazed! I tried to look casual. But my heart was trampolining; boing, boing, and my legs were all wobbly like the bones inside were melting.

'That was quick! Have you really been all that way?'

''Course!' I protested. 'Told you I'm a good runner.'

'All right then,' said one of them suspiciously. 'What did he look like?'

I started to tell her: tall, floppy brown hair, goofy teeth . . .

'No, no,' she said. 'I mean what did he look like when you told him the message?'

'Err, err.' I felt hot and sick. But I had to admit it. 'Never stayed to look,' I mumbled. 'Just took off again and ran here like mad. Do you want me to go back?'

It was a real relief when they just laughed. 'Well, next time,' they said, 'don't forget to stay long enough to see the expression on his face.'

I learned a lesson then. Because now I always hang around just long enough to see the expression on their faces. The people who send the messages almost always ask me about that.

Then Vicky flicked me ten pence. That was the next thing I learned – that people were willing to pay me to do their dirty work. 'Worth it,' she said, 'to have my own private Runner.'

Anyway, that was the start of it. After that, it sort of snowballed. It's got so busy that now I've got to think about taking on some help. Everybody wants to use me for their messages. It's the cool thing to do. Don't take them youself. Get Sparrow to do it for you.

I forgot about the nickname. I haven't explained about that yet. At junior school, when I was running in my shorts, they called me 'Sparrow-legs'. Even in this school, Sparrow-legs was my name. But all that changed after I became the Runner. People gave me some respect. If they're lucky, if I like them and they're not younger than me, they can call me Sparrow. But no one's allowed to call me Sparrow-*legs* any more. They'd better not. Because my head is crammed with secrets. I could cause big trouble for certain people, if I felt like it.

'And now,' Mrs Frink is saying, 'just complete this work sheet.'

Scribble, scribble. The trick is to look busy. You don't need to look interested, as long as you look busy. That way, you can just slide through lessons without making any ripples at all. But it's nearly time for the lunch-time bell and I'm worrying again about the messages.

They're stacking up again: Nicky's message; the fluffy bunny from banana ears, and now Stringer is hissing at me from the next table.

18

'Oi, Sparrow, tell Andy that it's paying-up time again. Else he knows what'll happen.'

I nod and mouth OK. No need to write this message down on my hand. I know it by heart. It's the same every week. Stringer pays me later, out of the money I collect from Andy.

Almost everyone is scared of Stringer, even teachers. But not me. Being his Runner protects me – I'm useful to him. Stringer's a hulk: big and slow with spiky red hair. He looks dumb but he isn't. He's intelligent and vicious. And very dangerous. They say he carries a knife round school. And I believe it. They say he's got a shotgun at home. So I'm extra careful to take his messages on time and bring all the money back. Then I'm safe from him. He never threatens me.

Brrinng! I stop doodling on the work sheet (I'm doing Nicky's name and mine inside a heart) and make a dive for the door.

'And this week's homework is . . .' Mrs Frink's voice is saying, faintly in the distance.

Messages are written on my hands and money's jingling in my pocket. But I'm still worried. Worried that I've got so much to do that I'll have to break my first rule. My first rule is: 'Speedy delivery guaranteed'. Sometimes I deliver within seconds. Sometimes it takes longer. But I've never once let a message hang over until the next day. By the next day gossip, secrets, rumours have all gone stale – they're yesterday's news. It's more than my reputation's worth not to deliver messages as fast as possible, while they're still fizzing.

'You're a victim of your own success,' I tell myself proudly as I sprint down the corridor with timetables and maps whirling round inside my head. 'And now you've absolutely, definitely got to get some help!'

CHAPTER THREE

Ten minutes into lunch break and already I'm way behind schedule. There are messages written half-way up my arms, bits of paper stuffed into my pockets. I'm hot and hassled – breaking out in a sweat. Things are getting out of control. And the trouble is that people are giving me more and more messages, until I'm bristling with them like the needles on a Christmas tree. I try to keep out of sight, use back stairs, fire escapes and basements. But everywhere I go it's 'Hey Sparrow, wait a minute!' and someone else shoves ten pence and a message into my hand.

I'm racing through the dining hall. Cauliflower cheese today: it stinks like old trainers. This is just a short cut – there's no time to stop and eat. Sometimes, rushing through a toilet block, taking messages to smokers, I'll shove my head under a tap, glug down a couple of gallons and let the cool water trickle on my face.

There's that boy – the brilliant runner who made me late for Mrs Frink's lesson. I skid to a halt. An idea just whizzed across my mind. It was a beautiful idea – like a shooting star.

21

I don't usually act like this – do things on impulse. Usually I'm a really cautious person. But I'm worried about the messages. Getting the messages delivered is more important than anything. And even as I'm going up to him, tiny warning bells are ringing in my brain. Why is he sitting on his own like that? There are people wandering about with loaded trays. But they avoid the empty places next to him.

Why is he eating his food like that? He's got an arm curled round his plate, protecting it. And his mouth is on a level with the table and he's shovelling in the mashed potato. He keeps peering round, like a dog guarding its dinner, as if somebody might steal his food away.

But I'm not suspicious – in fact I'm quite pleased. He looks stupid and that suits me fine. I prefer him stupid. All he'll have to do is run. He doesn't have to think. I'll do all the thinking.

He glares round again. And when he sees there's no danger he drops his head and carries on filling his mouth. I don't waste time on being friendly: 'You know who I am, don't you?'

His mouth falls open. Stupid, like I thought. All the tables round us have suddenly gone quiet. A tiny part of my brain wonders why that is.

'You know that I'm the Runner don't you? You've seen me round the school taking messages?'

He nods. I take hold of his chin and snap his mouth shut. It's gross, seeing all that food churning round in there.

'I'm a victim of my own success,' I tell him. 'I'm

just too popular. So I need someone to help me take the messages. And you're the fastest runner in the school. Faster even than me.'

It seems to take forever for my words to reach his brain.

'Look I haven't got all day. Do you want to be a runner or not? You'll get paid 5p for every message you take for me. You won't be running every day, of course. Just when things get hectic.'

I know the money's crap. But that's not the main thing. The main thing is the respect that comes with being a Runner. In this school, the Runner is a very important person.

He's still goggling at me, like I'm a three-headed monster or something. You'd think he'd be grateful to be asked. Most kids would give their right arm to be a Runner. But he's obviously a total loser – apart from being able to run.

There's not a sound from the tables round us.

And then, just as I'm moving on, his eyes light up. He's finally understood. And he seems really keen. He seems grateful, just like he ought to be.

His head'll drop off if he nods any faster. 'Yes,' he says. 'I'd like to be a Runner. I'd really like that.'

I'm not angry any more. I even flash him a quick smile. But then I get business-like. 'Right. But you'll have to do a time trial first. Make sure you're good enough.'

He's off, like a bullet from a gun. I give a heavy sigh. 'Come back here! You haven't got your messages yet!'

He spins round, looking embarrassed. It bothers me, just a little bit, that no one watching even sniggers when he comes trudging back. Usually, they jump on any opportunity to take the mickey.

But the seconds are ticking by. Quickly, I off-load some of my messages – the straightforward ones – then give him his instructions. He seems to be listening. But you can never tell. The crazy risk I'm taking suddenly hits me. What if he gets it all wrong? It's me that'll have to sort out the mess. At least I didn't give him any of Stringer's messages. I'm not *that* crazy.

'Five, four, three, two, one!' I count the seconds down and he's off again, skidding on a pool of greasy gravy. The swing doors flap like wings behind him.

I sit down in his place and give another deep weary sigh. It's great to rest my legs. His glass is still half-full of water – I gulp it down. It'd be so easy to fall asleep here, using my arms as a pillow. My head droops. Lower, lower . . . The dining hall noise shrinks away until it's just a buzz in the background . . .

My head jerks up again. Someone's calling my name. Not another message! But it's only Lexie, at the next table.

He's using a low, creepy voice like he's a ghost come to haunt me. 'Wake up, Sparrow. Don't you know about him, Sparrow? Don't you know why he was chucked out of his last school? I thought everyone knew that.'

I don't take much notice. Nobody takes much

notice of what Lexie says. 'Shut up, Lexie. You just talk rubbish.'

'You'll find out,' he whinges. He's got a smug smile on his face. 'You'll soon find out.'

But lots of other voices back me up. 'Yeah, shut up, Lexie.' They make me confident again. Lexie's warnings were giving me this queasy feeling in my stomach. Like someone walking on my grave.

I feel even better when my new Runner comes racing back into the dining hall. His face is still pale. In fact, he's hardly even worked up a sweat. I check my watch. Five minutes for five messages. Almost as good as me!

'You can't have delivered all those.' I glower at him suspiciously. My eyes are narrow slits. He'd better not be conning me on his very first run.

'Yes I have! Go and check if you like.'

He's hopping up and down in distress in case he can't make me believe him. But I do believe him. He doesn't look the devious type. He's probably too stupid for that.

'Hope you didn't mix them up,' I grumble. But secretly, I'm really pleased. I was scared that I'd made some terrible mistake, that there was something dangerous about this boy that everybody knew about but me. But he doesn't look dangerous. With that weedy body he'd have trouble breaking through the crust on a cherry pie.

'Was I any good then?' He sounds anxious. He's trying to pat down his wild, black hair. But it keeps springing up all over the place.

I say, casually. 'Good enough.'

'Yaaay!' he yells, punching the air. It startles me. But everyone at the other tables cringes back as if a firework had just gone off. Beats me why they're so twitchy.

'See you in the entrance hall tomorrow then, before first lesson. And I might have some more messages for you to take.'

'Don't I get paid? For the messages I just took?'

'Course not. That was just a trial. You don't start work properly until tomorrow.'

For a moment, it looks as if he's going to argue. But he just grabs a half-eaten bread roll from his plate and goes out, tearing at it with his teeth. He's got the table manners of a pig. But that's not my business. All that matters to me is that he can run like a cheetah.

Don't even know his name. 'Must ask him tomorrow,' I remind myself. But it's not important.

And now there's lots of time left to take Nicky's message to Heather. Mustn't forget Stringer's message either. That would be suicidal.

Heather's in the year ten common room. She's surrounded by crowds of fans — the centre of attention, like she always is. She's too perfect to be true. You never see her with a single spot. Like the good fairy waved a wand over her in her cradle and said: 'This child shall be blessed with a zitless skin!' This reminds me of the crater at the side of my nose. Feels like it's going to erupt again. Now I've remembered it I just have to stop to squeeze it.

The group won't let me in. So I prowl around the outside. But no one notices. They're sharing some private joke and laughing, in high shrieky voices.

'Message for Heather – it's from Nicky!'

It makes me feel powerful when they all stop to look at me, when people stand aside to let me through.

Heather gives me a kind and gentle smile as if she's going to pat my head, like you would a little dog.

Stuck-up cow, I'm thinking.

'What's the message then, Sparrow?'

'Nicky says he can't go out tonight. He says he's got better things to do than going out with you.'

There's a gasp of surprise. Everyone's looking at me. I'm the centre of attention now. It makes me feel really good.

'You *sure* he said that?' She looks more hurt than angry. She flicks aside her long blonde hair so she can see me better. 'Were those his actual words?'

'Course they were. I never change a message. You know that.'

'Sorry, Sparrow.'

'Well,' (my foot's tapping impatiently) 'is there any reply then? I haven't got all day.'

The girls around her are giving her plenty of ideas. 'Tell the creep to get lost!' 'Tell him you've finished with him, permanently.' But she seems too dazed to speak. They've shut me out again, so I race for the door, as if I'm far too busy to hang around.

On my way to deliver Stringer's message, Nicky's standing, laughing with his mates by the Coke machine.

I go panting up to him and tug at the strap of his school bag so he'll look down and notice me.

He looks puzzled, as if he's forgotten who I am.

'It's Sparrow!' I remind him.

'Oh yeah – Sparrow.' Did he wink then at his mates? No – I must be seeing things.

He's got these gorgeous brown eyes.

'She sent you a reply,' I hear myself saying. 'Heather did. She said, "Get lost, you creep. I never want to see you again."'

It's not an absolute lie. Someone said it, even if it wasn't exactly Heather.

'What!' He looks as if he can't believe it.

Then more words come tumbling out my mouth. Can't seem to stop them: 'Ditch her, Nicky. She's a stupid cow anyway. She's not good enough for you.'

'Just shut it, Sparrow!' he screams at me, his face twisted up and ugly. 'When I want your advice I'll ask for it. You don't know what you're talking about!' And he turns away, ignoring me. He and his mates close into a huddle, whispering together. Their backs are a wall, shutting me out.

'I thought . . . I thought . . .' I stammer. But nobody is listening.

Somehow I drag myself back up the stairs. My trainers feel like concrete blocks. At the top, I sit down to rest. People shove past me. Someone treads on my hand, leaving a muddy boot print.

It's not Nicky's fault. I shouldn't have broken my own rules. It's one of my strictest rules, never ever to comment on a message. Never to give my own opinion. Nicky's right. I should have kept my mouth shut.

But even deciding it's not Nicky's fault doesn't make me feel any better.

I'm so fed up that it's halfway through Computer Studies before it hits me, like a fist in the stomach: 'Ohmygawd, Stringer's message!' How could I forget?

In half an hour on the school bus home, Stringer will be expecting me to give him Andy's money. I don't have it. I'm dead.

Time for drastic action. Timetables click up in my brain. My luck's in – Andy's got Geography with Mad Maxwell.

My hand shoots up: 'Sir, Sir, I'm going to be sick!' I double over, puff my cheeks out, ram my fist in my mouth, just to make it look extra convincing.

'Are you ill?' asks Mr Walker. He doesn't sound very interested. So I lean over, as if I'm just about to spew up in his new laser printer. Then he goes hysterical.

'Quick, girl, quick!' (He doesn't know my name.) He's flapping his hands to shoo me out of the door.

'Yurgh! Yurgh!'

That's me, staggering out the room, making gurgling, choking sounds. It works every time.

Behind me everyone is sniggering. They realize it's all an act. But they won't tell on me. They know it must be an urgent message if the Runner has to work in lesson time.

Once outside the door I'm up and running. I've done this twice before, when things have been really desperate. It's risky though. You have to know what you're doing. Miss Donaghy, or Ferretface – you wouldn't dare interrupt one of their lessons, not unless you've got a death wish. But Mad Maxwell – no problem. There's so much racket going on in his classroom that he won't notice that I've been and gone.

It's eerie, slipping through empty corridors. As if I'm the only one left alive after a deadly plague has wiped out the whole school.

There's another survivor. He's in the next block – you can see him through the big windows. He's slumped against the wall outside a classroom, his head hanging down as if it's very, very heavy. Then he lifts his head. It's my new Runner. Only he looks weird, with two red spots burning on his cheeks and his eyes bright and frantic. There's no time to stop, no time to think. The only thing that's important now is getting Stringer's money.

You can hear Mad Maxwell's lesson from halfway down the corridor. It's guerilla warfare in there. I push the door open and slide inside. The noise makes your eardrums go *twang*.

There's kids swarming all over. Mad Maxwell's somewhere at the front buried in an excited crowd. They're waving maps at him, shouting questions. He doesn't notice me – he wouldn't notice the

Terminator if he came crashing through the wall. Easy peasy. Just find Andy and shoot off again. Now where is he?

He isn't here. Panicking, I grab the nearest kid. He lets his friend out of a headlock: 'Who are you?' Then he yells out: 'Sir, Sir, there's someone come to see you, Sir!'

'Shut up!' I growl at him. 'Just tell me where Andy Summers is. I can't see him. He's supposed to be in this class isn't he?'

The kid giggles. I'm really worried now. I grab him by his tie and snarl: 'Tell me where he is.'

'All right, all right, don't get violent.' He smooths down his tie. I'm nearly screaming with impatience. My clenched knuckles are dead white, like bone.

'He went home at dinner time. Had a headache he says. But if you ask me,' sneers the kid, 'he's keeping out of Stringer's way.'

I'm appalled. 'What's he think he's doing going home? I've got a message for him – from Stringer.'

'That's why Andy's gone home,' pipes up a girl from behind me. 'He can't pay Stringer today. He's broke.'

'Can't pay Stringer?' I'm horrified. It's me that's going to have to face Stringer, empty-handed. Me that's going to get slaughtered.

'I'll kill him!' I screech. 'What's he playing at, skiving off lessons! Not paying Stringer. I'll kill him when he comes back!'

Mad Maxwell lifts his head up from a scrum of

kids. 'What are you doing here, Charlotte?' I'm amazed he remembers my name.

I don't answer of course. I just slip away, like a mirage. He'll think his mind is playing tricks.

On the school bus Stringer's roaring from the top deck: 'Where's my Runner? Where's that little cow got to?'

He can't see me. I'm downstairs, sitting right next to the Exit doors for a quick get away. But I can't help shuddering, imagining his dog's breath hot on my neck, his great shovel fist slamming down on my shoulder. I'm scrunching up small in my seat, trying to make myself invisible.

Now we're slowing down for my street . . . I dive off before the bus stops moving, start running as soon as my feet hit ground.

'Hey, you!' the driver's yelling after me.

But I've already taken cover in the nearest alley. Crouching down, with litter blowing round my legs, I wait until it's safe to come out. Then start walking home.

It's been an absolutely rubbish day. Nothing but trouble. The one good thing is that I've got myself a new Runner. But why do warning bells start clanging in my head every time I think about him?

'Don't be stupid!' I tell myself. 'He's fast, isn't he? He's the best. He did the trial OK. So what else is there to worry about?'

I wish I knew . . .

CHAPTER FOUR

It's a long, hot walk from my house to school. But I couldn't risk taking the bus this morning. There's no way I want to meet Stringer — not before I've collected his money from Andy.

There's something going on over there in the bus park. An excited crowd of kids is whooping and yelling, as if they're cheering people on. It sounds like a fight. 'Keep right away,' I warn myself. 'The last thing you need is to get mixed up in that. You're in enough trouble already.'

There's Andy, creeping round the side of the school.

'Andy!'

I'm just about to race after him with Stringer's message when Lexie comes puffing up. He's got something bad to tell me. You can tell by the smug grin that's plastered all over his face.

'Your new Runner's in the middle of that lot,' he says, jerking his thumb over his shoulder at the mob of kids. 'He's really entertaining. A real good laugh.'

'What're you talking about?' I can't keep the surprise out of my voice. Lexie hears it and looks pleased.

'Told you you didn't know everything. Told you he was a head-banger. Go and look,' he sneers at me, 'and see for yourself.'

He knows he's got me flustered. It's a struggle to stay cool: 'You're a fat freak, Lexie. Has anyone ever told you that?'

It's a feeble insult. He's heard it a zillion times before. So I can hardly believe it when he looks at me like a puppy that's been kicked. People call him names all the time. You'd think he'd have got used to it by now.

But I'm wasting time insulting him. I dive into the crowd and start worming through to the middle.

And there, on his own, in an empty circle, is my Runner. A boy dashes into the space holding out a football. 'You want it,' he sniggers. 'You come and get it!' He dances about like he's teasing a starving dog with a bit of meat. My Runner grabs for the football but the boy whisks it away and dashes back into the shelter of the crowd.

And they're all capering about and yelling. They're playing games with him – showing him the football then throwing it over his head to someone else in the mob. And my Runner's whirling round and round, trying to see where the ball is. 'Give it back,' he's screeching. 'It's mine!' There's a look on his face like a hunted animal.

Don't like this, it's really scary. Around me they're howling and chanting – I've never heard that kind of noise before.

'What's happening?' But the girl beside me is too

34

busy jumping up and down to answer. Her face is ugly with yelling. It's Sophie, banana earring's friend, who can't sleep at night without her blue fluffy bunny under her pillow.

Someone dodges out from the crowd, roars, 'Where's your ball now then?' at my Runner and then darts back to safety. I can see the football – it's bobbing over people's heads to the back of the crowd. Everyone's hot and shoving and screaming and the air's crackling with excitement like they're waiting for something to happen.

My Runner pulls back his lips to show his teeth. And he's snarling, snarling at them all.

'He's going!' shrieks one girl next to me. And all the crowd pull back. They stop shouting. Someone near me gives this weird hissing sigh, like a balloon going down. Everyone's eyes are fixed on my Runner.

He's going crazy, as if something snapped inside him. He's berserk, out of control, charging round his little space like a mad tiger round its cage.

This is what they've all been waiting for. He's screaming at them, swearing, lashing out with his fists. But his punches are so wild they don't connect. They just make people howl with laughter. 'Psycho psycho psycho,' a group of kids are singing next to me.

There's only me now. Only me left in the space around him. 'Look out Sparrow!' someone yells. 'He'll get you if you go too close.'

But I'm so shocked I stand my ground. He's

charging at me! It's OK. He'll recognize me any second now. But his face is twisted with rage and tears and it's clear he doesn't know me, doesn't know where he is, doesn't even know who he is. But I still can't move . . .

They drag me back just as his hands shoot out to grab my throat. 'Great, isn't it Sparrow?' someone's babbling in my ear. 'It works every time! He goes crazy like this every time. It's what he was thrown out his last school for. He wrecked a classroom. Bust it all to bits when he got in a rage.'

'Oh great,' I mutter to myself. 'Trust you, Sparrow. Trust you to choose a raving maniac for a Runner.'

'Teacher's coming!'

Everybody scatters. Except me. I'm left alone, watching him writhing on the ground, spitting out curses, clawing with his hands trying to grab my legs. I step backwards out of his reach.

It takes three teachers to hold him down. And the whole school's peering round corners, hanging out of windows, enjoying the show.

They go past me, with my Runner kicking out and struggling. He stares straight into my face. But his eyes are mad and blank. He doesn't know who I am.

A teacher says: 'He'll kill somebody one day, when he's in one of these moods.'

They frogmarch him into the building. And he's fighting and cursing them every inch of the way.

The big doors crash shut behind them. Show's over. There's nothing left to see.

It's very quiet when they've gone in. Everybody's quiet. Even the rows of people hanging out the windows.

Kids begin to sneak out of their hiding places. Some are still smirking. But most look embarrassed. They don't look in each other's eyes.

They seem to have forgotten about the football. It's not even a proper football, just a cheap plastic one, the kind you get from Woolworth's. For some reason I pick it up, turn it round and round in my hands.

They should have left him alone. If the teachers had left him alone his anger would have burnt away, just fizzled out. They shouldn't have made such a big deal about it. He would have worn himself out, eventually. I know, because I used to lose my temper, just like that . . .

But it's really urgent that I find Andy. Plus I've got other messages to deliver. Even when the crowd was shouting loudest, two people crammed messages and money into my hand. So God knows why I follow the teachers into the building, still carrying the football. Just because he's my new Runner doesn't mean that I'm responsible for him. It'll only waste my time. I took him on to speed my operation up, not to slow it down. Better just to dump him altogether.

But, in spite of all the reasons not to, I still hang

about outside the door of the First Aid Room where they've taken him to cool down.

Booming voices are coming from inside. Teachers' voices telling him: 'If you don't grow up fast . . . if you don't learn some self-control, you'll get thrown out of this school too. And then where will you go?'

My Runner doesn't answer.

I wait until the last teacher hurries out and I know he's on his own.

Then, checking that there's nobody about, I push the door open a crack and slide inside.

CHAPTER FIVE

'Brought your football back.'

He looks terrible. He looks a wreck. His face is sick and pale, with red-rimmed eyes and he's shaking, as if he's so weak that he can't stay upright on the chair. There's a graze down his cheek where he scraped his face when he was writhing round on the gravel.

'You look terrible.'

I'm still wondering what I'm doing in this room. It's like cutting my own throat. I should tell him he's finished as a Runner, that he isn't on the team any more. Then, get out of here.

But instead I ask him: 'Why did you let them make you mad? You did exactly what they wanted you to do.'

'Can't help it,' he mutters miserably.

'Rubbish!' My voice is low, in case there are any teachers lurking outside. But I'm really angry. I hate to see such a good runner go to waste.

'And all over a stupid football!' I hiss, shoving the ball into his hands. But he doesn't seem to have the strength to hold it. His arms flop by his side and the football trickles off his knee into a corner.

I sigh and shake my head. No point in hanging around here – he's bad news. 'Look, got to get going. Got an urgent message to deliver.'

He doesn't respond, doesn't even raise his head. 'Just leave him,' my mind's telling me. 'He's a disaster area. Not worth the trouble. Remember your rules? Don't get involved. Getting involved slows you down.'

But he's murmuring something. I know I'm making a big mistake when I crouch down to listen instead of walking out the door.

'What? What did you say?'

'I wanted them to like me,' he's whispering. 'To make friends. So I brought the football. I thought we could play football. But they just took it off me and laughed at me and – '

'You didn't have to go berserk though, did you? It was a bit over the top, wouldn't you say? Just because they didn't want to play football with you?'

But my voice isn't as harsh as before. Because I remember how it felt, how desperate for friends I was, before I became the Runner. I understand about being lonely.

I decide to give him the benefit of my experience: 'I used to lose my temper.' It's a hard confession to make because now everybody thinks the Runner is cool.

He raises his bloodshot eyes. He seems interested: 'What you?'

I nod. 'That's right. I never lost it in public though like you do. Always in private. Some nights

I'd go home, shut myself in my bedroom and slam my fist into the wall. I used to rip up all my things, go wild, just like you. And do you know what I used to do to get myself out of a bad mood?'

I can't wait for him to shake his head and say no, because I'm so eager to go on, to tell him how he can solve all his problems. 'I used to run.'

'What?' A look of disappointment comes into his eyes. But I hardly notice it. 'Are you joking?' he says, scornfully.

But I'm deadly serious. I can remember, on the field behind our house, running until all the bad temper was sweated out of me. I can remember how free it felt — as if you could run for miles and miles, away from home, away from school, run off the edge of the world . . .

Then I'd drop, dog-tired into the grass, and watch the clouds go tumbling by.

But he's not listening to my advice. His head has slumped down and he even seems to be asleep.

I shake him angrily. 'Look, I'm trying to help you! You should listen when people give you advice.'

He yawns. 'People are always giving me advice,' he sneers. 'They tell me to count to ten. They tell me to take deep breaths. They tell me to walk away: "Just walk away!" they say. Now you're telling me to go for a run. Oh yeah, I'll just jog a few times round the sports track and I'll never ever lose my temper again. Why didn't I think of that before!'

'Well, there's no need to be sarcastic!' I'm in a huff now. 'And if you won't let anybody help you . . .' I knew it was a big mistake to get involved, to break my own rules. You only end up getting hurt. ' . . . You can forget about being a Runner,' I say viciously, heading for the door. 'You've had your chance.'

That'll teach him to make fun of my advice, to sneer at my most secret memories. Should have kept them to myself – that way nobody can spoil them.

'You're finished.' He doesn't have a hope in hell of being a Runner without me – he hasn't got the contacts.

'Wait a minute!' His sharp cry makes me turn round. 'Sorry,' he mutters. He raises his head. His eyes are watchful. They're intelligent. He's a lot smarter than I thought. It's a surprising discovery.

A little warning bell tells me that he won't be easy to control. But I ignore it because I'm so pleased he's apologizing.

'I didn't mean what you said was stupid, about going for a run, but just because it worked for you, doesn't mean it'll work for me. Got to find my own way of doing it.' He shrugs. 'Just haven't found it yet.'

I shrug as well. 'All right then. But you'd be no good as a Runner. If you get in a rage like that you'll frighten people. It's bad for business. Besides, it'll slow you down if you go bananas every five minutes.'

Suddenly, he livens up. He's almost pleading with me: 'Give me another chance,' he says. 'I'm the best runner in this school, aren't I?'

'Yes,' I admit reluctantly. 'But you've got this other teensy-weensy little problem.'

'That won't come into it when I'm running. I won't have time to get mad. I'll just take the message, then race away to take the next one.'

He can see I'm not convinced: 'You're telling me you won't lose your temper?'

'No.'

'How many times have you told people that?' I can't help mocking him the way he mocked me.

But he's deadly serious. 'I won't have time to get worked up. I'll be a blur, see, just whizzing round all over the place. I'll be going so fast they won't even know who I am.'

That makes me grin because it sounds so much like me.

Brrinng! Panic grabs me. Five to nine already. How could I forget about Stringer – and the other messages growing cold inside my pocket? I've wasted ten minutes of precious running time in this First Aid Room. And now there's no choice. If I don't take on extra help I won't get through the day.

'You'd better not mess things up,' I threaten him.

'I won't. I'll be the best Runner you ever saw.'

'Huh!'

He can see that I haven't got much confidence.

'Just give me a message,' he begs. 'Any message.'

He's not slumped in his seat now. He's hopping about like his feet are on fire.

An idea pings into my brain. Why not give him Stringer's message?

Stringer's out for my blood because I'm late delivering Andy's money. He won't listen to excuses. It won't matter to him that Andy wasn't even in school yesterday. But if I send a stranger Stringer will be so surprised that, by the time he gets mad, my new Runner will be long gone.

'What's your name?' I ask my new Runner.

'Scott.'

I nod. 'Right then.' I make my voice business-like. 'You know Andy Summers, in year eight. The one they call Andy the Alien?'

'Yes.'

'Well, at first break you go find him. He'll be somewhere near the technology block. And you tell him: "Pay up or you know what'll happen." Just say you're helping me. He'll know what it's all about. I take the same message every week.'

'What *is* it all about?'

I'm getting irritated now. 'Look don't ask questions. Runners never ask questions. Just get the money from Andy and take it straight to Stringer.'

'Stringer!' Scott hasn't been at this school long, but he's already heard of Stringer.

'It's all right. He won't hurt you. It's strictly business. Just give him the money then come back and report to me. I'll be outside Room Seventeen for two minutes, two minutes mind, at the end of morning school.'

'I'll be there.' But he still looks confused. 'What's the message mean: "You know what'll happen." What *will* happen?'

Last bell goes for morning school. I should be over in the maths block now. 'Oh, I don't know. It's just a threat, like they'll kick his head in or something. Look, *do* it will you? I'm late already.'

'All right,' he nods hastily.

I sneak out the door and look around. 'There's nobody out here.'

'They've probably forgotten all about me. Might as well go to first lesson.' He goes over to the corner to get his football.

'Why don't you pick it up later? It's got you in enough trouble today already.'

'No,' he says, as if he's had a brilliant idea. 'I'll just leave it here! I don't need it any more. Besides, it's bust anyway.'

He's right. While we've been talking, without us noticing, the football has been slowly shrivelling up. He stamps on it, jumping up and down until it's totally flat.

I raise my eyebrows. I'm about to say: 'Are you sure it's dead?' but I decide not to.

He kicks what's left of the football under the radiator, out of sight. 'That's that,' he says, as if he's done something really good.

And off we go together, racing up the stairs three at a time. Some little kid watches us speed by, his mouth hanging open in amazement. Me and Scott could make a really good team – if only these doubts would stop itching away inside my head.

CHAPTER SIX

It's first break and I'm too busy taking messages to check on how my new Runner's doing.

In the last ten minutes, I rushed Simon's brace back to him – again. It's made of slippery pink plastic and silver wires and he leaves it all over the place because he takes it out every time he wants to eat something. He pays me when I deliver.

I took a message to the top floor that said: 'Can't go out tonight I'm grounded.' And everywhere I went, I yelled out about my new Runner. So people know he's working for me. Know that he's the real thing.

Then I raced out to the sports field with a screwed-up piece of paper for Claire. She shrieked with embarrassed laughter when she read it. Her friends crowded round. 'Get lost,' she told them. 'This is private.' But I already knew what it said – some people have got really dirty minds.

Now I'm puffing back to the main building. It's a sweltering hot day. There's this girl, sunbathing in the warm grass, chewing daisies. She snaps off a dandelion clock and blows it, so the white seeds drift down like a summer snowstorm.

Can't help thinking: 'Wouldn't it be nice to be lazy, just for a minute.' But then I remind myself: 'What would you be if you weren't a Runner? You'd be nothing, a nobody.' And I zoom off to deliver my next message.

Lexie's gobbling chocolate as usual when I skid round the corner, yell, 'Thar she blows!' and dash off again. There's some kids in year eight whose main purpose in life is insulting Lexie. It's pitiful if you ask me, really childish. But it's their money . . .

I'm hurtling back to English class when an arm shoots out of a classroom, grabs the collar of my shirt and twists it. I have to stop running – or choke to death.

'Stringer!' is the one panicky thought that explodes inside my head.

It isn't Stringer, it's Nicky. 'Leggo Nicky. Joke's over. You're hurting me!'

But Nicky isn't wearing his smiling face. He's got his black-as-thunder face on. Something must have made him really mad.

He unscrews my collar and I stagger back against the wall, gasping for breath, rubbing the sore place on my throat.

'What's this about a Runner interfering between me and Heather?'

I gulp, remembering the messages I changed. That was really stupid – just asking for trouble.

My mind's already dreaming up some wild excuses when Nicky growls: 'You'd better sort out this new Runner of yours, Sparrow-legs. I gave him a message, just now, to take to Heather. I wanted her to know that I might, just might, think about seeing her again. If she's lucky. But my spies tell me that he didn't just deliver my message. That he's been giving her advice, like a flippin' agony aunt. He's been putting ideas into her head!'

I'm as shocked as he is. 'Sorry Nicky, sorry.' The bell rings for the end of break. 'Don't know what he's playing at. I've told him that a Runner never, ever gets involved. But he's just new, see. Doesn't understand the rules. I'll see him about it, Nicky. At lunch-time. Make sure it never happens again.'

'It'd better not,' he's muttering, as he walks off.

I'm really furious now. All through English my stomach's scrunching into knots because I'm so angry. What does Scott think he's doing? Me and Nicky have always had a special relationship. He's trusted me with all sorts of important secrets. Even when he was two-timing Heather, sending messages to this other girl, he knew I wouldn't tell. And now this new Runner's ruined everything. Why didn't I listen to Lexie's warning?

The dining hall noise wallops me in the face as I crash through the swing doors. Fish today – it smells like rotting socks. My stomach's churning worse than ever as I look round for my Runner. There he is, surrounded by a gang of little kids. I stride up and yank him out: 'Want to talk to you!'

'Sparrow!' That makes me scowl – only my friends are allowed to call me Sparrow. 'I was just coming to see you.' He sounds excited, really pleased with himself.

'Just what do you think you've been doing?' I hiss at him, keeping my voice low, so nobody can hear.

'What?' He looks bewildered. 'I've been delivering loads of messages. Listen!' He jingles the money in his pocket. 'Here.' He gives me a handful of silver. 'Aren't you pleased?'

I nod reluctantly. He's certainly been busy. When I speak my voice isn't quite as fierce as before.

'Look – Nicky's just complained to me that you've been changing his messages to Heather. Runners never, ever change messages. Thought you understood about that.'

He looks astonished. 'I never changed his message. I delivered it just like he said: "I might go out with you again. If you're lucky." That was the message. But then we got talking, me and Heather. And I said, "Look, to be honest, he sounds like an arrogant prat . . ." '

My mouth drops open: 'You said *that* about Nicky? You called him an arrogant prat?'

'Yes, and then Heather agreed and I said that she shouldn't waste her time on him. Do you know she thinks she's not pretty? She thinks she's got fat legs? Nicky told her that. So I told her there were boys queueing up to take her out and she said – '

My head's whirling. I can't believe what he's telling me. Finally I splutter, 'You don't get paid to solve people's problems. You're just a Runner.' I plead with him: 'Look, don't make complications. Complications slow you up. Just keep it simple. Deliver the messages and go.'

I'm worried – but I don't want to lose him. God knows how but he's made more money in one morning than I make in an entire day. And I need this money, desperately. I'm saving up for something.

He's still babbling on: 'Guess what? Someone tripped me up on the stairs. Put his foot out and tripped me up deliberately. And I was going to go crazy. You know, like I do. But I was in a hurry. Places to go, messages to deliver. So I never went crazy. And he looked really disappointed. He – '

'Yeah, yeah,' I say impatiently. 'But all this talking's wasting time. There's three messages here for you to deliver. And remember, this time keep your mouth shut, right? A Runner never, ever gets involved.'

He nods and holds his hand out eagerly. I write some instructions on the back in big red capitals so he can't get it wrong. 'And Mr Walker wants a message taken. He'll be in the library now. You got to watch him though – he's a real skinflint. He's always saying that he'll pay you later but he never does. Just tell him a Runner never gives credit. No money, no message. That's our rule.'

'We take messages for teachers too?' Scott sounds impressed.

I shrug modestly. 'Why not? It saves them time. They're always sending messages to each other. Like: "Can I have 8R's report books when you have finished with them?" It's dead boring stuff. But they always think it's urgent.' I stress the word 'urgent'.

'Right!'

He zooms away and just as he's about to dive through the swing doors I yell after him. 'You did take Stringer's message didn't you?'

But he doesn't hear me.

Can't remember the last time I ate anything at lunch-time. But there's one minute to spare – just time to wolf down a cold slice of pizza left on someone's plate.

I'm moving off, when a kid from year seven comes sneaking up to me. He's got a soft baby's face with pink cheeks and freckles. He looks like an eager little puppy.

'Well?' I say, in a kindly voice, to encourage him. A new kid like him is bound to feel nervous, meeting the Runner for the first time.

He kicks me in the shin.

'Ow! What did you do that for!'

'We want our money back!' he howls. 'You rotten twister!'

'Rotten twister?' I raise my eyebrows and rub my shin at the same time. 'Is that supposed to be an insult?'

He's dancing about with rage. 'That new Runner,' he roars at me. 'We gave him 10p. We wanted him to go and shout "Wobblebum!" at Lexie. But my friend was at the chocolate machine getting a Curly Wurly and he said your Runner didn't call Lexie Wobblebum at all. He said he gave him lots of advice about healthy eating and treating your body with respect! So we want our 10p back.'

'Get lost,' I growl. 'I don't give refunds.' He skips away into the crowd, still protesting.

When he's gone I groan. My head is starting to throb. Suddenly I'm getting tangled up in complications. And they're things I didn't expect at all. I thought the worst problem with my new Runner was going to be his temper. I could have coped with a Runner who goes berserk once in a while. After all, nobody's perfect. But a Runner who thinks he's an agony aunt?

'Trust you,' I snarl at myself, 'to choose somebody who wants to change the world!'

CHAPTER SEVEN

The only thing to do is find him and stop him before he gives any more advice – and causes me even more trouble. There are twenty-five minutes of the lunch break left. I start searching the school: clattering up stairs, bombing down corridors, diving in classroom after classroom.

Then I spot him. He's out in the sunshine, in the school yard, talking to Andy the Alien.

'Oh no,' I groan out loud. 'Please, please, don't let him start interfering in Stringer's business.'

But it's too late. As soon as I go out in the yard he rushes in my direction. He leaves Andy sitting all hunched up in the shadows of the gym wall.

Andy's the weirdest-looking kid. He's got a head shaped like a long narrow egg – and thin dangly arms that wave around like feelers when he gets excited. But that doesn't happen often, because he's almost always miserable. Today, though, there's a bright, hopeful expression on Andy's face. I've never seen him looking hopeful before. That's how I know my Runner must have done something drastic.

I go on the attack straightaway before Scott can even open his mouth: 'What do you think you're doing? Messing everything up! You know the rules. You take the messages no questions asked. A Runner never gets involved. I've told you that a dozen times, you total retard!'

Too late I remember his wild man act in the bus park. But I'm so spitting mad that I couldn't care less if he swells up, bursts out his clothes and becomes the Incredible Hulk.

But he doesn't show any signs of going berserk. I seem to be the one doing all the shouting. Instead he says, in a dead calm voice: 'Did you know that Stringer's got this protection racket going? Where he asks little kids for money or he'll cripple them if they don't pay up? And that you're part of it because you're taking his messages?'

Suddenly, I feel embarrassed. To cover it, I yell out in my most aggressive voice: ''Course I know! Think I'm an idiot or something? So what about it?'

'But did you know that kid over there,' he jerks his thumb in Andy's direction, 'is nicking money out of his Grandma's purse just so he can pay Stringer off every week?'

I shrug. I didn't know that. But it doesn't surprise me. 'Not our responsibility is it? It's between Stringer and Andy. We're just the Runners.'

Even talking about Stringer makes my palms feel greasy with sweat. I wipe them on the sides of my white school shirt.

'Look,' I whisper, peering round to see if anyone's listening. 'You're new at this school. So you don't know what Stringer's like. If you did, you wouldn't even think about poking your nose into his business.'

My voice is cracking – my throat seems to be blocked with dry gravel. I have to swallow once, twice, before it clears: 'Just . . . just be grateful that being a Runner gives you protection against Stringer. As long as you don't ask questions.'

Because he's new to this school, he doesn't understand what a precious thing that is: 'Look Scott, most people would give their right arm to be safe from Stringer and his gang. They control this school. And if they decide they don't like you, you're . . . you're better off dead.'

He laughs, a great big snorting laugh as if I'm exaggerating.

'No,' I whisper, looking over my shoulder. 'You mustn't laugh. You got to believe me. This is deadly serious – Stringer could make your life hell if he wanted to.'

I'm not an idiot. It was obvious from the start what Stringer was up to. The very first message he gave me was a threat. But I couldn't afford to think about that – I shut my mind to it. Better to do that than refuse to co-operate with Stringer. Anyone in this school with any sense would tell you the same.

'Look,' I plead with him. 'Don't mess things up. Everything's all right as it is.'

Scott ignores that. 'I've been talking to Andy.'

'Oh no.' My voice has gone hoarse again. I try swallowing but there's no spit in my mouth. 'What did you talk about?' The words come out as a croak.

'What?'

'You heard! What did you talk about?'

'Well, me and Andy were discussing things . . .'

'*Discussing* things?' Normally, I would've raised my eyebrows but, some how, I don't feel like being sarcastic at the moment.

'Yes, and I've taken Stringer a message. I left it in his locker. Don't worry, Andy paid me to take it.'

'That's not what I'm worried about.' My voice sounds shrill and desperate but I can't control it. He must have a death wish! Going up against Stringer is like handling a live grenade – it's absolutely guaranteed to blow up in your face. Why can't he understand that? You can't win against people like Stringer. You just keep your head down and keep off their hit list.

I hardly dare ask him the next question: 'What did this message say?' But I have to know, even though my mind shrinks away from his answer.

When he speaks it's even worse than I imagined. It's a nightmare.

'I told him that the Runners weren't going to take his messages any more.'

'You told him what?'

'I told him,' Scott continues, 'that we've got our reputation to think about. That we don't need his kind of business any more.'

'This is a joke, isn't it? You're winding me up?'

If only he would tell me it's a joke . . . But there isn't a trace of a smile on his face.

'People are right about you!' I gabble at him. 'You *are* crazy! You need locking up, you do! Have you any idea what you've gone and done? Have you got any idea at all!'

CHAPTER EIGHT

Maybe Stringer hasn't found the message yet – maybe I'll have time to race upstairs and take it out his locker before he sees it. Then we can pretend none of this ever happened.

'You didn't sign it, did you?' I ask Scott hopefully.

''Course I did. I signed it with both our names.'

'You complete and utter moron!'

I can't understand him at all. He doesn't seem to realize what a crazy, reckless thing he's done. It's as if he couldn't help himself. Like those teachers said, he's got no self-control. I'm a cautious person – when I cross the road I always stop and look both ways. But my Runner's like someone who dives straight into motorway traffic. He doesn't even *see* the dangers. And even though I'm mad as hell with him, I can't just run off and leave him. Someone like him needs somebody streetwise, like me, to protect them.

'We got to think of a way to get back that note!'

Just as my brain is whirling round, juggling with three plans at once, someone bellows from a top-floor window. I don't even have to look to know whose voice that is.

'He's found the note.' I feel deathly cold – shivering as if I'm out in a blizzard, even though the sun is beating down on my head.

Stringer's got his green and brown army jacket on. His mouth is making ugly shapes. We can't hear the words he's using, there's just a roaring noise. But we can see what he does.

He jabs his fingers at us out the window like he's stabbing with a knife. Then he takes the finger and pulls it across his neck as if he's slitting someone's throat. And then, just to make quite sure we understand, he jabs his finger at us again.

Then he disappears.

He's coming down.

'Let's go!' But my Runner's gazing up at the empty window, his mouth hanging open.

I yank his sleeve and his head snaps round. 'We got to go!' I'm screaming right into his face.

Then we're running. And suddenly my mind is sharp and clear. I plot a route, just like when I'm taking messages, searching the map in my head trying to find a place for us to hide.

'Bus park!'

I make a sudden swerve to the right and my Runner swerves too as if we're one person.

We're racing side by side now, round the corner of the school, our feet crunching gravel. But we can still be seen from a dozen windows.

Duck down three steps, praying that the door to the basement isn't locked. It's open – we plunge into the gloom, dodging stacks of chairs and ancient wooden desks all carved with names. The boiler's hissing and gurgling and pipes snake off into the darkness.

'Oi!' shouts a voice out of the hot darkness. There's something stirring in a dusty corner. It's the caretaker. He waves a wrench at us. 'Oi, you shouldn't be down here!'

Scramble over a coal heap. The pieces clink in all directions. We start a landslide and while the caretaker's threatening us and coal's rattling down, for one heart-freezing moment I'm spinning round in panic. My map's let me down. There used to be a door here!

My hands are scrambling along the wall like I'm trapped inside a tomb. My Runner's breathing down my neck, hot, gasping breath.

'Got it.' I twist the handle and we tumble out into the sun. We're right where I wanted us to be – on the other side of the school almost under the wheels of a bus.

I know about hiding on the buses. Because once, after a tip-off, I found Andy here fast asleep on a back seat, keeping out of Stringer's way.

The caretaker's not following. I knew he wouldn't. He's old and slow and he doesn't want any trouble . . .

The buses for the school run are old wrecks that belong in a museum. Two of them have open platforms without any doors. We just creep on board.

'Keep down!' I hiss at Scott. There's still a chance we could be seen from the windows of the school.

He crouches beside me on the sticky floor among the crushed drink cans and spat-out chewing gum. Peanut shells crunch under our shoes. You can always tell where Peanut, from year nine, has been sitting – by the trash he leaves behind him.

For a moment we don't speak. The only sound is a rattling, wheezing noise as we struggle to get our breathing back to normal.

I check my watch. Ten minutes to go until the start of afternoon school. We should be safe here, for a couple of hours at least.

Then it really hits me. We're in deep, deep trouble.

'It's your fault!' I snarl at Scott. 'I had a nice little set-up – being a Runner, earning money. Now you've ruined everything. Why did you have to interfere? Why couldn't you leave things alone?'

I'm so angry that I'm sick and shaking. But he doesn't answer. He just hangs his head and shuffles his feet about.

Then he says, very quietly: 'Couldn't stop myself. Just felt sorry for them. You know, for those people, Lexie, and Heather and Andy – '

'What!' I snap at him. 'I can't hear you! Did you say you felt *sorry* for them?'

He nods and looks miserable.

'Oh great!' I wonder how such a sad case as him, who goes berserk when kids take his football, has the cheek to feel sorry for anybody else.

'And,' he says, brightening up, 'they listened to what I'd got to say. I mean seriously listened.' He seems to feel really proud about this. 'I think I've discovered a hidden talent,' he tells me eagerly. 'I'm dead good at giving advice.'

I'm so mad that I could grab his skinny neck and squeeze until his eyes pop out. 'But giving advice isn't part of the service!' I splutter at him. 'We take messages. Right? That's *all* we do. We don't sort out people's lives for them. We don't get involved in their problems. That's asking for trouble.'

'But it's interesting though!'

I shake my head helplessly. Then I sink my face into my hands and rock backwards and forwards in despair. Stringer's after us. Nicky won't speak to me. There's a gob of chewing gum on my new school trousers. My white shirt's smeared with coal. My whole world's crumbling to pieces.

A grimy hand sneaks on to my shoulder. 'Don't worry, Sparrow. This may *look* like a crisis situation. But it's not that bad really. I've got loads of ideas to get us out of this. And, after all, every cloud has a – '

'Don't you dare say it!'

I can't believe it. He's giving *me* advice now. I shake off his hand and threaten him: 'Don't you start on me, you, you agony-auntie!' I know it's a feeble insult, but I can't think of anything better at the moment – my brain isn't working very well. 'Just keep your advice to yourself. OK? And remember that I'm Chief Runner. I do the thinking. I tell *you* what to do.'

He looks hurt. But I couldn't care less.

I try to pull myself together, think of something positive. But my mind's a black hole. I almost ask him what his ideas are but pride won't let me. Finally, I say: 'We'll have to miss afternoon school, go somewhere, figure something out. We can't stay on this bus.'

'Where will we go?'

'Just follow me. And keep down,' I mutter as we crawl commando-style over the peanut shells towards the exit.

CHAPTER NINE

It's really weird being on our estate when all the kids are at school – so quiet and empty that it's spooky. The only thing moving is the washing, flapping in the wind. It's like you're the only ones left on the planet. But then we see a stray dog, sniffing at some rubbish. And a toddler on a little yellow bike zooms out of a gate and pedals up the street.

'Are we going to your house?' Scott asks me. Perhaps he thinks my mum and dad are out at work and I've got a key. Dad is at work. He works for a haulage firm. He's driving a lorry to Germany and back like he does every week. But my mum is in. And she's having a bad day.

I shake my head: 'We're going somewhere else.'

Even if I wasn't playing truant, it'd be no good taking anyone home on one of Mum's bad days.

So we climb up the sloping field behind my house. At the very top there are some gorse bushes loaded with yellow flowers that smell like coconut. We crawl between the spiky branches. There's a den where it's cool and shady – I used to play here when I was little. Stringer won't get us here.

We sit huddled in the den. You can hear cars but

the noise seems to come from very far away. Up here it's quiet – the only sound is bees buzzing over the gorse flowers. You can see the whole estate spread out below us. There's my house, the one with the dark green door. I'm not afraid my mum will see me from the windows. She won't go near the windows today.

My mum's frightened of going outside. On good days she goes out in the garden. She even walks round the block. Once, on a very good day, she went as far as the shopping mall but she got in a panic, got all sick and dizzy. They couldn't prise her fingers loose from the litter bin she was clinging to. When they did, a woman had to bring her home. Sometimes, like today, she doesn't even get out of bed. She hides under the duvet. She doesn't look you in the eyes.

It's not her fault. But I get sick of it sometimes. Sick of making up lies and excuses for her, of doing the shopping. I wish she would look after me, instead of me looking after her all the time. Sometimes, she seems more like a little kid than a mum.

It's not her fault, but she never came to see me run when I was at junior school. She promised. Even got all dressed up once – put on her best lilac summer dress and some pearl earrings. She never made it past the end of the road.

I don't tell anyone about her. I'm not going to tell Scott either. It's embarrassing having a mother who's not like everyone else's mum. Who never goes out, who's got frightened eyes that dart about all the time. And anyway, it's too difficult to explain – my mum ends up sounding like a crazy person if I try to explain. She's not crazy. She just thinks the world is a scary place.

'This is the field,' I say to Scott, 'where I used to run like mad when I felt like smashing things up. I used to roll down the slope as well, over and over again.' The grass smelt fresh and green and juicy when you went rolling down and crushed it under you. But I don't tell him about the grass. He'll only be sarcastic, like he was in the First Aid Room.

But this time, he doesn't look sarcastic. He just looks miserable and hopeless.

'I'll get killed,' he's muttering, 'if I get thrown out of this school, as well.'

But don't ask me to feel sorry for him. It's his fault that we're in this mess. And I've got more to lose than him. If I can't be a Runner, then I'm nobody again.

'Why do you do it?' I snap at him. Thinking of what I've lost makes me want to be really cruel. 'Why do you go crazy and get yourself thrown out of schools? Why don't you behave like a normal person?'

He shrugs. 'It's a habit.'

'A habit!' I can't believe that he's given me such a feeble answer. 'A habit? Squeezing zits is a habit. Chewing your nails is a habit. Going bananas and busting classrooms up isn't a habit!'

'I didn't bust classrooms up. Who told you that? I

was "a disruptive influence". That's what they said. That's why they threw me out.'

'Don't blame them.'

He shrugs again. 'My dad used to wind me up. He used to get at me all the time. Saying things, making fun of me until I lost my temper. Then he used to laugh. He used to enjoy doing it. It made him feel good. My dad – '

He's about to tell me his whole family history. But I don't want to listen. So I deliberately interrupt: 'Where's your dad now?'

'Married to somebody else. He lives in New Zealand. They've got two kids.'

'Well, what's your excuse now then?' I can't help sounding vicious. 'What's your excuse for going berserk? Your dad's on the other side of the world, winding up some other kids. You ought to be able to stop doing it now.'

'I can't,' he says.

I sigh, as if he's a hopeless case. 'That's crap, that is. You *can* stop going berserk. You didn't do it today did you, when that kid tripped you up on the stairs?'

He brightens up. I didn't mean him to do that. I was trying to make him look useless and stupid. I even wanted to see him lose his temper. That would've made me feel good.

But instead he seems quite cheerful. 'I stayed really calm didn't I?' he says, as if it's some kind of big achievement. 'I think it was being a Runner that did it. I was good at it, wasn't I, being a Runner?'

I'm just about to explode with rage, tell him he's

the worst Runner ever, that he's ruined our chances of ever being Runners again, when suddenly he's clutching my arm.

'Look,' he hisses in my ear, 'there's somebody climbing up here. Look, down by the houses. Can you see who it is? It's not Stringer, is it?'

CHAPTER TEN

It's not Stringer lumbering up the slope. It's Lexie, puffing and red-faced. And behind him is Andy the Alien with his weird, egg-shaped head and long dangly arms, like a praying mantis. Nobody could possibly mistake either of them for Stringer.

'What do *they* want?' I hiss at Scott. There's an electric buzz of fear down my spine. Neither of them have any cause to like me. They might betray me to Stringer, just to see me hurt. I check my watch. Four o'clock. They must have just got off the school bus. I shrink back into the gorse bushes. Maybe it's a coincidence they're here. Maybe the gorse will give us cover and they'll just pass by.

When Lexie collapses beside us the ground shakes, like a minor earthquake.

'Hello Sparrow,' he gasps.

I poke my head out a yellow cloud of gorse flowers. 'How did you know we were here!'

He points vaguely back down the hill: 'Your mum said to look here.'

'You mean, she opened the front door?'

Lexie frowns at the surprise in my voice. But I can't explain, can I? I can't say: 'On a bad day, she usually hides under the duvet.' He'd think my mum was crazy.

''Course she opened the door,' answers Lexie, puzzled. 'Else she couldn't have told us, could she? She said to try up here. She said you sometimes come up here, after school.'

That surprises me too. Mum must have watched me running, from the kitchen window. Didn't think she'd ever watched me running.

'You haven't told her about Stringer have you? You haven't told her about me missing lessons?' My mum knows nothing about my life at school. I never tell her, even if she asks me. School and home are strictly separate. They're different worlds.

''Course we didn't,' Lexie says. 'Do you think we're stupid?'

Hope they didn't go upsetting her. I don't like anyone upsetting my mum. At the same time I want to ask Lexie: 'What did she look like to you? Did she look like anybody else's mother? Did she look you straight in the eyes?' But I can't ask those things – it'd be too embarrassing.

Instead I say: 'What do you want then?'

'We came to see if we could help.'

'Haw, haw!' – that's me, giving them my loud, sneery laugh.

The Alien still hasn't said anything. He's sitting with his long arms wrapped round his knees, picking at a crusty scab on his elbow.

'What, you two?' I'm using my best sarcastic voice. 'Help *me*?'

70

Slowly, slowly, the Alien lifts his egg-head. It looks like hard work, as if his head is really heavy. 'We didn't come to help you,' he says quietly. 'We don't care what happens to you. You're scum. We came to help him.' He points a long, bony finger at Scott. 'We came to help the new Runner.'

This shuts me up. I haven't got a single smart answer. An awful sick, empty feeling heaves in my guts. Just for something to do, I rip a buttercup out the grass and begin to shred it to bits, petal by petal. Would you believe it, there's tears itching under my eyelids. I have to hang my head so nobody sees. 'Stupid cow,' I mutter at myself.

Scott's speaking now. It's driving me crazy that they think he's more important than me when I've been a Runner for ages and he's only been one for twenty-four hours. He works for me – I'm Chief Runner. But they're paying me no attention at all, ignoring me as if I'm nobody. The buttercup leaves in my fist are getting mashed to a green pulp.

'Have you got any suggestions then,' Scott is asking Lexie, 'to get us out of this mess?'

A snigger bubbles up in my throat. I can't stop it. I mean, any plan Lexie suggests is bound to be useless.

'I've been thinking,' says Lexie.

A great snort of surprise bursts out of me. But nobody takes any notice. Except Andy's long narrow eyes slide round and look at me sideways. They inspect me and then slide away. He carries on picking at his scab. That silent and accusing look makes me flinch.

'There's no way we can fight Stringer. Not face-to-face.' Those are Lexie's words of wisdom.

'Incredible! You ought to be on Mastermind!'

But Lexie ignores me. I'd forgotten that neither of them care about me. He carries on. 'But we can destroy him another way.'

It's a mystery to me why the others are listening so hard, taking Lexie seriously. No one takes Lexie seriously. Do they?

Lexie turns to me, including me at last in what's going on. 'You know about rumours, don't you Sparrow? You know how they hurt people?'

He's getting at me. But I'm so desperate to be noticed that I'm listening now, just like the others. And for once I don't see how fat Lexie is. I just see his brain working.

He's right about the rumours. I've carried all sorts of rumours round the school – seen them grow and swell and turn poisonous. And once they've started, you can't stop them. It's like they've got a life of their own.

I boasted before that the Runner never refused to take a message. That's not a hundred per cent true. There's one I didn't take. Someone in my class had been off school for two months. He'd had a blood test for glandular fever. I know that for a fact because he lives in the same street as me. Next day, this girl in our class, with a really sick mind, came up to me and said, 'Take this will you, Sparrow?'

And she handed me this screwed-up piece of paper. I read it, of course. It was to a bigmouth in year nine and it said: 'Gary's had a blood test for AIDS. But don't tell anyone.'

I changed it. The Runner broke her own rules. I rubbed out AIDS and wrote in glandular fever and that particular rumour was killed stone dead before it ever got started.

'Are you saying we should start up a rumour about Stringer?'

'Right,' Lexie nods at me.

'What, like he's got AIDS or something?'

This time Lexie shakes his head, frowning. 'No, no,' he says. 'That's deadly serious that is. I'm not thinking about that kind of rumour.'

'What then?'

'You know how Stringer thinks he's really tough, really hard. How he poses all the time?'

I nod eagerly. You learn a lot about people being a Runner. Lexie knows a lot about people too. And I begin to see what he's getting at.

'So, we start some rumour that wrecks his reputation for being a hard man. You know, something that makes people laugh at him. Turns him into a joke.'

I think hard about that. The one thing you never do when you're with Stringer is laugh. Stringer's got no sense of humour. He'd hate it if people laughed at him instead of being scared of him.

'I don't know,' said Scott doubtfully. 'It sounds all right, in theory. But it would never work, would it?

Stringer's too powerful. He'd just find who started the rumour and kick their head in. And that'd be the end of that.'

But my mind is racing along. More than anyone else in the school, I've seen how cruel rumours can be. How, once they get their claws in, they're impossible to shift. You can't trace where they started. And the more fuss you make about them, the more it seems to other people that you've got something to hide.

'He won't know who started it,' I say excitedly. 'And I know who've got the biggest mouths in the school. Just tell this rumour to them, say, "Don't tell anyone else," and everyone'll know by lunchtime. All you have to do is – ' I stop, embarrassed. I'd forgotten that they didn't come to help me. But Lexie says: 'See, Sparrow knows what I mean.'

I look gratefully at him. If I was him, I'd hate my guts. Even Andy's listening. *He* hates me. But he hates Stringer worse.

Scott's looking worried. But he's not an experienced Runner like I am. He doesn't realize that spreading rumours could, if we do it right, do more damage than beating Stringer in a fight.

'Look,' I explain to Scott, 'what choices have we got? We can't hurt Stringer can we? I mean, not physically.'

Scott looks round at the four of us: he's got arms and legs like twigs; Lexie's like a sumo wrestler only he can't wrestle; Andy's like a creature beamed in from another planet. Of all of us, I probably stand the best chance in a fight with Stringer. And I don't stand any chance at all.

Scott nods reluctantly. I carry on, eagerly. 'So we've got to be sneaky. Right? We've got to find other ways to hurt him. Making him into a joke is a good idea. It just might work.'

'Doesn't mean he won't still be after us,' mutters Scott.

''Course it does,' says Lexie, gently. 'It'll finish him, won't it? Break him. If he's a joke no one will listen to him or take him seriously again.'

You can tell that Lexie's speaking from personal experience. All the insults that I've yelled at him come rushing back to me. They weren't my personal feelings of course, not my responsibility, but all the same, it makes me squirm. My face is getting hot, flushing bright red as he stares at me, I have to hang my head because I can't bear to look him in the eye.

Then Andy speaks, for the first time. I'd forgotten he was here. He's taken one trainer and one sock off so he can scratch his foot. He's got weird feet, like white floppy flatfish. 'So this rumour you're talking about,' he says, 'it's something like he sleeps with his teddy bear, right? Or he's scared of the dark. Or he cries when there's a sad film on the telly. Or he shaves his legs?'

'Shaves his legs?' Scott wrinkles his nose and looks confused.

'You know,' says Andy, 'like a girl does.'

Lexie interrupts: 'Something like that. Something that'll mean he can never act tough again.'

'But none of those is right,' I say thoughtfully. I'm pleased that they're all listening to me. They know I've got a lot of experience of this sort of thing. 'If we don't find the right rumour we might as well not bother.'

I'm giving them my opinion but I'm still not convinced about all this. It might work and it might not. Rumours have a strange way of back-firing on the people who start them. And it's going to be dangerous. Like defusing a bomb, defusing Stringer could end up with a big explosion. And we'll get caught in the blast.

Still, I try to sound positive. 'What we've got to do is think of the right rumour and work out the best way to spread it. We got to do it quickly before Stringer finds us. We haven't got much time.' I'm worried about this too. Sometimes rumours catch on quick, spread like forest fires. Sometimes they're slow burning – take ages to work up to a blaze.

'I don't know,' says Andy hopelessly. 'Why don't you say that when Stringer goes home his baby sister beats him up. Or that his pet gerbil beats him up. Or that his mother beats him up – that she bounces him off the walls!'

'That's stupid,' growls Scott. 'We're getting really stupid now!' He sounds irritated, as if he's working himself up into a rage. Great – that's all we need.

Suddenly Lexie says: 'It just might work.'

'What, about his gerbil beating him up?'

'No, no, about his mum doing it.'

There's silence while we think about it, turn

it round and round in our minds. Stringer is a big hulk, who thinks he's boss of the school. He swaggers about terrorizing people. The idea of his mother smacking him round the head like he's a naughty little boy makes me grin. Already, I'm less scared of him.

So I say: 'That's not a bad rumour. People'll want to believe it.'

Scott says, 'Will they really believe a feeble lie like that?'

'Oh yes,' I tell him. 'You'll be surprised what you can get people to believe.'

'Now,' says Lexie, 'we got to think how to make this work. We haven't got much time, like Sparrow says. We got to do it right.'

It's amazing. Only five minutes ago I would have rubbished anything that Lexie said. I wouldn't even have listened. But now I'm nodding in agreement.

'Lexie's right. If me and Scott go running all over the school spreading this rumour, Stringer will get us. He'll stop us before the rumour's really cooking.'

'We could be Runners too. Me and Lexie,' pipes up Andy.

In spite of my new respect for Lexie's brain, I can't help sniggering. By the time Lexie got to the top floor he'd be too puffed out to deliver any messages. And Andy would have tripped over his flatfish feet on the first two steps.

'The best thing,' I say, tactfully, 'is to spread the rumour when everyone's together.'

'Like in morning assembly?' asks Andy.

77

I shake my head. 'Not there.' The teachers are in rows down the side watching us like hawks. You've only got to open your mouth to get jumped on. I've tried it before.

Scott's been quiet for a while. Probably sulking because he thinks the rumour is too ridiculous for anyone to believe. But then he says: 'If a crowd gathered, then all three of you could go round, pick out the bigmouths, spread this rumour in five minutes.'

'You don't just pick out the bigmouths,' I point out. '*Stupid* bigmouths are the best. They'll believe anything you tell 'em. There's Sarah Roberts for a start. Or Peanut in year nine – he never connects his brain to his mouth.'

'All right, all right,' says Scott, angry at my interruption. 'But what I'm saying is, I could get that crowd together for you.'

Lexie has already guessed what he means. 'You're going to go berserk?'

'I'm going to *pretend* to go berserk,' Scott corrects him, as if it's an important difference. 'You know how Stringer and his mates always head straight to the toilets for a smoke soon as they get to school? Well, I'll set up this diversion then, in the bus park, and they'll never know what's going on.'

I'm proud of my Runner. He sounds cool and confident. But then he says: 'What do I look like, when I go crazy?'

'What do you mean; "What do I *look* like?" ' I mimic him. 'What kind of question's that?'

'When it happens,' he says patiently, 'there's this sort of red screaming in my brain. I don't know what I'm doing. So tell me what I do. Or it won't be convincing, will it?'

'Oh right.' I understand now. And all three of us are keen to tell him.

Andy stands up: 'You do this.' He whirls his gangly arms about, punching at the air. He stamps like a toddler in a tantrum. 'And you shout rude things at people.'

I flop about, banging my head until it dents the grass. 'Look, look! This is what you do when you *really* get going.'

'And,' says Lexie, 'if anyone comes near you, you grab at 'em. Like this.' Lexie's arm shoots out and locks round my throat.

'Gerroff, you're choking me.'

'Well we got to show him, or he won't get it right.'

'This is ridiculous! I can't breathe!'

Scott's mouth is hanging open, like he can't believe what he's seeing. He looks stunned. 'Anything else?' he asks.

'Yes, your face goes all red, like this.' Andy holds his breath until his face is a big crimson balloon.

'And your eyes sort of go all blank,' Lexie stumbles about like a mad zombie.

'But mostly,' says Andy helpfully, 'you yell a lot and try to kill people.'

Lexie nods and laughs out loud.

'It's lucky you're such a useless fighter,' Andy adds, 'or you might really hurt somebody.'

I don't like Andy calling my Runner a crap fighter. Or Lexie laughing at him. But I keep my mouth shut. If I got nasty about it, they might both remember all the reasons they've got to hate me.

Scott doesn't seem insulted. He just sighs and shakes his head: 'No wonder they're queueing up to see the show.' Then he says, 'Don't think I can do that. Not all at once.'

I've just thought of a brilliant idea. 'Why don't you let me work you up? You know, steal your football, call you names. Then you'll go berserk for real.'

'Nah, that won't work. I'll know you're doing it deliberately.'

'Well, everybody else does it deliberately. And you give them what they want, every time.'

'I know.' He looks thoughtful. 'But I don't think I can do that any more. I'll just have to fake it.'

'OK,' I shrug. 'Long as you make it convincing. So lots of people crowd round.'

'Don't forget . . .' says Andy. Hard to believe, but he looks almost cheerful – I've never seen him like that before. 'Don't forget that when the teachers come to get you, you've got to try to thump them as well.'

That's a snag I hadn't thought of. 'I'll warn you when the teachers are coming,' I say anxiously to Scott, 'and you run like hell. Right? You mustn't get caught. They'll throw you out the school.' I suddenly realize that I don't want my new Runner to get thrown out of school. Not after I've invested so much time and trouble in him.

'That's all right then,' I say when he nods. But, even while we're talking about details: what signals we're going to use, which bigmouths we're going to target, I don't feel that everything's all right. Like I said before, rumours are very dangerous things. When you're handling them, they sometimes blow up in your face.

CHAPTER ELEVEN

I was too pessimistic about this plan. It's coming together like a dream. Stringer and his mates are in a cloud of smoke in the toilets – they're safely out the way. The buses all arrived on time. And me and my other two Runners, Lexie and Andy, are in position, waiting for the show to start.

It all depends on Scott now. He'd better make his move soon. In three minutes the crowd will be inside the school and we'll have lost our chance. Tomorrow will be too late. Stringer will have caught us by tomorrow.

Wonder why Lexie got involved in all of this? He didn't need to – it's not his problem. Far as I know, Stringer isn't out to get him. Not like he's after me, Scott and Andy. I can't believe that Lexie's doing this just because Scott was kind to him . . .

Got to concentrate. The tension's getting to me. Stomach's churning, feel sick and my palms are slippery with sweat. Have to wipe them on my tie. Things are going OK – so far. But I've been a Runner for a long time. And I know how people let you down. They're unpredictable – they make promises they don't keep.

At least I don't have Mum to worry about. Dad is home for three days before his next trip. He'll take over. He'll look after her and do the shopping. And besides, it was a good day today. Mum got up this morning really cheerful. Even talked about going to the shopping mall. She won't, though. Talking about it is as far as she ever gets.

Concentrate. Don't know why my mind's jumping about like this. Yes I do – it's because I'm worried about this rumour. You never know with rumours: some fly right away, some crash – and some never get off the ground. You can't tell until you try them out. But I'm scared this one is so far-fetched that even bubble-brains like Peanut won't believe it.

My hand slides up to prod that crater – that massive zit tucked in beside my nose. I always squeeze spots when I'm worried. 'Don't!' I slap my hand to stop myself. That zit feels like a second nose. It feels like Mount Popocatepetl. That's a volcano – on the geography room ceiling right above my desk . . .

Things are happening. There's a great big splodge of black, white and red as school uniforms crowd together. With flashes of bright pink, silver and blue – that's school bags, bobbing on kids' shoulders as they run, shouting to each other.

Over their heads I can see Lexie, casually propping up a litter bin. He gives me the thumbs up sign. The show's on the road.

Time to get moving. We've all got our special

targets. I already know where mine are. Diving through the crowd, dodging, weaving, I hear one of them: Kelly-Ann Dixon. She's shrieking. 'Hey, look at 'im! Look at 'im!' Her voice could crack windows.

I'm shoving my way towards that voice. I smell hot sweat, *Fuzzy Peach* body spray, spearmint chewing gum. Bags bash my face. Sweaters tickle my nose. Suddenly a gap opens up and there's Scott. He's looking good. He's got to the 'Give me my ball back!' stage. Nobody would know he's acting. And if everything's going to plan, Lexie and Andy should be somewhere in this mob, doing the same as me, making the rumour work.

Will it save our skins? Who knows. But I feel the old excitement – that thrill the Runner gets from being slap-bang in the middle of the action.

Kelly-Ann's mouth is a big square hole that's yelling without stopping: 'What's 'e doing now? Look at 'im! 'E's crazy! 'E's – ' She looks round as I yank her sleeve.

'Heard the latest?' I hiss into her face. 'Heard about Stringer? They say he's scared stiff of his mum. They say she beats him up – smacks him round the head. And he cries just like a little kid. They swear he cries his eyes out!'

I've just thought of this last bit, about Stringer crying. I'm proud of it. It's a nice touch.

I repeat the rumour to make sure she gets it. Her eyes go wide and goggly, like a frog's. Her mouth makes an 'O' shape. She's thinking about it. This takes a long time.

'But promise you won't tell anyone,' I whisper. I almost forgot about that bit.

Suddenly she shouts out in excitement. 'Honest? You're kidding me, Sparrow. Stringer *crying*? You hear that, Laura? Stringer's mum hits 'im. She makes 'im cry!'

'True,' I say solemnly, wiping her spit off my face. But what I'm thinking is: 'Christ, she believes it. She's stupider than I thought!'

But I'm cheering inside because she's fallen for it. She can see the picture in her mind, same as I could, of Stringer's mummy bouncing him off the walls and Stringer, the hard man, crouched in a corner sobbing his heart out like a baby.

It's working. It's actually working! See, you never can tell with rumours.

Kelly-Ann's already passing it on, adding bits of her own. I knew she would – bigmouths like her are so predictable. 'Yes,' she's blabbering, 'and I know it's true because I know someone who's seen it!'

It's amazing the lies you can get people to swallow, especially if they're desperate to believe them.

Got to move on. The crowd is buzzing, whether with our rumour or Scott's show, I can't tell. But you can feel the heat, see the pushing, shoving, getting frantic. Someone's elbow crunches in my ribs.

'Gerroff!'

And in the background Scott's roaring, cursing, turning the air blue. A twist of panic stabs my guts. He sounds very, very convincing.

'Teachers!'

I've only told three more bigmouths when the warning cry goes up. I promised Scott I'd be alert, watch out for danger. But buried in this shrieking mob, I'm as good as blind.

'Teachers coming!'

Everyone scatters. Except me. I head in the opposite direction, fighting against the stampede to rescue my Runner.

My heart almost stops. There, in an empty space, Scott's lying, stretched out on the ground — eyes closed, his face grazed and bloody and deathly white.

Oh no. He didn't act. He went berserk — he went berserk for real.

I kneel by him. 'Scott! Get up, there's teachers coming. You'll get chucked out the school!'

For one awful moment I think he's dead. 'Get up!' I shake his arm. 'Get up Scott!'

Then he opens one eye and winks at me. There's a huge grin on his face. He scrambles up. 'Fooled you,' he says. 'Fooled them as well. I was pretending all the time.'

'Idiot!' But there's no time to be angry. We're running now, with everybody else, taking cover. So that when the teachers come puffing up, there's nothing left to see but a patch of trampled grass.

CHAPTER TWELVE

There's no need for the Runners to do any more work. We just sit back and watch things happen. The rumour's hot and getting hotter. There's no controlling it – it's rushing from room to room, up stairs, down corridors. Soon the whole school's jumping with it. People want to believe it. Even if Stringer's never threatened them personally, they're still scared of him. They're thrilled to get the chance to destroy him.

I know it's working when someone passes the rumour on to me, the person who started it in the first place. 'Sparrow,' this little kid gasps into my ear as he's racing by. 'Have you heard? Stringer's terrified of his mum! He wets his pants every time she shouts at him! She makes him dust the house with a feather duster. He has to wear a frilly apron. Honest! And she hammers him if he doesn't do it! Can you believe it?'

No, I can't believe it. But I knew it was a lie in the first place. The rumour is so strong and powerful now that I even risk saying, 'Come on! You don't expect me to believe that crap, do you?'

'It's true,' he says, scowling at me. 'Everybody says so.' And he dashes off to tell somebody else.

No one's seen Stringer. He's not swaggering round the school at lunch-time like he usually is. His mates are about but they're keeping a low profile. They look worried. So would I if my leader was the school's biggest joke.

We Runners stick together. We watch our backs. You can't be too careful. But I'm getting restless, sitting here in the dining hall, just waiting. My legs are twitchy. I should be running now – there are messages to take, and I need the money. I'm saving up. But Lexie warns me: 'Stay with us. Don't go off on your own just yet.' He's worried Stringer might be hiding somewhere, still out to get me and Scott.

'Nah,' says Scott, 'he's finished. He's probably crawled into a corner to die.'

Wish I felt that confident. I can't help looking over my shoulder. Wonder where Stringer's really got to? It all seems too easy. Hard to believe he's going down without a fight.

The macaroni cheese has set like rubber on my plate – my knife bounces off it. Ever smelled a dish-cloth that's been used to wipe up milk and then gone sour? That's how this macaroni cheese smells.

'You want this?' I say to Lexie, pushing my plate towards him. Even Lexie doesn't want it. It must be disgusting.

The spot on my nose starts throbbing like it's got its own heartbeat. My hand creeps up towards it. To take my mind off it I say to Scott: 'I was worried back there, when you pretended to go berserk. I thought you really had!'

'It was brilliant,' says Andy. Because he never says much we all turn to look at him. He's chewing an apple, turning it round and round in his bony fingers like a praying mantis crunching up an insect. We wait for him to say something else, but he doesn't. He's a weird kid. But I don't feel like making fun of him just now – in case he slides those long eyes in my direction and makes me feel guilty again.

Then Scott says: 'I didn't lose my temper. I was in control all the time.' He seems really proud of this.

I'm in a mean and edgy mood – must be because I'm not running. 'So you're telling us,' I sneer at him, 'that you've cracked it. That you'll never, ever lose control of yourself again?'

'Don't know,' he answers. His voice is quiet and deadly serious. 'I probably will. But right now, I don't feel like I need to anymore.'

That shuts me up. Can't think of a single smart reply. So I drag my knife along the table top. Scrape, scrape, scrape. It's a really irritating noise that makes you clench your teeth.

'For Chrissake,' says Lexie, 'why don't you go and take some messages? You'll drive us all crazy if you sit round here much longer.'

I look at him gratefully, growling at the same time: 'Don't need *your* permission.' But he just grins and waves 'Bye bye' as I rocket out my chair and race away.

Timetables, plans of the school building, flash up in my brain. Now I'm back being a Runner, I feel alive again.

And if Stringer's out there waiting, well it's just too bad.

By afternoon break I'm busier than ever. And everywhere I go the rumour's still sizzling. 'He's scared of his mum. He wets his pants – she makes him wear nappies.'

Because the Runner always has the freshest news, knows everything that's going on, people check with me: 'Have you heard about Stringer?' I have to hide a secret grin when I nod and say: 'Yeah, I've heard. But it can't be true can it? Not Stringer.' And then they convince themselves even more when they tell me: 'It's a fact. Everybody says so.'

Stringer's tough mates have gone quiet. Which is strange because, usually, they shout their mouths off all the time. The rumour is too powerful for them to stop. Stringer won't be able to stop it. The more he throws his weight around, trying to deny it, the more people will believe it's true.

I read once about this monster – when you hacked its head off, two more grew in its place. Rumours are like that. The more you try and cut them down, the bigger and stronger they get.

There's no escape. Stringer's finished. No one will take him seriously again. And all because of me and my Runners.

'Yay!' I punch my fist into the air, once, twice. Runners rule, OK!

Wish we knew where Stringer was though. No one's seen him since this morning. He's gone to ground. I'd feel even better if we knew where he was . . .

Five minutes into afternoon break and already I'm behind schedule. Someone paid me to insult Lexie but I gave the money back and said no way – Lexie's one of us now. They were angry. They grumbled: 'But it was all right before.'

I just snapped: 'Well, it's not all right now!' The Runner doesn't have to explain herself. But I won't be making a habit of turning down messages. It's bad for business.

Simon's brace is rattling in my pocket. He never wears it – he's going to look like Goofy all his life. Someone found it in a toilet bowl, bobbing about like a pink jellyfish. I trace my route inside my head. Can't use the basement to reach Simon in the art room – the Caretaker might still be mad. Have to take a short cut through the bus park . . .

I'm skidding to a halt, leaving deep grooves in the gravel. Now, I'm creeping backwards. Can't believe what I just saw. Should have known this was going too smoothly; that Stringer wouldn't shrivel up and die like a slug that you put salt on.

He's got Scott. He's holding Scott hostage in the back of the bus. I can see them – Stringer's spiky red hair and Scott's black mop-head – and hear Stringer's roaring voice. And I can't believe that I forgot just how scary Stringer is. That I let myself believe we'd won so easily and that he wouldn't take revenge.

Don't know what to do. My mind's frozen up. So I just crouch down by the side of the bus and cram my fist into my mouth, trying to stop myself whimpering with fear.

CHAPTER THIRTEEN

I'm sneaking on the bus to rescue Scott. Haven't got a clue how to do it. But I'm trying to be brave. I keep telling myself that Stringer's not a big scary bogeyman any more. He's just a joke. The rumour's taken all his power away. He's nothing but a stupid hulk, like Bluto in the Popeye cartoons. But my fists are clenched so tight that my nails are stabbing me. There's little red beads of blood on my hand. I lick them off.

Then, between the seats, I get a glimpse of Stringer's face, battle-scarred from fighting. It looks like it was chopped out of rock. And his eyes aren't stupid, they're horribly alert and dangerous. The old fear comes back, twisting deep inside me, making me gasp with pain.

I duck down again and squash myself flat, wriggling under the first two seats. It was a big mistake to try this on my own – Stringer looks as deadly as he ever did. But it's too late now. I'm trapped here, just like Scott.

'You're dead.' This thought spins round and round my head like a lonely piece of washing in a tumble dryer. 'You're dead, Sparrow.'

I'm usually a very cautious person – steer clear of messy situations, never get involved. But over the last few days, I've broken every one of my own rules. I don't understand what's happening to me.

Typical – letting my mind drift when I'm up to my neck in trouble. Stay alert. Concentrate.

Stringer's voice sounds like a growling Rottweiler. Can't hear what he's saying. My face is pressed against the gritty floor so I can only see their boots: Scott's battered white trainers and Stringer's massive red leather boots that lace nearly to his knee and shine like polished apples. Stringer's really proud of his boots.

Concentrate!

Scott's speaking. Incredibly, there's no trembling in his voice, no pleading. No fear at all. My ears strain to listen. I can't be hearing right.

'I didn't know what was going on, Stringer,' Scott says, quite clearly. He sounds as if he's trying to be friendly. 'I didn't know anything about it.'

My mind's sparking now, giving me electric shocks. Scott's betrayed me, gone and joined the enemy. Why else would he be sliming round Stringer, pretending he had nothing to do with the rumour? I remember, from this morning in the bus park, how good he is at pretending. Bet he's told Stringer that I'm to blame for everything. Bet that's what he's done.

That's what you get for trusting people. There's a bitter taste in my mouth like sucking on a lemon. I thought that being a Runner meant something to

Scott. He said it did. But it can't have done, can it, if he can land his partner right in it like this? Should have kept it a strictly solo operation. People are too risky. They make promises they don't keep. And even though I'm trying to be angry, there's a great ache inside me. I really did believe that my new Runner liked me. I thought we were a team. Serves me right. Shouldn't have been so stupid.

Suddenly, I can't bear to listen any more. Wriggling backwards off the bus, my foot clanks against metal. Shush! My whole body freezes. But there's no reaction from them. Their heads are close and they're muttering together, as if they're plotting something.

Then I'm free, weaving through the bushes along the school drive, heading for the main gate. Mad Maxwell's chugging in in his rusty old Ford just as I'm sneaking out. He stops and winds the window down: 'Shouldn't you be in class, Charlotte? Is something the matter?'

For a split second, I almost tell him everything. I must be crazier than I thought – what with the shock of seeing Scott and Stringer ganging up against me. I pretend to be deaf and run on. He won't follow. And anyway, his car is such a wreck that even Lexie could outrun it. There'll be trouble tomorrow. But facing Mad Maxwell is the least of my problems.

I run through the quiet spooky streets of my estate, keeping close to walls, dodging down alleyways. I don't think. Running stops you thinking. The rhythm takes over and you go into a trance.

Safe at my house, I yank down the door handle. And wrench my wrist. It's locked.

'What the hell – !'

My mother's never out. She's always home – I always know exactly where she is. Where's she gone? How could she leave me stuck out here with nowhere to hide?

Bet my Runners are spreading rumours about *me* now. By tomorrow I'll have taken Stringer's place as the school's biggest joke. I won't be able to hold my head up any more. And nobody will even notice when Stringer comes to get his revenge.

I rattle the door handle again and prowl about peering in the windows. But the house is still and empty. My dad must have persuaded her to go out.

'Where is she? What the hell's she think she's doing, locking me out?' It feels like everyone's deserted me. My bottom lip starts trembling. I bite it so hard that salty blood trickles in my mouth. 'Stupid cow!' I rave at myself. 'Don't tell me you're crying!' I'm not usually this much of a wimp.

The only safe place left is the field. So I trudge up there and crawl into the gorse to hide, chewing my nails, with yellow flowers shivering all around me. There's a bee in here with me, buzzing round my den like it's trapped inside a bottle. It finds the entrance and zings out into the sunshine.

Minutes pass. I should get myself together, make plans, think about a way out of this mess. With my experience of being a Runner, I've seen loads of people in desperate situations. But I've never hung round long enough to see how they get out of them. There's a flappy bit of skin down the side of my nail. It hurts. So I munch on it some more. Ages pass. It's unreal up here. Like being in a glass bubble. You can't even hear the cars on the road. I've no idea what time it is.

My mind's wandering, like the time I was delirious with chicken pox. That girl, the one I saw sunbathing on the school field, chewing daisies, drifts into my head. She's doing what she did then — blowing seeds off a dandelion. They parachute into the wind. If only I could do that now, with all my problems. One little puff of breath and they'd all just float away . . .

Stay alert. Concentrate. Stop thinking soppy thoughts.

Voices! Coming from the bottom of the field. I part the gorse to make a spy hole. My hand is shaking so much it knocks a cloud of golden pollen out the flowers.

'Achoo!'

'Sparrow! There you are!'

It's them. Should have known they'd come to get me. I'm convinced by now that Lexie and Andy have changed sides too. That they've put all the blame for the rumour on me.

For a moment I feel dead tired; so drowsy I could curl up like a little kid and go to sleep. 'Get it over with,' a voice in my head whispers. 'It's no use running. They'll get you sooner or later. There's no escape.'

Then fear takes over.

Fear drives me into the open, running like I've never run before. They'll never get me. I know this field. I know every stone, every rabbit hole that might trip me up.

'Sparrow, wait! We only want to talk!'

Nobody can catch me. I'm springy, light, smooth as oil, I'm flying . . .

Risk a backward glance.

Scott's right behind me.

My legs collapse. Burning liquid pumps into my throat, makes me retch. I'd forgotten. Forgotten that he can run like a cheetah.

Perhaps I could've outrun him. But I just wait, kneeling doubled over in the grass clutching my sore stomach. It looks as if I've given in. But I haven't. Because, like magic, my brain's stopped whirling. It's clear and still. And it's whispering to me. 'Get him where it hurts most. Use his weakness.' You learn that as a Runner. The most cruel messages, insults, rumours, hit people in the rawest places, where they're already hurting.

Scott staggers up, gasping. I'm pleased to see that catching me has been such hard work.

'Sparrow, what did you run away for? We wanted to talk to you, that's all.'

'Who's with you?'

Back down the field, there are people moving, closing in.

'Only Lexie and Andy.'

'What, not Stringer? So he's sent you three to get me, has he? You're working for him now?'

Scott looks puzzled, as if he can't understand my questions: 'What are you talking about?'

But he can't fool me. I know what's happened. They've taken over, crowded me out. I'm back outside again, with no friends, no respect, just like before I was a Runner.

Fear and desperation make me vicious.

'Did it make you feel important?' I sneer at him. 'Running to Stringer, laying the blame on me?'

You can see what I'm doing. I'm hitting that raw nerve, trying to make him go berserk, lose control. Then I'll just stroll away, laughing. And he won't be able to do a thing to stop me. It won't solve my problems. I'll still be on the run from Stringer and all the other people my ex-Runners turned against me. But now, at this moment, it's going to make me feel really good.

'You don't understand,' Scott's saying.

His face is grim, his mouth set in a tight line. Suddenly, getting him in a rage, flinging punches, looking like an idiot, seems the most important thing in the world. So I turn the screw a little bit more.

'Oh yes, I *do* understand!' I spit the words at him. 'You're a born loser, aren't you? You were born sad and lonely. A reject with no friends. Shouldn't be surprised if you fake losing your temper to make yourself more *interesting*. Just to be the centre of attention.'

'I don't! I did fake it this morning in the bus

park. But not all those other times!' You can tell that hurt him. I feel a stab of pleasure. Out the corner of my eye I see a bulky shape struggling up the hill. It's Lexie, finally catching up. I knew all the time that he hadn't forgiven me for delivering those insults – I wouldn't have forgiven me if I was him.

I hit out again: 'I must have been crazy, choosing you for my new Runner. Giving you the chance to be somebody.'

Scott's fists are clenched, his face is getting flushed, his eyes blazing. Excellent. Seeing that drives me on.

'You were a hopeless Runner. You never had a clue did you? Did you?'

Instantly I know that I've said the wrong thing. Because Scott's eyes soften, as if he's remembering good times.

'I was a great Runner,' he says simply. 'I didn't do it the same as you. But I was a great Runner, all the same.'

And he shakes himself like a wet dog climbing out of a deep dark river. He's back in control. He's not going to lose his temper.

Confused, I start to back away. 'You were on the bus with Stringer. I saw you! Chatting like you were best friends!'

'Oh.' His face clears. 'I understand now.'

Lexie, with Andy trailing behind, has reached us at last. Lexie collapses on the grass, groaning. Andy says: 'We couldn't find you, Sparrow. What you doing up here?'

'I thought . . .' I begin to say. Then stop – I don't know what I think any more.

'She saw me talking to Stringer. She thought we'd sold out, gone over to his side.'

Andy's mouth drops open. It does that when he's amazed about anything. 'Why should we do that?' he manages to gasp. I shrug and try to look apologetic. 'That rumour worked like a dream,' he tells me. 'Stringer's finished. He's just a joke now.'

'Then what was Scott doing on the bus with him? It didn't look like he was laughing at him.'

Scott's face has an odd, sympathetic expression on it. I recognize that expression. 'Wait just one minute! Don't tell me you were doing your usual trick. Don't tell me you were giving him advice. I don't believe it. You weren't doing your agony auntie bit with Stringer!'

He nods and I'm pleased to see he looks a bit ashamed. I can hardly speak. I just splutter: 'For God's sake!'

But then Scott says in a calm voice: 'Did you ever wonder, Sparrow, why that rumour worked so well? You didn't think it would, did you? And did you ever wonder why Stringer just crumbled, went down without a fight?'

I have been thinking about these things – all the time. 'I did wonder,' I confess, 'why that rumour made such a big impression. It wasn't even a very good rumour, was it?'

Scott's voice is quiet and serious. 'Oh, it was the best rumour we could ever have thought of. Because it's true. Some of it anyway. All the best rumours have a bit of truth in them.'

'What?' I can't help laughing. 'You're having me on.'

Scott shakes his head: 'I saw Stringer on the bus,' he says. 'And I knew he wasn't dangerous any more. Just by looking at him.'

'So you climbed on to the bus? To talk to him?'

Scott nods at me.

'You *are* crazy,' I tell him.

But he just shrugs as if that isn't important. As if that insult can't hurt him any more.

'Anyway, Stringer told me some things. He told me about his mum. He says she hits him.'

'So we're supposed to feel sorry for him?' Andy pipes up, taking time off from prising a scab loose.

'I never said that,' Scott says.

I'm raking about in my mind. I've seen Stringer's mum. Once. This big strong woman, tall as Stringer. I remember it, because I was walking past the house where Stringer lives. Most kids avoided Stringer's territory altogether. But I didn't. In those days I believed I could go anywhere – that being a Runner gave me special protection. Anyway, Stringer's mum came out with washing. And what I remember about her was her arms. Big, muscly arms like a boxer. And bright red hair, like Stringer's.

'Why doesn't he hit her back?' Andy's asking Scott. 'He hits everybody else.'

Scott shrugs: 'Dunno. I never asked him that.

102

Because he loves her, I suppose. Because he doesn't want to hurt her. And because he's scared of her.'

'Phaw!' Andy makes a snorting noise to show how ridiculous he thinks that is. 'That doesn't make sense. How can he love her *and* be scared of her? He was just having you on, trying to get some sympathy.'

Lexie's scowling as if he's puzzling something out. 'Wait a minute,' he says. 'When I was in the same class as Stringer at junior school, when we used to get changed for games, we'd see bruises on his legs and on his back. Green and yellow bruises, old ones. And fresh purple bruises. But everybody thought it was from fighting. Stringer was always fighting.'

None of us remember that. Stringer is older than us. Lexie's the only one who's the same age as him.

'What else did he say?' Lexie seems curious now.

'What's it matter?' Andy sounds really worried. Even talking about Stringer makes him jumpy. 'Let's forget him,' he begs. 'Let's not think about him any more.'

But Scott can't help it. I get the awful feeling that solving people's problems has become his latest bad habit, now he's given up going berserk.

'Stringer says he tries to keep her in a good mood. But he's always doing wrong things. Things that make her mad. And she beats him up.'

'Phaw!' Andy just can't believe it. He can't believe that Stringer would cower in a corner and let somebody hammer him.

I'm thinking all this over. I look seriously at Scott.

'You're not trying to say, are you, that we should try to stop this rumour or change it somehow?'

'You can't feel sorry for Stringer!' Andy's squeaking at us. 'I don't believe it! Think of all the little kids. Little kids had nightmares about him. They hid under desks when he came in the classroom. They wet their pants they were so scared of him!'

'We can't stop it now,' Scott says. 'Or change it. Even if we wanted to. It's gone too far. And anyway, Andy's right. We've done a good job. Everybody's pleased. We've done everyone a big favour.' But he still doesn't sound convinced.

I know what he's thinking. Me and my new Runner, we're a good team. We can read each other's minds, some of the time.

'You can't help him, Scott. Don't get mixed up in this. You can't get involved between Stringer and his mum.'

'It'd be suicide,' Lexie adds bluntly.

'I know,' Scott says.

'You won't, will you?' I plead with him.

He shakes his head. 'I'm not that stupid. I can't do anything. Wouldn't know where to start.'

But I still get the feeling that he wishes he *did* know.

'Where's Stringer now?' asks Andy, looking round fearfully, as if just talking about him can make him appear.

'Who cares?' I shrug. Andy grins with relief. He likes this answer.

Scott's face is still deadly serious. Then he shudders, as if he's waking up from a bad dream and begins to smile, with the rest of us. 'Yeah, who cares?' he tells Andy. 'Nobody cares where he is. We don't have to worry about him any more.'

CHAPTER FOURTEEN

Friday night. And I've got a date. I'm waiting for Scott in the shopping mall, on those bright yellow seats by the fountain – the one that shoots out pink water, just opposite McDonald's. There are crowds of people about, doing late night shopping. Security guards are prowling round in navy blue uniforms with two way radios sticking out their back pockets.

We arranged to meet here. Scott's not my boy-friend or anything. I don't fancy him. We're just friends – we joke with each other all the time.

It's more than twenty-four hours since Scott, Lexie and Andy came to find me on the hill-side to tell me that the rumour about Stringer was true. A lot of things have happened since then. I thought seriously about not being a Runner any more, about breaking up the organization. It was getting me into too much trouble.

But this morning, soon as I got into school, Mad Maxwell yelled at me along a corridor: 'Sparrow, come here a minute!' I thought it was about missing lessons yesterday but he seemed to have forgotten about that. He wanted me to take back Simon's brace. He'd noticed it on his geography room ceiling, stuck with chewing gum to a mountain range in Central Asia. 'Wonder how it got there?' he said, looking puzzled. Mad Maxwell's got this crumpled face that looks permanently puzzled.

After that, lots of people gave me messages. So it was business as usual, as if nothing had happened.

Scott's still my partner. And I sort of promised Lexie and Andy that they could be Runners too, when things got hectic. Stupid decision to make – all of them will slow me down, what with Scott doing his agony auntie bit and Andy falling over his flatfish feet and Lexie taking half an hour to get to the top floor, especially if there's a chocolate machine on the way. But I suppose I can live with that.

Nicky's stopped giving me dirty looks. He's even talking to me again. He said, 'Hello, Sparrow, how's it going?' as he strolled by with his mates. He's in a good mood because he and Heather are back together again. I told Scott about that and he just shrugged: 'Well,' he said, 'it'll end in tears. You wait. I mean, I told her he had a terrible personality. Plus, he looks like a weasel. But if people won't listen to good advice . . .'

While I'm waiting, I jingle my money around in my pocket. There's lots of it. We could go and have a McDonald's, go to the cinema and get popcorn and hot dogs and Coke. There's a good film on. And I don't care what I spend – I'm not saving up any more.

It was a really funny thing. I've been saving up for ages for these shoes. Not that thrilling really, saving up for a pair of shoes. But I loved them the first time I saw them. They're in the window of that sports shop just by Woolworth's. And they're very expensive trainers – high ones of soft black leather with a pink and silver trim. And the laces are pink and silver too. 'Good running shoes,' I thought soon as I saw them. And dead smart too.

But when I got home from school today my mum gave me a box. It was full of crinkly white paper. I lifted it up and my shoes were underneath, my running shoes.

'Hope they fit,' my mum said. She had a big smile on her face. She looked pleased and proud.

I couldn't believe it. 'How did you know I was saving up for these shoes?'

'Because you told me,' she said. 'You said how much you wanted them.'

I couldn't remember saying that. 'Did you send Dad to get them?'

'No, I went on my own.'

'Honest?' I was lacing the shoes up now.

'I'll take them back if they don't fit.'

'They fit just great.'

'She was determined to go,' my dad said. 'Just to get you those shoes.'

I was touched. I really was. No one but me and Dad could appreciate how brave she had to be to go into the mall, with all those people crowding her in. I'm not kidding myself that it'll last. It may be a bad day again tomorrow. But it was a good day today. And that's something.

I'm wearing my new shoes now. There's a speck

of dirt on the silver streak – I bend down to flick it off. It's ten past seven. Scott should be here by now.

There's a boy over there with spiky red hair. I can see him by the glass lift that goes up to the car park. For a moment it looks like Stringer but then he turns round and it's not Stringer at all.

Stringer's disappeared. This morning at school there were all kinds of rumours. Someone said they'd seen him sleeping rough in a skip. Someone else said he'd run away and hitched down to London to get away from his mum. And then they said he'd got arrested for getting fighting drunk last night and smashing all the windows in his house. He even tried to set fire to it. But they're all just rumours. Maybe none of them is true.

By this afternoon no one was talking about Stringer any more. He's yesterday's news. Today's hot news is: Mad Maxwell's having an affair with Mrs Frink. It's all round the school. Someone knows someone who's seen them kissing in the geography cupboard. But that's one rumour I don't believe. You'd have to be brain dead to fancy Mad Maxwell. He's got these bushy hairs sprouting out his nose – it's gross. And he smokes a pipe. But you never know with rumours. Maybe it's true. Maybe I should offer to take their secret love notes. Discretion assured!

It's surprising though, how soon Stringer was forgotten. How nobody even mentions his name. You don't notice he's gone – there are plenty of others ready to take his place, just dying to step into his shoes. But I hope they don't want me to take their messages. I'll say no if they ask me. Or better still, I won't give them the chance to ask me. I'll be running so fast they'll just see a blur. They'll think their mind is playing tricks.

'Hello.' Scott plonks himself down beside me. He looks different. His wild mop is all flattened down and glossy. He's been putting hair gel on it.

'Sorry I'm late. I didn't have a watch.'

'What's that on your wrist then?'

He glances down at the watch on his wrist. 'Oh that. It's the wrong sort of watch. I borrowed it off my sister. But it's got hands see, a little hand and a big hand. I can't tell the time by that sort of watch. I can only use a digital one.'

'For Chrissake! Didn't they teach you *anything* at junior school?'

He shrugs. 'I must have been in the drama room the day they did telling the time. They used to put me in there to cool off. It was soundproofed, see, with all these mats spread out so I couldn't hurt myself.'

'What a sad case you were, weren't you? A real reject.'

He grins: 'Nice shoes you've got there.' He lifts his foot.

'Don't you dare stomp on them!' I shriek at him. 'I'll kill you if you do!'

It's all right. You can have a joke with Scott now without him going berserk. We insult each other all the time. That's what I mean about fancying him. You can't fancy someone you insult all the time. Can you?

GRAPHICAT

Marilyn Watts

For my mother and father

CHAPTER ONE

It was five minutes to three, on a boring Friday afternoon. Tim stopped pretending to write his story and yawned. He checked the clock again. He'd have to be quick to get there first.

Very carefully and quietly, so that Mrs Edmonds didn't see, Tim closed his book. Next was the difficult bit. He watched for a moment. Mrs Edmonds was busy writing at her desk, with her head bowed. When he was sure she wasn't looking, he opened his desk drawer and put his book and pen inside. Then he closed the drawer slowly, but it wasn't slow enough because she looked up. Tim held his breath, she couldn't have seen . . .

'It's nearly three o'clock,' she announced. 'Finish what you're writing and put your books away. If you're helping with the posters for the fête, then go to Miss Grant's room now. The others can choose what to do for the rest of the afternoon, so long . . .'

Before she had finished, Tim was already on his way to the side of the classroom.

'Timothy!' barked Mrs Edmonds. 'Where are you going?'

'I've put my things away, Miss.'

'I can see that. Where are you going?'

'To the PASHT.' Tim jerked his thumb at the computer. 'You said we could.'

Mrs Edmonds sighed. She turned to the rest of the class. 'Is it Timothy's turn on the computer?'

Silence. Twenty-eight pairs of eyes looked at her and then looked down again. Of course it wasn't: Tim Pascall was always playing with the computer, but no one was going to dare say that. They didn't want to meet Tim on the way home, alone, and have to explain.

'All right, Timothy,' Mrs Edmonds said. 'But you must share with someone. Joanne, you have a go as well.'

Jo looked up in horror. 'Oh no, Miss. I – '

'Go on, Joanne. Don't argue.'

Jo knew that Mrs Edmonds wouldn't change her mind. And because Caron, her best friend, was on holiday, she couldn't even pretend she'd arranged to join in with someone else. Eddy Edmonds knew that, of course. Jo got up and started to walk across the classroom, between the desks. Everyone else was getting ready to do what they wanted, and Jo wished she, too, could choose to paint, or read. Anything would be better than this.

'Why did you come?' Tim hissed, when she got there.

'I had to, didn't I?' she hissed back.

'Well, I'm busy.'

So Jo sat and watched. Tim had already switched on the computer, and at each stage of the loading program he keyed in an answer, almost before the questions had come up on the screen. Then, when the index files appeared, he moved the cursor down until it picked out a game.

A: GRAPHICAT

PRESS ENTER TO START

This was too much for Jo. She didn't mind wasting an afternoon, but she did mind ending up in the middle of one of Eddy's grand explosions. 'Tim! What are you doing?' she whispered. 'You know we can't play games during school.'

'Shut up,' he said. 'I play games all the time and she's never caught me.'

'You're stupid.'

'So are you, then.'

Tim pressed the *return* key and the screen cleared. Then there was a picture which built up line by line; a squarish cat's face, looking out of the screen. A blue cat, with red eyes and long whiskers. GRAPHICAT, it said along the bottom of the picture. The cat blinked, once, and then the screen changed again and Tim was into the game.

It was a street scene, with a dustbin, a saucer and a garden gate.

The cat had to come out of the gate, eat the fishhead which was sticking out of the dustbin, and drink the milk. Tim moved the cat along by pressing the cursor keys, his fingers working fast and sure over the keyboard. Jo was impressed, even though she didn't want to be. Then a square dog appeared, and the cat jumped on to the dustbin, up on the

115

garden wall, and pushed the dustbin lid off. The lid fell down on to the dog, and it went flat. The screen cleared again.

'That was good.' Tim was so pleased with himself that he even sounded normal. 'It was quick, too. Now it goes to level two.'

'Can I have a go after?' Jo was itching to see if she could move the cat so quickly.

'Sshh.' Tim frowned at the screen.

'I'm not just sitting here all afternoon,' Jo snapped, but it came out louder than she meant.

'What are you two doing?' Mrs Edmonds was sounding angry.

Jo spun round, guiltily, just in time to see Eddy knock a whole, beautiful tub of colour off someone's desk. A few seconds longer and she would have caught them, but now she was too concerned with trying to stop more paint going over her skirt.

'Timothy, you're not letting Joanne near the computer,' she said, dabbing at the material. 'I want you to share.'

When Jo turned back to the screen, there was a row of columns in black and white standing there, innocently. At the side it said HEIGHTS OF CHILDREN IN OUR CLASS, and along the bottom was a list of names. As she stared, Tim said,

'It's Jan Margett's maths project.'

By the time Mrs Edmonds arrived at the PASHT desk, Jo was carefully shading in the different columns.

Five minutes of shading was plenty. 'Can I play the cat game?' Jo asked.

'I'll play it first,' said Tim.

There wasn't any point in arguing, so Jo moved over and Tim changed the discs back and called up the cat. This time the first screen only lasted for a few seconds, because the fishhead disappeared into the dustbin again before the cat could eat it. The second time, too, Tim was slower, and the cat had hardly finished the milk when the dog came bowling along. But Tim held his breath, his fingers flew over the keys – cursor left, up, up again, *enter* – and the dog was flattened.

'It's my go now,' Jo said. 'Come on.'

'No, I'm doing level two. Shut up.'

'You'll just keep playing and playing.' Jo didn't mean to sit and watch for the rest of the afternoon. 'Sssh.'

Level two was full of feet – legs hurrying along, wearing spiky heels or heavy boots. The cat had to weave between them, not touching, in order to reach home, which was on the right of the screen. There were holes along the bottom of the picture for it to hide in. As the cat got further towards the right-hand side, there were more legs, and they came quicker. From time to time Tim hit *escape* and the cat reached out a paw and scratched the nearest leg. The leg would stop for a moment, and the cat could run on again.

'No. I'm not going to shush.' Jo tried to reach *escape*, but Tim knocked her away with his elbow.

117

'What d'you think you're doing?' he snapped. 'Let me finish.'

'No.'

They were almost fighting now. Tim took a hand off the keyboard, and grabbed her wrist. But with his right hand he was still pressing the cursor – right, right, right – and, amazingly, the cat missed all the threatening legs. It reached the side of the screen, and still the cursor was saying *right, right, right!* Jo expected the computer to bleep a warning, but there was no sound. The cat squashed against the frame. And then, silently, carefully, it walked out of the screen.

Jo stared, dry-mouthed. The cat left the screen, it grew bigger and bigger, and it changed. Its hind legs were square but along its body the angles disappeared. As the cat came towards her, walking on to the desk top, she watched unbelievingly as its smooth, fine paws found a grip on the shiny wood. It gazed at her steadily, out of unblinking red-orange eyes, and as its last foot left the picture, it slunk out of its last squareness.

Jo was terrified. She couldn't move. The cat stared at her. It seemed too frightening to be a real cat, but it was, down to its velvety grey paws with the odd bluish tinge. It walked along the bench, past her shoulder, and Jo didn't dare to turn round to follow it. Instead, her glance slipped past where it had been. She looked at Tim's face, and wished she hadn't. It didn't help to see that he looked simply petrified.

For a long time, Jo stayed still. The hairs on the

118

back of her neck prickled, and she knew the cat was somewhere behind her, but she couldn't move. She and Tim just stared at each other in horror.

Slowly, Jo realized that the room was still noisy. It seemed the only safe thing to hold on to. Perhaps that meant that this was all some silly trick of the imagination. She forced herself to breathe again, and turned away from Tim's stare. But then he gasped, and Jo turned to look.

The room was full of movement and chatter, and no one was paying them the slightest attention. Except for one person. Opposite them, pencil hovering in the air and mouth wide open, Vicky was sitting, very still . . . staring at something behind Jo's head.

CHAPTER TWO

But when Jo looked behind her, the cat had vanished.

Together, she and Tim turned back to the screen. There were the legs, still hurrying, the holes and the house, but no cat. No cat anywhere.

Slowly, Tim started to press the cursor keys. Questioningly, once, then again, and again. Left, left, left. Trying to bring the cat back into the picture. He started tapping the keys more quickly – up, down, left, left, left – but nothing happened. No cat appeared. There were just the legs, still moving, walking jerkily across the screen. 'It's gone,' he said. It sounded so helpless, so final.

'Come out of the program and try again,' Jo said. 'It might be there, then.'

She didn't really think it would work, and she knew Tim wasn't convinced. But they had to try something. Tim pressed *exit* and went back one step in the program.

A: GRAPHICAT

PRESS ENTER TO START

Enter. Nothing. He tapped the key again.

'Let me have a go.' Jo pushed him over so that

she could reach the keyboard, and took the program back to the menu.

'Graphicat,' she murmured, glancing down the list.

'Cat!'

Jo froze, staring at the screen.

'Who let that cat in here?' It was Mrs Edmonds' voice. The class stopped what they were doing and looked up. A couple of people grinned with delight. This was more like it! Jo and Tim were the last ones to look. But when they did, there it was . . . sitting on the Display Table, elegantly washing its paws.

The cat looked at them, blinked once, and disappeared.

'Catch it, someone!' Mrs Edmonds called, but it wasn't a good thing to say. The group nearest the table rushed forwards, eagerly, and the cat slipped easily between their feet. Not touching. Like a game.

'All right everyone. Stop. Stop!' Mrs Edmonds was holding back the knot of people beside her. 'We'll frighten it. *Stop!*'

Eventually, most of the class stopped. No one had managed even to touch the cat. So they simply watched as it paused, then walked very slowly and deliberately across the room, picking its way between the table legs, until it jumped up on to the computer desk.

Please, oh please, thought Jo. She didn't know what she wanted. Just for it to go back. To go away. As if somehow, with all the class watching, it could still slink back into the dots and squares of the computer screen. But instead the cat sat down on the desk, next to Tim, and put its tail neatly round his neck. For a second, Jo thought it smiled at her, as if it were sharing a joke. And then it started to purr.

Mrs Edmonds was amazed. She stared – and then she began to be suspicious. 'Is that your cat?'

'No – no!'

'Timothy?' It was obvious that she didn't know whether or not to believe him.

'No, honest, Miss. It's not mine.'

Mrs Edmonds smiled. 'Well, it's nice and friendly.'

Friendly? thought Jo. She looked at Tim. The cat gazed back at her. It opened its mouth slightly to show little pointed teeth, its face close to Tim's ear. Superior, threatening, in control.

No, she thought. *Not friendly.*

'Anyway, Timothy,' Mrs Edmonds went on. 'You obviously have a way with cats. Can you pick it up? Careful, though. Mind it doesn't scratch you.'

At first Tim looked as though he didn't dare to move. *It is threatening*, Jo thought. *He can feel it, too.* Tim slid his neck away from the cat's tail, and stood up, next to it. The cat flexed a paw, opening the white claws. Tim stretched out his arms. The cat didn't move. Slowly, Tim picked it up in both arms.

'Good,' said Mrs Edmonds. Then, when Tim still didn't move or speak, she said, 'Can you take it outside, Timothy? Into the playground?'

'I'll help.' Jo jumped up. 'I'll – I'll open the doors for him, Miss.'

122

'Thank you, Joanne.' Mrs Edmonds smiled at her. 'Take it into the playground and let it go.'

'Yes, Miss. Of course, Miss. We'll take it now. Come on, Tim.' Jo knew she was babbling, but she had to get Tim and the cat out of the room. What was the matter with Tim? Why didn't he move? She grabbed the sleeve of his jumper and started to pull him towards the door.

Outside in the corridor, they stood staring at each other. Over the blue-grey head of the cat.

'What are we going to do with it?' Jo whispered.

Tim shook his head. 'We can't let it go. We'll never find it again.'

Jo looked round. 'Well, we can't just stand here. Someone's bound to come along in a minute.' She thought, hard. 'What about the old storeroom? We can put it in there and . . . and . . .'

'Okay. Anywhere. Then we'll think. Quick!'

They ran round the corner of the corridor and into the narrow room. It was dusty, and unused. Tim opened his arms, and the cat flowed to the ground in one quick movement. And stayed there. Jo and Tim both darted to the door in case the cat tried to run out, but it simply sat on the floor, looking at them.

Jo closed the door behind them with a sigh of relief. They couldn't lock it, but that didn't matter. After all, cats couldn't open closed doors by themselves.

'We'll come back after school,' she said. 'And

then we'll – ' She couldn't think of anything at all. 'Then we'll do something,' she finished lamely.

They walked back to the classroom. Tim said nothing, just walked along, watching his feet.

'Tim?' No answer. Jo couldn't understand it. Usually Tim bossed everyone around. She didn't like that very much, but she didn't like him like this, either.

'What's the matter?' Jo asked. Then she looked at Tim and realized what it was. 'You look like Caron does just before she faints.' Then she giggled. 'Even your hair's standing on end.'

Tim stopped walking. He ran a hand over his short, spiky haircut, but he still didn't speak.

'Okay,' said Jo. 'You don't have to tell me. And you can go and get the cat. You started it, you were the one who had to – '

Tim looked up at her and she stopped at once. He looked awful. All white.

'What's the matter?'

He opened his mouth, closed it, swallowed, and looked at her with terrified eyes. Then he said, quietly,

'It's a big cat, isn't it?'

'I suppose. Quite big.' Jo frowned. 'Why?'

'When I picked it up, I couldn't feel it. *It didn't weigh anything!*'

CHAPTER THREE

That's impossible, Jo thought. But before she could say it, Mrs Edmonds' head appeared in the classroom doorway.

'All right, you two,' she said loudly. 'When you've quite finished chatting, I want you in here, now. What's the matter with everyone? I can't get any sense out of Victoria. What an afternoon!'

Vicky! Jo and Tim walked down the corridor (NO RUNNING IN THE CORRIDORS) as if they were in a race, and into the classroom. Eddy was standing in front of Vicky, hands on hips, which meant she really was getting angry.

'I asked what's wrong, Victoria. You haven't done a thing for the last quarter of an hour. The excitement's over, you know.'

'The cat – ' Vicky stopped and looked past Mrs Edmonds to where Jo and Tim stood in the doorway. She sneezed. Jo glared at her. She *couldn't*, she *mustn't* say anything.

'Yes, the cat. What about it?'

Jo could hear Tim breathing beside her, and she crossed her fingers behind her back. Without taking her eyes off them, Vicky said, slowly,

'Nothing about the cat, Miss. Nothing at all.'

She sneezed again, then bent her head and began to write, furiously. Mrs Edmonds waited for a moment, then just said, 'I think you need a handkerchief, Victoria,' before turning to the rest of the class. 'Ten minutes to go, everyone,' she said briskly. 'Start clearing up any paints if you're using them. Oh, Joanne, turn the computer off, please.'

Jo hesitated when she got to the computer. She had a feeling she was doing something dangerous; losing the last link with the cat in some way. But she switched it off and the screen monitor as well.

It was odd. Even without looking at Tim, she could still feel how worried he was – like invisible signals across the room. *The cat will know we're scared*, she thought, and then made herself stop. How could it? It was silly to think like that. What she had to do was to work out how they could get to stay behind. Jo twitched her ponytail forward over her shoulder, and chewed the end, thoughtfully.

Five minutes after school was over, Jo was walking round the classroom, extremely slowly, watering every plant she could find.

Her idea had worked. Mrs Edmonds always made a big fuss about pupils being responsible for their own classroom, but she had been very surprised when Jo suddenly insisted that the plants needed watering and Tim offered to put all the chairs straight. They had both deliberately avoided Vicky, who had hung around too until Mrs Edmonds told

her to go home at once and take her cold with
Vicky left, and they could hear her sneezing all the
way along the corridor as she went.

Eventually, Mrs Edmonds picked up her bag. 'I
can't stay any longer, I'm afraid. Why don't you
finish that another time?'

Jo looked very serious. 'But Miss, the plants are
all drooping already, and if we wait until after the
weekend, it might be too late.'

Then Tim joined in, all concern and innocent
blue eyes. 'And I can't sort everything out when
there are people here, Miss. It'll be so tidy for
Monday.'

Mrs Edmonds looked at them, and then smiled.
'Well, all right,' she said. 'But I want you out of here
by quarter-past.'

Jo nodded and tried to look responsible as she
watered a plant for the third time. But as soon as
Mrs Edmonds closed the door behind her, Jo put
down the jug.

'Come on.' She grabbed her bag and coat, and
raced Tim to the door. They watched until Mrs
Edmonds disappeared into the staffroom, and then,
as there didn't seem to be anyone else around, they
slipped out and started to run along the corridor. It
was eerie, just the two of them in the quiet school
with no one else there. But then the staffroom door
opened further down the corridor, and there was a
sudden babble of voices.

For a second they didn't move. Then Tim slipped
behind the nearest open door, and Jo dashed after

him. The voices got louder and nearer, until someone exclaimed, 'Damn, I've forgotten my shopping!' Another voice said, 'We'll wait,' and the whole group of teachers stopped right outside the open door. Jo could see them through the crack along the hinges. They were less than a metre away – surely they must know she was there? Tim glared, with a finger across his lips, although Jo shook her head to show that she wasn't going to make a sound. Soon there were footsteps again, the teachers all moved off, someone laughed, and then the noise was cut off as the outside doors closed behind them.

Tim looked round the door, and then they went out again into the silent corridor. Neither of them said anything until they reached the storeroom, but when they got there, Tim stood back to let Jo go first. Her hand was shaking on the door handle, but she took a deep breath and pushed open the door.

She couldn't see the cat anywhere.

Jo and Tim stood and stared at the room. It was darker than the corridor outside, with only one small window at the end, and it took a few moments for their eyes to adjust. Then Tim jabbed Jo in the ribs and whispered, 'There it is.'

Jo looked along the rows of empty shelves, and saw it. The cat was sitting on a shelf above their heads, watching them. They could only just see the faint outline of its body, but the amber eyes gleamed out. Jo walked into the room and Tim followed her. As she walked, a voice inside her was saying *It's all right, it's only an ordinary cat*. But when she reached it and looked up, she knew that that wasn't true.

The cat didn't move. It sat there, impassively, staring out of the screen – no, it was air of course, real air – with its front paws tucked underneath it. *It's like the Cheshire Cat in Alice in Wonderland*, Jo thought. *But it's not grinning. And that cat vanishes. I don't think this one will*. She shivered. 'The *Alice in Wonderland* cat's frightening,' she said out loud. 'It's not funny at all.'

'What are you talking about?' Tim replied, angrily. 'I want to know what we're going to do? What it is.'

The cat's eyes opened wider. They looked more red than orange. They opened very wide, and Jo screamed. Where the colour should have been round, and slanting at each side, it wasn't. The red area of its eyes was totally, impossibly, square.

And then they heard the angry shouts behind them, and heavy footsteps in the corridor. 'Hey you kids, what are you playing at? Get out of there!'

They ran for it. They were faster than the care-taker and anyway they had a head start. Bags and coats flying, Jo and Tim ran out of the room, through a classroom, and down the hall steps into the playground. They were so busy running that they didn't notice the cat, running with them. And they didn't see it slip past their legs and disappear into the bushes.

They ran out of the school gates and round the

corner. Then Tim stopped and leant against the railings.

'Do you think he saw us?' Jo asked, not knowing whether to stop or not.

'Nah. Not enough to recognize us, anyway,' Tim said. He sounded very calm, and Jo thought of some of the stories that went round the class about him. He did a lot of running away from trouble. What was she doing, being chased by care-takers with Tim Pascall? She ought to have her head examined. But when her heart began to stop pounding, she found she was quite enjoying herself. They'd made it away, after all. It was lucky she was a fast runner.

Tim looked back at the school. 'I wonder where it is?' he muttered.

'It must be still in the storeroom,' Jo answered. 'Do you think he'll find it?'

'No.' Tim shook his head. 'No.'

'But he won't just shut the door, will he? Oh, Tim, that means it'll be locked – '

'No.' Tim shook his head again, but angrily this time. 'I mean, it won't be there any more.'

'How do you know.'

Tim looked at her, blankly. 'Because it isn't. Can't you feel it?'

It was Jo's turn to look blank.

Tim turned to the trees and houses on the other side of the road. 'It's out there, somewhere. And I don't know what we're going to do about it.'

'Perhaps we don't have to do anything,' said Jo.

'Perhaps it's an ordinary cat and it'll just go away and eat Kitekat and mice and things.'

'And we'll go home and go to school and play GRAPHICAT,' Tim said, sarcastically. 'All safe and normal. It's all right for you. Go and have your tea, then.'

'Okay,' Jo snapped back, and hitched her bag over her shoulder. 'See you.'

She started to walk away, towards the main street of shops, but when she got to the corner she glanced back. Tim was still standing by the railings, and still looking across the road, as though he were watching something in the gardens opposite.

CHAPTER FOUR

By Monday morning, Jo was looking forward to getting out of the house. Even school was better than staying in and remembering the Row.

Saturday evening had been the worst time, when it had all blown up. Her mother had been so pre-occupied and busy, as she got ready to go off for the week. Jo was feeling fed up to start with, and thought she deserved more attention herself. After all, the weekend wasn't being much fun with Caron away.

At first, Jo's mother asked if she would like to help her pack. Jo said no. Then her mother asked her to help wash the salad. Jo said there was a television programme she wanted to watch instead. Then her mother and father had ganged up on her.

'It's only for a week, Jo!'

'And you know your gran's finding it difficult to cope on her own,' added her father.

Jo privately wondered why her aunt couldn't go and help, but she didn't dare say that out loud.

'We ought to be glad it's only her wrist that's broken,' said her mother, encouragingly. 'It could have been a lot worse.'

It didn't work, so they ignored her. Jo sat and

watched her mother dashing round, collecting things to take, bringing various bits and pieces downstairs. Jo's father watched television and at the same time ironed his way steadily through a growing pile of clothes.

Jo sulked. And when her parents said she was sulking, she got angry instead.

'There's no need to be in such a bad mood,' her mother snapped. 'It's not my fault that Caron's away.'

'I'm not in a bad mood!'

It had ended with Jo storming up to her bedroom.

Her dad hadn't been saying much since then. Last night, he had cooked tea and then told Jo to eat it on her own. He wasn't hungry, he said. He sat in front of the television all evening, and didn't notice that Jo stayed up until eleven o'clock. Jo wished he would notice. But in the end she was so tired that she had to give up and go to bed, anyway.

Jo kicked the pavement as she walked. It was lonely going to school on her own, but Caron's family weren't coming home for another week. And Mum would be back by then, anyway. Jo suddenly wished she hadn't been quite so awkward about her mother going away. It made her feel uncomfortable, so she told herself that it wasn't her fault, and kept walking.

Jo was so busy trying to convince herself, that she reached her classroom before she remembered that there was anything wrong. It was all much more noisy than usual. People were running around, and there was a group of children huddled by the computer desk. *The cat!* She looked for Tim, but he wasn't there. And then Mrs Edmonds came in, walking fast, with Tim trailing behind her. She saw Jo, and pounced.

'Joanne! What's happened to the computer?'

Jo stared at her. Not this as well! She didn't want to think about computers and strange animals. But Mrs Edmonds went on, loudly,

'You were the last one to touch it, weren't you?'

'Miss?'

'It won't work. It's broken.'

Jo felt herself going bright red. She mustn't, not in front of everyone. They'd think . . .

But Mrs Edmonds saw her face, and started talking more quietly and slowly instead. 'It's all right, Joanne. I'm sure there's nothing you could have done.'

'I just switched it off, Miss.'

'I know.' Mrs Edmonds sat down heavily on the chair beside her. She looked flustered, but she gave Jo a little smile. *She is trying to be nice*, Jo thought.

'And I saw the screen before you switched it off,' Mrs Edmonds said. 'It looked normal. Was it a list of files?'

'Yes, Miss. We were looking at the menu.'

Mrs Edmonds sighed. 'Then I don't see what the problem is. I tried to use it first thing this morning, and I couldn't get it to do a thing. Neither could Miss Thompson, and you know how good she is with computers.'

Jo nodded. Miss Thompson was the school expert, and very enthusiastic. Her class boasted that they could get out of doing any writing for a whole afternoon just by asking her questions about computing.

Mrs Edmonds got up. 'Don't worry about it, Joanne. Or you, Timothy. We'll have to get someone in to have a look at it.' Then she walked to the front of the classroom, raised her voice again, and in three minutes they were all quietly having the register taken.

It took a while to get down to the end of the list of names. And that was when Jo and Tim realized that Vicky Willis wasn't there. *Well, it saves us having to explain to her,* Jo said to herself. But she felt uneasy.

After morning school, Jo and Tim tried to stay in the classroom to look at the PASHT, but they were chased out by Mrs Abbey, the dinner lady. No one ever dared argue with her. There was no point in trying to sneak back in, either, so they ended up sitting by the playground wall, arguing.

'There's nothing we *can* do,' Tim said, fiercely. 'I don't know how to program a computer. Not properly. And neither do you.'

'I know more about them than you do, anyway,' Jo snapped back. 'At least I don't just play stupid games.'

'So what are you going to do, then?' he sneered.

Jo shook her head. 'I don't know. I don't even know what we've *done*.'

They sat for a while, without talking. Then Tim said, slowly,

'Have you seen it — since — ?'

Jo knew at once what he meant. 'No,' she said. 'Have you?'

'No.'

'Perhaps it might have gone away,' Jo said, carefully. 'It makes sense. We haven't seen it again.'

'And the computer's broken! So perhaps it's safe now.'

'That's all right, then.'

'I suppose.' Tim laughed. 'Yes, I suppose it is. And they'll just get someone in to fix the computer —'

'And I bet I beat you at GRAPHICAT!' Jo grinned back. 'Even though you've had more practice.'

'You're on. I'll give you a game.' Tim jumped up. 'Now, I'm going to play football.'

'Best of three!' Jo called after him, as he ran off.

Jo felt a lot better now that Tim had stopped worrying about the cat so much. It meant that she could stop worrying, too. Anyway, she said to herself as their sitting went in to dinner, there was nothing she could do. She knew she hadn't imagined it, but what other explanation was there? So she tagged along behind the girls from her class and tried not to think about anything except whether she wanted fish pie or spaghetti.

But it wasn't that easy. Why was Vicky away from school? It had to be just a coincidence. And anyway,

Vicky wouldn't have seen exactly what had happened, would she? Jo tried to remember how she and Tim had been sitting. Would someone behind them have been able to see the screen?

Jo followed her line to the nearest table and sat down, still thinking. After one slimy mouthful of spaghetti, she wished she'd had pie instead, but it was too late to change. So she ate and listened to bits of the conversation around her, and said 'yes' when anyone expected her to join in. And as soon as she relaxed, the cat walked into her mind. Beautiful, lean body and hungry eyes; thin, velvety legs and sharp claws. No, she couldn't have imagined it. Not something as lovely and threatening as that. It was nothing like a real cat, and it was everything like a real cat – all at the same time.

Then Kay Jones, who was sitting at the end of the table, suddenly squealed, 'Oh, look!'

'Close your mouth, Kay,' someone said. 'I can see all your chewed fish.'

'Look, isn't it sweet?'

They all looked. A cat was sitting on the window sill, watching them. A large, grey cat, with its whiskers pushed against the glass.

'It's probably hungry,' Kay said.

'Not for our school dinners!' Dawn called over.

'Don't choke, Jo,' Kay laughed. 'It wasn't that funny.'

Jo went to get some water, to stop herself coughing. She hadn't laughed. There was a huge crash outside the window. Jo saw Mrs Abbey run across the playground, clapping her hands together and shouting at something underneath the window. There was more noise, and then Mrs Abbey marched into the dining hall and went over to the counter. Jo followed her at a safe distance.

'Can you tell Cook that some cat's been at the dustbins?' Mrs Abbey said to one of the servers.

'It must have smelt the fish. It's made a right mess, though.'

Jo ran out of the door and into the playground, but the cat was nowhere to be seen.

'Hello,' said a quiet voice behind her. And when Jo didn't move, the voice went on, 'You're Jo, aren't you? Jo Reynolds?'

Jo spun round. She didn't know what she had expected, but it was a relief to find it was only Miss Thompson.

'Hello, Miss,' Jo said. But all the time she was thinking furiously. *Where had the cat got to? What was going to happen next?*

'It's your class's computer, isn't it? The one that's broken?'

It's your class's computer? It's your computer. The words said themselves over and over again in Jo's mind. *Of course!* She thought quickly. Miss Thompson was looking at her strangely, expecting an answer. So, give her an answer and then ask.

'Yes. Mrs Edmonds said you couldn't find anything wrong with it.'

'And I had a good look. But then it's an odd computer, of course.'

'Odd?' Jo's voice came out sounding small and strangled. She wished someone else was with her, to help her think.

'Well, it's not a usual make,' Miss Thompson said. 'I'd never heard of a PASHT before I came to this school. And the other computers here are BBC micros, of course.'

'Can it – can it do different kinds of things, then?' Jo asked.

'What do you mean? It uses the same software as the other computers.'

'So why is ours different from the others, Miss?'

'I don't know. But it doesn't really matter, does it?'

Jo wanted to scream. Miss Thompson didn't understand. Jo could hardly just stand there and ask her why cats walked out of their particular computer.

'And anyway, Jo, if you really want to do some computing in the meantime, Mrs Edmonds and I can arrange something. But we'll have an engineer in to look at it soon.'

Jo couldn't think of any engineer who could catch escaped cats. But she smiled, and said thank you, and walked off to think again. She spotted Tim playing football with a crowd of boys, and knew that she couldn't talk to him, even if she wanted to. But she didn't want to. Anyway, what did it matter if the cat helped itself to some disgusting school fish? It was welcome to it. For a second, she knew there was something wrong with that. Something very wrong. But she could not remember what it was.

In the end, Jo didn't have to remember what was wrong. It came to her instead, without her having to work it out.

She was crossing the playground for the start of afternoon school, when she saw a group of girls at the gates, crowding round something in the middle. Jo's stomach suddenly felt very hollow – she thought she knew what they must be looking at. But when she reached the group, there was a person in the middle, not an animal.

'Who is it?' Jo asked, as a couple of girls left the circle and started to walk towards her.

'That little kid, Tracey Wright,' one of them said.

'Her dog's got hurt,' said the second girl, as they turned to go into school. 'She's really upset.'

Tracey had been crying so much, that her eyes had gone all red and scrunched up. She was a nice kid, even though she was only a first year, but Jo was just relieved that it wasn't the cat, there in the playground. She didn't hear what Tracey was saying at first, and it was difficult to hear, anyway, through her crying. Then Tracey took a deep breath.

'There was all this blood,' she wailed. 'All round his eye.'

'He'll be all right, Trace,' someone said.

'But the vet, the vet said . . .'

Jo never did hear what the vet said. The two girls she'd passed before were coming back across the playground, looking very important, and dragging one of the teachers with them. Jo felt sick. She knew what had happened. She didn't need to hear them telling the teacher.

'Tracey's dog's got attacked, Miss.'

'By a great big cat, she says.'

'It's ever so badly hurt, Miss.'

'Tracey's ever so upset.'

Jo didn't stop to hear any more. She raced over to her classroom. She had to tell someone. And Tim was the only person who'd believe her. She didn't know what else to do. When Jo walked into the room, she was cornered by people wanting to know what was happening out in the playground. But there was no sign of Tim.

Everyone knew the dog, because Tracey's mother used to bring it when she collected her from school. It was a big, bouncy, golden-coloured dog, which used to bark its head off when it saw Tracey coming. Jo wished she could sit down on the ground, like Tracey, and cry her eyes out, too. But she was a bit too old for that. She had to *do* something.

Where was Tim? She'd never live it down if she asked anyone in the class where he was. But Mrs Edmonds could ask the class, of course, and did so; and they said he'd suddenly run off, in the lunch hour. 'Perhaps he was ill, Miss?'

Perhaps he heard about the dog, thought Jo. Well, there was no one left to talk to. Unless . . .

On Friday afternoon, Vicky had been sitting in one of the chairs by the bookcase. Jo walked to one chair and looked over at the computer, trying to imagine her and Tim still sitting in front of it. Then she tried the next chair, and the next. She thought that Vicky could have seen the game, even with people there.

'Is this a private game of musical chairs, Joanne, or can anyone join in?' Mrs Edmonds was in one of her sarcastic moods, and those were always the worst.

Jo felt herself go red. 'No, Miss,' she mumbled, and slipped back to her own table. But she'd decided: she'd got to talk to Vicky after school.

CHAPTER FIVE

Jo stood at the front door of Vicky's house, feeling awkward. She'd rung the doorbell twice, and there'd been no answer, but she was sure there must be someone inside. Vicky didn't just bunk off, and anyway, her mother wasn't the sort to let her. There was an alley at the side of the house, and the gate wasn't locked. So Jo opened the gate, walked through – and yelled out.

There was something round her legs, tripping her up. Something which darted off as soon as she looked down. And then a tall woman appeared at the end of the passage, who saw Jo, picked up the cat in one quick movement, and started to walk towards her.

'Who is it?' Vicky's mum looked puzzled. Jo wasn't surprised. She probably wasn't used to people walking into her back garden and then screaming their heads off. And the cat, now that she could see it clearly, was a little, stripy thing and nothing like It at all.

'Hello, Mrs Willis. I'm Jo. I'm a friend of Vicky's.'
'From school?'
'Yes,' Jo said. 'I – we – she wasn't at school.'
'And you've come to see how she is?' *Not quite,*

thought Jo, but she nodded hard. 'That's very nice of you, dear. Come in.'

Mrs Willis bent down to drop the cat and stopped. 'Don't you like cats. Tigger wouldn't hurt . . .'

'No, I mean, yes. I mean, cats are fine.'

Mrs Willis looked at her slightly oddly, but then she put her smile back on and led the way into the house. At the bottom of the stairs she called up, 'Someone to see you, Vicky,' and then said to Jo, 'The door's open. Straight ahead at the top of the stairs. I'll tread mud everywhere if I go up.'

So Jo walked up, followed by the little cat, who was keeping her distance because she didn't want any more shouts. It was easy to find Vicky's room, because that was where the sniffing was coming from. Vicky was sitting up in bed with a funny crochet thing round her shoulders. Jo had two like that, from Gran, and she had refused point-blank ever to wear them. It seemed that Vicky felt the same about it. For a moment, she looked surprised to see Jo; then she quickly pulled her duvet up to cover her shoulders.

'Hello,' Jo said. 'Can I come in?'

Jo had never actually been inside Vicky's house before, even though they were both part of the same group of friends at school. She looked round. The room was painted yellow and white, with frilly cushions and lacy mats on the chest of drawers. Vicky saw where Jo was looking and said, quickly,

'My gran makes those.'

'My gran makes them, too.' Jo made a face. 'We have to use them, in case she comes.'

She looked at Vicky. Vicky suddenly let go of the duvet. 'And these, too?'

'Yup,' Jo said. 'In bright green.'

Vicky grinned, sneezed, and then wriggled up to leave a space for Jo to sit on the bed. Tigger promptly jumped up and started to make herself comfortable there, so Jo sat on the floor instead.

'What's the matter with you, Vicky?' Jo asked, looking at Tigger.

'I'm all right.' Vicky sighed, then sneezed again. 'Mum fusses.' And she carried on watching the cat, too.

'Vicky . . . on Friday . . .' Jo gave up and stopped. It all sounded so ridiculous, what she was going to say.

But Vicky made it easy. Without taking her eyes off Tigger she said, slowly, 'About the cat? I saw it.'

Jo held her breath.

'I couldn't believe it,' Vicky went on. 'I'm not sure I believe it now.'

'I don't know what to do,' Jo said, very slowly.

'Do you have to do anything?'

So Jo told her, about the game, and about the cat at the window and Tracey's dog and Tim running off. And Vicky stopped watching Tigger and stared at Jo instead.

'D'you think I'm being stupid?' Jo asked, when she'd finished.

'I don't know. If I hadn't seen it . . .' Vicky

shrugged. 'But it's all so stupid that you're making sense. So what do we do?'

We. That sounded better. Safer.

'Are you coming to school tomorrow?' Jo asked.

'No, she is not.' Mrs Willis appeared in the doorway, holding a tray. 'Not for a while yet.'

'Mum!'

'I'm sorry, Vicky, but it's no good making a fuss. Now, here's a drink for you both.'

'Thanks, Mum.' Vicky made a face, but Mrs Willis just made a face back at her, and went out again. They drank the orange juice and tried to get the jammy centres out of the biscuits in one piece. Jo was the best. She held up her complete jam circle so that the light shone through it, while Vicky gave Tigger the biscuit plate to lick. And then they talked again about how impossible the cat story sounded, and how no one would believe them.

'I wonder what sort of a cat it is,' Vicky said.

'How can it be a real cat?'

'It might be. I'll look it up. We've got a big book all about cats, for Tigger.'

'Why? Can he read?' Jo giggled.

'It's a she. Yes, probably.' Vicky scratched the little cat between the ears, and Tigger rubbed against her hand, and purred.

'Okay,' said Jo, getting up. 'I can't think of much we can do. We'll have to see if Tim has any bright ideas.'

'Come back tomorrow.'

'Yes, if I can,' Jo promised. 'Bye.'

She was half-way out of the room when Vicky called after her.

'Jo! Wait! Ask Tim what happens after the dog.'

'What do you mean?'

'After the dog. The next screen in the game. Find out what happens.'

'Okay,' said Jo, though she couldn't understand why Vicky was so keen to know. 'I'll ask.' And she waved goodbye and started to walk down the stairs.

CHAPTER SIX

That night, Jo woke up screaming. It was dark in her bedroom, but at least she could breathe now that she was awake. In her dreams it had been black night, with air so heavy that it stopped her from moving. She couldn't even turn her head, although she tried to. There was something behind her. Out of the corner of her eye she could just see a dark shadow and red points of light. Eyes? A cat?

Suddenly the hall light went on, then her bedroom light. And her father was standing in the doorway, asking if she was all right. Jo looked down at the bed in surprise and saw that she had kicked off all her bedclothes into a heap on the floor.

'Hey, Jo,' her dad said, softly. He walked over the blankets and sat down on the edge of the bed.

'I couldn't breathe,' Jo whispered.

'Poor thing. Come here.' He pushed the hair away from her face and hugged her, still talking quietly. 'You've had a nightmare. It's okay now.'

'It's not. It won't go away.'

'What is it? Tell me.'

Dad would know what to do, Jo thought. Could she tell him? Even though it sounded so impossible?

For a moment, Jo thought she might. But then she realized how crazy it would sound. He couldn't believe her – he'd think it was just a bad dream.

'What's the time, Dad?' she asked, instead.

'I don't know, love. One o'clock – something like that. Can you go back to sleep?'

'I suppose.'

Jo lay down, and her father gathered up the bed-clothes and started to lay them back over her.

'Do you want a drink?' he asked.

Jo shook her head. 'No,' she said. 'It's all right, honest.'

'Call if you want me, okay? Good night.'

Jo listened to her father going back downstairs. He left the hall light on and he didn't shut the door to the front room, either. She could hear faint music. Jo thought she'd never go to sleep again, but she must have done so very quickly, because she didn't even hear the end of the song that was playing.

But out in the garden, the cat heard it. It blinked, and its red eyes disappeared into the darkness. It walked away, softly, behind the bushes and through the fence.

Four roads away, Tim was lying awake looking up at the ceiling that he couldn't see because of the dark. He knew it was very late, but he couldn't sleep. The bedclothes felt too hot until he pushed them away, but then he immediately started to feel cold again.

In the next room, his brother was playing music,

149

too loud. Tim wanted to go and tell him to turn it down, but he didn't want to get into a fight. Rick was a lot bigger and older than Tim, and had been in a bad mood all evening. Tim sighed. He wouldn't risk it. He tried putting a pillow over his face, but decided he'd rather listen to rotten music than suffocate. Suffocate? What made him think that? It wasn't that hot.

And then he knew.

Suddenly Tim stopped feeling hot, and a cold shivery feeling ran along his shoulders as if someone had touched the back of his neck with an ice cube. Very slowly and quietly, he got out of bed. The door to his room was closed, so there was no light. But if he put the light on, anyone – or anything – would be able to see in. In the darkness Tim felt his way between the bed and the wall, and then moved along slowly to the window. The curtains were drawn, and Tim carefully lifted up a corner so that he could see out.

At first he could only see a corner of the garden. It was all shadows. But there was more light outside than in his bedroom, and as his eyes got used to the dimness, he could make out more objects. He couldn't see very well through the little gap, so he pushed his head under the curtains and looked properly.

The eyes were there, looking back at him. Tim breathed in so fast that he felt dizzy for a second, but when his head cleared, they were still there. Two red lights, like a warning, or a challenge. Saying, *I'm*

*here and what are you going to do about it? I can come
and go as I like.*

Tim's breath was gradually steaming up the
window until the eyes were no longer clear, and he
looked away from the garden as he wiped the mist
away. That movement broke some kind of spell. Tim
stood there, then, feeling calmer. The music was still
playing, reassuringly. His room was warm, and, after
all, the cat was two floors down and behind doors
and windows.

The eyes were gone when Tim looked into the
garden again. He left the window and went back to
bed, lying facing away from the garden, and with
the sheet drawn up over his head.

Out in the garden, the cat walked twice round,
beneath Tim's window, and then disappeared into
the dark. It was part of the night.

Tim finally settled down, but he had forgotten
what other things were part of the night. A great
panther walked through his dreams, and when he
woke up, he wished that Rick's music had managed
to keep him awake all night after all.

When Jo got to school, Tim was hanging around
the entrance, waiting for her. He looked tired and
upset, even paler than normal. Jo didn't feel much
better herself. Her dad thought that she'd had the
nightmare because he'd cooked them a bad meal or
something, and he was acting as if it were all his
fault. Jo didn't know whose fault it was.

Tim jumped off the wall and walked with Jo into the playground.

'I saw it last night,' he said, abruptly. 'It was outside our house.'

'It was outside ours, too . . .' Jo replied, and then stopped. How did she know that? ' . . . I think.'

'What are we going to do?' he asked. Jo would have laughed, if she hadn't been so worried. The great, tough Tim Pascall asking *her* what to do!

'We'll have to make a plan. And decide,' Jo said. That sounded good, even though she had no idea what plan. 'At dinnertime, okay?'

'Okay, see you then.' And Tim vanished into a game of football.

But bits of the plan came without Jo having to think about them. When they went into the classroom, the PASHT had gone. Mrs Edmonds told them that an engineer was already working on it in Miss Thompson's computing 'cupboard', as it was called. And half-way through the morning, he carried the PASHT back into the classroom. Mrs Edmonds raised her eyebrows in a question, but he shook his head. Then they had a quiet conversation about it by Mrs Edmonds' desk. Jo and Tim both tried to listen in. They couldn't hear what was said, but when the man left, Mrs Edmonds spoke to the whole class.

'The computer does seem to be broken,' she said. 'The engineer can't understand it, either. It might have to go away to be mended . . .'

What would happen then? Jo thought.

'But he's going to order a new spare part, to try

that. If that doesn't work, then he will have to take it away.'

How long would that take?

'I'm afraid we might lose some programs, or some work,' Mrs Edmonds went on. 'But we'll do our best not to.'

Lose programs? Graphicat! No! Jo felt ill. *Then there wouldn't be a program for the cat any more.*

'It's no one's fault,' Mrs Edmonds said, 'so, Joanne and Timothy, there's no need to look so worried. This sort of thing does happen sometimes.'

Jo and Tim stared at each other, horrified. Both thinking the same thoughts. *What about the cat? Would it be free? And what would happen then?*

Mrs Edmonds was still talking. 'It might just take a while to sort out, because it's an unusual make of computer. But I'm sure we can do some work using the other classes' equipment. Now, let's all settle down. This afternoon we're going to be doing an experiment, so we need to set up . . .'

But Jo and Tim never did hear what they were supposed to set up. They were too busy thinking.

After morning school they both managed to take so long packing their things away, that everyone else left. They hid by the cupboard until Mrs Abbey had gone past on her corridor check, and then they came out and sat on the desks.

'What plan?' said Tim.

Jo didn't want to admit that she didn't have a brilliant plan all worked out. So she sat there,

swinging her feet and trying to look as though she
wasn't worried.

'I wonder how long it'll take to mend it?' Tim
said after a while. 'I didn't know the PASHT was so
unusual.'

Unusual. You can say that again, thought Jo. But
there was something . . . what was it? Someone had
said that before. Not Mrs Edmonds, someone else.
And then she remembered.

'Miss Thompson said that,' Jo blurted out. 'About
the computer.'

'What?' Tim asked, confused.

'Yesterday. Miss Thompson. She said "It's an odd
computer". And she ought to know.'

'But the cat, Jo! What are we going to do?'

Jo stared at him. 'That's not it! Don't you see?
Stop thinking about the cat. And start thinking about
the computer.'

Tim walked over to the computer desk. He stood
there for a moment, looking at the PASHT, and then
he put the plugs back into their sockets. He tried all
the switches, in different combinations, but there
was just a whirring sound and nothing else. Even
though the screen flickered on, there was nothing
to be seen on it. The machine sat there, broken,
useless.

Tim looked across at Jo. 'Why was Miss
Thompson talking about the computer anyway?' he
asked her suspiciously. 'You didn't tell her!'

'Of course not! I met her in the playground,
when I went out to find . . .'

The cat. But she didn't want to tell Tim that. He was even more affected by it than she was. But then she hadn't touched it, and she hadn't been the one to call it out of the screen.

'Anyway,' Jo went on, 'she said it was an odd make. Different from the other school computers.'

'Why?' Tim was speaking quietly, almost to himself.

Jo tried to remember what else Miss Thompson had said. 'She said it used the same software as the others, though. That's all.'

That had an effect. Tim suddenly grabbed the box of computer discs, opened it, and started flicking through them. He took out a couple of discs, compared them with each other, and then grinned.

'How odd!' he said, and dashed out of the classroom.

By the time Jo got to the door, Tim was halfway down the corridor, running. Jo followed him. What was he doing?

'We're going to ask Miss Thompson if we can start a computer club,' he called out.

'What?'

'If we can use a computer. Now!'

Next thing she knew, Jo was standing there with Tim, waiting for Miss Thompson to come out of the staffroom. And that was when Jo realized that there were advantages in being a 'difficult pupil'. She could imagine the reaction if she'd asked to do something in the middle of a teacher's lunch hour.

But because Tim could be a 'problem', Miss Thompson made a big effort. She wasn't going to give up her lunch. But she did say that they could stay for a little while after school.

'It'll only take a minute, Miss. Honest,' Tim assured her. 'But I've got some maths work on this disc and Jo wanted to see it.'

'Liar,' Jo muttered, as they walked away.

Tim looked at her and laughed. 'It worked, though, didn't it?'

'What's really on the disc?' Jo asked.

'HEIGHTS OF CHILDREN IN OUR CLASS,' said Tim, innocently.

'Oh, yeah?'

Tim kept grinning, maddeningly. 'Yeah. But on *this* disc . . . we'll see.' He pulled out a second disc, hidden in the same paper sleeve.

'Is that the disc that GRAPHICAT's on?'

Tim suddenly went serious again. 'I don't know,' he said, quietly. 'I don't know if it's still there. But we'll find out tonight.'

CHAPTER SEVEN

Miss Thompson's computer 'cupboard' wasn't really a cupboard at all; it was a small room off the main classroom, where everything was set out. Miss Thompson helped Tim and Jo switch the computer on and set it up, and stayed long enough to see the floppy disc running. Then she left them to it. They could hear her bustling around in her classroom, and every now and then there was the sound of a staple gun accompanied by a grunt as she forced staples into the wall.

'Is it safe?' Tim muttered.

'Yes.' Jo stood to one side, so she could see the screen and also see through into the classroom. 'Go on.'

Tim swopped the floppy discs over and called up the list of files on the screen. There it was:

A: GRAPHICAT

Tim pressed some more keys.

RUN: GRAPHICAT

The words shone at them out of the screen. Tim didn't move. Miss Thompson was just starting on another row of pictures, stapling them up. Jo looked at the words and then at Tim. Now they'd know.

Either the cat would be in the pictures or it wouldn't. She leaned over the keyboard and pressed *enter*.

Nothing. For a long time nothing happened at all. Then the screen cleared and began to scroll, faster and faster, showing lines and lines of nonsense. Symbols, letters and figures. Nothing that made any sense at all. The scrolling stopped, and then started again, the meaningless lines jerking upwards.

Tim never moved. He just watched. Jo pressed *escape* and switched the discs back. 'Play with the graphs, Tim,' she said. 'I'm thinking.' She leaned against the wall and started to chew the end of her ponytail.

''ive 'ore 'inutes,' Miss Thompson called out. It sounded odd because she was holding some staples between her teeth. *Five minutes!* What had Miss Thompson said before? *It uses the same software.*

'Get up.' Jo elbowed Tim to one side and put the GRAPHICAT disc in. Quickly she went to the list of files. 'What other games are there?'

'Play a game?' Tim gasped. 'Now?'

'No, idiot. Which one's a game?'

'MAZE is.' Tim pointed half-way down the list. 'But you can't . . .'

RUN: MAZE

Jo pressed *return*. The screen cleared, and then a picture built itself across the screen. Not lines of nonsense symbols this time, but a green and yellow maze. A little figure appeared at the bottom of the screen, standing at the entrance to the maze. Jo pressed the cursor keys at random, and the figure moved towards the gates.

'Jo!' That was Tim.

Jo pulled out the disc and switched off the computer and the screen faster than she would have thought possible. And *that* was when she realized that there were also advantages in being known as a 'good' pupil. Miss Thompson looked a bit suspicious at first, but Jo knew that she could make her come round. By the time Jo had finished smiling and saying thank you and how interesting the maths graph had been, Miss Thompson was smiling too, and Tim had safely hidden the second disc.

'You two had better get off home,' Miss Thompson said. 'Or your parents will be wondering where you are.'

Not with Mum away, Jo thought. *Dad won't be home yet.* That was one advantage, she supposed. Normally she wouldn't have been able to stay like this.

'You can always come back tomorrow,' Miss Thompson said kindly. 'You could even print your graphs out if you like, on our new printer.' She pointed to it, with a soppy smile on her face. 'It's a lovely printer. We've only just bought it.'

That was when Jo had a brainwave. *New printer!* 'Miss,' she asked. 'Where did our class's computer come from?'

'What do you mean, "come from"?'

'Because it's different from the others. Did you get all the computers at the same time?'

'I doubt it.' Miss Thompson frowned. 'That

would be very expensive. And the school doesn't
have that much money. But I wasn't here then, of
course, so I don't know. Now, off you go.'

On the way back to their own classroom, to put
back the discs, Tim asked,

'What was all that about? You don't want to buy
a computer, do you?'

'Yeah, with my pocket money!' Jo laughed.
'Don't be daft.'

'Why did you want to know, then?'

Jo stopped walking. She had to concentrate. It
was difficult to put into words an idea that was only
beginning to come together.

'Well,' she said, 'if something strange happens, or
something goes wrong, you ask why. And there's got
to be a reason. Suppose . . . suppose . . .' And then
she had it! She went on, her words rushing out.
'Suppose you're walking along and you find you've
lost your bus fare. And you go back to find it, but
you can't, it's not there, not lying in the street or
anything . . .'

'Jo, WHAT are you going on about?'

'But it's not there because you never had it.
Because it's at home and you never took it with you
in the first place. You can't solve the problem,
because you've got to go back even further. Back
one more step, to home.'

'Ye-es.'

'That's why I asked about the computer.'

'You mean we go to the shop where they bought
it?' said Tim. 'And what then?'

'I don't know. I'm not really sure what it's got to do with anything. But I'm sure we've got to go back further than the cat.' Jo shrugged. It all sounded hopeless, and even though she was sure she was right, she didn't see why.

But Tim pulled both the discs out of their sleeves and turned them over in his hands, comparing them.

'They're different,' he said at last.

'What do you mean, "they're different"?' Jo pounced on the discs. 'You didn't tell me!'

'I didn't realize. I didn't think of checking before.' Tim held the discs up, side by side. 'They've got different labels, too. Look!'

Jo looked. One disc was grey, while the other was black. And the grey disc had a funny-shaped label in one corner. The label was already beginning to peel off.

'That's the GRAPHICAT disc.' Tim waved the grey disc in the air.

Two minutes later, Jo and Tim were in their classroom and sitting by the PASHT, with floppy discs all over the table. They went through them one by one, but it didn't take long. All the other discs were black, and although the labels were different colours, they were all the same type of label, and stuck on to the discs in exactly the same place.

'D'you think this came with the computer?' Jo asked, pointing to the grey disc. 'It's older than the rest.'

'Perhaps. Eddy says the PASHT is the first computer they got. And we have to have it!'

'So it's not just the computer that's different,' Jo said, wonderingly. 'It's the disc, too.'

'That must be why the other computer couldn't read it,' Tim started, then he shook his head. 'But it could. It read MAZE all right, and that's on the same disc.'

'I feel like *we're* in a maze,' Jo said. 'All we know is that the computer and the disc are both odd. And that they might belong together.'

'Jo,' Tim said slowly. 'How could the computer read MAZE but not GRAPHICAT?'

'I don't know.'

'But all that rubbish going up on the screen.'

'It wasn't rubbish. It was the GRAPHICAT program.' Jo thought carefully. 'I think it means that the machine can't run the game properly. But it shows us the program. Bits of the actual programming. I think.'

Tim shook his head. 'It doesn't make any sense. The cat – then this disc.'

'The cat doesn't make any sense,' Jo agreed. 'But the disc has got to make sense. So has the computer.'

'Huh. Tell the computer that.' Tim grabbed the discs and started stuffing them back into the box.

' "*Computers are logical*," ' Jo quoted. 'That's what Miss Thompson always says.'

'This whole thing's illogical if you ask me. Come on, we'd better get out of here.'

'Computers are always logical,' Jo repeated. 'So that's where we've got to start.'

CHAPTER EIGHT

It was Vicky's mother who solved the immediate mystery, without even knowing.

After Jo and Tim had put away the PASHT discs, Tim walked off straightaway. But Jo hesitated. She didn't want to go home, not into an empty house. Then she remembered her promise to Vicky.

This time, when Jo knocked at Vicky's house, the front door was opened almost immediately. There was Vicky's mother, looking rather flustered, but beaming down at her.

'Hello – Jo, isn't it? Vicky *will* be pleased. She's getting very bored. She . . .'

Her voice trailed off, and that was when Jo first heard it. A wailing sound, like a baby crying, that rose higher and higher.

'Oh no, not again,' Mrs Willis moaned, looking round. Then she looked back at Jo and waved her hand. 'Come in, come in. Can you go up – you know where it is. Oh, shut the front door! Quickly! Tigger doesn't like . . .'

The sound was getting louder. It made shivers go up and down Jo's neck. It was an awful, frightening sound.

'I must go. Sorry!' And Vicky's mother disappeared into the kitchen.

Jo stood there, bewildered, the door shut behind her. She didn't know Vicky had a kid sister, or brother. Imagine living with that noise!

Vicky was out of bed by the time Jo got up the stairs, standing by the door, listening. The sound only came in snatches now, and Jo could hear Mrs Willis talking soft baby-talk downstairs.

'I didn't know you had a baby!' Jo blurted out. Vicky stared at her as if she'd gone mad. 'I mean your mother . . .'

'What baby?'

It was Jo's turn to stare. She pointed down the stairs. 'That one, of course.'

Vicky shook her head, angrily. Then she pulled Jo into the bedroom and pushed the door to, behind them. 'I'm not meant to be out of bed,' she said, taking a flying leap on to the bed, and pulling her duvet around until she was back underneath it.

Jo stayed at the door, listening to the noise quieten down.

'What do you mean, baby?' Vicky snapped at her. 'Haven't you ever heard a cat?'

Jo opened her mouth, saw Vicky's furious look, and decided she'd better be careful. So she shook her head and said, gently, 'Not sounding like that.'

Vicky sighed. 'I've never heard Tigger like that, either. Before. Sometimes you get cats making a real racket round here at nights. But this is different.'

'Is he ill?'

'She. No, we don't think so.' Vicky paused and looked at Jo as though trying to decide something. Then she seemed to make up her mind. 'I think she's scared,' she went on.

Jo didn't say anything. She just looked at Vicky, but inside she was saying *No, please, you don't mean that. It's not here as well. It can't be.*

Vicky didn't say anything either. She just nodded.

Suddenly there was a sound of padding steps, light on the stairs. Jo jumped automatically, then turned round, annoyed with herself for being so silly. It was only Tigger. The cat pushed the door open with her head, enough to squeeze through, then dashed into the room and under the bed.

'She was under there all last night,' Vicky said. 'She kept making funny noises. And then this morning she went out as usual but came straight back.'

'As if she was terrified by something,' Mrs Willis's voice broke in, and Jo jumped again. This time she moved away from the door. 'Tigger's back up here, is she? Better leave her. I'll bring her some milk in case she's hungry. She still hasn't eaten her dinner.' And she walked off downstairs again.

'Poor Tigger,' murmured Vicky, reaching over to look under the bed and nearly falling out in the process. 'Come here. Come on!'

Tigger ignored her outstretched hand. Jo knelt down so that she could see Tigger, sitting exactly in the middle of the carpet under Vicky's bed. She was only a young cat, with a pretty face and little white paws where the stripes ended. Jo reached out her hand and made what she hoped were friendly noises. But Tigger certainly wasn't going to come out.

Mrs Willis came back, carrying a saucer with milk in it. She got down on the carpet next to Jo and pushed the saucer along under the bed, towards the white paws.

'Do you know what frightened her?' Jo made herself ask it, but the answer she was dreading didn't come.

'No idea,' Mrs Willis said. 'I went to have a look outside, but I couldn't see anything at all. Never mind, she'll get over it. Better let her stay here until I get back from Kathleen's.' She got up, brushing bits of carpet and drops of milk from her trousers. 'Vicky, are you sure you'll be all right?'

'Of course I'll be all right!'

'Your father'll be home soon anyway. But we must finalize the arrangements for Saturday, and then there are the tickets, of course.'

'Mum, I'll be *fine*!' Vicky was beginning to sound exasperated. She looked past her mother, at Jo, and raised her eyebrows.

Mrs Willis sighed. 'I know, I fuss. But I bet Jo thinks her mother fusses, too?' She looked at Jo and smiled, as if they were sharing a joke. Jo managed a half smile. Mrs Willis really must think she was weird, screaming at cats and not answering friendly remarks about mothers.

'Are you on the PTA?' It was all she could think of saying, but at least it was something normal.

'Yes. And there's the fête on Saturday, you know. So make sure you find us some old toys or something during the week, or else you won't get your new hall piano. The school doesn't have much extra money.'

'Do you buy us other things? Computers?' The words were out before Jo had even thought about them.

'Yes. I think we did buy one computer.' Mrs Willis frowned, remembering. Jo held her breath. 'It was a while back. There was some special arrangement – the last one of that particular model or something.'

'That must be the one we've got,' Vicky broke in. 'A PASHT.'

'I don't know what type it was,' Mrs Willis said. 'But I'm glad it's ended up in your class. And now, if I don't go and do these tickets, you won't get anything else!'

She waved goodbye, smiled at Vicky, and went out of the room. Jo followed her on to the landing.

'Where did you get it from – the computer?' she asked, desperate for an answer.

Mrs Willis looked at her questioningly, and frowned.

Jo thought quickly. 'It's just that my dad was interested in it. He wanted to find out how much they'd cost,' she burbled.

Bringing in an adult was a good move. It was obviously all right for grown-ups to want to know things like that.

'Oh, I see,' said Mrs Willis. She thought for a

167

moment. 'It was from a firm, I think. Something like Folus or Phenex. No, of course!' She laughed and nodded. 'I know. I remember thinking it was funny at the time. The name was Felix – you know, like the cat food. It's the only thing Tigger will eat.'

Jo stared at her in horror.

'Tell your father that,' Mrs Willis went on. 'And if that's not enough, then he can phone me and ask.'

'Er, yes,' said Jo, meaning 'no'. Mrs Willis carried on down the stairs and Jo stood at the top, watching her go.

Jo walked home slowly, her mind racing. She and Vicky had gone through the telephone book and the Yellow Pages, but there were only two Felixes, and neither of those looked like a company. 'I suppose it doesn't have to be a local firm,' Vicky had said. For a moment, Jo felt like giving up.

Now, as she walked, she went over the possibilities. There weren't many of them, but they had to be checked through, at least. They'd probably need a map, and bikes. Vicky couldn't come with her, but perhaps Tim would.

There was a flicker of grey, a sudden movement on her right. She took no notice, but when the grey flickered again she looked up. And stared.

The cat was walking along the wall beside her. No, not walking – it glided, as if it wasn't actually touching the bricks. Tail high and neck arched, it ran ahead until its legs blurred with speed. Then it stopped, and looked round at her before settling

168

itself down on the top of the wall. Jo walked towards it, carefully. Its tail was whipping backwards and forwards, hitting the wall. The cat opened its mouth, showing the pointed white teeth at the front.

But when Jo was only a couple of metres away, it got up, sauntered off for a bit, and then settled down again. She moved forward a few more steps, with the cat watching her, and then stopped. *It's a game*, she thought. *It's teasing. It won't let me catch it. And I'm not going to let it play with me.* The cat stretched a paw towards her; its sharp, hooked claws were out.

Something in the back of Jo's mind was saying that she was crazy. That this was the only chance she'd have to get near the cat. But she ignored the voice. She turned her back, and crossed the road, away from the wall. Then she spoilt it all by looking over her shoulder. The cat was watching her go, and it seemed to be smiling.

CHAPTER NINE

When she got to school the next morning, Jo realized why the cat had been smiling. She walked into the classroom and into a nightmare scene.

The room had been horribly vandalized. There was a knot of people standing silently by the door, looking at the mess. All the plants had been overturned and smashed, and had covered the floor with earth and dirty water. The books that had been on display were knocked down as well, and there were papers thrown everywhere. The bits of floor that didn't have earth on had a wonderful mixture of powder paint colours instead. Jo looked at the table nearest to her. It had red paint over it, and in the paint was a mark, like a pawprint. Without thinking, Jo wiped it away, and then wiped her hand on her sweatshirt, and that was when Mrs Edmonds came in.

Mrs Edmonds was trying to keep her temper, but not very successfully. She spotted Jo and headed straight for her, looking suspiciously at her hands and clothes.

'Come with me, Joanne. Now,' she ordered, and marched straight out of the classroom again, followed

170

by Jo. Jo was followed by a mixture of sympathetic glances and whispered questions.

'D'you think Jo *really* did it?'

'What, you mean . . .!'

'No, not Jo! I don't think . . .'

Next time she watched a cops and robbers film, Jo decided, she'd feel sorry for the robbers.

She had to walk behind Mrs Edmonds' back all the way to the school office. Tim was already there, looking as if he wanted to hit someone, or something.

'Now you two,' said Mrs Edmonds. 'Miss Thompson tells me you stayed after school to use her computer. Did you go back into the classroom afterwards?'

'Yes,' said Tim. 'We had to put the discs – er, disc – back.'

'Was the room all right then?'

Jo and Tim nodded, firmly.

'You're sure?'

She doesn't believe us, Jo thought.

'We'd have noticed if it'd been like *that*,' Tim grinned, but stopped when he saw Mrs Edmonds' face.

'It's not at all funny,' Mrs Edmonds snapped. 'And you should tell me, too, if you're staying after school. What were you doing, anyway?'

Jo couldn't think of a thing to say. But Tim started to talk enthusiastically about computers and maths projects, and he went on for so long that in the end Mrs Edmonds stopped him and told them both to go with her, back to the classroom. 'We've got some clearing up to do,' she said, unnecessarily.

As they trailed along the corridor, Jo got a little bit of revenge by making faces at Mrs Edmonds' back. 'It's not fair, thinking we did it,' she grumbled to Tim.

He shrugged. 'Teachers do that all the time.'

'It was the cat,' Jo whispered.

'I know.'

They had two addresses, which Jo had copied out of the telephone book. She showed them to Tim after morning school, and told him all about Tigger and Vicky's mum and the PTA, feeling rather pleased with herself. Tim obviously wasn't prepared to be impressed, but he grabbed the piece of paper out of Jo's hand and read it carefully.

Felix, Don, The Minories, 143 Ladulfus Road
Felix, G. Z, 64 Conston Street, Branley

'Branley's miles away,' Tim groaned. 'There's no way we can cycle there.'

'Okay,' said Jo, reasonably. 'Let's try the first one first. Only I've no idea where Ladulfus Road is.'

'I know where it is,' said Tim. 'That's the trouble. It's all houses round there, no shops or offices or anything like that.'

'There might be. Sometimes you get a couple of shops in the middle of an ordinary street.'

'Yeah, computer shops. Very likely!' Tim broke in. Then he stopped, and sighed. 'What's a Minory, anyway?'

'Dunno. But we ought to go and have a look.'

'Okay. After school tonight?'

'Okay.' Jo knew she ought to ask Dad first, but immediately decided that she wouldn't. He wouldn't be around till late anyway.

Concentrate on the computer, Jo told herself. *You can do something about that, perhaps . . .*

They met at the end of Jo's street at half past four. Jo had to try not to laugh when she saw Tim's bike. It was very small, much too small for him, and he looked like a hunched-up monkey on it. But the look on Tim's face dared her to say anything, so she didn't.

It took them over half an hour to cycle there, with Tim leading the way. Ladulfus Road was the other side of the main shopping centre and over a steep hill, and Jo was relieved when they stopped at the turning into it. It was a wide road, with trees along the pavements, and houses set back from the road. Jo and Tim wheeled their bikes along, not talking, counting off the house numbers as they went: eighteen, twenty-four – cross over the road – forty-nine, seventy-seven . . . They walked quite slowly, and neither of them suggested riding their bikes along. They didn't want to get to number one-hundred-and-forty-three too quickly.

At first they walked by bungalows, and normal-sized houses standing in little rows of four or six together. Then the houses began to space out more

– ninety-one, ninety-seven, and there were big trees
in the front gardens, and high hedges.

'I told you,' Tim said, as they passed number one-
hundred-and-twenty-one. 'There can't be any shops
here.'

Jo shrugged. She had never been to the posh side
of town before, and was enjoying herself, looking
over into huge gardens, with ponds, and carved stone
ornaments, and lights all the way up the paths to the
front doors.

Finally they got to number one-hundred-and-
forty-three. Tim checked the number on the plate
and stood there, kicking the wall. 'Told you,' he said.
'This is stupid, coming all the way here.'

Jo looked up. The wall was quite high, and there
were iron gates in the middle of it. She looked
through the gates, expecting to see another old
house, with a pond and ornaments.

What she saw was quite different, and dis-
appointing. The house was modern, much smaller
than most of the other houses, and instead of a
garden there was just gravel all the way from the
gates. It didn't look like an office, either.

'We might as well ask,' she said.

Tim waved his hand at the gates and the wall.
'It's not worth it.'

He started wheeling his bike away, back the way
they had come. Jo hesitated before going after him
– all that cycling for nothing! They couldn't even
just walk up to the front door. The gates were closed,
they looked old . . . She stopped watching the house

and focused on the gates instead, looking at the pattern.

The gates were wrought iron, as high as her head. The black metal was curved and twisted into shapes, lines like candy twists, little circles and other, larger shapes. She stepped back to see them properly. The shapes moved as she looked at them and re-focused themselves into another pattern. No, not a pattern — a picture.

'Tim! Tim!' Jo tripped over her bike, hauled herself and the bike up together, and dashed to catch him up. 'It *is* the house. It *is*. Don't stop,' she added as Tim turned to stare at her. They walked on together.

Jo told him about the gates, how each half of the gate had a picture worked into the metal. 'You can't see it close up,' she explained, 'because you think it's just circles and curly bits. But it's a cat — two cats, one on each gate. You see it if you step back. And I'm going to phone Dad.'

'W–what!' Tim stuttered, but Jo had already climbed on to her bike.

'There's a phone box further down, we passed it,' she called. 'Have you got ten pence?'

Tim cycled after her, looking murderous, and caught up outside the phone box. 'You can't tell him!' he yelled.

Jo just pulled out a handful of sweet wrappers and coins. 'Don't worry, I've got one.'

'Jo!' Tim dived in front of her and stood in front of the telephone. 'You mustn't tell him. He'll never believe you.'

'Oh, I'm not going to tell him about the *cat*, you berk,' Jo said, crossly. 'But if you think I'm going into some strange house without telling him where I am, then you're really stupid. Mind you, he might not be in.'

Jo's father was in, and he was furious. Tim could hear both halves of the conversation, her father was shouting so loudly.

'I didn't know Mum would call!' Jo shouted back.

'Well, she did. And she thinks I'm not looking after you properly. Going off like that.'

'All right. I'm at a friend's house. With, er, Kay.'

'Who?'

'Kay. 143 Ladulfus Road, Dad. We're at 143 Ladulfus Road. She's asked me to stay for tea.'

'Well, I suppose . . .'

Jo smiled. He was calming down. 'Sorry, Dad. I won't be ages.'

'I'll give your mother a call. She'll probably phone later to talk to you.'

'Okay. Bye.' Jo put the phone down.

'Right,' said Tim. 'Here goes.'

CHAPTER TEN

They walked back up to the house and propped their bikes against the wall. There was no one about, and very few cars went past. Jo looked around. It was all so empty – very different from her own small, friendly street where there was always someone walking along, or people standing in the road, chatting.

Tim went up to the gates, then stepped back to see them properly.

'You have to step back, don't you?' said Jo. 'It's like the cat and the computer – you always have to go back one stage further.'

'THAT'S VERY GOOD.' A voice, crackling out of nowhere. Tim jumped and Jo whirled round, but there was no one there. Jo was poised, ready to run. Tim automatically moved away from the gates.

'HELLO?' said the Voice. And then Tim pointed.

On the right-hand gatepost, set into the stone, was a metal sheet with a grille in it. 'It's an entryphone,' he whispered.

'OF COURSE. AND YOU ARE?'

'We're . . .' began Jo. 'Well, we're from Ravenscroft School, and, er . . .'

'AH, YES. THE GATES ARE OPEN. COME IN.'

Jo stepped forward and touched the gate, very lightly. It moved. 'It wasn't open before,' she whispered to Tim.

They pushed the gates, leaving their bikes outside, and went through. Their feet crunched on the gravel, and then there was another crunching sound behind them. The gates had swung again. Shut.

'Well, come in!' she said cheerfully, stepping backwards into the hall. 'Come in if you're coming in.'

Whatever Jo and Tim had expected, it wasn't this. They had stood at the front door, looking hopelessly for a bell, or a door knocker. There was nothing. But then there was a faint buzzing sound and the door had swung open, slowly, like the gates.

There was a woman standing there, smiling. She was carrying a little girl on one hip, and the child was very busy trying to put a toy lizard on to her mother's head.

The woman stepped away from the door, gestured Jo and Tim into the hallway, and then disentangled the toy from her hair. 'Ow!' she said. 'Don't do that with Lizzie.' But the little girl just giggled and made the lizard twitch even more.

'Mr Felix said he was expecting you,' the woman went on. 'I'm his wife, and this is Kate, our youngest.' She settled the girl back on her hip.

Kate waved the toy at them. 'Lithie,' she announced. The lizard looked almost real.

Mrs Felix nodded to them and walked off down

the hallway. Jo and Tim exchanged glances, and then followed her. 'He's in the back room,' she told them over her shoulder. Jo was glad Tim had gone first. She looked around her as they went, but there was nothing to see, just closed wooden doors and cream-painted walls. She heard the front door close behind them as they walked.

At the end of the passage the woman stopped and opened the last door. She nodded to them. 'Go in, then!' she said. And she smiled again and went off with Kate, leaving them standing in the doorway.

Jo leaned over Tim's shoulder to see in. It was a large room, with big windows all along one side, rather like a conservatory. Outside the windows was a garden, with grass and trees this time instead of gravel. There were lights reflected in the glass, coloured lights that winked and flashed. It was all Jo had time to see before Tim walked forward and she fell into the room.

'Hello?' said the Voice. It was the same Voice as on the entryphone, without the crackling.

'Hello,' said Tim.

And then, as Jo finished tripping over and got her balance back, she saw him.

He was sitting in a low, sagging armchair, which had papers balanced on the arms. He had reddish hair, a round face, and baggy eyes, and he was smiling at them – but it wasn't a simple, friendly smile. It had questions in it. Tim obviously thought so too, because Jo heard him swallow nervously before he spoke.

'I'm Tim,' he said.

Silence. The man glanced at Jo, still smiling.

'I'm Jo,' said Jo. It didn't sound very much, so she added, 'Jo Reynolds.'

Still silence. The man picked up a sheaf of papers and placed it on top of another pile. He sighed and rifled the pages, which fell down again, heavily, into place. 'So much paper. You'd think we wouldn't need paper.' And he waved a hand to one side.

Jo and Tim looked where he pointed. It was where the lights had come from. A bench ran along the length of the wall, and it was filled with machines. Jo knew what some of them were: the computer screens, the printers, the keyboards. But there were other things, boxes with switches on the front and one large metal board with slides and rules marked on it, that she'd never seen before.

'Wow!' That was Tim. He went over to the bench, reaching out his hand to the nearest keys.

Jo expected the man to shout at Tim, or stop him. But he didn't move. He just watched, as Tim walked slowly along, looking at the machines on the bench.

Then, when Tim reached a printer that was chuntering quietly to itself, the man suddenly said, 'That's connected to America. Right now. It's getting information from the computer that runs the space program.'

Jo started. A computer spy! She'd heard about them. But the man looked at her and laughed, as though he could read her mind. 'Lots of computers over here are linked up,' he said. 'You just pay for it, like a phone call.' Jo didn't know whether to believe him or not. The chuntering went on.

'What information?' Tim's hand was hovering over the printer, as if his fingers had eyes and could read.

'Oh, various things,' the man said. 'Not very interesting, really. And not much fun. The next computer – the one on your right – that's something you might be interested in.'

Tim turned, and Jo moved forward too, so that she could see the screen. It was blank.

'Press *control* and *alt* together with one hand,' said the man, 'and then press *return*.'

Tim found the keys, and did so. The screen flashed white, went dark again, and then filled with colour.

'It's probably the fastest game you've ever seen. Go on, see if you can beat it.'

Tim didn't need telling twice. He was already bending over the keyboard, watching the screen, frowning with concentration to see how the game worked. Jo couldn't help watching, either. It was a battlegame, and the graphics were amazing: a whole city of skyscrapers, where the spaces between the buildings made a kind of maze when seen against the sky. The speed with which the attackers flew in along the lines and the spaces was breathtaking. They came in hovering machines which dived and zig-zagged and spun upwards again to avoid the lasers. The person playing the game moved two figures –

two armed men against all the spacecraft, and the view of the city shifting every few seconds to show new buildings and new attacking, flying craft.

Tim lasted two seconds. The next game was over even more quickly, but after a few more games he could hold off three attacks – almost ten seconds. Then, as his players were annihilated yet again, Tim shook his head and got up. 'Your go,' he said.

Jo was itching to try it. She thought she had seen a pattern while Tim was playing, but when she turned the lasers to where the spacecraft should be, they changed direction at once. It was as if the machine could think, and was working out what Jo expected and then doing the opposite. It seemed to be using one formula against Tim and a completely different set of tactics when Jo played.

'I told you,' Mr Felix said. Jo started. She had almost forgotten he was there, she had been so wrapped up in the game. Her fingers jumped off the keys and the game ran on without her. Her men soon vanished from the screen. 'It's one of my best,' he went on. 'Of the new batch, anyway.'

'You write computer games?' Tim asked.

'Yes. Other things too, of course. But the games are just for fun.'

'It's brilliant. What are the others?'

Mr Felix didn't answer. He just sat and looked at Tim, questioning, until Tim asked again. 'The other . . . games . . .?'

'Lots of games, about different things.' Mr Felix

watched them carefully as he spoke. 'Space fights, cars, mazes . . .'

'Cats . . .'

'Aaah.' Mr Felix leaned back in his chair. He nodded, slowly. Smiling. 'Cats. Or cat.'

'Cat,' Jo said, deliberately.

'So that's why you've come. That's very clever. Which of you was it? Or both?'

Tim and Jo looked at each other, bewildered. After a while Mr Felix sighed. 'I mean, who worked it out.'

'Worked what out?' Jo asked.

It was Mr Felix's turn to look confused. 'The game. The – what shall we say – special effect. Who did it?'

'I suppose I did,' said Tim. 'But it was an accident. I didn't mean to.'

'An accident? Really?' Mr Felix frowned. 'That's not possible. Tell me, how *did* you work it out? How long did it take you?'

'I didn't.'

'He didn't!' Jo burst out. 'We don't know what you're talking about. We were arguing, and Tim just kept pressing the same key, and then it happened.'

There was no reaction. Jo looked away, angrily. In front of her was a sofa, covered in papers, and lying on the papers was a small, plump dog, fast asleep. It looked like a spaniel, except for the fact that its coat was an odd shade of red, which gleamed in the light from the windows. Between the sheets of paper Jo could see old-fashioned material; a pattern of flowers, yellow, and green, and faded.

'Is that all you did, Tim?' Mr Felix asked.

'Yes.'

'Oh, I see. I see. I thought it was rather . . .' He shrugged. 'You must be wondering what I'm going on about. But never mind, it really doesn't matter. I'm just sorry that you've had a wasted journey. Now, if there's nothing else, you must both be wanting to get back home.'

'But what are you going to do?' asked Tim.

'About what?'

'About the cat?'

'What should I do?'

'I don't know.' Tim's voice was very quiet.

'Well, then,' Mr Felix said, calmly, spreading his hands in the air.

'You can't just leave it,' Jo broke in. 'It's dangerous. It − it's hurt a dog.'

'Dad!' There was a sudden noise in the hallway and a boy ran into the room, knocking into Tim as he skidded to a stop. 'Dad, Maggy wants . . .'

'That's a visitor you've just crashed into,' Mr Felix said calmly.

'Sorry.' The boy glanced at Tim and then turned back to the armchair. 'Can we have Lewis? Maggy said I had to ask you this time.'

'He's been running around all day.'

'*Please*, Dad.'

'Oh, all right.' Mr Felix nodded at him. 'I suppose so.'

184

'Great!'

'But don't wear him out between you.'

'Okay.' The boy dashed over and grabbed something off a table, and then scooped up the dog. It didn't seem to mind. In fact it hardly seemed to wake up, as he snatched it up off the sofa. Jo and Tim were watching him, so it took them a moment to realize that Mr Felix was talking.

'The dog got hurt,' he said. 'Do you *know* the cat did that?'

'Not exactly, but – '

'It might have been an accident. Anything could have caused it. Cause and effect: they're not necessarily the same.'

'Honestly, Dad,' the boy called over. 'How d'you expect anyone to understand you sometimes?'

'Do you want Lewis or don't you, Danny?'

Danny grinned and rushed out of the room. Jo and Tim turned to watch him go, so they both saw the dog looking back at them with strange half-closed eyes. The eyes were intensely blue – surely they were too blue for any animal to have. For a split second Jo thought she began to understand, but Mr Felix was still speaking and she had to turn back to listen.

'There's no proof,' he pointed out. 'No scientific evidence, if you like.'

Jo sighed. It was like trying to argue with their Headmaster – it was impossible.

'And after all,' Mr Felix went on, 'it's just a game – fun – isn't it? Graphicat?'

'No,' Tim said, quickly. 'It's not. Not now.'

'But you've just played another game, haven't you?' He nodded over towards the bench and the screen where still, in silence, spacecraft were shooting through the sky and crashing into buildings. 'You enjoyed zapping the people in the space flyers. They *are* people, you know.'

Tim hesitated. 'The dog's not fun!'

'It should have moved faster. But dogs can't, you know, when they're up against a cat. That's the first part of the game.'

'But – '

'But you didn't care about the people, did you?' Mr Felix asked, innocently. And Tim turned round to look at the screen, concentrating on the images as they flashed past.

Jo was busy thinking of something else. *Dogs and cats!* 'That dog just now,' she began. 'Why – ?'

Mr Felix glared at her then. 'Now, you really must go.' He walked over and stood by the doorway, waiting for them to leave.

'You don't understand,' Tim muttered. 'You can't just leave it like that!'

'Of course I can,' Mr Felix said. 'What your school does with its computers is up to them. And I don't want people bothering me about it. Do your teachers know you're here?'

Jo shook her head. She had no idea what to say next to make him understand about the cat. She was so sure it was dangerous, threatening.

'In that case I think you'd better go straight away,

don't you?' Mr Felix went on. 'And then I shan't have to tell them.'

The thought of Mrs Edmonds finding out they'd been annoying him made Jo feel quite sick.

Tim sighed. 'Come on, Jo,' he said, already starting to walk out of the room. 'It's no good.'

Jo opened her mouth to argue, but she realized that there was no point, not if Mr Felix might complain to the school about them. She could never explain that to her parents. So she gave up, and followed Tim along the hallway − no sign of the woman or the boy − and out through the front door. The door closed behind them without them having to push it shut, and the gates opened before them as they walked back down the gravel path. It felt as though they were being watched, but when they were back on the pavement outside and Jo turned round, there was no one at the windows.

The gates closed. In the pattern of metal there were still two cats, one on each gate. But now, as Jo looked, she could see another picture: a maze, that twisted and turned out of the black iron.

CHAPTER ELEVEN

'The ancient Egyptians used to worship cats.'

'Thanks, Vicky,' said Jo. 'That's really useful.'

'And in the Middle Ages people thought they belonged to the Devil, or witches. You had to cross your fingers when you saw one coming. There, you see. I told you I'd look up that book.'

Vicky had finally stopped sneezing, and her parents didn't mind her being up and dressed, as long as she stayed indoors. So Jo had called round again after school.

They were in Vicky's room, lying comfortably on the carpet and looking through a huge book called *Cats: Their History and Their Care*. 'Tigger's Book', Vicky called it. Tigger helped by trying to sit on it every time they turned a page. The book seemed to cover every possible subject, and there was even a whole chapter at the end on how to wash and brush your cat to get it ready for a cat show. Jo couldn't imagine that bit ever applying to Tigger, but she didn't tell Vicky.

'The Egyptians had a goddess called Bastet, or Pasht,' Vicky went on. 'There are all these pictures showing her, with a cat's head. And Egyptian cats were stripy, like Tigs.'

She scratched Tigger's back, and Tigger purred. Jo looked up. 'Called what?'

'Pasht.'

'That's the computer! Programmable and Scientific High Technology.'

'I think your Mr Felix has a rotten sense of humour.'

Jo had told Vicky all about their visit to the house. She hadn't been sure that Vicky would believe her, but she had. 'He's crazy,' Vicky had said. 'Or we are. But it's three to one then, not that that helps us much.'

'Do you think he's really crazy?'

'I dunno.' Vicky shrugged. 'He sounds like my gran. She's not mad or anything, but she's always going on about people in telly programmes like they live next door to her, and wondering what they're going to do next and all that.'

'He said they were real people, that we shot down,' Jo reminded her.

'There you are – Gran again. She watches telly too much. Half the time she doesn't seem to know what's real, either, and what's not.'

Jo sighed and looked at the pictures in the book. They showed stiff Egyptian figures, turned sideways, wearing pleated white robes. The bodies were people, but each one had the head of an animal: a falcon, a jackal, a cat. They looked strange, and rather frightening. Jo turned the pages. In the middle of the book there was a section of colour photographs of every imaginable cat: cats with tails; cats without tails; cats with curly coats; cats which loved swimming and pined if you didn't throw them in the bath every now and then.

'No blue cats,' Jo pointed out, 'with red eyes.'

'There are loads of blue cats!' Vicky said. 'Look, here – blue Persians.'

'They're grey.'

'No, they're not. Well, they're called blue. Lots of grey cats are. How about this one, a Burmese Blue.'

Jo looked. It was rather like a Siamese cat, but bigger, heavier. It stared out of the picture, sleek and arrogant, its fur shining with a strange tinge of colour.

'It's the nearest so far,' Jo said. 'But it's not the same. Its eyes are the wrong colour.'

'They don't do red eyes,' Vicky snapped, and read out the text.

' "The Burmese breed was created by the mating of a Siamese cat with a dark-coated cat of unknown origin. The coat of the Blue is a soft grey, with a velvety sheen, so that the cat seems to glow." '

'Like it was on a computer screen,' Jo chipped in, sarcastically.

' "The body is solid, lithe and muscular, with slender legs, the back legs being slightly longer than the front ones. The head is wedge-shaped, and . . ." Oh,' Vicky said, disappointed. 'It can't even have orange eyes. Only yellow or gold.'

'But it's not a real cat – the cat out there, I mean,' Jo insisted. 'It can't be.'

'Better to have a look through, just in case,' said Vicky, sensibly. 'Your computer man isn't going to be much help. Hey, listen, did you know that "the cat has evolved as a most efficient hunting machine. Its physique, stamina, speed and intelligence combine to enable it to seek and catch its prey, while its highly developed vision, even in very dim light, means that it can hunt effectively at night." '

Jo shivered, and crossed her fingers just in case.

Tigger walked on to the book again and pushed at Vicky's arm, making little pleading noises. 'There's no need to miaow, Tigs,' Vicky pointed out. 'If you're hungry, go out and grab something yourself. It says here that "the domestic cat will kill small mammals such as birds, mice and voles, and sometimes even larger prey". So there. And don't forget you're closely related to leopards and lynxes and things.'

'Tigers,' said Jo. 'They're nearer, with all the stripes.'

'You see, Tigs,' Vicky laughed, 'we've even called you after one.' But Tigger continued to miaow, and Vicky stopped reading and gave in. 'Oh, all right,' she said. 'Come on, Jo. Let's get her some milk.'

They went downstairs and left the book behind. But the next day, when everything got much worse, Jo remembered it. And she remembered what the book had said about how powerful and dangerous even a small cat could be.

CHAPTER TWELVE

The next day was Friday. It was the day before the school fête, and it was a strange day right from the start. As soon as Mrs Edmonds finished going through the register, she announced that they'd all do their normal work in the morning, but that in the afternoon some people might be asked to help with the preparations. 'And it's not an excuse to mess around, Damien,' she said at once, 'so sit down.'

What actually happened was that Mrs Edmonds spent all day running in and out of the classroom, and the other teachers seemed to spend all day popping in and out of their classrooms, too. In the end, everyone gave up trying to work. It was much more fun to sit and chat, and wonder who would reappear next.

Jo went over to the library corner, and tried to find a book on cats. There wasn't one. So she picked out a book about computers instead and started to flick through the pages, holding the cover up so that anyone looking over could see it. It worked. Tim walked over a few minutes later. He pulled a book out from the shelves without even glancing at it, and sat down next to her. Jo saw the title, and giggled.

It was called *The Reluctant Ballerina*, with a picture of a thin-looking girl on the front, dressed in frills. Tim saw her laughing, looked at the title, and jumped up at once. He came back with *Hamsters for Beginners*.

They talked quietly, behind their books, watching the door for Mrs Edmonds to come in again. There wasn't much to say, and there didn't seem to be any point in going round to the Felixes' house again. Jo told Tim about Vicky and the book, but she knew that it hadn't got them much further. She thought Tim would be interested to know what they'd read, and she got as far as telling him how the Ancient Egyptian for cat was *Mau*, because of the sound they make. But Tim couldn't care less – Vicky Willis always had her nose in some book or other – and Jo soon shut up. After all, they still didn't know what the cat was, or what to do about it.

'We don't even know *where* it is,' Tim said, gloomily.

'It might have gone away. For good.'

'No.' Tim shook his head. 'But what do we do when it comes back?'

Jo sighed. She didn't know, either.

When it happened, though, it took them by surprise.

By the time the afternoon came, most of Mrs Edmonds' class were involved in getting ready for the fête in one way or another. And because Jo's group were over in the sports hall, sorting out piles of old cups and plates, she saw it. Or at least, she thought she did.

The hall was full. Some people were tying the stand decorations together, or finishing off notices. In the middle of the floor lay a piece of white card with the stalls marked on it; the various stands grouped around the big goldfish game that was going to be the centre of the fête. Kay Jones was carefully writing the names of each stall on the chart, in her best writing, because it was going up at the fête entrance.

At one end of the hall there was a line of tables, all with different kinds of jumble on them. Jo's group had quite a solid table, which was lucky because they were putting out china, but some of the tables were old and sagging in the middle. 'I bet Dawn's table doesn't stay up,' said Sue. 'It's bending already. Look at it.'

Jo looked. And she saw, not the table, but something gleaming from underneath it. Two things – two red points of light. The teapot she was holding crashed to the ground and shattered into tiny pieces.

'Jo! What are you doing?' gasped Sue, jumping at the noise.

'Joanne, really! Do try to be more careful.' Mrs Edmonds came swooping over and stood in front of them, blocking out Jo's view of the table. By the time Mrs Edmonds had gone again, muttering about dustpans and brushes and daydreaming pupils, the cat had disappeared. Until the shouting started.

'Hey! Look!'

'Miss! Over there.'

'How did that get in here?'

'Isn't that the same cat as . . .?'

Even Mrs Edmonds couldn't get a hall full of excited people to stay still and be quiet. Everyone started trying to catch the grey streak. It darted suddenly across the hall. When at least half the runners had followed it to one side of the hall, the cat doubled back through their legs. Jo watched it as it ran, straight through the middle of the fête plan on the floor, heading for Dawn's table again. As the cat darted past, Jo thought it glanced at her, but everything happened too quickly to be sure.

The cat dived under the table. Dawn screamed, whirled round, and lost her balance. She began to fall, and reached out to stop herself falling – but she grabbed the table instead, and pulled it after her as she went down. The trestles collapsed, and soon Dawn was buried under a pile of old clothes and the remains of the table top.

A couple of teachers ran over and started to lift the table away. Eventually Dawn was pulled out, crying and laughing all at the same time. After they had lifted a tablecloth away, and the last pair of trousers from off her head, Dawn bent down and rubbed her leg.

'It scratched me,' she yelped. 'Ow. It's bleeding!'

Mrs Edmonds bent over her. 'You'd better go along to the school office. Ask Mrs Abbey to put something on your leg.'

'It was that cat. It scratched me.'

Mrs Edmonds, and Dawn, and everyone else looked round. There was no sign of the cat.

'It's gone,' said Miss Grant. 'All this shouting will have scared it off.'

'Perhaps it was the table,' Mrs Edmonds suggested. 'It's quite sharp. You really must get that cut cleaned up. Off you go.'

'The table wasn't . . .' Dawn began, but stopped when she saw Mrs Edmonds' face. She got up, and limped off heavily. It was partly for sympathy, partly because they didn't believe her.

But Jo believed her. She looked at the collapsed table and the mess on the floor and felt light-headed. How could one cat do so much damage? And what would it do next?

What would it do next? The words hit Jo so hard she could almost feel them, and she put her hand over her mouth to stop herself shouting out loud. But her face must have given her away, because Mrs Edmonds took one look at her and sighed.

'I'm sorry, Miss Grant,' she said, heavily. 'I really don't know what's got into my class today. They can't even help out sensibly.'

Jo knew very well that Mrs Edmonds was talking to her, not really to Miss Grant at all, and it didn't help that the girls behind her were still giggling over the sight of Dawn going down under the collapsing table. So when Jo was sent back to the school and her classroom 'to do something quietly', she wasn't very surprised. But it suited her. She raced back along the corridors, looking for Tim. She had to ask him . . .

Jo found Tim standing by the windows, watching a game of football that was being played out on the fields. He wasn't very pleased to have Jo rush up and interrupt. He tried to ignore her at first, until he realized what she was talking about.

'I've seen it – it's in the hall! Well, not in the hall now, but – Tim, listen – '

Reluctantly, Tim stopped watching the football and watched Jo instead, waiting for her to stop gabbling.

'And it's what Vicky said. And you've got to tell me!'

'Tell you what Vicky said? I don't know what Vicky said.'

'No, stupid.' Jo took a deep breath, and started again. 'She said to ask you what happened next. In the game.'

'Next after what?' Tim relaxed and looked out of the windows again. It didn't seem so urgent after all.

'Next after the cat knocking the dog out, and all the feet – you know.'

Tim watched the ball go out of play before he answered. The cat seemed a long way away from real life, which was football and wanting the bell to go for the end of school. He remembered the screen, and the bright colours – just a little picture in his head.

'If you get it past all the legs,' he said, 'it goes

into the next screen. It's difficult. You really have to scratch your way through the last crowd of people. But then it gets to the good bit.'

He sighed. Nothing about the game was good, not now.

'What?' Jo almost screamed it at him.

'The third screen. It's a crowded market. An Eastern Bazaar or something. There are all these stalls, and they make a kind of maze, with traps along the alleys. And there's another cat there, too. It's a race.' Tim stopped, his eyes wide. 'You have to get your own cat to the centre of the market first, to the well and the magician's tent, so it can touch the crystal. And then, then it grows bigger and changes.'

'Changes?' Jo whispered.

'Yes, you know. Like the films. It sort of becomes like a lion – or a puma, I suppose – and then you can . . .'

'No!'

Tim stared at her. 'What do you mean?'

'The cat – it scratched Dawn. Badly. Just now, in the hall.'

'Like it does on the screen. And then . . .' Tim stopped. The fear at the back of his mind grew bigger, nearer. He leaned his forehead on the window, against the cool glass.

Neither of them dared say aloud what it was they were scared of. But they both knew. *A lion?* thought Jo. *That's crazy.* But she knew that it wasn't any more crazy than the cat existing in the first place.

198

'We've got to go and see Mr Felix,' Tim said at last.

'It won't do any good.'

'It's got to. He's got to do something.'

'He didn't do anything before,' Jo said obstinately.

'It's all we can do. Come on.' Tim levered himself up. 'Let's go.'

'Now?' Jo glanced at the clock. Only ten past three. 'We can't!'

'Are you coming or not?'

Jo thought of Mrs Edmonds. Then she thought of cats, and lions, and Tim going to see Mr Felix on his own. Then she gulped and followed Tim out of school.

CHAPTER THIRTEEN

'Why ever didn't you tell me?'

Mr Felix was sitting in the same chair, still surrounded by the piles of paper. He picked up a small remote control and balanced it in his hand as he spoke. Jo shook herself. She didn't believe she was hearing this.

They had gone round to the house. This time the gates opened at a touch, and when they got to the front door they found that it had opened as well. They didn't even have to knock. 'It's like he knows we're coming,' Jo had said, and a Voice from nowhere had crackled, 'I DIDN'T KNOW YOU WERE COMING. BUT I KNOW WHO IT IS. COME IN. YOU KNOW THE WAY.'

So they had walked in, along the corridor and past all the doors. Jo thought of *Alice in Wonderland* again, except that Alice didn't have boring dark brown hair. She half expected a white rabbit, or perhaps a dormouse, to appear suddenly out of one of the rooms. But no one appeared. She could hear people talking and calling to each other, but the voices came from another part of the house.

'How did you know it was us?' was the first thing

Tim said when they were in the back room. The room looked just the same. The lights were still flashing, the printers whirred, and the dog was asleep again on the sofa.

'There's a scanner by the gates. I use it to check up on people. And when you got to the front door, I weighed you.'

'Eh?' Tim asked, confused.

'I weighed you. You stood on a pad there. It's to check no one else has slipped in. You weigh about twelve stones, between you. I don't know how much that is each.'

'Kilos,' Jo said. 'You weigh people in kilos.'

'I don't.' Mr Felix shrugged. 'I'm too old-fashioned for that. So, tell me, why have you come this time?'

Tim and Jo looked at each other, and then told him everything, falling over their words and each other's sentences, trying to get him to understand before he told them to leave again. They explained about the cat, and nightmares, and the dog, and the scratches on Dawn's leg.

'It's not a game any more. And it's a real dog! It's not just a square on a computer screen,' Jo told him, urgently. 'It's a yellow dog. It's very friendly, and it belongs to a girl called Tracey who was really upset . . .'

'And then Jo asked me what happens next on the screen, after the cat starts scratching people,' Tim joined in. 'So we had to come and see you.'

201

'And it frightened Tigger.' Jo caught Mr Felix's glance and mumbled, 'Tigger's a cat.'

'Vicky's cat,' Tim added.

They stopped together, out of breath, waiting. And, amazingly, Mr Felix smiled at them. A real smile.

'Why ever didn't you tell me?' He stood up and walked over towards the windows. 'I didn't realize you'd come about that. I thought . . .' He waved a hand, as though gesturing something away. 'Oh, never mind what I thought.' Then he tapped on the window and called, 'Danny! Maggy!'

'We tried to tell you.' Jo followed him across the room, indignant. 'And you wouldn't listen!'

He didn't answer, just shook his head and looked pleased. 'So that's where she is,' he murmured, to himself.

Jo and Tim heard running footsteps along the corridor, and then the boy, together with a girl, burst into the room. They both looked about twelve – dressed the same, like twins, in jeans and sweat-shirts, and both with very short, wavy hair.

'This is Maggy, and Danny,' Mr Felix said. 'Now, you two, Jo and Tim here have come to tell us about Cleo. They've seen her.'

Tim frowned, first at the strange tone – which sounded like some kind of warning – and then at the looks that Maggy and Danny exchanged with their father. But he shrugged it off, and concentrated on telling his bit of the story.

But before Tim and Jo had finished, the little girl

toddled unsteadily into the room. They all looked round at the noise. In front of her was the toy lizard, running along on the carpet. For a moment Jo was sure it was real – but people don't give lizards to babies to play with! The lizard stopped for a moment and raised its head to look round. It was emerald green with bright red eyes, and, as Jo watched, it flickered its tongue and blinked. Jo blinked too. They were all standing there, watching, when Mrs Felix followed Kate into the room.

'Kate!' she snapped. 'If you don't stop teasing Lizzie, I'll take your control away and TURN HER OFF!'

Jo gasped. Mrs Felix looked round, saw the group of people standing staring, and just sighed and closed her eyes, as if she didn't want to know that Tim and Jo were there.

Silence. Then Tim said, wonderingly, 'Turn her off?'

And suddenly everyone was talking at once. Mrs Felix stood holding Kate, looking worried; the twins were babbling about how their mother didn't mean it, that it was a joke, and Jo and Tim were trying to make sense of all the ideas that were running through their heads. In the end, Mr Felix yelled for everyone to shut up.

'I think we'd better tell them,' he said. Maggy and Danny looked sullen. 'After all, they might be able to help. We can't just leave Cleo out there, you know that.'

'She'll come back.' That was Maggy, but she sounded uncertain.

'I don't think she will,' said Mr Felix, patiently. 'It's not as if she was pulled out by a normal control.'

'Where is she, then?' Danny asked Tim. 'If you've seen her.'

Tim looked at him. Then he turned to Mr Felix and said, 'Tell us what?'

'They're new,' Mr Felix said. 'No one knows about them yet. We mustn't let anyone know until we've got them right.'

'What are "they"?'

Mr Felix picked up the control pad again from the armchair and pressed a button on it. 'This is Lewis,' he announced. 'He's been missing Cleo, too.'

The dog lifted his head when he heard his name, yawned, and opened his eyes very wide. They were unusual eyes, bright blue, and quite, quite square. Jo shook her head, trying to focus. But when she looked back the eyes were just the same blue and just the same shape.

Lewis barked once, fiercely, but Mr Felix just tutted and murmured, 'Oh, go on with you!' Then he pressed the button again.

'What does the control do?' asked Tim.

'That.' Mr Felix waved a hand towards Lewis, who had already settled down again on the sofa. 'Lewis likes his sleep, so I have to turn him off. Otherwise he'd get too excited, what with all these visitors we've been having lately.'

Jo gulped, and moved away from the sofa.

'Don't worry. He won't hurt you,' Mr Felix laughed. 'He's old and soft. The cat's a bit different, though. It seems to have gone wrong.'

'You shouldn't have had that game,' Danny said. 'It shouldn't have been in with the school computer discs.'

'Does anyone else know?' asked Maggy.

Tim and Jo shook their heads. Then Jo smiled. 'It's not the sort of thing you can tell the teachers.'

'D'you think they'd have believed us?' said Tim.

'I see what you mean,' said Danny, and he and Maggy grinned back at them.

'Lewis is a Compupet,' said Maggy, suddenly.

Jo and Tim looked blank. Then Mrs Felix came over and held out a leaflet for them to read. 'Here,' she said. 'This explains about them. They're a brand new invention.'

Jo took the sheet of paper from her. There was a big heading at the top:

COMPUPETS – ANIMALS FOR THE MODERN HOME

and underneath:

NEW! No feeding! No trouble!
Compupets mean fun and company without
work or mess!
THERE'S A COMPUPET TO SUIT YOU!

'Computer pets?' said Jo, slowly. 'Lewis is one?'

205

'He's the first,' Danny told her. 'He's mine.'

'He's both of ours,' said Maggy.

Tim glanced at Lewis. He looked just like a normal dog, sleeping comfortably. Tim frowned and carried on reading the leaflet. It described how each animal would look and behave just like a real one, and how it was activated and directed by remote control. The leaflet went on to talk about high-definition graphics and three-dimensional imaging until Tim gave up and stood and stared at Lewis instead.

'We sell a computer disc with the program on,' said Mrs Felix. 'For whatever kind of pet you want. All you need is a home computer with a display screen. The special control pad comes with the disc.'

'Stop it, Mum! You sound just like the brochure,' said Danny.

'Well, I did write it, don't forget.'

'You run the program on your own computer,' said Maggy, beginning to sound like a brochure as well, 'and the animal appears on the screen. Then you use the remote control to pull it off the screen and into the room.'

'They look ever so real,' added Danny. 'You thought Lewis was a real dog, didn't you?'

Jo nodded. *And the cat fooled everyone, too*, she thought, remembering.

'And later,' Maggy went on, 'Dad's going to try to work out a cheaper version and get pets from ordinary television screens. They'll be for old age pensioners, for company. Better than just watching television.'

'That's only a trial publicity sheet you've got there,' Mrs Felix explained. 'We haven't started selling the pets yet. In fact, we're still working on the prototypes – we have to get those right to start with. These Compupets, they were Danny's idea in the first place.'

'I wanted a dog,' Danny told them. 'But Mum wasn't sure I'd look after it properly.'

'I bet you wouldn't have taken it for a walk *every* day,' added Maggy.

'I would've!'

'Not in the rain you wouldn't, I bet.'

Danny ignored her. 'So I said to Mum, why can't we have a pet that doesn't have to be taken for walks if you don't want to?'

'Or brushed. Or fed every day if you're on holiday,' Maggy said.

'And doesn't have to go to the vet!' Jo added, eagerly.

Tim looked up from the leaflet. 'I suppose,' he said, 'you could call Lewis a Compup!'

Jo tried to think of another one, but couldn't.

Maggy laughed. 'And Rabbytes!'

'And what about Cleo?' asked Jo.

'The Graphicat!'

Then Mr Felix brought them all down to earth again. 'It sounds as if it's time we got our Graphicat back, you know.'

'Can you do that?' Jo asked, and held her breath.

She could see Tim crossing his fingers behind his back.

Mr Felix made a face, but didn't reply. Instead, he went over to the bench, sat down in front of one of the computers, and started typing. The others crept over to watch. Jo and Tim realized without being told that they mustn't interrupt.

Lines of type started scrolling across the screen. Mr Felix pressed a key to stop them, typed in another line, and then started it scrolling again. He did it quite a few times. Then he came out of the file. The screen went blank, and then a word appeared.

READY

He pressed a key and sat back. Nothing happened. He touched the key again, and then started typing. Suddenly lines started flashing up on the screen.

ERROR

ERROR

ERROR

'Oh dear,' Mr Felix murmured, still staring at the screen. 'It's got that far, has it? That's difficult.' He pressed a key and then spun round on his chair. The screen went blank.

'How far away from the school do you live?' he asked.

Tim looked a bit surprised, but answered him. 'About four roads away.'

'And you, Jo?'

'Another few roads more than that.'

'Less than half a mile?'

Jo laughed. 'Well, less than a kilometre, anyway.'

'And you both saw the cat in your gardens. Jo, are you sure about the girl — the one who got scratched?' he asked.

'Sort of,' said Jo. 'I couldn't see, though. Dawn said it was the cat, but it could have been a table.'

Mr Felix shook his head. He looked at them both, carefully. 'It's very important that we stop her. And you want me to get her back, don't you?'

'Yes!' Tim blurted out, and Jo breathed, 'Oh, please!'

'And you'll help, if you can?'

They both nodded, hard.

'We'll help, too,' said Danny.

Mr Felix thought for a moment. 'I think there'll be a limit to how far away she can go,' he said. 'Where's the GRAPHICAT disc?'

'It's by our computer at school,' Jo told him. 'In a box with all the others.'

He nodded. 'Okay. And the school's the centre of her range. I need to get on to the PASHT then, back to the original computer. How do we arrange that?'

'The PASHT's broken,' said Jo.

'I doubt it,' said Mr Felix.

'It doesn't work any more. We tried,' said Tim. 'And then we tried to run the GRAPHICAT disc on Miss Thompson's computer, and it wouldn't go.'

'Well, GRAPHICAT wouldn't,' Jo pointed out. 'But the other games were there. MAZE was all right.'

'And you don't understand why?' Mr Felix

asked. 'And when you first came here I thought you'd managed to work out something so much more . . .' He stopped abruptly and shook his head.

'Instead of the GRAPHICAT game I think we just saw the program,' Jo said, hesitantly. 'Was it the program – lines and lines of nonsense?'

'It's not really nonsense,' Mr Felix answered. 'It only looked like that because the computer couldn't read it properly. What you saw was the computer trying to interpret the program.'

'The PASHT just whirrs when you switch it on now,' Tim said. 'That's all it does.'

'It's not broken,' Mr Felix said. 'But they won't be able to mend it. There's a code. Now that the GRAPHICAT program has gone, um, wrong, you need to key in the code before the PASHT will recognize any program at all.'

'That's why the other computer ran MAZE.' Jo nodded, seeing what he meant. 'But it couldn't read GRAPHICAT because the code was in there.'

'You see, it's really quite simple,' said Mr Felix. 'Perhaps in a few years you'll be working – other things out, too.'

'Dad has this theory about kids and computers,' Danny teased. 'He says the computer geniuses of the future are all under fourteen now, and you only have to hide a few problems in . . .'

That time his father really did glare at him. And Danny went very red and shut up at once.

'You'll have to be quick, whatever you do,' Tim

said. 'They're going to take the PASHT away if they can't mend it.'

'And tomorrow's Saturday already,' Jo began, and then she cheered up. 'But it's the fête. Can't you come to that, Mr Felix?'

'What, and win a goldfish?'

'No, to see Miss Thompson. She's the computer teacher.'

'And she'll let you in. As it's your computer.' Tim grinned. This was going to work.

As they cycled home together, Tim was whistling. *He sounds cheerful*, Jo thought. *Like it really is going to be all right.* She concentrated on pedalling, round and round, head down into the wind. Round and . . . suddenly, Vicky's voice came into her head: 'Ask Tim what happens after the dog. The next screen in the game.' Jo frowned. She'd been so stupid, she'd never asked Tim until now. And Vicky had got the connection right away. She must tell her what was happening.

'Tim! Tim, stop!' she yelled out, and braked at the corner. There was a phone box with an old woman in it, who was shouting into the mouthpiece at someone. The conversation seemed to be about tea bags. Jo waited until Tim doubled back and came up alongside her.

'What are you doing?' he asked.

'Have you got any tens? I want to phone Vicky, and tell her.'

'Tell her what? Why?'

'What we're doing. Because she was right all along, and she's been worried, too. Come on, I only want one more.'

The old woman was beginning to glare at them.

'Why's she looking at us like that?' said Tim, loudly.

'Ssh,' said Jo, embarrassed.

'We're not talking as loud as she is.'

'Ssssh,' the woman hissed at them.

Jo closed her eyes and leant against the outside of the box. *Great*, she thought. *The old Tim Pascall again, and I'm stuck with him. Welcome back!*

The old lady finally left, tutting loudly, and Jo got through to Vicky. It took up the first ten pence to tell her what had happened at the Felixes, and what they were going to do the next day.

'But I thought you weren't going to go round again,' said Vicky, puzzled. 'I thought you said it wouldn't do any good.'

'That was before Tim told me about the game,' Jo explained. 'Then we had to. You were right, and I forgot to ask.' She told Vicky all about the last screen, and the lion. Tim moved away from the phone box. There was a silence on the other end.

'Vicky?' Jo asked. 'Hey, Vicky. It's going to be okay.'

Silence.

'You know, about the lion,' Jo went on, wanting to hear someone talk, even if it was only her own voice. 'I got this picture of a huge, great lion, with a mane and everything. That's silly, isn't it?'

Still silence.

'I – I mean, it *is* silly. Cleo's a female, anyway. A lioness. She wouldn't be so strong, or dangerous. Lionesses are a lot smaller, aren't they? She wouldn't even have a mane.'

Tim had left his bicycle lying on the pavement, and was staring out over the road. It made Jo feel more uneasy. It was too much like the first time, after school, when he had said he could feel the cat out there. Then there was a strangled noise on the phone.

'Hello?'

'Jo.' Vicky's voice sounded very small and faint. 'Jo, don't you understand?'

A little shiver ran up Jo's back and on to her neck. She didn't want to listen to what Vicky was going to say next, but she had to.

'The male lions don't really do very much,' Vicky went on, carefully. 'They don't usually kill to eat. The ones who hunt – they're the *females*. The lionesses. They often hunt alone. And, Jo . . .'

Nothing. Jo shook the phone, and then saw that the sign was flashing for more money. She didn't have any more. And anyway, it wouldn't be of any use now. She swallowed. Her heart was beating fast, as though she had been running, but there was nothing to run away from. Not yet. She put the phone back on to its cradle, slowly, and looked at Tim. He walked back and picked up his bike. She couldn't tell him – it wouldn't do any good. She couldn't tell anyone. But now, the fête didn't seem to be a very good idea any more. It was too scary, too dangerous.

CHAPTER FOURTEEN

Jo woke up the next morning feeling headachy and exhausted. It was Saturday, and her mother was coming back, but she couldn't look forward to it. When she told her father that she wouldn't be at home when Mum arrived, he started to look annoyed.

'You're not going to be moping around all weekend, are you, Jo?' he asked. 'You've been funny all week.'

'I haven't!'

'Well, don't.'

'I'm not being funny. But it's the PTA fête this afternoon, and Miss Thompson's asked me to help out,' Jo lied. 'It's very important. I can't not go. I promised.'

Her father had to give in then. 'Okay, if you've got to. But try to be here when your mum arrives.'

'I'll try. I hope she's brought me a present.'

'And be nice to her!'

Jo glowered at her father's back. Sometimes he had no idea. No idea at all.

The fête started at two o'clock, and Jo and Tim

were lurking at the school gates half an hour early. There were groups of screaming kids, and parents who ran pushchairs over other people's feet, but no sign of Mr Felix or Maggy or Danny. 'D'you think they're coming?' Jo asked, trying not to panic.

'They've got to.' Tim shrugged his shoulders, and carried on picking black paint off the railings.

It was half past two before the car arrived. It was bright lizard-green, so they would have noticed it anyway, even without Maggy and Danny waving at them out of the windows. Jo and Tim walked across, following the car in the queue to the parking area.

The fête was crowded by now, and there was a steady stream of families crossing between the cars and the stalls. The people all seemed so relaxed and cheerful that Jo wanted to go up and start shaking them, to make them realize. Everywhere she looked she could see little children, and helpless dogs. No one would be able to do anything against a big cat. It could be hiding among the cars, or under the stalls – it could be anywhere. Her nerves were on edge. She saw a flash of movement out of the corner of her eye, and stopped, spinning round to try to follow it.

'What's the matter?' asked Tim, and without waiting for an answer he grabbed her arm and pulled her along. 'Come on.' They stepped over the rope to the car park, and met the Felixes as they piled out of the car and on to the grass.

Mr Felix had a briefcase with him, and Maggy pulled a holdall out of the boot. 'Here you are,' she announced, waving a control pad in each hand. 'There's one each.'

'How does it work?' Tim wanted to know. He held his control out and pressed some keys at random. Suddenly there was a loud barking, and Lewis jumped out of the car and ran straight for him. Tim was nearly knocked off his feet. Maggy started laughing at the look on his face, but Mr Felix pounced on them.

'Not here!' he hissed. 'There are too many people around.' And as if to prove his point, a little boy called out 'Doggy!' and tried to drag his parents towards them.

Danny walked over to Lewis. Anyone watching would have simply thought he'd picked the dog up, but Jo realized that really he'd turned him off first. He put Lewis back into the car.

'That's a good idea,' said Mr Felix. 'Let's all get in, and then we can go over what we're going to do.'

It was warm inside the car, and very squashed, so Maggy sat on Lewis to make a bit more room. 'It's all right,' she said, when she saw Jo's shocked expression. 'When they're switched off, they're nothing, really. That's why they're so good. You can't break them.'

'If we don't get this cat back,' her father interrupted, 'it's going to do something so dangerous that we'll never get the chance to sell any of them at all, let alone break them. Now listen. Jo and Tim, you see the red button at the top? You press that once to activate the Compupet.'

He showed them how to use the control pads. There were four main input keys: *stand by, activate, freeze, turn off*. It was just like learning how to use a remote control for a video recorder. 'But the difference,' he explained, 'is that we've linked them all up. Normally there's only one control pad for each animal, but any of these four should control Cleo.'

Jo noticed that he said 'should'.

'Now, which is your classroom?'

Jo pointed it out. The fête stalls had been set up on the grass between the car park and the school buildings. There were streamers and flags flying, and big balloons in the air to mark the middle of the fête. Hundreds of people were milling around the fête, laughing and shouting, and the school itself was grey and deserted behind the colourful stands. Mr Felix looked past the fête and drew imaginary lines from the main school out into the playground. Then he told everyone where he wanted them to stand.

'Usually the controls are effective to about one hundred yards . . .'

'Metres,' said Danny.

'But you might have to get nearer. Perhaps a lot nearer, I'm not sure. If the cat's generating her own counter force, you might have to get very close indeed. I hope you can run.'

They nodded. 'Jo's good,' said Tim. 'She's fast.'

I can run, thought Jo. *But I don't think that's going to be enough.*

218

They bought their entrance tickets from Mrs Wood by the car park, and walked across on to the playing fields. Jo and Tim tagged along behind, until they saw Miss Thompson. 'That's her,' Tim hissed, pointing. 'The one in the blue dress.' Then he hung back with Jo while the Felixes went across.

Miss Thompson was looking busy and preoccupied. She smiled politely when Mr Felix went up and introduced himself, but it was clear that the last thing she wanted to have to cope with was the broken computer. And while they were talking, a little first year ran up as well, calling out. 'Miss Thompson, Miss Thompson! Miss Grant needs some more change.'

'Oh dear,' wailed Miss Thompson, looking more harassed than ever. 'I . . .'

'Here goes,' muttered Tim, and he walked up, innocently, as if he'd never seen Mr Felix or Danny or Maggy before in his life. 'I'll show them, Miss,' he offered, trying to look particularly helpful. 'The PASHT's in our classroom.'

Miss Thompson looked at him, warily. And when Jo went up, too, looking equally eager to be helpful, Miss Thompson started to look positively suspicious. But she couldn't leave the playing fields, and the first year was hopping from one foot to the other in front of her.

'Would you mind if I don't come in with you?' she said to Mr Felix. 'I'm supposed to be on duty here. I'm sorry. Jo and Tim – show the gentleman where your classroom is then, please, and come straight out again. All right?'

Jo and Tim nodded, and Miss Thompson darted off towards the stalls.

None of them spoke as they walked to the school buildings. Mr Felix was frowning, and when Jo looked she saw that he was holding his briefcase so tightly that the knuckles on his hand were white. He was obviously more worried than Danny and Maggy realized, because they were bouncing along quite happily. Tim kept glancing around as though he expected to see the cat suddenly appear. *It can't be far away, if Tim's so jumpy*, thought Jo. She wanted it all to be over. She wondered what the others were thinking.

The corridors were silent, except for the echo of five pairs of feet. Tim clutched his control pad hard, waiting for something to happen. It wasn't like school at all. The doors were closed all along the passages, and he felt there could be all kinds of things hiding behind those doors. But they got to the classroom without seeing anything.

Mr Felix switched on the computer and took out the GRAPHICAT disc. 'I have to do this bit on my own,' he said. 'And you lot might have to react quickly. So go off, and make sure you're ready as soon as the cat appears.'

There were so many questions Jo wanted to ask. But she didn't dare. *What happens if it doesn't come?* she thought. And then, more worrisomely, *What if it's out there already, and we can't stop it?* Tim wasn't

220

moving, either, so she grabbed his arm and dragged him away.

'It'll work,' she said, even though she didn't fully believe it.

'You can't watch, anyway,' said Danny. 'Dad has to be on his own when he's concentrating.'

'Don't worry,' Maggy added.

'Don't worry!' Tim yelped. 'Oh yeah! Let's have a nice time while we don't know . . .'

'You could look at the fête.'

'Great!' Tim pulled a face. 'What d'you expect me to do? Try to win a goldfish?'

'It's cruel, having goldfish,' Jo butted in. 'You could win some chocolate for us, instead.'

Along the corridor, a shadow moved. None of them saw it.

When they got back into the playground, Tim nudged Jo and nodded in the direction of the fête. Miss Thompson was standing by the stalls, but she was looking over towards the school, and had seen them.

'Look normal,' said Tim. So they all sat down on the school steps, in a neat row, as though they were waiting for Mr Felix to finish. But as soon as Miss Thompson disappeared into the fête, Tim and Jo darted back round outside the school, with Danny and Maggy after them, until they reached their own classroom. Quietly, they moved to the window and looked in.

Jo gasped. She didn't know whether it was shock or relief, but there was a cat there. It was blue-grey, and not golden. Perhaps everything was going to be all right after all.

The cat was walking across the desks. It jumped from one table to another, carelessly and elegantly, swishing its tail as it went. Mr Felix seemed to be talking to it. They couldn't hear what he was saying, but he was shaking his head. In spite of everything, Jo thought how wonderful the cat looked. The light shone off its coat, turning it to silver. She saw the wide head, the soft, pointed ears and the clever face.

Jo shuffled back away from the window. 'I wonder if my parents'll buy me a cat,' she whispered.

'After all this?'

'Yes.'

'You could have a Comp . . .' Danny began, before Maggy elbowed him.

'I never want to see another cat in my life,' Tim hissed back.

'I think we'd better move.' That was Maggy.

They fanned out, moving slowly and quietly, until they reached the edges of the playground. Danny was by the school gates, and Tim was by the main entrance. Jo and Maggy stood opposite each other where the playing fields started, and not far from the fête itself. Jo checked for the third time that she was holding her control the right way round. Her fingers hovered over the keys: *stand by, activate, freeze, turn off*. She hoped she could remember the right order.

Tim kept looking along the school building, trying to decide where the cat was most likely to come from. Mr Felix had said it would probably run when he tried to alter the program to get it back, but he couldn't be sure. And first he had to try to get the cat back into the screen. That would be the safest way, if it worked. But if the cat didn't respond, and the screen couldn't absorb it, then it would be really free. And as Mr Felix couldn't use a control pad so near to the computer itself, it was up to the group of them waiting outside.

And while they waited, Tim remembered the game he'd played so often. The graphics turning into a great cat, a hunting lion. He tried to imagine a lion, golden against the grey of the playground, but failed. He looked at the stalls instead, at the bright colours and the people wandering around. And then he felt very sick, because he suddenly knew what Mr Felix must know but hadn't told them. What had he said? *If we don't get this cat back it's going to do something so dangerous . . .* They weren't there just to get back a scientific prototype before someone found out about it. They were there to stop something because they had to, because of the danger, and this might be their only chance.

Suddenly Danny was waving his arms and calling out. 'It's all right, look, she's here!'

'It's not a game,' Tim muttered to himself. 'And he'd better stop dancing around.'

Tim was right. The cat saw Danny, stopped, turned, and ran back in the opposite direction, straight for the stalls. Jo and Maggy started to run forwards. Jo was very fast, but to Tim it looked as if she were running in slow motion. Then the sun caught the cat's coat, turning it golden, and Tim found that his legs had come unstuck and he could move.

'No! Stop!' The yell came from behind, making Tim nearly overbalance. 'Wait!' Mr Felix was running out of the school, waving his arms and screaming at them. Danny started to run over, and Maggy stopped too when she heard her father. Only Jo kept running, and as Tim hesitated she disappeared round the edge of the fête.

'Dad! Are you all right?' said Danny, grabbing at his arm.

Mr Felix ran on for a bit, dragging Danny after him. But then he came to a halt and stood there, burying his face in his hands.

'What is it?' Maggy ran up, looking panic-stricken.

Mr Felix glanced round at them. 'Where's Jo?' he shouted. 'Where is she?'

'She's gone after it,' said Tim. 'Like you told her to. What's happened?'

'Get her back!' Mr Felix snapped, and started running himself.

'What's happened?' Tim grabbed Mr Felix's other arm, to stop him. 'What's gone wrong?'

'The game. You were into the game.'

'What do you mean?'

'When you switched the computer off. You hadn't come out of the game. I went in – it was into the third screen already. I wasn't quick enough.'

'Dad,' said Maggy, softly. 'It's all right. We'll get Cleo back. We'll have another go.'

'No, Maggy.' Mr Felix shook his head. 'It's not safe any more.'

He looked at Tim, and Tim knew what he was saying. The third screen of the game was the one where the cat changed, in the bazaar. Tim jerked his head up and looked at the fête. A market – people, stalls. The image on the screen was a reflection: this was the real thing. And it was out there somewhere. And where was –

'Jo!' he yelled, and started running. It was all his fault; he had to get her back.

Tim dashed straight for the fête. There was no sign of Jo, and it was difficult to move fast because of all the people. Everything seemed normal. Then someone screamed – he whirled round, but it was only someone winning a prize. There were loud shouts from the coconut shy, and a little girl yelling because she'd dropped her ice cream. He couldn't possibly find Jo in all this. Or the cat, if it was still a cat. But it wouldn't be if it had reached the centre. If it got there. Then he realized. The centre – the well and the magician's tent. The big goldfish game was right in the middle of the fête, and next to it –

Tim turned right round and started to run back to the school, faster than he'd ever run in his life before.

Jo wasn't running. She wished she were an animal instead of being human, and could sense or sniff out danger. She was holding the control pad so hard that her fingers were cramping, but she didn't believe that it would do any good. Not any more. There had to be something else, something Mr Felix wasn't telling them. Or perhaps he didn't know, either.

She walked slowly, hesitantly, through the fête. Past the sweets tables, past the 'Space 2000 by Class 3' model rocket and on to the exotic 'Our Animal World in Danger' stall. Every time she came to the edge of a stand she looked both ways before slipping round on to the other side. It seemed that everyone was enjoying themselves, except her. It was all so noisy and busy, she knew she'd never find an animal that didn't want to be found. Then she thought. There was something Tim had said. Something about the cat in the game always going towards the middle, to the water well. And then she saw the big yellow balloon, shaped like a goldfish, floating above the stalls in the very centre of the fête. Carefully, she began to make her way towards it.

'I know it's out there,' said Tim. 'I just do.'

'But where?' Danny said, reasonably. 'It could be anywhere among that lot. We'll never find it.'

'We've got to try the game. There's a pattern to that, isn't there?'

Mr Felix scratched his fingers through his hair, and nodded.

'Can you start it up again?' Tim persisted. 'From the first screen? Because then it will have a new cat.

And if I take it to screen three, and get to the middle first . . .'

Mr Felix stared at him then, as though he had never seen him before in his life. 'Yes. Yes, I can. Are you good at this game? Very good?'

Tim nodded.

'Right. Danny and Maggy, go and wait for the cat. But be careful.'

'Wait for her? Where?'

'Don't you remember the game at all? Go right into the *middle* of that lot.' He pointed to the fête. 'It's probably around that goldfish thing. The cat'll go there, it always goes towards the centre in the game. AND BE CAREFUL. Come on, Tim.' And he headed back to the classroom.

They got to the PASHT, Mr Felix exited from the program and they waited while the computer processed the password. Tim's hands were sweating as he sat there, watching the blue and red cat's-face logo come up on the screen, line by line. Then the screen changed again and he was into the game.

No time to wipe his hands. His fingers flew over the keyboard in the old, familiar pattern. The dog appeared – cursor left, up, up again, *enter* – and he was on to level two.

Tim bit his lip. The legs seemed to be faster this time than he could ever remember. No time to play safe, and hide the cat in holes – he had to make it run and hope he was lucky. Just scratch and scratch to get through. He kept one finger constantly on the escape key, which meant that he had to move the cat along with just one hand, and it was difficult to work out quickly which cursor keys to cover with which fingers. He wondered what was happening out in the fête, and where Jo was. *Don't think*, he told himself. *Concentrate!* He had just glimpsed the edge of the screen, when a group of legs all came along together. He couldn't do it! And what would he do if the same thing happened as last time he played? Tim pressed the cursor key just once, kept his finger on *escape*, and closed his eyes.

He didn't see the screen change. But when he heard Mr Felix breathe out, loudly, he took his fingers off the keys and dared to open his eyes. They were on to level three. There was the brightly coloured scene, the squares and dots that stood for market stalls and traps – and there was only one cat! Not two, as there had been every other time he'd played the game. Tim whistled with relief, and had started to move the cat along, into the first part of the maze, when he stopped and stared. Above 'his' cat, there was a blip on the screen.

'That's not part of the graphics.' He pointed to it. The blip was white, reversed out of the colours on the screen.

'No. And you need to keep your cat away from it,' said Mr Felix. 'That's where the other cat should be, or is. And it's nearly got there.'

That was when Tim realized that the white blob was moving steadily towards the centre of the maze, fuzzing over the screen picture as it went and leaving a blank trail behind it in the graphics. He'd never catch it in time, unless he made his own cat take the direct route, over all the traps. He took a deep breath and started to move the cursors. The blip was almost in the centre now. He couldn't do it – there wasn't enough time. But he got his cat safely through the Closing-Gate trap, and when he looked again, the white hole was still in the same place. It hadn't got any further. It was jerking backwards and forwards as if it had run up against some invisible barrier. Tim took a deep breath and pressed the cursors again, as fast as he could.

Jo was standing still, backed up against the rough tent material behind her, not daring to move. She was in a nightmare, where nothing made sense and where she couldn't believe what she was seeing.

From beneath the stall opposite her, two unblinking eyes were staring out. Around the edge of the stall, the cut-out goldfish shapes threw moving shadows on to the grass below. But Jo could only look at where the cat was. One moment it was a dark grey shadow; then it turned to gold as the sunlight shone through the plastic fish. *It's still only a cat*, Jo told herself. But she wasn't convinced. Surely it was too big – bigger than she remembered? That couldn't simply be a trick of the shadows. And there was something different about it that she couldn't quite place. It looked heavier, and its tail was wrong. She thought of the time she had seen the cat on the wall, lashing the bricks with its tail. That tail had been thin and whip-like, but this was different. It had a kind of tuft on the end, and Jo knew that ordinary, domestic cats never had tails that shape, only . . .

Then the cat snarled. Jo would have run, but her feet wouldn't work and she knew, deep down, that there was nowhere she could run to. The cat got up. It stretched out its front legs and opened its mouth, and its muzzle drew back in loose folds, unlike any cat Jo had ever seen. And she knew it wasn't a cat any more. But there was nothing else to do, so still she refused to move.

And then, as if in slow motion, the cat opened its eyes wide, drew itself together, and jumped forwards. A sideways pouncing leap over the grass, and then it sprang towards the gap in the tent behind Jo. She saw the open mouth, the long teeth, the front claws stretched towards her, and she screamed and stepped backwards. Her foot caught in the tent. She found herself falling heavily into the material. And as she fell she saw the cat hang in mid-air, judder and fall sideways. Someone screamed to Jo's right, there was a shout, and Jo ended up sitting on the floor with suffocating darkness all over her.

It would have been nice to stay there, safely, like that. But there was Maggy, pulling the blankets away. Jo looked round. A woman with a tea-towel on her head was sitting at a little table, looking embarrassed, with an upside-down goldfish bowl in front of her. Another woman, sitting opposite, was looking even more embarrassed. Kay Jones's mother – 'Madame

Jay will tell Your Fortune' – was wishing she'd never got into this.

There was a pause. Then a voice yelled out, 'Where's that lion, then?'

And another voice called back, 'I'm bringing it over to the animal stall now. With the zebra.'

Suddenly a man walked past, with a cardboard cut-out lion under one arm and a zebra under the other. Jo closed her eyes, but when she opened them again he was still there. He walked calmly across the grass and disappeared past the goldfish stand, leaving Jo staring after him.

Fortunately the people nearby had seen the funny side of the collapsing tent, and gathered round to help pull the material back over the stand. Maggy dragged Jo up, and started steering her back through the crowds. Jo looked round wildly for those crazy, flat animals, but all she saw was Danny instead, carrying something carefully in his arms.

'Has he got her?' she gasped.

'Yes. I don't know what state she's in, though. Don't worry about Danny. He'll be all right with her, she likes him. But she stopped! They must have managed to get through the game. Tim won!'

'What?' Jo closed her eyes again. She didn't understand any of this.

'Come on back to the school,' Maggy said, holding her arm. 'We'll explain then.'

Maggy's explanations were too much for Jo after the shock of the cat and the tent, and then the sheer relief of not having to be frightened any more. She remembered the man solemnly carrying the flat, cut-out animals, and started to giggle instead, louder and louder.

'Don't,' hissed Maggy. 'You're getting hysterical.'

Jo laughed until the tears were running down her face, and she couldn't stop them.

'Jo, don't,' Maggy squealed. 'Everyone's looking.'

'I don't care,' Jo called out, waving her arms in the air. 'I don't care. I DON'T CARE!' And she started running back to the school.

In the classroom, Mr Felix and Tim were sitting in front of the PASHT, looking at a screen which was filled with a single image: a shining, golden lion.

'I got to the crystal first,' Tim yelled at Jo, as she walked in. 'It was nearly in the middle, and then it stopped.'

'Jo stopped it,' Maggy said. 'She was standing there, right in front of the tent. She wouldn't move.'

'I *couldn't* move.'

'Cleo didn't notice us. We were really close, and then Danny went in to get her and she went all funny.'

'That was when Tim got his cat through the maze and took the crystal,' Mr Felix said. 'The cat out there couldn't win, it couldn't change.'

'And it really worked?' Tim asked.

'Yes.' Maggy beamed. 'Danny's taken Cleo off. I don't think anyone noticed – they were too busy with Jo pulling the tent down.'

'But whatever did the cat think Kay's mum's gold-fish bowl was going to *do*?' said Jo, bewildered.

'Nothing. She didn't "think" at all, she had no choice. Once I'd gone into the PASHT, I set the program off again. Outside, the fête was like a huge version of the GRAPHICAT game. So she just started running, as though she were in the game itself.'

Jo was quiet for a moment. 'What are you going to do with the Compupets?' she asked.

Mr Felix sighed. 'I don't know. I'll have to go back a bit. There's a problem. I didn't realize before, but it looks like the Compupets can cross over into other programs that are running on the same computer. That's how Cleo became part of the GRAPHICAT game. It could get too dangerous. I need to make sure that they can't cross over, if I can. And if not . . . what do you think, Tim?'

Tim shook his head. 'I don't know.'

'And *I* don't know how you got in here, Timothy Pascall. You really are the limit. Playing computer games in the middle of the school fête?'

'Er, this is Mrs Edmonds, our teacher,' Tim muttered.

Mr Felix switched on a huge smile. 'Good afternoon! I think we may have managed to sort out your machine, Mrs Edmonds,' he said. 'And these two pupils of yours have been, um, extremely helpful. I wonder if I could have a word with you, or your Head. It's about a computer . . .?'

Jo and Tim stood by the school gates to say good-bye as the car drove off. Mr Felix hooted, Lewis barked, and Maggy and Danny waved at them.

'We were going to try to do a horse as well,' Maggy called. 'Come and try it, if they work in the end.'

'Not on your life,' Tim called, waving back.

Jo watched until the bright green dwindled into a dot. 'Tim,' she asked. 'What do you think is going to happen when they sell them?'

'The Compupets? I dunno.'

'Do you think they will, after all this?'

Tim shrugged. 'Well, I don't want one.'

'But Tim, even if he does put barriers up between the programs, I bet people could find ways round them. I bet you could. What if there's a space invaders game, and . . .'

'I don't want to think about it,' Tim said, finally. Then he suddenly jumped up and stretched his arms above his head. He was grinning. 'Come on,' he said. 'I'm going to win that goldfish.'

Much later, when they got to Jo's front gate, the car was back, and Jo's father was busy hauling things out of the boot.

'Mum's inside,' he called.

Jo ran in and flung herself at her mother. 'It's nice to have you back.'

'It's nice to be back. Is everything all right?'

Jo nodded hard. Everything was all right, now.

'Have you been very bored?' her mother asked. 'I'm sorry it was when Caron was away. It wasn't very good timing, was it?'

'No, but it was okay. I've been too busy. After

the cat . . .' Jo realized she couldn't tell Mum about that, and then she remembered Tim as well. She dragged her mother out into the front garden. 'This is Tim. We won a goldfish!'

'I haven't got a tank at home,' Tim said.

'I'll find something.' Jo's mother took the goldfish from him. 'It's lucky we don't have a cat,' she pointed out. 'The fish'll be safe here. What's his name?'

'Cleo,' Jo and Tim said, at the same time.

Jo's mother looked surprised. 'That's an odd name for a goldfish,' she commented.

'I like it,' said Jo. 'Wait till I tell you what we did this week!' Then she caught Tim's warning glance. 'Well, some of it, anyway,' she added.

On the Monday morning, Mrs Edmonds was in an amazingly good mood. She forgot all about taking the register, and started by telling the class how successful the fête had been.

'We are very grateful to the PTA,' she announced. 'We've raised enough money for the hall piano, and there is some over. We did think we'd have to put it all towards mending the computer, or perhaps getting another one, but then we had some very good news.'

Mrs Edmonds paused, and everyone waited. She was obviously working up to a surprise for them. Jo and Tim glanced at each other. Vicky looked up, mouth open. Caron saw the looks and decided that she'd have to *make* Jo tell her what had been going on while she'd been away. She'd obviously missed out on something very interesting.

'The PASHT came from a local firm,' Mrs Edmonds went on. 'When they heard that it was broken, the owner of the firm came to look at it personally. It can't be mended properly, so he has offered to replace it quite cheaply. With a newer model.'

Jo gulped. She had a horrible idea that she knew what Mrs Edmonds was going to say next.

'So that's good,' Mrs Edmonds smiled round the class. She noticed Tim staring at her, and nodded. 'And there are even some games on it – for after-school use only, of course.'

'Real games, Miss?' Dawn called out.

'Yes. With much better graphics than the old one. There are dinosaurs, and space invaders, and a game with sharks, too, I think.'

'So Tim Pascall can play them all the time,' someone muttered.

But Mrs Edmonds was in too good a mood to rise to that. 'Well, Tim,' she said. 'I thought you'd be pleased.'

Tim looked at her, then at Jo. 'Actually,' he said, solemnly, 'I prefer writing stories.'

THE PRESENT TAKERS

Aidan Chambers

CHAPTER ONE

LUCY BEWARE MELANIE PROSSER
SHE IS OUT TO GET YOU Angus x x x

How do you know? And stop sending me notes.

I HERD x x x Angus

'Wait here,' Melanie Prosser said at the school gate. 'Then we won't miss her.'

'In her daddy's posh car,' Sally-Ann Simpson said. 'Showoff pig.'

'I'll put an armlock on her,' Vicky Farrant said. 'I'm amazing at armlocks.'

'Not till we've got her behind the cycle shed,' Melanie said. 'Be all smarmy smiles till then.'

From the corner of the school hall Angus Burns watched the three girls hanging about by the gate.

He knew they'd wait for her today, being her birthday. Just like Prosser to think of that. He also knew what he would like to do to Prosser: kick her fat teeth in.

Angus swept the hair out of his face and scanned

the road, the school field, and then the drive right up into what he could see of the playground, looking for Clare Tonks. They'd be giving her a day off today while they had a go at Lucy. Poor old Clare, all she ever got was days off when they were bored with her, and were giving themselves a change by tormenting somebody else.

Angus spotted Clare at last. He could hardly miss her if she was in sight, she was so big in every direction. Tonks the tank. She was standing inside the cycle shed just out of view of the gate, and watching Angus.

'A new pencil case will do for me first time,' Sally-Ann said. 'My old one is grotty.'

'Could put a neat half-nelson on her,' Vicky said. 'With a wrist-lever to screw on the agony.'

'Save something for another day,' Melanie said, as patient as a granny.

'Or put her down with a hip throw, do a step-over toe hold, and really make the silly bitch scream.'

Melanie yawned.

Sally-Ann giggled. 'You and that wrestling. I reckon you're a bit loopy.'

Lucy Hall came downstairs wearing her new blue birthday shoes. She could hear her father backing the car out of the garage.

'Is it such a good idea to wear those?' Sarah Hall said meeting Lucy at the door to say goodbye.

'Stop fussing, Mum.' Lucy gathered her things into her school bag.

'Don't complain if they get scuffed.'

'They won't.'

Jack Hall blew the car horn.

"Bye, Mum, see you this after.'

They kissed before Lucy ran to the waiting car.

Last five weeks, Sarah thought, then the holidays and after that she goes to the High. Seems only yesterday she started at Infants. Where does it go?

She waved as the car drove off.

'Morning, Mrs Harris,' Melanie said as the teacher hurried through the gate.

'Morning, girls,' Mrs Harris called, stopping to look. 'What are you doing here? Can't you play in the yard?'

'Lucy's birthday, miss,' Melanie said, sweet as candy floss.

'Got a surprise for her,' Sally-Ann said, simpering. She was good at simpering, because she thought she was right in every way to play Annie in the musical, and had practised a special simper so that she would be ready when the call came.

'I'd forgotten,' Mrs Harris said. 'And, heavens, isn't she on hamster duty today? I'd better see to them myself. Have you a nice surprise?'

'Smashing,' Vicky said flatly, her eyes on the road.

'How thoughtful of you.' Mrs Harris strode away up the drive.

'Old bat,' Sally-Ann muttered.

'Shut it,' Melanie said.

'Mrs Harris,' Angus said, stepping into the teacher's path.

'Hello, Angus. Early for a change.'

'Lucy's birthday.'

'So I gather.' Mrs Harris glanced back at the group by the gate. 'She's popular all of a sudden.'

'I thought – '

Mrs Harris waited. 'Come on then, dear. I haven't all day.'

' – I thought you might meet her.'

'Meet her?'

'Her birthday and that.'

'At the gate, you mean?' Mrs Harris laughed. 'No, couldn't do that, Angus. I'd have to meet every one of you on your birthdays if I did. I'd never be done. Anyway, Melanie and Sally-Ann, and, what's her name, Vicky Farrant are there with a surprise. We'll all sing "Happy Birthday" after registration as usual, so the occasion will be properly celebrated, won't it? She isn't royalty after all.'

'It's just – '

'Yes?'

Angus blushed. Or, at least, what little of him Mrs Harris could see blushed. His face was mostly hidden by his hair. Luxuriant you might call it; long certainly.

Mrs Harris laughed again, louder this time. 'Well, I never! You of all people, Angus Burns! A dark horse, you are. You've good taste though, I'll give you that.'

She stepped around him, about to go inside leaving Angus rooted to the spot with embarrassment; but stopped.

'There is something you can do that would help Lucy, and me as well, if you want.'

Angus brushed the hair out of his eyes and managed to look at the teacher. 'Miss?'

'Feed the hamsters. Lucy's meant to – '

'But, miss, I – '

'You'll see her later. And think how pleased she'll be.'

Mrs Harris took Angus by the shoulder and drew him with her into school. Angus looked back furiously at the group by the gate as he went inside.

Jack Hall stopped the car a safe distance from the gate.

'Friends of yours?' he asked nodding in the direction of the three girls who had come out on to the pavement.

'Same class,' Lucy said, busying herself unnecessarily with her bag.

'Pleased to see you from the way they're waving.'

'Just being silly. 'Bye, Dad.'

'Happy birthday again, sweetheart.'

They leaned together and kissed, Lucy pulling away quickly and getting out.

'See you later,' Jack said.

'Bye.' Lucy slammed the car door and watched

her father drive away. She would rather he was out of sight before she faced Melanie. Till that moment she had pretended to herself that it wouldn't happen. Not to her.

But Melanie and the others came pelting towards her.

'Hi, Lucy!' Melanie called breathless with gush, grabbing Lucy's spare hand in what might have been a friendly grip if, looking on, you didn't know better. She gave Lucy an awkward hug.

Sally-Ann and Vicky frisked and stomped on either side.

'Sure,' they said. 'Happy birthday!'

'Ten today!' Melanie said, an announcement to the world.

'Eleven, if you have to,' Lucy said, trying to pull her hand away.

'*Eleven!*' Melanie's eyebrows rose and her grip tightened. 'Isn't that great, everybody! Lucy's *eleven* today!'

Sally-Ann giggled.

Other children, passing by, gave them a wide berth.

'All growed up,' Vicky said.

'Give us your bag, then.' Sally-Ann snatched it. 'I'll carry it for you today What an honour!'

Lucy swung her hand to snatch her bag back, but found instead that her arm was grabbed by Vicky and twisted up behind her.

'Let me go!' she shouted, trying to wriggle free.

She had heard people shouting like that before as the same thing was done to them, but she had never interfered, as nobody did now.

'Run!' Melanie ordered, and she and Vicky towed Lucy along the pavement, through the gates, and took her stumbling up the drive, across the playground, all unhindered, and round behind the cycle shed, where they were out of sight of the school building.

All the way Melanie and Vicky, and Sally-Ann bringing up the rear with Lucy's bag hugged to her like something precious, laughed and whooped.

From the classroom where he was feeding the hamster Angus heard their noisy progress. He threw the rest of the food into the cage and dodged across the room to the windows overlooking the playground. He was just in time to spot tail-end Sally disappearing behind the shed.

Some of the other kids were watching, but no one was following. Angus searched for Clare Tonks, at first could not find her, then saw her shadow looming at the back of the shed, leaning against the wall. Only the bricks, Angus thought, were separating her from what was happening on the other side. She could probably hear every word Prosser and her goons were saying. He'd ask her later.

Angus turned from the window. Mrs Harris was paying no attention, busy with work at her desk.

'Can I go now, miss?'

'All done?'

'Think so.'

'The fish?'

'Yes, miss,' he lied. He'd see to them at break. They wouldn't die before. Lucy was more important.

'All right.'

He sped away.

'We only want to *talk* to you,' Melanie was saying.

Sally-Ann had thrown Lucy's bag at her feet. She and Vicky held Lucy's arms out, pinning them against the cycle shed wall. To avoid Melanie's eyes, Lucy stared across the field at the houses on the other side of the road.

'Want to hear all about the fabulous prezzies you got this morning,' Sally-Ann said.

'Some fancy stuff, I bet,' Vicky said, 'your dad owning a shop and that.'

Melanie nudged Lucy's bag with a foot. 'What've you brought to show off?'

'Nothing!' Lucy's reply was a note too triumphant.

Melanie's face lost its grin. 'Must have.' She crouched and slowly unzipped the bag, watching Lucy's face all the time.

Lucy forced herself to keep quiet.

'Best make sure,' Sally-Ann said. 'Don't mind, do you, Luce.'

Melanie started rummaging.

Her temper fraying, Lucy could not help crying out, 'Leave my things alone!'

'Shut up, Whining Winnie,' Vicky Farrant said

between clenched teeth, and gave Lucy's arm a sharp nip that made her catch her breath.

Running feet echoed round the shed. Angus burst into view, skidding to a stop at the corner. He glared at the little group frozen into statues by his arrival. But the hair closed over his face at once. Melanie stood up, glaring back. 'Had an eyeful?' she said, hands on hips.

'Leave her alone,' Angus said unimpressively.

'What's it to you, you hairy beanpole?' Sally-Ann said. She had a voice that sliced your ears when she wanted it to.

'Just leave her, that's all.'

'He do fancy her,' Vicky said, matter-of-fact.

'Oooo – d'you think so!' Sally-Ann hooted.

'No I don't!' Angus said too quickly.

'Yes you do,' Melanie said, not even smiling. 'Well, you needn't worry. We're only talking. No harm in *talking*, is there? So you can just bug off, Angus Burns, because what we're having with your *sweetheart* – ' she paused, challenging him, 'is a *private* conversation.'

There was a silence. Angus opened his mouth, then shut it. He looked sideways as if someone out of sight round the corner were talking to him.

'Have you got some of your stinky friends with you?' Sally-Ann shouted. 'They don't scare us. You know what'll happen if we tell Mr Hunt you boys have been bothering us girls.'

Angus shifted on his feet, looking back and away.

Finally he brushed the hair out of his face and said, 'Just watch it, Prosser, that's all.'

'I'd rather not watch your ugly mug at all, if you don't mind,' Melanie said. '*Yuk!* Put your hair over it again!'

'I'm warning you,' Angus said, straining against his anger.

'Don't forget old Hunt,' Melanie said.

Angus hesitated; then, seething, slowly backed away round the shed corner.

As soon as he was gone, Melanie turned on Lucy. 'Rotten friends you've got. No bottle.'

'Not half as rotten as yours,' Lucy said, unable to restrain herself. 'And Angus Burns isn't my friend.'

'Not good enough for you, eh?' Vicky said.

Sally-Ann said, 'Never mind all that. What about the prezzies?'

'Nothing much in her bag, just the usual stuff,' Melanie said, her eyes not moving from Lucy's. She had unsettling eyes, like a cat's, grey, and they didn't blink much.

'I told you!' Lucy said.

'Funny what you notice though,' Melanie said, 'when you get down to earth.'

'What she on about?' Vicky said to Sally-Ann.

Sally-Ann looked down, and hooted; 'Ooooo yes!'

'Eh?' Vicky said.

Melanie, her eyes still unblinkingly on Lucy's, pointed with a finger. 'We'll have to teach Pukey

Lukey some manners,' she said. 'No prezzies, but showoff new shoes.'

'So she has!' Vicky said. Lucy felt the grip on her arm tighten.

'Happy birthday, Lukey,' Melanie said, and, moving very close, pushed her lips, exaggeratedly wet and pursed, into Lucy's face. Lucy twisted her head to avoid the soggy kiss. Melanie's lips landed, squelching, on her ear.

Melanie stepped back. 'All right, little Miss Stuckup, we'll just have to show you what happens to people who won't be friendly.'

'It shouldn't be bad *this* time,' Sally-Ann said like a nurse comforting a patient before an operation.

'Ready,' Melanie said.

Vicky and Sally-Ann each raised a foot above one of Lucy's.

'Stamp!' Melanie ordered.

The hovering feet pounded down on Lucy's toes, screwed this way and that, and lifted off.

Lucy cried out, and instinctively tried to bend down to grasp her feet and comfort them. But Vicky and Sally-Ann pinned her against the wall; all she could do was squirm, and shift her toes about inside her shoes, trying to wiggle the hurt out of them. Tears filled her eyes. Through them, as she bent her head to hide her face, she saw the scruffed and dented surface of her birthday shoes.

She had been wanting them for weeks. Her father had made a special trip to Gloucester to buy them for her, and this morning, longing to wear them, she could not resist the temptation. Now the pain in her toes was nothing to the distress she felt for her ruined gift. She hated Melanie for that.

As soon as she recovered her breath and could see properly again, she glared her hatred at Melanie, who laughed, as if pleased by such passionate dislike.

'Come on, Pukey,' Melanie said. 'Tell us all about your other presents.'

Lucy shook her head.

'You must have millions,' Sally-Ann said. 'Stuckups like you always do.'

Lucy shook her head again, fighting herself to say nothing.

'Think you're something, you do,' Vicky said. 'Coming to school in that poncy car.'

'Other people come in their parents' cars.' She could not help herself. Why should they get away with saying such stupid things about her?

'I don't,' Vicky said, twisting Lucy's arm a turn.

'And not in showoff big ones like your dad's,' Sally-Ann said.

'He has a big car for his work. He has to carry a lot.'

'Work!' Vicky sneered. 'Call what he do *work*. Owning a shop.'

'Doesn't own it. He manages it.'

'Same difference. Up the workers.'

'What do you know, Farrant!'

'Here,' Vicky said, 'don't get fresh with me.' And she banged her forehead against Lucy's.

Lucy's eyes swam again.

Vicky observed the results with close interest. 'Head butt,' she said. 'Might make it my speciality.'

Sally-Ann said, 'Vicky's going to be a wrestler, aren't you, Vick?'

'As if we didn't know!' Lucy said.

'She watches it every Saturday on telly and even goes and sees them live when they're at the Leisure Centre, don't you, Vick? She's going to be the first woman champion of the world. Over the men as well as the women, of course. Aren't you, Vick?'

'As you've no prezzies with you,' Melanie said, 'you can invite us to your party tonight.'

'Not having one,' Lucy said, still battling her tears.

'Too mean,' Vicky said.

'Having it in the holidays, if you must know.' Lucy was furious at herself for letting them provoke her into telling them anything.

'Can't wait till the holidays,' Melanie said. 'You'd better bring me a present tomorrow to make up for it.'

'Me as well,' Sally-Ann said.

'And for Vicky,' Melanie added.

'Something nice,' Sally-Ann said. 'Something lovely and new.' She placed a finger on the end of Lucy's runny nose and began pressing slowly.

'Like a squashed tomato,' she said.

'You won't forget, will you, Lukey, dear?' Melanie said.

At that moment Mrs Harris came striding round the corner.

'Now, girls, what are you doing here?' she called.

Melanie stood back; the others let go; Lucy wiped at her face with the back of a stiffening hand.

'Nothing, Mrs Harris,' Melanie said brightly. 'Just a game. Lucy is a robot that's broken down and we're repairing her.'

'Well, I'm sorry to spoil your fun, but you should be inside. You'll be late. Quickly.'

Melanie snatched up Lucy's bag and ran off. Sally-Ann and Vicky grabbed Lucy's hands again and pulled her along with them. All friends together.

They let go as they entered the building and made for the cloakroom.

'Don't forget,' Melanie said cheerfully, 'see you tomorrow before school.'

CHAPTER TWO

Mrs Harris led the class in singing 'Happy Birthday'.
Lucy pretended to be pleased but was really too
upset to care. One or two of her friends gave her
cards, but more diffidently than they might have
done, knowing what had just happened outside.
Samantha Ling gave her a little brooch made of
something that looked like red fruit gum with yellow
Chinese writing on it.

'Your name,' Sam said. 'Hope you like it.'

'It's pretty. Thanks, Sam.' Lucy looked round to
see if Melanie had noticed, but luckily she and Vicky
and Sally-Ann had their heads together round their
corner table. Plotting, Lucy thought.

Samantha said, quietly, 'What were they doing to
you?'

Lucy, looking closely at Sam's present to avoid
her eyes, said, 'Nothing.'

'They weren't getting on to you, were they?'

Lucy shook her head, though she couldn't think
why she lied. 'I don't want to talk about it.'

'If they were, you should go straight to Mr Hunt.'

Lucy kept quiet.

'You're not going to be friends, are you?'

'Course not.'

'What was going on then?'

'Nothing.'

Sam waited.

'Look,' Lucy said, 'I've told you. I don't want to talk about it, that's all.' She turned away.

Samantha stiffened. 'All right,' she said, 'be like that!' And she went off and made noisy conversation with Mary Gardiner, who, as usual, was busy organizing Mrs Harris.

Half-way through the morning Angus came gangling over to Lucy.

'Borrow us a needle, Loo,' he said, leaning his spiky elbows on her table and talking through his cascading hair.

'My name is Lucy, if you don't mind,' Lucy said, not stopping her work.

'I've got some paper to stitch for that book we're making.' He waited but got no reply. 'I hate stitching.'

Lucy said at last, 'You should have brought your own needle.'

Angus had a scrappy piece of paper held between his fingers. He dandled it between Lucy's eyes and her work.

'I had one,' he said. 'But I lost him.'

'You would,' Lucy said, pushing his dandling hand away with her pen. 'Being stupid.'

'Can't all be geniuses,' Angus said, putting the

piece of paper on the table and fiddling about with it. 'Did the hamsters for you though, didn't I.'

'The hamsters!' Lucy said, hand over mouth. 'I clean forgot.'

'Birthday present,' Angus said, pleased. 'Sort of anyway.'

'Thanks,' Lucy said but not sounding grateful. 'I'll do it when it's your turn.'

'Borrow us a needle, then.' He flipped the piece of paper on to the page where she was writing.

Anything to get rid of him. 'Here,' she said, fishing one from her bag. 'Now go away.'

Angus took the needle and ambled back to his place.

'Dropped her a note, I think,' Sally-Ann whispered to Melanie, who made no move to look.

'One throat chop, he'd be out like a light,' Vicky said. 'He's a weed.'

'Is she reading it?' Melanie asked, working away.

Sally-Ann bobbed up from her seat, pretending to ease her skirt. 'Letting it lie.'

'He's not that bad, I expect,' Melanie said. 'Under all that hair.'

Sally-Ann leaned closer. 'Don't fancy him, do you, Mel?'

Melanie looked up from her maths and winked.

Five minutes later Lucy could not help herself. She poked at the grubby scrap with her pen.

It had to be another of Angus's notes. She was

half fed up, and half amused by them. He'd been giving her one every day for the last two weeks. The first she had discovered sticking out of one of her shoes when she got back from a games lesson. The second had been glued to the bottom of her pencil case with a piece of chewing gum. The third had been delivered to her home; written on the envelope in large red letters were the words: SECRET AND PRIVAT AND CONFIDENSHAL. There was no stamp so he must have brought it himself, either very early or late the night before.

But today's note – the tenth – was the only one he had almost handed to her. Must be getting brave, Lucy thought. Or desperate. And she had to admit that she was keen to know what this one said.

As casually as she could manage, she unfolded the scruffy page.

2DAY 1700 RAILWAY CROSSING
GOT PLAN 2 STOP PROSER
x x x Angus

Lucy smiled for the first time since arriving at school. All Angus's notes were attempts to get her to meet him, but were never subtle. PLEASE MEET ME AFTER SCHOOL OUTSIDE GATE – that kind of message. One of them, the eighth, had begun U R THE GREATEST and was the first to finish with an x. Lucy thought them so funny she had kept them, safely tucked away in a small pocket inside her bag, so that she could read them and cheer herself up when she was bored.

Twice she had taken him at his word, and met him. The first time to satisfy her curiosity; the second, after his note about her being the greatest, because she took pity on him. Both times she went home afterwards wishing she hadn't bothered. Angus had done nothing but bumble about, paying her hardly any attention, and dragging her across muddy fields between school and Whiteshill. There he abandoned her outside his house with hardly a word. This was not Lucy's idea of a date.

Not that she had ever had a proper date. Melanie Prosser had, of course. Several, if what Sally-Ann said was true. All of them with much older boys from the High School, which all the other girls seemed to think was very daring. And judging by what Sally-Ann said happened, Lucy's meetings with Angus did not count as dates at all. They were just mucking about. Kids' stuff.

Lucy glanced across at Melanie's table and met Sally-Ann's eyes gazing back at her over the top of Melanie's bent head. Spying, as usual. Sally-Ann twinkled her fingers in a brazen way.

Lucy looked away, and pushed Angus's note into her bag with the others.

What was all this 1700 nonsense and having a plan to stop Melanie? Was it just a dodge to get her to meet him again? And she wished he'd just forget about Prosser and what had happened this morning. She wished they all would; everybody would be talking about it. She hated the thought; the whole thing made her feel unclean. Small. A mutt. She couldn't find the right word.

And anyway, Prosser could eat Angus for breakfast and still feel hungry. Angus. Aberdeen Angus. A kind of cattle they make steaks out of. Angus Steak Houses. She had seen them in London. Her father would not take her to eat there because he said he wanted fish and somewhere quieter.

Aberdeen Angus. A rather stupid bull. Hardly a bull yet, though, more like a skinny calf. A long streak of steakless stupidity. She found herself smiling again. But he was good for a laugh, and that was something.

Though you only had to look at him and then straightaway look at Melanie (who was still bent over her work, chewing the ends of her hair as she often did when she was trying to concentrate) and you could tell that Melanie knew about a thousand times more than Angus about everything to do with the hardest parts of life. Like making other people do what you wanted, and how to be nasty without really trying. They were both the same age and both in the same class, but Angus looked like a boy and mostly behaved like a boy, whereas Melanie – well, Melanie wasn't exactly a woman yet but you could tell she knew what it meant.

Not that she, Lucy, was any better than Angus. Beside Melanie she felt like a rake. She had hoped being eleven might make a difference. But of course, it hadn't. And what Melanie had done this morning only made her feel more like a kid than ever. Some birthday present – being made to feel more childish just when you were wanting to feel grown up.

'What's this, Lucy?' Mrs Harris said, coming up from behind. 'You don't seem to have done much.'

'Thinking about my project, miss,' Lucy said, pulling herself together.

'You look very glum for a birthday girl. Are you all right?'

Dragging energy from the pit of her stomach, Lucy managed a birthday-girl smile.

Mrs Harris gave her a studied look, but left her to get on.

At the end of afternoon school Mrs Harris clapped her hands for silence.

'Mary tells me you want to hold a meeting,' she said, 'and I gather I'm not wanted. I don't know what this is all about but here's what I'm going to do. You're all on your honour to behave. Mary is in charge. I'll go off to the staff room for, let's see – ' she consulted her wristwatch – 'for about ten minutes. That should do. Then I'll come back and see you off home.'

She went, closing the door firmly behind her. Mary Gardiner was already at the front, standing behind Mrs Harris's desk.

'Some of us have been talking,' she said. 'These are our last few weeks in this school. Some of us thought we'd like to give a present to Mrs Harris because she's been so terrific. We wondered if the rest of you would like to join in. Everybody would give money and we would buy something with it. What do you think?'

There was a brief pause while the suggestion sank in. Then, as usual, some of the boys jeered. After that people started chattering all at once, till Mary broke in and made them put their hands up if they wanted to say anything. After that the usual few did all the arguing.

Lucy said nothing. She sat at her table, chin in hands, half listening. She had heard enough about presents for one day.

Samantha came over and sat next to her.

'Don't know how she does it,' Sam said. 'Nobody would let me hold a meeting.'

'Nor me,' Lucy said. 'Not that I want to.'

'Nor me neither,' Sam said. 'Nobody else could do it,' she went on, full of admiration at Mary's command. 'There'd be a riot if anybody tried.'

'Melanie could,' Lucy said.

'Sure,' Sam said. 'Except she'd do all the talking and we'd have to sit and listen.' She gave Lucy a sideways glance. 'You certain you aren't being friends?'

Lucy couldn't even be bothered to reply. Sam, rebuffed again, moved back to her own place.

In a way, Lucy thought, Mary and Melanie were two of a kind. Only Melanie used whatever it was they both had to bully and squash people, so they did as she said and hated her for it, while everybody liked Mary (except Melanie and her hangers-on of course) and elected her class leader every time.

It was sickening, Lucy grumbled to herself as the discussion heated up around her, how Mary seemed to know exactly what to do and exactly how to do it, and was good-looking as well. If one person in the class could stop Melanie, it was Mary. But of course they both made sure to keep out of each other's way. Almost as if they had a secret agreement.

'Okay,' Mary was saying, 'I think we've decided that we'll give as much as we want. Anybody who doesn't want to doesn't have to. The present will be from the class, but we'll put in a special card that only those who have given some money will sign. Those in favour put up a hand.'

Lucy held up hers because it was obvious you would have to.

'Against,' Mary said.

Roland Oliver raised a hand, but he would, just as a joke, Roland having elected himself class comedian. Sally-Ann put hers up too, turned, grinning, expecting to see Melanie's in the air as well, was surprised that it wasn't, and rather sheepishly let her own drop again.

'Only Roland against,' Mary said. 'Great. There's one more thing. I don't mind collecting the money but I think someone else should buy the present. Any suggestions?'

Silence.

Then Melanie's voice: 'Lucy Hall.'

Lucy braced, startled out of her dumps. 'No!' she called. 'I don't want to. Why me?'

Melanie said, 'Your dad owns a shop. You'd be good at picking presents.'

'Hear, hear!' Gordon James shouted, mocking.

'Good idea,' Mary said.

'But – ' Lucy spluttered.

Before she could say anything more, Mary asked, 'Who agrees?'

A forest of hands. Cheers from the usual boys.

Mrs Harris came in. 'Sounds like you've had a good time.'

'Thanks, Mrs Harris,' Mary said. 'We've just finished.'

And that was that. They all scattered for home, leaving Lucy trying to gather herself together again.

'See you tomorrow, present picker,' Melanie muttered into Lucy's ear as she brushed by on her way to the door.

Lucy wanted to scream.

CHAPTER THREE

Sarah Hall sat cross-legged on the living-room floor surrounded by a clutter of bills and invoices and cheques and account books. Her fingers flicked over the keys of a pocket calculator lying at her side. The remains of her lunch – scraps of cheese, a bread crust, and an apple core turning brown – lay on a plate behind her.

Stopping in the doorway, Lucy thought: she'll have forgotten the plate is behind her and she'll either sit on it or knock it over. Why does she have to be so untidy? And why does she have to work with her stuff all over the floor?

Sarah glanced up quickly. 'Hello, sweetheart. Wishing you'd had a party after all?' Her fingers didn't pause on the keys. Lucy always admired the speed at which her mother could tap the keys; when she tried it, the calculator went crazy and the answers were billions wrong. 'We could still do something to celebrate if you want.'

Lucy shook her head. 'No. It'll be better in the holidays.'

'Can't say I'm sorry,' Sarah said. 'The VAT man

threatens. Got to finish this before supper. Could you make yourself some tea today?'

Lucy nodded.

'Okay at school?'

'Average boring,' Lucy said, turning away and crossing the passage into the kitchen.

'Never mind,' her mother called, 'soon be holidays. Then the High. You'll enjoy that.'

Maybe. Weeks away. So who cared? Melanie Prosser was tomorrow.

Lucy had rushed home meaning to talk to her mother about what had happened. Usually she talked to her mother about everything. Sarah was that kind of mum. Which some were not, Lucy knew. A few of her friends came and talked to her mother quite often because they couldn't talk to their own.

But today, when she saw Sarah sitting in the middle of the floor poring over the shop accounts, Lucy felt for the first time that she did not want to talk to her about something important. Not only did she not want to, but could not. It was as if what she wanted to say was too private, even to tell her mother.

Important? Private? Standing in the kitchen surrounded by so many familiar things all higgledy-piggledy as usual, the whole thing seemed silly. Three girls teasing a fourth for a bit of fun. That's what the story would sound like, wouldn't it? Who would take it seriously?

For a few seconds Lucy wondered if the scene behind the cycle shed had really happened. Or at least had been as bad as she remembered. It couldn't have been, could it?

One glance at her wounded shoes and she knew.

But if she told her mother, she'd want to know all the stupid details, all the ridiculous chat. (Sarah was a great one for knowing what everybody said, and as a rule Lucy enjoyed telling her.) And certain sure she would be stomping-mad. She would want to do something drastic about Prosser. Dad would have to be told, and Lucy couldn't bear the thought of his hearing about it. She knew he would feel more hurt than she felt herself – he always did when anything unpleasant happened to her. And this, he would say, was not just unpleasant; it was sordid. Sordid was one of his biggest hate words. And hearing him say it would only make her mother even more agitated.

No, she wouldn't tell them. Interfering parents she could do without. Anyway, tomorrow might be different. Prosser might only have been trying to scare her today because it was her birthday.

Lucy realized with a start that she had been staring into the cluttered sink for five minutes without moving. She gave herself a glass of iced milk and five Tango biscuits – her favourites but banned at tea time – as a reward and comfort for having survived horrible, rubbishy Prosser, and for keeping her mouth shut, instead of blurting everything all out straightaway to her mum.

On the third biscuit, it occurred to her that, if her mother saw the state of her shoes, keeping her mouth shut would end there and then. Sarah was also a first-rate interrogator. So she flipped the shoes off, stuffed them into her bag, and as coolly as possible made for her room upstairs, clutching her now bulging bag, her half-finished glass of milk and the two remaining biscuits.

With her room door safely shut, she transferred her shoes, after a close, regretful examination of their scars, to a box where she kept old toys hidden at the back of her clothes cupboard.

Looking carefully at her shoes had brought vividly to mind every second of her ordeal behind the cycle shed. Instead of feeling relieved, she felt sick. Sick with Prosser's disease, otherwise known as The Nasties. So far not thought to be deadly. But there was always a first time.

It was as if even her clothes were contaminated. She pulled off her skirt, her blouse, her socks, threw them all into her laundry bag, and put on a favourite red jumper and knock-about jeans and trainers.

This made her feel a little better; but not knowing what to do next – as if she were standing in a waiting room with nothing to do but wait – she sat on her bed and stared at herself in her mirror. Short hair curling round her head, framing a thin triangular face. A nose she always thought was stubby. Thin long neck. Square shoulders showing bonily through her jumper. Flat chest. Flat, flat chest. How could anybody like her? Even Angus, the steakless wonder?

Lucy stared herself defiantly in her green eyes. 'I will not cry,' she told herself.

Sarah Hall finished the accounts and sat back on to her plate of leftovers. 'Blast!' she said, and cleared up.

Finding no Lucy in the kitchen, she went to the bottom of the stairs and called. A faint and delayed reply.

'Want to help with supper?'

No answer, but sounds of movement.

Lucy wasn't herself, Sarah decided. It wasn't like her to mope. There had been something wrong when she came in. But what?

Sarah went back to the kitchen and set about preparing food.

Lucy arrived looking pale, even perhaps a hint weepy.

'Clean some lettuce?' Sarah suggested.

Lucy stood at the sink where Sarah had dumped a head of lettuce fresh from the garden, its milky juice still oozing from the stem.

Sarah peeled and chopped and mixed.

'No gossip?' she asked when they were well started.

Lucy shrugged. 'They did the usual. Some of them gave me cards. Sam gave me a brooch with my name on in Chinese.'

'Nice of her. Can I see?'

'It's upstairs.' With surprise, Lucy realized she hadn't even bothered to look at it or the cards since she had been given them that morning. Prosser's disease really did things to you.

'Show us when Daddy gets in.'

267

'Okay.'

'What are you going to do with the ten pounds Uncle Bob sent?'

'Don't know yet.'

They worked for a while in silence but for the clack of the kitchen clock. Twenty to five. Sixteen forty!

'Angus Burns gave me another of his silly notes.'

Sarah laughed, glad of something to lighten the conversation. 'Probably his idea of a present.'

'Wants to meet me at the crossing at five.'

'How romantic.'

'Mum!'

'Well it is. Crossroads of life. Trains rushing by to exotic places like Swindon. Two beautiful people keeping a secret tryst.'

'Yuk!' Lucy was cheering up again. 'I'm beautiful, naturally. But Angus Burns . . .!'

'You I'm not so sure about. Angus – I think he's gorgeous.'

'You've only seen him once. When you picked me up from school the other day.'

Sarah gave her daughter a glancing kiss on the brow as she went by to a cupboard. 'Know-all. I've seen him more than that.'

'When?'

'In the shop. Buys screws, gardening stuff, tools now and then. Quite the handyman. Can't be for him. For his dad I should think.'

'You didn't tell me.'

'Didn't think you wanted to know. Always grumbling about how boring he is.'

'Well, he is. He's stupid and skinny and all floppy hair, which I'm sure isn't clean, and he's clumsy.'

'You wait. In a year or two bumbling Angus will metamorphose into a knockout.'

'You do talk rubbish, Mum. And he isn't getting better, he's getting worse. This year he's got really scruffy.'

'Have it your own way.'

'I don't see how you can tell. Mostly he's just hair and mud anyway.'

'Let's say it's something you know when you're me that you still can't know when you're you.' Sarah took away the lettuce and plonked a bowl of potatoes and a peeler in their place. 'Exercise your fingers on those.'

'Do I have to?'

'Do *I* have to?'

'Okay, okay, don't start! What's left for Dad?'

'Washing up the breakfast things, clearing out the waste bin – '

'All right!'

' – bringing in the laundry, plus he wants to mow the lawn because it hasn't been done for five weeks and there are probably elephants lost in it.'

'You needn't go on, Mum – I'm sorry I asked.'

'Want to help him?'

'No thanks.' Lucy jabbed at a potato eye. 'Is most of being grown up so boring?'

'Is boring today's word?'

'Forget it.'

Ten minutes to five. Sixteen fifty. Could he really have a plan?

'I might as well go and meet Angus if that's okay. I might catch him at it.'

'At what?'

'Meta-what-you-said.'

'Metamorphosing.'

'Could be fun.'

'Is he less boring than the spuds?'

'O, Mum!'

'As it's your non-birthday birthday I'll finish them. But don't be long.'

'Thanks. I won't. He never has much to say.'

'Hello, is that you?' Mrs Prosser shouted from upstairs.

Melanie switched on the television and flopped on to the sofa. 'No,' she said, 'it's the milkman.'

Her mother's voice went on, 'Your tea's in the kitchen.' Then the noise of her clopping feet on the stairs and the smell of her scent coming before her like fog. 'You'll be all right, won't you?'

Melanie glanced up. Her mother had tipped the contents of her everyday handbag on to the top of the drinks cabinet and was selecting the few things she wanted in her funbag.

'There's some of your favourite ice-cream in the fridge and a new video I bought specially for you on the table.' She stopped sorting and looked across the room at her daughter. 'I did tell you, didn't I?

I'm meeting your dad after work and we're off to a new club in Bristol. I did say, didn't I, I do remember saying something, and I'm running a bit late. You know how he goes on if I'm late.'

Melanie turned back to the television. 'Go on, shove off.'

Cynthia Prosser grabbed up her funbag, glared at her daughter, said, 'Ungrateful brat,' and left, slamming the front door behind her, and over-revving the car.

As Lucy strolled up the lane to the railway crossing she saw Angus sitting on the top bar of the gate. A spaghetti-style gnome.

'Thought you weren't coming,' he said. 'Again.'

'I'm only having a walk before supper, so don't excite yourself,' Lucy said, stopping in front of him.

An old woman carrying a loaded shopping basket came plodding across the tracks and stood making faces. Lucy nodded towards her, Angus saw at last, and all but fell off the gate. The old woman edged through, eyeing them both suspiciously.

Lucy said, 'Are you going to keep me here long? I'm not sure it's safe to be seen with you.'

'We could walk along the line. There's some interesting stuff, birds and plants and that.'

'I'd rather stay alive, if it's all the same to you.'

Angus hitched his jeans and stared sideways across the railway.

Lucy could not understand what her mother was talking about. No sign of any metamorphosing that she could see. He was a head taller than she, which meant he was tall for his age, and he was so slim his grubby blue T-shirt was slack on his body, though this could also be from losing its shape because of needing a good wash. As for his jeans, they might well have no legs inside them for all she could see, except for worn and bony points where his knees must be, one of which, the left, had a hole torn just above it.

Angus glanced at Lucy, aware that she was staring at him. With his right hand he flicked his hair from his face, a habit almost as irritating as his hair hanging there in the first place. But only with his hair pushed back could Lucy see that he had big brown eyes that gave her a shock, they were so unexpected. His hands, however, were long-fingered and filthy, and to hide her surprise she said, 'Your dad a coalman?'

'No, why?'

'You look like you've been digging coal.'

Angus inspected his hands as if he had never seen them before. 'Been planting lettuce,' he said, rubbing them down the side of his jeans, where they had clearly been rubbed many times before. 'For my rabbit,' he went on. 'He works at Daniels.'

'Your rabbit works at Daniels?'

Angus grinned. 'No. My dad. He's a fitter. On the night shift.' He examined his hands again, which on the whole looked worse than before. He stuffed them into his pockets. 'Don't see him much. Weekends mostly. He's a bit grumpy sometimes when I get in from school. He's just got up, you see, and sorting himself out for work. He was like that this after, so I put off asking him.'

'About the lettuce?'

'About Prosser.'

Wary of that name, Lucy said, 'What about Prosser?'

'He'll know what to do.'

'Angus Burns!' Lucy said, rearing. 'Was that your plan? Is that why you dragged me out here to meet you?'

'I thought you were just having a walk.'

'What if I don't want you asking your rotten dad about Prosser, or about anything to do with me?'

'He's not rotten and – '

'Maybe I'm going to ask my own dad. Maybe he knows more than your dad about anything you care to mention.'

Furious, Lucy was about to stalk off again when Angus said, as if reaching a difficult decision, 'Yeah, he might.'

Lucy swung back, hands on hips. 'Who might what?'

'Your dad.'

'Just be careful what you say about my dad, Angus Burns!' She wagged a finger at him. 'You don't even know anything about him. You haven't even met him.'

'Yes, I have. In his shop. I often ask him about things I have to buy for my dad. My dad says your dad has the best shop in town for tools and gardening gear and stuff like that and knows about them – '

'O shut up!' Lucy plonked herself down on the grass verge and leaned her back against the fence.

The things parents didn't tell you! 'I don't want to talk to anybody about Prosser, if you must know,' she said. 'So I think your plan is a real *futt*.'

The warning bell above the gate started clanging, preventing speech with its deafening harshness. The five-nineteen to Gloucester went rattling by. When the bell stopped, the silence itself was a sound for a few seconds.

Melanie picked up the telephone and dialled.

'Hi,' she said. 'Guess what! Want to come over?'

She listened.

'A new viddy. You'd think she'd left the crown jewels. A rubbishy one as well. Bring one of yours.'

More listening. She giggled.

'You aren't half rude!'

She listened again.

'Not till late. After your bedtime anyway.'

She laughed.

'See you,' she said, and put the receiver down.

'Wasn't going to talk to my dad about *you*,' Angus said, sitting an arm's length from Lucy. 'If you'd only listen.'

'I am listening. Get on with it.'

'I wouldn't have said it was you. I'm not that stupid. And I didn't say that was my plan.'

'So?'

Angus shuffled. 'I was reading this book — '

Lucy chortled. 'You – read a book!'

'Why not?'

'What sort of book?'

'A story sort of book, why?'

'You never read books.'

'Yes, I do. All the time.'

'I've never seen you.'

'You're not there all the time.'

'When then?'

'In the evenings mostly. After my dad's gone to work.'

'Story books?'

Angus rounded on her. 'I thought you wanted to know my plan?'

Reading story books – Angus Burns? Lucy stared at him: another surprise. And which books? She was dying to know. But she said, 'All right, get on with it.'

'In this story,' Angus began, and sounding, Lucy thought, as if he were going to tell her every word of it exactly as in the book, 'three boys were getting on to another boy – '

'I'm not a boy.'

'I know you aren't, but who cares?'

'I do. And I thought you did too, Angus Burns.'

'I only meant – '

What Lucy could see of him went red. He turned away bending his head to look at the ground between his knees, his hair falling like a curtain over his face.

Why don't I keep my big mouth shut, Lucy

thought, but said brightly, as if nothing had happened, 'Go on, then.'

Angus hitched, brushed the curtain open, picked at the hole in his jeans. 'The kid they were after kept running and hiding and everything.' He paused while he watched a stray scallywag dog pottering by, sniffing at garbage on the other side of the lane.

'And?' Lucy said, nursing her patience. With Angus, she was realizing, you needed lots of patience.

'They kept after him. He kept imagining how he might get rid of them, and his friend wouldn't help, and his mother wouldn't listen, and his dad was away, and there was nobody he could turn to, so in the end – '

'At last!'

' – he decided he just had to stand up to them whatever they did to him, so he and the biggest of the bullies had a punch-up, and the kid got a busted nose, but he hurt the bully as well, and in the story it said how the bully didn't seem as big after that, and didn't bother the kid any more.'

Angus glanced at Lucy, waiting for her reaction.

'Yuk!' Lucy said.

Having reached the railway tracks, the litter-hunting dog turned back and came trotting down the lane, paying no attention to Lucy and Angus sitting against the fence.

Angus said, 'I haven't told it very good, but the book's okay and funny as well. I'll borrow you it, if you want.'

'No, thanks. Are you trying to tell me that your plan is for me to have a fight with Prosser?'

'I'm only suggesting.'

'Then don't. Because what you're suggesting, Angus Burns, is that I get myself duffed up. Prosser and Farrant and that creepy Simpson would mince me into little pieces. Look what they do to Clare Tonks.'

'They wouldn't if she stood up to them.'

'How can she? What could she do?'

'The kid in the story did.'

'You and that silly story! It doesn't happen like that. Haven't you noticed? To start with, the big bully probably wouldn't have fought him on his own. The three of them would have got on to the kid all at once. Then where would he be?'

Angus said nothing, but kicked at the grass with a foot. Which, Lucy noticed, wore a running shoe caked in mud and split along the toes.

'He'd have been okay if his friend had helped.'

'Nobody helps Clare, or any of the others Prosser goes after. None of my friends helped me.'

Angus muttered, 'I tried.'

'You call that help! And who said you're my friend?'

'Clare Tonks was trying to help.'

'Clare Tonks?'

'Yeah, she was standing by the wall and going, "Don't, don't, you'll only make it worse for Lucy." And I listened. But she was wrong.'

Lucy sniffed. 'She was right.'

'No, she wasn't.' Angus startled Lucy with his sudden anger. 'I've been thinking.' He stubbed at the grass so hard a tuft went skipping across the lane. 'I should have kicked them to death.'

Lucy could not help herself feeling pleased at his vehemence on her behalf. 'It wouldn't have worked,' she said quietly. 'They'd only have got you in trouble with Mr Hunt.'

Angus pushed himself to his feet. 'I hate Prosser,' he said. 'She's sick.'

Above their heads, the warning bell started clanging again. The five forty-four from Gloucester to Swindon. Lucy got up and brushed herself off while the train clattered by. Angus leaned on the gate, chin on hands, watching it pass.

In the after-silence Lucy said, 'They probably won't bother me again.'

'Yes, they will,' Angus said, not turning around. 'And next time I'll pile in.'

'No, don't,' Lucy said, feeling panic in her stomach. 'You won't stop Prosser and everybody will laugh at you. At me as well.'

Angus said nothing.

'Do you hear, Angus Burns?'

He turned at last and leaned back against the gate, his hands jammed into his pockets. 'Yeah, I hear,' he muttered, staring, as far as Lucy could tell, at his feet.

'I've got to go,' she said.

The hair nodded.

'Angus Burns,' Lucy said, exasperated. 'Do me a favour.'

'Yeah, what,' Angus said, too eagerly pushing the curtain out of his eyes.

'If we have to be friends, at least wash your hair and get it cut. It's *awful*.'

Angus, unthinking, put a hand to his head.

'That's right,' Lucy said. 'The stuff that grows on your noddle.'

And she set off down the lane.

Melanie answered the door. She had changed into a pair of tight red jeans and a clingy white T-shirt with ZAP printed across the front in zappy black letters.

'Hi,' she said. 'Come in quick. There's a right old nosey next door.'

'For someone who's boring, you talk a lot about him,' Lucy's father said at supper.

'It's just that he's so weird,' Lucy said.

'Doesn't seem a bit weird to me,' Jack said.

'Nor to me,' Sarah said.

Lucy ignored them. 'And he's so scruffy. Why doesn't his mother do something about him?'

Sarah laughed. 'Why doesn't his dad?'

'His dad works night shift all the time. Angus hardly sees him. Except at weekends. You'd do something about me if I got into the state he's in.'

'No,' Sarah said. 'You'd do something about yourself.'

Jack helped himself to more salad. 'You must like him or you wouldn't go on so much.'

Lucy said, trying to laugh this off, 'I do not, Dad. I'm just curious, that's all. Like a scientist who's found a new kind of gruesome maggot.'

Sarah and Jack grinned at each other across the table.

As soon as his father had cycled off to work, Angus took the scissors from his mother's workbox and went up to the bathroom. He studied himself in the mirror from as many angles as he could manage. Then he started clipping.

'She sounds a right nerd.'

Curling up on the sofa, Melanie said, 'She is.'

'Just asking for it.'

'That lovey-dovey father and that know-all stuckup mother.'

'Vomit-making.'

'I called her Pukey Lukey this morning. She could have killed me.'

'She might try.'

'With Farrant around! Farrant's as thick as frozen porridge but she has her uses.' Melanie pulled a gormless face and flexed her biceps like a body-builder.

'Hey, that's nice! Do it again.'

'Fink!' Melanie said and kicked out.

They both laughed.

'We've got a terrific thing going.'

'Tell us, then,' Melanie said.

Not altogether sure about his evening's work, Angus checked the doors were locked, that the stove was safely off, found his book, turned off the television, and went to bed, forgetting, as usual, to wash.

Lucy lay in the dark of her room. She could hear her parents two floors below and a background of music playing not quite loudly enough for her to pick out the tune.

She couldn't sleep. Melanie Prosser kept invading her thoughts. She broke into a cold sweat each time.

Since coming to bed she had been trying to decide what to do. Hope Melanie wouldn't bother her again? Take some small presents and hope that would end it?

Or maybe Angus was right: Prosser wouldn't forget or give up. But what would Prosser do if she didn't take anything tomorrow? Hurt her a bit? Say vile things? Not much else. That was the trouble. Most kids gave in straightaway, just at the thought of what Prosser was supposed to do to you. All because of the stories that went around about her. But take nothing the first time, and more than likely Prosser would find someone else to pick on, wouldn't she?

It was worth a try.

Lucy squirmed on to her back, sighed and tried to settle down again.

The front door slammed, shutting in arguing voices.

Melanie scrambled to her feet. 'Yikes, they're back early!'

She tore round the room, tidying it and herself. The sitting-room door flew open: Bill Prosser came with it.

'It was lousy!' he was shouting over his shoulder. But was stopped short. 'What's all this?' he said, his tone changing to danger. 'Who the devil are you?'

'A friend of Mel's.'

'Mel's? You mean Melanie, don't you? And who said you could be here at this hour of night?' Bill Prosser glanced at the clock above the fire-place. 'Quarter past eleven!'

'O, Dad!' Melanie protested.

'Don't O, Dad, me, madam! And you – ' Bill said, pointing, ' – out!'

'We weren't doing anything,' Melanie shouted.

'And you – ' Bill pointed at his affronted daughter, ' – bed, Now!'

Melanie stomped from the room, her friend careering ahead of her.

Cynthia Prosser appeared in the doorway. 'What are you going on about now, you great lump.'

'I hope you've seen to her, that's all,' her husband said, marching around the room.

'Stop yelling,' Cynthia said, opening the drinks cabinet and pouring herself a large tumblerful.

Melanie's bedroom door slammed, shaking the house.

'You'll have to talk to her,' Bill Prosser said, slumping into his chair.

'Talk to her yourself.' Cynthia Prosser poured a glass for her husband. 'She might listen to you. She doesn't listen to me, that's for sure.' She handed him the glass. 'Here, swill this down and shut your face.'

'And next time,' Bill Prosser said, 'find somewhere more exciting than that dead hole.'

CHAPTER FOUR

Next morning Lucy contrived to be late for school. Sarah was cross with her for not having her things ready. Jack grumbled that she was making him late for the shop. But one way and another she managed to delay leaving the house long enough to be sure that the bell would have gone by the time Jack dropped her off at the school gate. As they arrived, she saw with relief that the playground was deserted.

'Not like you to be late,' Mrs Harris said.

'Couldn't find my games things,' Lucy said. 'Sorry.'

She carefully avoided glancing in Melanie's direction, but saw at once that Angus was not in his place. As she settled in her seat, Samantha smiled across at her, repairing yesterday's breach. Lucy smiled back vaguely. Not because she wanted to put Sam off, but because her thoughts, she found to her surprise, were on Angus. Why was he so late?

After a few minutes a note arrived in front of her. She thought for a second that Angus must be there after all and looked quickly round. Only to realize that the note couldn't be his; it was clean and too neatly folded. At once her eyes met Melanie's coolly looking back from her corner table.

Trying not to appear disturbed or much interested, Lucy unfolded the note.

10.30 PENS REST

She had to puzzle at it for a while before she understood what it meant. And then the day closed in, as though she had been shut into a box. Melanie was not going to give up.

Angus arrived at ten past ten. He was wearing his winter anorak with the fur-lined hood up and its draw-strings pulled tightly around his face.

'So you've decided to grace us with your presence,' Mrs Harris said. 'Late even by your standards.'

Angus stood by the teacher's desk. There were titters from various parts of the room. Melanie Prosser coughed significantly.

Mrs Harris went on, 'It's not raining, is it?'

'No, miss,' Angus said.

Warily, knowing Angus of old, Mrs Harris said, 'Then why the anorak? And the hood? You'd think we were in January instead of June.'

Angus did not reply, just gazed back. Expectant faces waited.

'Well,' Mrs Harris said, 'take it off and get to work.'

'I don't want to, miss.'

With heavy patience, Mrs Harris said, 'You don't want to take it off, or you don't want to start work?'

'Take it off, miss.'

'Whyever not?'

'I've got a note.' Angus handed over a crumpled envelope.

Mrs Harris took it gingerly, peered at it, smoothed it out, decided it wouldn't explode, sliced it open with her red pen, and took a page from inside. As Mrs Harris read the letter, Lucy was sure she saw a smile flicker in the corners of the teacher's mouth. But when Mrs Harris looked at Angus again, her mouth was as unsmiling as usual.

'Does Mr Hunt know about this?'

Angus shook his hooded head.

'Never mind now.' Mrs Harris folded the letter again and put it into her handbag. 'But he'll have to be told. I'll take you to him at playtime.'

She surveyed the ear-flapping faces.

'Angus has had a slight accident,' she announced in her no-nonsense voice. 'You might as well hear about it now so we can it get it over. Don't you agree, Angus?'

Angus looked as though Mrs Harris were suggesting she pull out all his teeth with a pair of pliers and no anaesthetic.

'Just remember,' Mrs Harris said to them all, 'about people who live in glass houses. Anyone – *anyone* can have an accident.'

Roland Oliver chuckled. Mrs Harris glared him into silence.

'Now, Angus,' she said when she was sure everyone was subdued and ready, 'off with that anorak.'

Unwillingly, Angus untied the draw-strings, bent forward, and began tugging at the clinging garment. Once it was over his head so that he couldn't see, his hands got tangled in his sleeves. Lucy wanted to rush out and help him, but as it was, Mrs Harris came to his rescue. She took hold of the anorak by the shoulders and with one strong pull emptied Angus out.

There was a moment's suspended pause before everyone, even Mrs Harris, burst into squalls of laughter. Unprotected, Angus forlornly braved the storm.

The accident had happened, of course, to his head. In place of the lank curtain of unruly hair, there was now a dome of short and spiky tufts, looking, Lucy thought, like an old brush that's been chewed by a dog.

But this was not all. From having been a muddy sort of brown, Angus's hair had changed to brightly coloured blotches of various shades of yellow. And the shades ran into each other in a melting sort of pattern.

Once they had taken it in, most of the boys cheered, as if Angus had scored a goal. The girls went on roaring with laughter.

'Looks like a frightened hedgehog!' Priscilla Moulton yelled.

'He's fallen in the Flash!' Sue Dodson shouted.

287

Angus blinked unhappily at them.

But Lucy all of a sudden was not laughing any more. Angus, she knew now, was not at all what she had thought. He was quite a different person. Her mother was right. Only the metamorphosing hadn't taken a year or two; it seemed to have happened overnight. Now that drooping hair no longer blurred his features she could see his nose and mouth and chin. They were firmly shaped, with clean, neat lines. But what held her attention most was the eyes. Large, appealing brown eyes she had first caught a proper glimpse of last night at the railway crossing. Now they were glancing here and there, pained with embarrassment. And his embarrassment became hers because she knew why his hair was in such a state.

She wanted to scream at them to shut up and leave him alone. That it was all her fault.

'It seems,' Mrs Harris said at last, quietening the class, 'that last night Angus decided to cut his own hair. And as if that wasn't enough, he tried to shampoo it with what turned out to be a sachet of colour rinse. How anyone can possibly manage such a stunning feat of ineptitude, I cannot imagine. But, Angus, if anyone can, you will.'

There was more laughter, though of the exhausted kind this time. Laughter for laughter's sake.

Mrs Harris let it blow itself out before saying firmly, 'I hope we can all forget Angus's little mishap now, and get back to work. Go and sit down, Angus.

Maybe after school this afternoon you'll do something to put right last night's disaster, eh?'

Angus trailed to his place, and fiddled distractedly with his gear, carefully avoiding his friend's eyes. He looked, Lucy thought, on the outside as she felt for him in her inside.

The bell went for playtime soon after.

Angus was at once set upon by a chattering, cheering, questioning mob.

In the crush, Melanie, Vicky and Sally-Ann hustled Lucy out into the yard, and round behind the cycle shed. Only Clare Tonks paid any heed, and followed.

Meanwhile, Mrs Harris shooed the mob away from Angus, arrested him by the shoulder, and led him off to Mr Hunt's room. A small band of determined and ebullient boys tagged along at a safe distance, only to be waylaid by Mrs Fletcher, patrolling the corridor on duty; she herded them, bleating protests, into the playground.

'*Nothing!*' Melanie's eyes narrowed. 'Didn't ask for nothing, Pukey.'

'Asked for *presents*,' Sally-Ann said, nipping Lucy's thigh so painfully she cried out.

'What's in her bag?' Vicky said, shifting her grip swiftly from an armlock to a half nelson, leaving a hand free to snatch a hank of Lucy's hair.

Sally-Ann tipped Lucy's bag upside down on the

ground. The contents spilled at Lucy's feet. She squirmed to break free.

'Wouldn't jump about if I was you,' Melanie said. 'You'll only tread on your own rubbish.' She squatted beside Sally-Ann and the pair of them picked through Lucy's belongings.

'Get your filthy hands off my things!' Lucy cried, struggling against Vicky's grip even though it hurt.

'Shut up, stinky,' Vicky growled, yanking at the handful of hair.

Lucy screeched. Tears came, which she couldn't stop. They seemed to have been poised, ready to flow. Anger at their coming added to the insult that was causing them.

At this moment Clare Tonks drifted around the corner.

Lucy tried to hide her face.

'Push off, Tonks,' Vicky yelled.

Clare did not budge, but watched from a safe distance.

Melanie glanced up. 'Forget her,' she said. 'She doesn't matter. She'll pay later.'

'This pencil sharpener isn't bad,' Sally-Ann said, matter-of-fact, as if choosing goods in a shop. 'There's a fairly okay key ring with Snoopy on it. And there's a nice felt tip in green. You'd like that, Vick. Green's your colour. And, oooo, look at these, Mel!'

Sally-Ann held up some scraps of scruffy paper. At the sight of them Lucy went wild. She writhed, and tugged, and twisted, and wrenched. She tried to kick; she even tried to bite. But Vicky held on, seeming to enjoy the tussle. Until, panting and trembling with rage, Lucy gave up.

'You haven't had enough practice,' Vicky said.

'Beast!' Lucy gasped. 'Pig!'

Vicky laughed and gave Lucy's arm a sharp twist that sent pain shooting into her shoulder, making her cry out again.

Melanie said, with mocking pleasure, 'They're little love letters from her boyfriend.'

'Angus Burns,' Sally-Ann said, jiggling on her toes. 'Yellow mop. Read them out, Mel.'

Melanie performed, an actress reading a script:

' "Outside the gate after school." "You are the greatest."'

Sally-Ann, peering over Melanie's shoulder, said, 'Oooo – kisses!' and swooned dramatically against the wall. 'Tell us all about it, Lucy. I bet you had a fab time outside the gate after school. Is that what made his hair shrink and change colour? You must be *dynamite*! All his strength went into snogging. Wasn't an accident at all!'

'Cow!' Lucy shouted.

'Snob!' Sally-Ann yelled, piercingly, back.

'Creep!'

'Smelly, toe-jammy, nitty sow!'

Lucy blustered, but could think just then of nothing really insulting to say.

Vicky muttered into her ear, 'You haven't had enough practice at that either.'

Melanie said, 'Don't know whether he can kiss

but he definitely can't spell.' She was unfolding the last of the notes. Her face broke into a wide grin. 'Listen to this. "Lucy, beware Melanie Prosser, she is out to get you. Angus, ex ex ex." '

'The nerk!' Sally-Ann sneered.

Melanie went on, ' "Today seventeen hundred. Railway crossing. Got plan to stop Prosser. Ex ex ex, Angus." '

'The worm!' Sally-Ann said. 'That must be the one he dropped yesterday.'

'What was the plan, Pukey?' Melanie came close up. 'Going to blab about us, was he?'

'No, he wasn't,' Lucy said. 'And I wouldn't tell you anyway.'

Melanie tried to outstare her, but couldn't. 'Don't matter,' she said, turning away. 'Hopeless Hunt never does anything anyway.'

Sally-Ann performed a twirling dance step. 'We say we didn't do it, it's all lies, and he gives up.'

'But you'll have to give us extra presents to pay for chatting about us behind our backs,' Melanie added.

'Yes,' Sally-Ann said. 'We'll want really great prezzies tomorrow. Specially as you've brought nothing today.'

Lucy said, 'I haven't been chatting about you and I won't bring you anything.'

'Yes, you will,' Melanie said, holding Angus's notes up and waving them under Lucy's nose. 'If you want these back.'

Sally-Ann giggled. 'Otherwise, we might have to

stick them up for other people to have a good laugh at as well.'

'You wouldn't dare!' Lucy exploded with a fresh assault of rage.

'Yes, we would,' Melanie said flatly. And she walked away. 'Let her go,' she ordered without turning when she was well out of range.

Vicky released her grip and she and Sally-Ann ran after Melanie, and all three disappeared round the corner.

Mrs Harris followed Angus out of Mr Hunt's room, closing the door behind her.

'Don't forget what Mr Hunt told you,' she said. 'That awful hair has to be seen to by tomorrow or you're not to come to school. Tell your father. We can't have a rash of yellow scrubbing brushes among the boys. If you do things like that now, heaven knows what you'll do when you're a few years older. But it won't be my problem then, thank goodness.'

'Yes, miss,' Angus muttered, his mind on Lucy and what they might be doing to her. He saw from the school clock that playtime was nearly over. He'd be too late to help.

'And you're to stay in the classroom at dinner time and go straight home after school – '

'But, miss – '

' – I don't want any more scenes like this morning. False heroes I can do without, thank you. Now, go along and catch up with the work you missed. I'll just get my coffee and I'll be there to see you.'

Lucy gathered her scattered belongings and carefully repacked her bag.

Clare Tonks sidled up on feet the size of dinner plates and just as flat.

'You shouldn't let them see you cry,' she said.

Lucy sniffed, but did not look up. 'What are you on about, Clare?'

'They like it, you see. If you cry they treat you worse.'

Lucy stood up, still not able to look Clare in the face.

'Couldn't help it,' she said. 'They're such — ' There wasn't a word bad enough.

'Next time,' Clare said, 'look at me. It'll help, honest.'

Lucy had never had a conversation with Clare before. But she had watched her suffering the same treatment that she herself had just received. She felt guilty about that now.

'Why should looking at you help?' she said.

'Having someone who knows what it's like.'

'How do you know there'll be a next time?' Lucy said irritably.

'There will be,' Clare said. 'You haven't given them anything yet. And them notes — '

'Shut up, Clare. You dare even mention those to anybody — Anyway, I'm not going to give them anything. Rotten thieves.'

'They'll go on till you do.'

Lucy stared feebly at her. Tonks the tank. But she still wasn't big enough to stop Melanie. So what could Clare know?

The bell rang for the end of playtime.

Lucy turned away and hurried into school alone.

CHAPTER FIVE

'But it *was* an accident.'

Angus had appeared from behind a tree as Lucy walked home. He was encased again in his anorak. Looking, Lucy thought, like a rumpled stick insect. He might be successfully hiding his hair, but he was also making himself more conspicuous in the warm afternoon sun. And if there was anything Lucy disliked, it was being the object of attention from strangers. So she was refusing to stop and talk.

'No one can have an accident like that,' she said, not turning to look at Angus and hoping that people in the street wouldn't think they were together. 'You wanted to look big in front of the other boys, that's all.'

'I didn't. There was these packet things – '

'Sachets.'

' – Sachets, and I thought they were all shampoo but they weren't. Some were dyes. Rinses. I dunno. Hair colour stuff.'

'Learn to read.'

'I can read. I keep saying – it was an accident.'

Angus trudged along for a while in silence. Lucy hoped he had given up and would go away. But no.

'It's all your fault,' he said morosely.

Lucy stopped in her tracks and swung on him. 'What did you say?'

Angus stopped short and took a step back. 'You told me to cut my hair and get it washed. I did it for you.'

'Don't blame me, Angus Burns, for *that* mess,' Lucy said all the more vehemently for knowing she was in the wrong. 'I did *not* ask you to cut your hair with the lawn mower and wash it in custard powder.'

'If you hadn't of told me, I wouldn't of tried.'

'Then please do not do anything I tell you ever again, thanks very much.' Lucy swung on her heel and set off once more. All she wanted was to get back to the safe comfort of home, away from beasts like Prosser and apes (even metamorphosing ones) like Angus. She had had enough of everybody for today.

But Angus followed doggedly behind as if towed by an invisible rope. She tried to pretend he wasn't there.

At last, however, by the corner of her own road she could bear it no longer. And she didn't want him following her all the way home, because her mother might ask him in. So she stopped, took a deep breath for patience, and said, 'Why don't you go home?'

'I daren't go yet.'

'Are you trying to annoy me?'

'No,' Angus said with genuine surprise. 'I thought after yesterday – '

'What about yesterday?'

' – you know. At the crossing.'

With warning in her voice, Lucy said, 'What about the crossing?'

'Well – ' Angus swallowed. 'That we – ' He shifted on his feet, watched the traffic, shrugged. 'Nothing.'

'Then go home,' Lucy said.

'I've told you. I *daren't.*'

'I'm getting fed up of you.'

'It's my dad,' Angus said, as though Lucy ought to understand. 'When he saw my hair this morning he went mad. I was really scared, honest. He said if I didn't have it right by this after he'd skin me, he'd cut it all off himself. And old Hunt said it wasn't the school's job to see to it and I had to tell my dad to do it. But he'll go wild again, and he always does what he says, my dad, so he will, he'll shave it all off. I'll be bald, honest.'

'Don't be silly,' Lucy said. 'Your mother won't let him.'

'How can she stop him?'

'Well, she isn't going to stand there and let your dad make you bald, is she? Mine wouldn't.'

For a moment Angus looked suspiciously at Lucy, before he said, 'But my mum doesn't live with us.'

'O!' Lucy said and, feeling the need of support, leaned against the corner wall.

'She went,' Angus said, 'before Christmas. With a friend of my dad's. They used to go fishing

298

ogether. My dad and him. I thought everybody knew.'

Lucy shook her head, unable to think of anything to say.

'It was funny, she didn't take anything, only some of her own stuff in a case. Just went. When I got up in the morning she wasn't there. She'd been okay when I went to bed. She didn't say anything about going or anything. Just left a letter on the mantel-piece with Dad's name on it. I haven't seen her since. I don't even know where she is. And my dad, he won't say much about it. Says I won't understand.'

Angus was talking so quietly now that Lucy could hardly hear him above the noise of the traffic. Sud-denly, standing there seemed all wrong. And she was noticing again how much Angus had metamor-phosed, and how nicely.

'If you want,' she said, 'you can come home with me. I expect Mum will know what to do about that hair.'

'They're staying in,' Melanie said quietly into the telephone, 'and some of their twitty friends are coming. They'll be drinking and viddying all night.'

She played nervously with the telephone cord while she listened.

'We could go down the park.'

Clattering sounds from the kitchen told her she was still safe.

'But why not? . . . I couldn't help last night.'

She did not pause for long but her face crumple at what she heard.

'Just because of that?' she said then, almost shouting. 'You know what you are? You're a spotty-faced, horrible creep is what you are!'

She slammed the receiver down, ran upstairs, and locked herself in her room.

Hearing the commotion, Cynthia Prosser flung open the kitchen door and scurried to the bottom of the stairs, steaming saucepan in hand.

'Melanie!' she shouted. 'Were you on that phone? You know what your dad said. Stay off it!'

No reply.

'Talk to yourself, Cynthia,' she shouted up the stairs, and scurried back into the kitchen, shoving the door closed with her backside and attacking her pans again.

Douglas Burns waited with his bicycle at the garden gate. He had been there ten minutes, looking anxiously up and down the road.

David Waller came along the pavement on his skates.

'Here, Davey,' Mr Burns shouted after him.

David freewheeled back.

'Seen our Angus at all?'

'Not since school,' David said, wanting to be off.

'Did he seem all right?'

David grinned. 'Got a right going over for his hair.'

'But you didn't see where he went after school?'

300

'Ran off Cainscross way. Everybody was ribbing him, but Mrs Harris made him go. She didn't want us talking to him about his hair.'

'And you haven't seen him since?'

David shook his head.

'Okay, thanks.'

David scurled away.

Douglas glanced up and down the road again. Thought for a moment. Then swung his bike round, and pushed it to the back door, leaned it against the wall, and went inside.

'It'll have to have another rinse later,' Sarah Hall said.

'You'll wash my head away soon,' Angus said, his voice sounding hollow in the basin, 'and I'm whacked.'

'Serves you right,' Lucy said. She was sitting on the edge of the bathtub, watching.

Sarah said, 'Wrap this towel round your head and come downstairs.'

They drank Coke in the kitchen while Angus dried out. Sarah snipped at his hair until it was an even length all over.

'They used to call that a crew cut,' she said.

Angus looked scrubbed and polished, and his hair was neat and soft and a sunbleached brown instead of custard yellow.

He's metamorphosing even more, Lucy thought, hardly able to take her eyes off him. She smiled to herself but then thought of Angus's notes, which reminded her of Melanie, and of tomorrow, and the inside smile evaporated. She'd die if the notes were put up for everyone to read.

Sarah said, 'I think he should keep his hair the colour it is now. Suits him.'

'Not bad,' Lucy said sipping her Coke.

She and Sarah sat in silence regarding Angus. Then Sarah looked at Lucy, grinned, and said, 'Told you.'

Lucy smiled back and shrugged, not daring to say anything.

Angus, unaware of what all this meant, said, 'My dad probably wouldn't let me keep it like this.'

Sarah plonked her scissors down in panic. 'O, my goodness! Does he know where you are?'

Angus looked startled. 'Dunno.'

'The poor man'll be worried to death.' Sarah glanced at the kitchen clock. Five forty.

'He'll have gone to work by now,' Angus said. 'Night shift at Daniels.' His face paled, the new-scrubbed bloom gone.

'I'll phone him there,' Sarah said. 'Just in case.'

She was out of the room before they could stop her.

Now that they were alone, Lucy found she couldn't look at Angus. She stared with restless eyes at the crockery littering the table and the wreckage of that morning's breakfast. She heard Angus sniff urgently. She gave him a sideways look; their eyes met and Angus raised his eyebrows as if to say 'O, lord!'

From the hall outside they heard the carefully

calm sound of Sarah's voice. But she put the phone down much too soon for everything to be all right.

'Apparently,' Sarah said when she came back, 'he hasn't turned up yet.'

They studied one another with closed faces.

'He'll be home, waiting,' Angus said bleakly.

Sarah said, 'Lucy's dad has the car. He won't be in until six thirty. I'll walk home with you. It'll be better than phoning.'

Resigned, Angus nodded.

Sarah went fussing around the kitchen setting switches on the oven and absent-mindedly moving things from one place to another. Angus dressed himself ready to leave, discarding the towel and pulling on his T-shirt, which looked more drab than ever now that his face and hands were so clean and his hair so trim.

'I'll come too,' Lucy said, but knowing.

Sarah shook her head.

'Why not?' Lucy asked unnecessarily.

'Wouldn't help,' Sarah said, a hand on Angus's shoulder to guide him ahead of her. 'Daddy will want to know what's happened. While you wait, sort out things for supper, there's a good girl.' She paused at the door and gave Lucy a brief kiss. 'Won't be long. Best for Angus this way.'

They left the house at a busy pace, Angus casting a regretful look back at Lucy, who, watching them go, felt deserted. Jealous for both of them.

'Let me in, you hear me, girl!' Bill Prosser shouted,

losing his temper, which never took him long, and hammering on Melanie's door with his fist.

'No!' Melanie yelled back. Apart from the lock, she had wedged a chairback under the door handle.

'I'm telling you, Melanie,' Bill Prosser said, 'open this blasted door or you'll stay there for the rest of the day.'

'Don't care.'

From the bottom of the stairs, Cynthia Prosser shouted, 'Leave the silly twit. Come and eat your meal.'

Bill Prosser fumed.

'She'll come off worst,' his wife shouted. 'She's the one who'll get nothing.'

Her husband rattled at the door handle again. The door shuddered.

'Stupid bitch,' he bellowed, and stormed off into his bedroom, slamming the door behind him.

Cynthia Prosser went into the sitting room and poured herself another drink. 'One's as bad as the other,' she grumbled to herself. 'Let them rot, Cynthia.'

'Thanks for fetching him,' Douglas Burns said.

Sarah said, 'No bother. Enjoyed having him. Hope we see him again. 'Bye, Angus.'

Angus waved disconsolately.

When Sarah had gone, Douglas shut the front door. By then Angus was in the living room trying to look normal, and not managing.

Douglas came in and leaned on the corner of the

sideboard. Defeated by his father's angry gaze, Angus
gave up pretending to be normal, hitched up on to
the edge of the sofa, and looked uncertainly across
the room at his father.

But the storm didn't burst. Instead, Douglas said
quietly, 'Might of come home first.'

Angus said, shamefaced, 'You said I hadn't to till
my hair was right.'

'Aye well. But couldn't you have gone to the
barber's?'

'I tried. Straightaway this morning. I walked all
the way into town. But they wanted five pounds
twenty just to change the colour. I didn't have more
than seventy pence. I had to walk all the way back
to school. I was late.'

'How late?'

'Ten past ten.'

'One mess after another,' Douglas said.

'But I did try, Dad.'

'You should have asked. I'd have given you
enough.'

'How could I?'

'What d'you mean, how could you?' Douglas was
getting worked up again: the storm perhaps after all.
'Are we not speaking or something?'

'After last night?' Angus said weakly.

There was very little between anger and tears.

'Last night,' Douglas said, coming to the centre
of the room and standing over his son, 'I got a bit
upset, that's all.'

'Worse than before.'

'Good heavens, Angus, you'll have to buck up, you know. Life isn't easy. You're growing up now. People aren't always nice to you. You'll have to get used to that.'

'It wasn't people. It was you.' Angus bit his lip. His breath was catching. 'You've never hit me before. I thought – '

His voice choked.

Douglas took a deep breath.

Angus sniffed, wiped his nose on the back of his hand.

'Now then,' his father said, quiet again. He took hold of Angus, and drawing him to his feet, hugged him. 'We're both a bit on edge these days.'

Neither said anything for a while.

'Not been easy since Christmas,' Douglas said at last. They sat together on the sofa.

'Your hair looks better this way.' Douglas stroked his hand over it. 'One good thing.'

'Is she never coming back?' Angus said.

He felt his father go tense. 'That's what she says.'

'I don't understand.'

'No,' Douglas said. 'It's hard.'

'Can't you explain?'

Douglas shook his head. 'Another day, maybe. Not today.'

There was silence again.

'This morning,' Douglas said, 'when I saw you with that hair. You reminded me of her.'

Angus waited, tense himself now.

'But I shouldn't take it out on you,' Douglas said.

Lucy in bed, Sarah and Jack cleared up for the night before settling to watch television.

'She's been in a funny mood the last couple of days,' Sarah was saying.

'Maybe it's just her age,' Jack said.

'Maybe.'

'Angus whatsisname.'

'Burns. Nice lad.'

'Well, then.'

'She says she doesn't like him.'

'You didn't like me to start with.'

Sarah laughed. 'Not sure I do yet.'

'Thanks!'

'But there's something else. She's moody. That's not like her.'

'Growing pains.'

They looked at each other, wondering.

'Should we encourage this Angus thing or not?' Jack asked.

Sarah thought before saying, 'He's probably just a phase. Bound to happen sometime soon.'

'And at least he's bearable.'

They smiled at each other.

Their chores done, they switched on the television and sat together to watch.

Lying in bed, Lucy prayed for rain. Rain, she had decided, was her only hope. Preferably with lashings of thunder and lightning as well. And arrange, please, she asked God, for it to happen just before school, during playtime, all through dinner, and again at home time. Then everybody will be kept inside and Prosser won't have a chance.

If He did all that, Lucy promised God, she would not grumble one word, even if she got soaked, just about drowned in fact, all four times, so long as the storms came when required. She wouldn't even grumble at having to do things like helping in the kitchen or cleaning her room on Friday evenings.

And if for some reason known only to God this was not possible, could Prosser please be made to twist her ankle by falling off a wall while showing off on the way to school tomorrow and have to be taken straight back home for a week in bed. And by the way, she added, a wall is not absolutely necessary; anything high enough to fall off will do.

Not that she had found God entirely reliable in the past, she reminded herself, giving up the Almighty as an ally. And there were, now she came to think of it, other ways of getting the better of someone like Melanie. By cunning, for example.

Perhaps she could smarm up to Prosser and offer to share a fizzy lemon drink from her Snoopy vacuum flask. Tomorrow would be bound to be hot, God deliberately not having provided the required storms as asked, so Prosser would be thirsty. But — ha ha — the lemon fizz would be mostly Andrews liver salts, or some other bog-booster diluted in lemon squash. Prosser, being so greedy, would glug it all down before realizing the fizz was not altogether what it appeared to be. The resulting lurgy would keep Melanie occupied for one day at least; she'd be too busy pooping to bother anybody at all.

But there was also the business of Angus's notes. She'd have to get them away from Prosser somehow. Maybe she could do a trade. A good swig of lemon drink in return for the notes?

Lucy fell asleep rehearsing to herself a satisfying drama in which Melanie took the bait, became bedridden for days on end from weakness because of Lucy's bomb, and never bothered anyone ever again.

CHAPTER SIX

God did not answer Lucy's prayers next day – not the way she wanted Him to at any rate. Nor did she go off to school armed with lethal lemonade. She had not really expected anything better of God, but her own timidity depressed her. And the thought of Melanie letting everybody see Angus's notes was the worst prospect of all.

The day stretched ahead gloomily. As she got out of the car it seemed as if an army of Melanies stood between her and the moment when she would arrive back in the safety of home. She would have given anything to be able to jump back into the car and be driven away to be with her father all day. But the car drove off, Jack giving a cheery wave, leaving Lucy feeling abandoned and helpless at the school gate – a fearful kind of loneliness she had never felt before: a desolation.

Half-way up the drive Melanie waited, with Vicky and Sally-Ann on either side, a barrier of bodies blocking her path. Had Lucy known just how awful that day would be, she would have run off home regardless.

'Tie her up,' Melanie ordered.

They must have planned it, for they were well prepared. Or maybe they went around prepared all the time. Sally-Ann produced a length of pink ribbon from under her skirt and tied Lucy's hands behind her back, while Vicky held Lucy in a headlock.

Lucy didn't struggle or call out. There was no use making a fuss. She had decided that from the moment Melanie waved Angus's notes at her as she came through the gate. And anyway, Clare was right: they enjoyed themselves more if you resisted. So let them get on with it, she thought; they would have to stop when the bell went.

This time they had not taken her behind the cycle shed, but stayed openly in the middle of the playground, as if they wanted everyone to see. Which is just what they did want, as it turned out. Clare Tonks hovered about a few paces away, making sure she could see Lucy's face. This time, Lucy stared back at her, and in some unexpected way it did help, like holding hands in the dark, only it was eyes and minds that were being held now.

A small crowd gathered like a ring of spectators at a circus. They knew they were in for some kind of show. 'They're yellow,' Angus said later. 'You weren't kicking up a row so they thought they were safe and they could have some fun watching what Prosser did to you.'

But what Melanie did was not what anyone expected.

Angus was not in the playground to watch because he was in Mr Hunt's room having his hair inspected. (He told Lucy afterwards that he was being given a wigging, which Angus thought a great joke.)

Mr Hunt was saying, 'I suppose it's an improvement.'

Angus did not reply but squinted at the head teacher from under furrowed brows.

Mr Hunt picked through as if looking for nasties. 'Is it likely to make further changes overnight,' he asked tartly, 'or can we hope for time to recover from the shock of this latest hue?'

No reply.

'Well?'

'Don't know, sir.'

Mr Hunt wiped his fingers on his handkerchief with elaborate care and sat himself at his desk, regarding Angus with a resigned smile.

From somewhere outside a jeering cheer went up.

'Ladies and gentle-men,' Melanie repeated as the cheer that greeted her first show-biz announcement died away. She paraded like a ringmaster. 'We 'ave 'ere a speci-woman of that strange and 'orrible h-animile – a Diddicums.'

She paused, hand and arm dramatically pointing at Lucy. On cue, the crowd cheered again, as they knew they were meant to. Wasn't it all part of the game?

312

Melanie went on, 'The name of this per-ticlar Diddicums is – Pukey Lukey!'

Most of the crowd laughed; some of the boys gave shrill whistles and clapped.

'This speci-woman, Diddicums Lukey, 'as been captured and brought 'ere at great h-expense for your per-ticlar h-entertainment.'

More cheers and clapping. Lucy took a deep breath, as though about to dive under water for a long time, and hung her head. Clare's eyes weren't strong enough to save her any longer.

Melanie, grinning, held up her hands for silence. 'But before we see Pukey perform, 'ere with a lyric specially composed for the h-occasion, is the very loverly, the very wonderful, the talented Saucy Song-stress – Sally-Ann Simpson.'

Louder cheers and shriller whistles and more clapping. The crowd, warmed up now and in the spirit of things, was totally absorbed.

Enter Sally-Ann. She had slipped away behind the cycle shed and made a quick change while Melanie was gathering the crowd; now she appeared in a flouncy pink blouse and slippery wet-look bright red jeans and white tap-dancing shoes.

At the sight of her the cheers became deafening. They brought Mr Jenkins, the duty teacher, into the yard. He peered over the heads of the spectators. 'What's going on?' he asked the nearest girl.

'Some sort of game, sir. They're pretending to give a show.'

Mr Jenkins assured himself that nothing untoward

was happening, looked at his watch, said, 'Not long before the bell anyway,' and went back inside.

Sally-Ann, making the most of every second of her big opportunity centre stage, acted the acclaimed star with practised confidence.

Tired at last of applauding, the crowd fell silent.

Sally-Ann waited, smiling sweetly. And at the very second when some impatient spectator might have been tempted to catcall, she suddenly let rip.

Not even Melanie, knowing what was coming, expected such a performance. Some girls in the crowd jumped, and had to ram their hands over their mouths to stop themselves gagging from shock. The usually jeering boys, never having seen anything like it before, were silenced by amazement. None of them could take their eyes from the parcel of irresistible energy that was Sally-Ann Simpson The Saucy Songstress. Only Vicky, standing guard over Lucy, was unaffected. The evening before she had watched Sally-Ann rehearse in the garage of Sally's house.

Sally-Ann not only sang, she also clapped, danced, gyrated like a star from *Top of the Pops*: the showgirl of showgirls.

'*Yeeee-ow!*' she began with ear-splitting force.

'*Yeeee-ow!*' she repeated, pirouetting recklessly.

'*O – yeah!*' she sang.

'*O – yeah! – Let's hear it now!*'

'Let's hear it!' shouted back some of the boys.

And hear it they did, a song-and-dance routine that went:

'This is the story
Of a diddicum girl,
Sweet as sugar –
Keeps her daddy in a whirl.
O – yeah! (two three) –
O – yeah!'
  (*Turn, kick, spin, a quick tap-dance rhythm, clap.*)
'Name of Pukey Lukey –
Jus' look at her smile –
Makes everybody
Want to throw up all the while.
O – yeah! (ain't it right?)
O – yeah!'
(*Gyrations from Sally-Ann. Loud guffaws from some of the crowd. More high kicks, spins, taps, and accompanying hand claps from Sally-Ann.*)
'This is how she walks –
I'll show you if you wish.
Nose in the air
And tail out like a fish.
O – yeah! (bump! bump!)
O – yeah! (wanna see?)'
Some of the boys shout, 'Go, Sally! Go!'
And now, encouraged by Melanie, almost everyone is clapping in time.
'SHALL I DO IT?' Sally-Ann yells.
'Yes – DO IT! DO IT!' they yell back.
Submitting to popular acclaim, as every great artiste must, Sally-Ann goosesteps up to Lucy. Stops. Eyes the crowd. Turns sideways to Lucy. Takes up an exaggerated posture, nose stuck in the air, chest

thrust forward, bottom poking out backward. Then, keeping to the rhythm of the clapping, sets off round the circle in a stiff-kneed, waddling strut that tickles everyone into gales of laughter.

'O – yeah!' she sings at bellow-pitch as she goes, 'O – yeah!'

She returns again to the centre. Pauses. Makes come-here gestures to the crowd, who, like well-trained dogs, edge closer. And she sings very quietly:

'Tell you what it is
Makes Lukey such a puke.
Got a mammy who's a walker
And a daddy who's a fluke.'

Roars of laughter. Through which, breaking into her high-kicking, spinning, tap-dancing, clapping routine again, she sings:

'O – yeah! (That's so)
O – yeah! (Ho ho)
O – yeah! O – yeah! – yeah!
O – o – o – o – yeah . . .! (Man!)'

The end of the song is greeted with wild cheers, whistles, applause, foot-stomping. Sally-Ann bows, curtsies, does an encore of high kicks for good measure. Would have started again: but Melanie joins her. They bow together. First to one side, then to the other. Then, the deepest bows of all, towards Lucy.

Shouts of, 'More! More! Sing it again!'

But Melanie walks slowly towards tethered and guarded Lucy.

Instinctively, the crowd knows this means a new

turn of events, a different excitement. The ovation drains away.

Melanie stops, hands on hips, square in front of Lucy. Only then do most of the crowd notice that tears are running down Lucy's cheeks, and dripping from the end of her chin. The crowd shuffles into a tighter circle, the better to see and hear.

Melanie waits, as Sally-Ann had waited, smiling.

When the crowd is still, she says quietly, 'Not clapping, Lukey? Didn't you enjoy it?'

She pauses for an answer. Tears or not, Lucy forces herself to say nothing, nor to make any movement that might suggest a reply.

'Everybody else loved it,' Melanie says. And then with sudden understanding, 'O, but you've got your hands tied. No wonder you weren't clapping! Untie her hands, Vicky.'

Vicky undoes Sally-Ann's tight little knots.

The bell for school goes, but no one pays attention.

Vicky steps back. Lucy's arms fall to her sides.

Melanie says, 'Well – go on, Lukey. Now you can clap. You wouldn't like to be *the odd one out* – would you?'

Somehow, in the way Melanie says those few simple words, Lucy hears a terrible message. And when Melanie takes from her jeans pocket Angus's crumpled notes and holds them up, Lucy's will fails. She finds her eyes flicking away, not wanting to see the scraps of paper. It is as though she is dazzled by a sharp light. Tears come freely and fast now. Her

317

eyes drown; she can see only blurred faces surrounding her. Her thoughts drown too in waves of unhappiness.

'Go on, Pukey,' Melanie orders without any pretence of friendliness now. 'Clap!'

With torturing shame, Lucy claps.

'They're having a great time out there,' Mr Hunt said to Mr Jenkins as he released Angus from his room. 'But better call them in.'

Mr Jenkins went out into the yard again and bellowed to the crowd, 'All right, everybody, let's be having you. Bell's gone.'

Angus tried to dodge past, but Mr Jenkins grabbed his arm and hauled him back. 'Too late, Burns. Fun's over. Back inside.'

In ones and twos the silent crowd broke up and drifted, still silent, into school.

'Gone quiet all of a sudden,' Mr Jenkins said as some of his class went by. 'Makes a change.'

But no one replied. All he got from a few brasher spirits were sheepish grins and quickly averted eyes.

'Too much excitement,' Mr Jenkins said. 'Not good before school.'

Half-way through the morning, sitting distractedly at her work, Lucy felt a nudge and saw a note lying on the table in front of her.

THATS FOR STARTERS
PENS REST TOMORROW OR ELSE

CHAPTER SEVEN

That night, in bed, Lucy reviewed her day. Since arriving home she had shut school and Prosser out of her mind. Even Angus as well, who had waylaid her again from behind his tree.

But now, lying in bed with summer evening light still glazing the sky outside her window, everything came sickeningly back.

Her stomach clenched. Though covered only by a sheet, she suddenly felt too hot, and threw the sheet off. Then she felt exposed, defenceless, and pulled it back over her again.

The hot flush turned into a cold sweat. She curled up on her side and tried to lie completely still, hoping this might help her to get to sleep. But scraps of her day floated through her mind like flotsam in a stream, the fragments all belonging to one broken object, but jostling by in any old order and swirling away before they could be rescued.

Angus stalking along beside her after school.

'Tomorrow I'll be there. They won't keep me in tomorrow. I'll get there early, really early, and hide somewhere. Just let Prosser start on you!'

Lucy replying desperately, 'You can't do anything.'

Pens rest tomorrow or else.

Clapping.

Mrs Harris checking Lucy's sums. Most of them wrong.
  'You don't usually make such silly mistakes, Lucy. It looks like carelessness to me. Were you paying attention?'
  And Melanie, moments later, grinning round at the class in a glow of self-satisfaction as Mrs Harris, marking, said, 'Very good. Excellent. One thing you do well, Melanie, is your maths.'

Lucy standing in a hidden corner behind the school kitchen during dinnertime. How could a warm summer day feel so cold? No one playing with her; but she didn't want anyone.
  Clare Tonks plodding into view.
  'You shouldn't cry, Lucy. I tried to be where you could see me. But you stopped looking.'

Clapping.
  Lucy clapping.
  Everybody standing silent around her, watching.
  And Lucy alone clapping.

Lucy turned from one side to the other.

She could not bear anything like that again, she just knew it.

She could have stood Farrant's stupid pinching and twisting and ridiculous wrestling. And bitchy

Simpson's twitting talk. She could even stand Prosser's threats, and mean, jealous, spiteful tricks.

But she could not stand being made a fool of in front of everyone, and hearing them all laugh at idiot things being said about her mother and father. And worst of all she could not stand the thought of Angus's notes on show. It wasn't that Angus had written them, or that they were from a boy – she was secretly pleased at that. It was that they were private. They had nothing to do with anyone else. They were hers. For herself. Not for others to read and say things about. And it was because they were private that everyone would laugh if they were put on show, and make fun of her.

She loathed Melanie for that.

Afternoon school. Sally-Ann flouncing up to Lucy during games on the field, saying, 'If you don't bring prezzies tomorrow, Pukey, we'll put your silly notes up, and tell everybody that you go with Angus Burns after school every day and do filthy things in Randwick woods.'

Lucy saying, 'You dare and I'll kill you, Simpson.'

Sally-Ann going on cheerfully, 'And I'll tell everybody the reason Angus Burns cut his hair short is that he's got plaguey nits and the colour is really the stuff they use to kill them.'

'You're vile, Simpson.'

'Which means, you know, that you've got nits as well, because nobody can do what you two do after school and not catch each other's nits, can they?'

'I'm not listening to you any more, Simpson.'

321

'And besides, Melanie's got something reeeally terrific lined up for you tomorrow, Pukey, you'll see. Reeeally ace. Everybody will be amazed.'

Sally-Ann runs off to rejoin her own team.

'We've got to get tough,' Angus was saying. 'Somebody has to stop her.'

'What's this about we, Angus Burns! I'm the only one that's being picked on. And nobody has stopped her yet. Not even teachers.'

'Well, somebody ought to stand up to her.'

'It shouldn't depend on just one person to stop a gang like Prosser's.'

'Then we should gang up on her.'

'Sure! You and whose army?'

'A few of us might. Olly and Gordon and Samantha.'

'Like today, you mean. Who did they all gang up on today?'

'It wasn't against you.'

'It felt like it.'

'They thought Simpson was funny. They were laughing at her. What Prosser did at the end — they didn't like that.'

'How do you know?'

'We were talking about it this after.'

'Talking behind my back?'

'No!'

'You're on their side now.'

'I'm not! I'm just explaining.'

'Don't explain to me, Angus Burns. It was me it all happened to, remember? I don't need telling. You weren't

322

even there. How do you know what they were laughing at!'

'I was just saying — '

'Don't say! All you do is say.'

'But I've got a plan — '

'And don't tell me about your plans. I know all about your plans, Angus. They're drippy. Stupid. Fliddy. Okay? Now leave me alone. I'm going home.'

Lucy turned on to her back and shook her head to banish the memory.

Now the sky was dark. The patch of acid orange glow from a street lamp was reflecting on the wall in its usual place.

What might Melanie be planning for tomorrow?

Lucy wished tomorrow would never come. But could not sleep for worrying about what it would bring. Prosser wasn't going to give up, she knew that for sure now. How could she, after today?

Tomorrow was Friday. Get through tomorrow and for two days she wouldn't have to worry about Prosser or any of them. She would be at home. Do what she liked.

She longed for Friday evening to come.

In twenty-four hours she would be lying in her bed, just as she was now, only she would not be feeling so awful. She would lie here and remember tonight, and how she felt now, and know that tomorrow was done with, was over. Tomorrow would be today and finished. And perhaps by Monday, after two days of not having her to pick on, Melanie would lose interest and get fed up and decide to find a fresh victim.

But tomorrow still had to happen.

Her skin broke out again in a sweat. And inside, her body prickled as though her blood had turned to fizzy bubbles, and her bones were splintering into needles.

No one could help. That was the truth of it. So there was only one thing to do and she would do it.

CHAPTER EIGHT

'What've you got?' Melanie demanded next morning.

'Better be something sensational,' Sally-Ann said.

'Carbohydrate,' Vicky said.

'You what?' Sally-Ann said.

'Carbohydrate,' Vicky said. 'Got to eat more of it.'

'But what is it?'

'Bread and spuds and that.'

'Why?'

'Training. Body needs it.'

Sally-Ann said to Lucy, 'Is that what you've brought − carbonflybait?'

'No,' Lucy said.

'Thank goodness,' Sally-Ann said.

'Get on with it,' Melanie said. The prospect of actually receiving a present at last seemed to make her irritable.

Lucy took an old envelope out of her pocket and handed it over half-heartedly.

Melanie might have been given a filthy handkerchief. 'What's this?'

'Having us on.' Vicky flexed her muscles.

'Give it here,' Sally-Ann said, snatching the envelope from Melanie's disdainful fingers and tearing it open.

Melanie snatched it back before Sally-Ann could look inside. 'I'll do it.' She fished inside, cautiously, as though it might be contagious, and drew out a ten-pound note.

There was a silence.

Then: 'Money!' Sally-Ann said flatly as she might have said 'Cabbage' or 'Toothpaste' or anything else she thought dull.

'Ten quid,' Melanie said. 'That isn't good, Pukey.'

'O, I dunno – ' Vicky started to say.

'Shut it!' Melanie snapped.

Another silence. Melanie crinkled the note between her fingers.

'It's all I've got,' Lucy said at last.

Sally-Ann said, 'Money doesn't count.'

Vicky laughed.

'What's so funny?' Sally-Ann asked sourly.

'Money,' Vicky said, 'not counting.'

'That's funny?'

'Yeah. Counting. Sums. You know.'

Sally-Ann ignored her.

Vicky spat at Lucy's feet.

Melanie said, 'Money isn't presents. You don't give money to friends.' She sounded hurt.

Lucy said, 'My uncle sent it for my birthday.'

'He must have a really vivid imagination,' Sally-Ann said.

'Anyway,' Lucy said defiantly, 'you're not my friends, and that's all you're going to get.'

Sally-Ann went rigid. 'You're going to give us some nice prezzies, pig face,' she said through clenched teeth, 'or next week we're really going to get nasty with you.'

She gave Lucy a vicious nip on the arm. Lucy cried out and tried to push away but Vicky grabbed her from behind.

'Twit,' Sally-Ann went on, nip-nip. 'Nobody. Bean pole. Smelly-nelly.' At every word she pinched Lucy again, now on the body, now on the leg, now on the arm, faster and faster. 'Squirt. Goofy-creep.'

'Stop it!' Lucy cried. 'Stop it! Let me alone!'

Tears came again, though she had determined they would not, shame, and most weakening of all, despair. She was soon sobbing breathlessly as she struggled to break free.

'Let her go,' Melanie ordered at last when it seemed that Lucy might become hysterical.

Vicky stood back. Lucy raced away up the path and into school.

'Blubber mouth!' Sally-Ann shouted shrilly after her.

The other two laughed but without amusement.

When Lucy was out of sight, Melanie said, 'I'll keep this,' and stuffed the ten-pound note into her jeans pocket. 'Not a proper present, so it's no use to you two, is it.'

WANT 2 TALK 2 U

No

Y

Stop sending stupid notes.

Having avoided Angus all day, Lucy was determined not be ambushed by him after school. She knew if she talked about Prosser and his notes she would not be able to control herself. All she wanted was to be at home on her own. She was starting to hate everybody, not just Prosser and her lot. Except her father; and her mother of course.

As soon as school was over she slipped out of the side gate and walked home the long way round.

Angus waited behind his usual tree. Not having a watch he couldn't tell how long he had been there; but longer than on the other days, he knew. He kept spying round the tree trunk but still no Lucy

Then suddenly beside him, having come from a direction he wasn't watching, there was Melanie Prosser.

'Hi Angus. Been stood up?'

He swung round, scowling. 'Push off, Prosser.'

Melanie smiled as if Angus were being as friendly as anyone could want. 'She won't come now.'

'Who won't?'

'You heard what happened this morning?'

'The sun rose.'

'Very witty.' Melanie enjoyed the joke. 'Morning has broken,' she sang, mocking Mr Hunt's favourite hymn at assembly. And then said, not able to hide her gloating, 'And so has she.'

Angus kept very quiet, but only with an effort.

'She didn't give us prezzies. You heard. But she did give us this.' Melanie fingered in her jeans pocket and pulled out the corner of the ten-pound note.

'Liar!' Angus said.

Melanie tossed her hair. 'Ask her, then.'

Angus stared at Melanie who smoothed her hair and gazed idly down the street, posing herself.

She said, 'Mind, I don't care whether you believe me or not. You'll soon find out.' She gave Angus a wide smile. 'She's just like the rest. Nothing really.'

Angus leaned back against the tree.

'Nobody likes being made to look a fool.' Melanie was still relishing the memory. 'Specially stuckups like her.'

'Yesterday, you mean?'

'That was just for starters.'

'I don't get you.'

Melanie gave him a sly glance. 'That'd be telling.'

'So?'

'You'd tell her.'

'Can't, can I. She isn't speaking.'

'But you're still friends.'

'Might be.' Angus shrugged. 'Might not.'

'You send her notes. Wait for her here.'

'Been spying have you?'

'Watching *you*.' Melanie tossed her hair again.

Angus regarded her silently.

'Anyway,' Melanie said, 'I only tell things to my friends.'

Angus laughed. 'And you haven't many of them.'

'Shows what you know, Angus Burns. Only they're not drippos from our crummy school. They're older. From the High actually.'

Angus sniffed.

Melanie took the ten-pound note from her pocket and crackled it between her fingers. 'We could do all sorts with this.'

'Like what?'

'Movies.'

'Here!'

'Gloucester. It'd pay the fare as well.'

'You're full of bright ideas.'

'*The Murder of Dracula* is on at the Odeon.'

'So?'

'Think I'll go.' She gave him a sideways glance. 'Want to come?' And she added with a grin, 'After all, your girlfriend is paying.'

Angus thought for a moment. 'What about all them friends from the High?'

'What about them?'

'Won't they be jealous?'

Melanie screamed with laughter.

'O well,' Angus said, 'let them suffer, eh?'

Which sent Melanie into a fresh bout.

'Hey,' Angus said, apparently enjoying himself, 'reckon I should be on telly.'

Lucy stayed in her room most of that evening, listening to her transistor and rearranging her books on their bookcase. They had been in order of the ones she liked most. But from time to time the order changed because she decided she liked others better.

Tomorrow there would have been two more; she had planned to spend some of the money she had given Melanie on new ones. Now there wouldn't be.

She sat on the edge of her bed and stared at her books till the memory faded.

Last night she had lain in bed thinking that by this time today she would be free from Prosser and feeling happy. But she wasn't; not free or happy. The thought depressed her even more.

She switched off her radio. The noise was replaced by the sound of the vacuum cleaner coming from downstairs. The Friday night house clean. She thought Friday evenings should be for having fun. Going out; enjoying not having school for the next two days. Not for dusting and polishing and tidying. But her parents said that Friday evenings were the only time in the week they could do it.

Tonight, though, Lucy somehow found the activity comforting. She went on to the landing and called down.

'Dad.'

'Hello?'

'If you fetch the vacuum up, I'll do my room.'

'Good heavens! Can this be true? Are my ears deceiving me?' Jack climbed the stairs with the cleaner. 'You're not ill, are you?'

Lucy laughed, a relief in itself.

In the interval Melanie bought two ice-creams with the last of Lucy's money.

'You could have a great time,' she went on as soon as she sat down again, 'with your dad out at work every night.'

'You reckon?' Angus slurped his ice-cream.

'I do when mine are out. Which is most nights. My dad's a builder. Has to socialize with his customers.'

'Must be loaded.'

'Mountains.'

'Doesn't pass it on though.'

'He does! Whatever I want.'

'Why d'you have to take stuff from other kids then?'

Melanie gave him one of her sly glances, and grinned. 'Fun, cloth-head.'

'Don't seem fun to me.'

'Try it and see.'

'On Lucy?'

Melanie laughed. 'She's starting to bore me. Not that she isn't boring all the time, wouldn't you say?'

'Why bother with her then?'

'Probably won't much longer. Just a couple of times. Till she's got used to the idea. Then you can have a go if you want.'

'You're dead generous.'

Melanie chuckled. 'Big-hearted, that's me.'

The lights dimmed. She flipped her empty carton

into the air over the heads of the people in front and slunk down in her seat.

Sarah answered the telephone.

'Hello?'

'It's Douglas Burns here, Mrs Hall.'

'O yes, hello, Mr Burns.'

'I'm sorry to bother you, but I wondered – have you seen Angus? He's not with you, is he?'

'He isn't, I'm afraid.'

'It's just – well, he hasn't come home.'

'You mean, not even from school?'

'No.'

'Goodness! Just a minute, I'll ask Lucy.'

Sarah called upstairs. Lucy came to the banister. 'Did you see Angus after school?'

'No, why?'

'But he was in school?'

'Yes. What's the matter?'

Sarah went back to the telephone. Lucy hurried downstairs and sat on the bottom step listening to Sarah's end of the conversation.

'No,' Sarah said, 'I'm sorry. Lucy didn't see him after school.'

'It's not like him to be so late,' Douglas said. 'Not without telling me. Half past eight.'

'Is there anything we can do?'

'No, no. I'll give him a few more minutes, thanks, Mrs Hall, then I'll ring the police.'

'Dear me! Seems a bit drastic. Get in touch again if we can help.'

Lucy could hardly contain herself. 'What's happening? What's he done?'

'Calm down,' Sarah said, replacing the receiver. 'I thought you didn't like him?'

'O, Mum, not that now. What's *happening?*'

'He's late home and his dad's worried, that's all.'

'Can't we go looking? He'll be picking stuff for his rabbit or up in the fields playing. He forgets things. Time and things.'

'How do you know?'

'I just know. Mum, can't we look?'

'No, no, he'll be all right. He'll turn up, you'll see.'

'You're hard, Mum, honest.'

'Hard!'

Lucy stomped upstairs to her room.

Sarah watched from below, wondering what on earth had brought on such an outburst. Surely not the news about Angus? Not that alone? Something was upsetting her these days, Sarah could sense it. But whatever it was was something more than first-boy trouble.

Jack, hearing the row, came into the hall. Sarah took him back into the living room to give him the news.

Douglas Burns decided to give Angus till ten o'clock.

Five minutes before the deadline Angus came rushing in, breathless.

'I thought you'd be at work,' he panted.

'Never mind where I should be. Where the devil

have you been?' Having kept his patience all this
time Douglas was seething now as much from relief
as from anger.

'Pictures,' Angus said, knowing he was for it.

'The pictures! Couldn't you have come home
first? Or telephoned even?'

'Couldn't.'

'What are you talking about? Couldn't ring your
own father? Who were you with?'

'Just somebody.'

'Don't you somebody me. Who?'

'You don't know her.'

'O, it was a her was it? Is that why you couldn't
ring?'

Angus nodded.

'Or didn't dare?'

'No, no! It was just – I can't explain.'

Douglas laughed dryly. 'I'll bet you can't. So who
was she? It wasn't the Hall girl, that I know?'

'How?'

'Telephoned and asked, that's how.'

'O Dad!'

'Who was it?'

Angus mumbled, 'Melanie Prosser.'

'Prosser? Prosser the builder? His girl?'

'Suppose.'

'You suppose! Must have had a lot to talk about
if you didn't find that out. And here – where did
you get the money for the pictures? You hadn't
enough this morning.'

Angus stared at his father speechless.

Douglas couldn't believe it. 'You didn't let her pay for you, did you?' He sank heavily into his chair. 'I don't know what's got into you lately, Angus. This is the second night this week I've missed work, you know. They'll be sacking me next.'

Angus sat on the edge of his chair across the hearth from his father, hugging himself. 'I'm sorry, Dad.'

Douglas sighed. 'I shall have to go on days. It's no good me being on nights. You on your own.'

Angus said nothing. He had been wishing his father would make the change, but he knew this was not the moment to say so.

'If they'll wear it,' his father went on, 'jobs the way they are at present. They'll not be keen.'

Douglas and Angus looked at each other. So much to say. But how to say it?

'I nearly had the police out.' Douglas smiled.

'You never!'

'Five more minutes.'

'Yikes!' Angus went weak at the thought.

'So mind — never again.'

Angus shook his head.

'Time you were in bed,' Douglas said, standing.

Angus got up, agitated, remembering. 'I've just got to ring Lucy — '

'Lucy? Now? This time of night? No you don't!'

'But it's important.'

'Rubbish! One girl takes you to the pictures and as soon as you get in you're wanting to ring another.'

'But, Dad, it's not like that — '

'Don't care what it's like – bed for you.'

'But it's about tomorrow.'

'Let's get tonight's fuss over before you start wrecking tomorrow.'

'But, Dad, Prosser is going to do something terrible to Lucy tomorrow. I have to warn her.'

'Lucy can look after herself. All you've got to do is go to bed. NOW. I'll bring you something to eat.'

'But I've got to tell her,' Angus shouted.

Exasperated, Douglas took his struggling son by the shoulders and propelled him upstairs, saying, 'Enough! I've had all I can stand for one night. You're tired and you're going to bed this second and that's the end of it.'

And for Angus, for that night, it was. Douglas stayed home from work to make sure.

CHAPTER NINE

On Saturday mornings Lucy earned extra pocket money by helping at the shop. While Sarah and Jack looked after customers and staff in the shop itself, Lucy worked in the store room behind, tidying, opening new deliveries, doing whatever odd jobs she was given.

She was there that Saturday morning when Sarah came looking for her.

'There's a girl asking for you,' Sarah said.

'For me?'

'She said to tell you it's Melanie.'

'Melanie! What does she want?'

'How should I know, sweetheart? The shop's busy, so whatever it is, don't hang about in there.'

Sarah hurried back to work.

Lucy fumed. How dare Melanie come here? For a second she thought of ignoring her, of letting her wait till she got fed up and went away. But at once Lucy knew this was not a good idea; Melanie would do something embarrassing to attract attention. She might just as well go out and see her, and get rid of her somehow.

It was nine thirty before Angus woke up.

Furious with himself, he ran downstairs to telephone Lucy. No answer, of course.

'O – knickers!' he swore, and scrambled back to his room to dress.

'Hi, Lucy,' Melanie called in loud friendliness as Lucy approached through the busy shop.

'What do you want?' Lucy kept her voice down and was as unwelcoming as she could be.

But Melanie lost none of her cheeriness. 'Thought I'd come and see you, that's all.'

'Come outside.' Lucy led the way.

Angus had washed and was almost dressed when it occurred to him that Lucy might be at the shop. He almost fell over himself in his rush back to the telephone. But first he had to find the number. This seemed to take decades. Then a hurried woman's voice he did not recognize said, 'Handy Hardware.'

'Is Lucy there, please?'

'Lucy? Who's this, please?'

'It's Angus Burns. She'll know.'

'I'd better get Mr Hall.'

'No . . . no!'

But the voice was gone with a clatter of the receiver.

Angus champed. Centuries went by.

'Hello, Angus. This is Lucy's dad.'

'Is she there, Mr Hall? It's sort of important.'

'She was just now. Hang on.'

Clatter again. A millennium passed.

Then: 'Sorry. Apparently a friend called for her.'

'Who was the friend, Mr Hall?'

'Didn't see, sorry.'

'Was it girl or a boy?'

'Girl I think. We're a bit busy, Angus . . .'

Angus desperately wanted to tell, struggled with himself, took a deep breath to keep it all in. 'Thanks,' he said, and straightaway decided he would have to cycle into town to find them. He might just be in time.

'What do you want?' Lucy asked when she and Melanie were away from the shop.

'Nothing.'

'Makes a change.'

'Just being friendly.'

'After this week?'

'O, come on. Just a bit of fun.'

'Not for me.'

'You shouldn't take things so serious.'

'You shouldn't take things.'

'Very witty,' Melanie said, sharp as a knife. 'Like your boyfriend, you mean?'

Lucy stopped and faced Melanie. 'What are you on about, Prosser?'

'Hasn't Angus told you?'

'Told me what?'

'We went to the movies last night. Had a *great* time.'

'Don't believe you.'

340

'O, but I nearly forgot. *You* paid for the seats, didn't you.' Melanie was blubbing with such enthusiastic gratitude that passers-by turned and looked. '*And* for the train fare. Thanks a million, Luce.'

She leaned forward and pecked a kiss at Lucy's cheek.

'I still don't believe you,' Lucy said, pushing Melanie away but believing every horrifying word. She felt weak from the shock of such betrayal.

'Ask him yourself,' Melanie said, and launched into a loud song right there on the pavement, words and movements.

Lucy turned on her heel and set off back to the shop.

'Hey,' Melanie called after her, 'hang on. What about this morning?'

Lucy stopped dead in her tracks.

Melanie dodged round her, blocking her path. She took Angus's notes from her jeans pockets and held them up in Lucy's face. 'Today,' she said encouragingly, 'I know what I want.'

Lucy sucked in her breath.

'Not money,' Melanie went on. 'Money's so boring.' She grinned. 'Well usually. Not last night though.' She waited for Lucy to say something. When she didn't, Melanie pushed the notes at her. 'By the way, here's your love letters. You can have them back.'

Lucy might have been made of stone. Melanie shrugged and dropped the notes into the gutter.

Lucy watched them fall among the litter of ice-

cream wrappers and orange peel and disgusting cigarette ends and used bus tickets. Was that all they
were: bits of rubbish to be thrown carelessly away?
And was that all she meant to Angus?

The thought of betrayal drove all the fight out of
her. And yet, it was only at this moment, staring at
his notes abandoned in the gutter, that she realized
how much she liked him.

'Come on, Luce, let's go.' Melanie tugged at her
sleeve. 'After all, he's only a boy! Who cares? You
and me can be real friends.'

What point was there in resisting? Might as well
get it over with. Just as Clare Tonks gave in day after
day. Clare Tonks, who Lucy had always thought of
as someone pitiful, even ridiculous, for allowing
herself to be picked on. But now here she was
herself, standing in a busy street outside her own
parents' shop, being picked on in just the same way
and behaving exactly like poor Clare Tonks.

Poor Clare Tonks? Then poor Lucy Hall. Ridiculous Clare Tonks? Then ridiculous Lucy Hall.

In a mood of deep self-loathing, Lucy said, 'Okay,
show me.'

There was no mistaking the look of triumph on
Melanie's face.

As Angus stood on his pedals and pumped his bike
up Rowcroft hill he saw Melanie, with Lucy trailing
after, cross the road ahead and go into Woolworth's.

Sprinting the last stretch, he threw himself off his
bike and dumped it beside others against the wall

outside, but then got stuck behind a large man and his wife encumbered with loaded shopping bags, and had to follow them slowly into the store. Inside, the crowd was so thick he couldn't see where Melanie and Lucy had gone.

They were standing in front of the music counter. On the wall above was a huge poster of The Pits, top of the charts this week. Oil-smeared skin showing through ripped and tight-fitting garage-mechanics' gear, screaming hair dyed blue, pink and green, the group were swarming over an old banger of a car and threatening the viewer with hammers and spanners, their faces fixed in mocking snarls.

'Aren't they hypnotic!' Melanie was raving. 'But I mean *explosive!*'

'No,' Lucy said flatly.

'But they're fabulous ace. I could eat them, Luce, honest.'

She might too, Lucy thought, from the way she was drooling. This was a Melanie she had never seen before. Not cool, sharp, and in command. But pop-fizzy, just like everybody else.

'I'm dying for their latest album,' Melanie said as she scrabbled through cassettes banked on the counter. 'Here it is. *Rev, Baby, Rev.*' She turned to Lucy, her fizzy bubble frozen to dry ice. 'This is what I want.'

Lucy shrugged. 'Don't have any money.'

Melanie laughed. 'You are thick. Don't want you to buy it, Pukey. No fun in that.'

Lucy went as cold as Melanie looked.

'It's easy,' Melanie said.

Lucy shook her head, her stomach clenching now in panic.

'You'll have to learn sometime.' Melanie was as matter-of-fact as if she were explaining a maths problem. 'That's the way we get all our prezzies.'

'No,' Lucy managed to say.

Melanie chuckled humourlessly. 'Got news for you.'

'If you want it,' Lucy muttered, 'you take it.'

'Don't be twitty, Puke. Then it wouldn't be a prezzie, would it? And you'd best be quick or somebody is going to start wondering why we're hanging about.'

Lucy did not, could not, move.

At which Melanie lost her temper. 'Honest, you're so *wet*! There's nothing to it. This time I'll help. But next time you're on your own.'

And suddenly, another quick change, Melanie was all smiles and loud talk, giving a performance as a Saturday morning shopper. 'O, look, Luce,' she sang in a bright honest voice, 'there's a new one from Sweet'n'Sour. Aren't they just terrif!' Aside she muttered in Lucy's ear, 'Stay close.' And all the time her hands were rapidly picking up cassettes and putting them down. '*And* from Charlie Chase. I just loved his last one, didn't you? Ooo, and Hector Protector. I just don't know which to buy. There's too much choice this week. What d'you think, Luce?'

Melanie stopped. Looking back along the

counter. Looked round the rest of the store, quite unable to make up her mind, sighed, and said, 'Let's go round town while we think about it and come back in a while.'

She hooked an arm firmly through Lucy's and guided her with unhurried steps towards the exit. As they threaded through the crowd, Lucy felt something being tucked into the waistband of her jeans.

'What are you doing?' she protested.

'Shut up and keep going,' Melanie said, tightening her grip.

But Lucy used her free hand to remove the object. A cassette of The Pits' album.

They had almost reached the doors. Lucy tried to pull her arm free. Melanie said, 'Stop it, stupid nellie!'

And suddenly there was Angus, bursting through the crowd right in front of them, waving his hands.

'Don't go, Lucy,' he was saying. 'Don't leave, you'll get caught, stay inside.'

At once, trembling with rage, Melanie snapped back at him, 'Don't you dare, Burns, you pig!'

A laden shopper squeezed by. 'Now then, you kids,' he said, 'go and play outside.'

Lucy was confused. What on earth was happening? What was Angus doing here? Why was he flapping his hands about and shouting mad things at her?

But when she opened her mouth to ask, what came out in flat mechanical tones was a quite different question.

'Did you go to the pictures with her last night?'

At which they began shouting at each other all at once.

ANGUS:	LUCY:	MELANIE:
I'll tell you in a minute. But you mustn't leave. Have you taken anything? She said she was going to make you take something. Has she? Have you pinched anything?	If you did, I never want to speak to you again, Angus Burns. You said you wanted to help me and all you've done is make things worse, and now she's trying to make me *steal*.	I'll get you for this, Angus Burns! You just wait! Think you're clever, don't you. But you aren't clever enough. When I start on you, you – you rotten stinking brickhead!

It was the word *steal* that ended the row. The sound of it seemed to go off like an explosion around their heads so that everybody must hear it. Though, in fact, no one stopped, or even looked.

But Melanie wasn't waiting to find out. 'I'll get you two,' she said, letting go of Lucy's arm. 'You wait till Monday!'

And she was gone.

'Have you taken anything?' Angus repeated urgently, paying no attention to Melanie.

'What?' Lucy said, still trying to gather her senses.

'*Have you taken anything?*'

'No – but – '

346

'But *what* – ?'

'This – ' Lucy showed the cassette clasped tightly in her sweating hand. 'She stuffed it in my jeans.'

'Give it here.' Angus snatched it from her.

'What are you doing?'

'Putting it back.'

And he was away, weaving through the crowd before Lucy could say anything more. She glimpsed him as he approached the music counter, then her view was blocked by shoppers.

As Angus reached out to put the cassette back a man's hand grabbed his wrist and held it tightly enough to hurt.

'All right, young feller, you'd better come with me.'

Angus was swung round, and found himself facing a towering man in shirt sleeves, who might have been any other shopper.

'I was only putting it back,' he said, squirming.

'I've heard that one before, old lad,' the man said, grinning wryly.

When the music counter came into view again, Lucy could not see Angus.

But then, her heart sinking for she knew what it meant, she saw him being led by a tall, heavy, shirt-sleeved man through a door marked STAFF ONLY.

Later, thinking back over all that happened, Lucy realized this was the moment when she made her decision. She had had enough of Melanie Prosser.

She had had enough of her life being spoiled, of giving in, of doing nothing in the hope that all the nastiness would go away. And she knew she liked Angus enough to be upset if he got hurt, or bothered with another girl, or was in trouble.

She was determined to do something about it. All of it: her own life, and Angus. Starting now.

None of this went through her head then. What she felt was a surge of energy.

She spotted the sales supervisor standing by a check-out and made for her.

'Excuse me,' she said in the politest voice she could muster.

'Yes?'

'A friend of mine has just been taken through that door by a man. Could I speak to him, please?'

'O?' The supervisor looked at her closely, suspicion sharpening her eyes.

'All right,' the manager said, glowering across his desk while the detective guarded the door. 'So you were only putting it back. What proof have you?'

Silence from Angus.

The manager leaned forward. 'Do you know that shoplifting is the country's biggest crime? Do you know that stores like this lose millions every year because of it? Do you know it is a crime of epidemic proportions among young people like you?'

Angus shook his head. From the fierceness of the manager's gaze, he felt he himself must have thieved all the millions of pounds' worth of goods and be so contagious he ought to be in an isolation ward.

'If,' the manager went on, '*if* you were only putting this cassette back, why did you take it away in the first place?'

'I didn't,' Angus said before he had time to think what his answer meant.

But the manager knew and pounced. 'So there *was* someone else!'

'No – !' Angus said, fearful now, but realized where this would lead, decided the truth would be best, and added: 'Well – yes.'

'Ah!' The manager nodded at the detective.

'But she wasn't taking it. Not stealing it, I mean.'

'She? The plot thickens.' The manager was becoming quite jaunty with success. 'Look, lad, I haven't time to mess about. Let's have the truth and get this over. Otherwise, it'll be the police and your parents and maybe even a court case.'

Angus felt himself turn sickly white.

The manager's telephone rang. He picked it up crossly. 'I'm busy, Peggy, what is it?' As he listened he began to smile. 'Is that right? Well, well! Bring her in, will you.' He replaced the receiver. 'Your accomplice, I gather, young man. Given herself up apparently.'

The door opened; Lucy was led in by the supervisor.

Lucy and Angus stared balefully at each other while the three adults, heads together, held a whispered conversation.

When the manager sat down again he said, 'Should I expect more of you?'

No answer.

'Well, who's going to begin?'

'It was all my fault,' Angus and Lucy said together. Which made them break into giggles; even the detective smiled.

The manager, though, was busy giving Lucy a closer examination. 'Aren't you – ' he said, searching for a name, ' – yes, Jack Hall's girl, what's your name – ?'

'Lucy.' The giggles vanished.

'Lucy Hall, that's it. Well, well!'

There was a shocked silence. Lucy's mouth went dry.

'Thanks, Mrs Wilson,' the manager said to the supervisor. 'You get back to the floor. You too, Bill. I'll cope with this. Thanks for your trouble, both.'

The supervisor and the detective left the room.

'Now then,' the manager said. 'I'll have the story straight, please. No frills. Then we'd better get your dad over here, Lucy.'

CHAPTER TEN

They were sitting in the Halls' living room: Lucy, Angus, Douglas, Sarah and Jack.

Everything had come out and been discussed over and over till Lucy was sick of it. Melanie, the bullying, Angus and his hair, Lucy and her birthday money, Angus and the pictures, even Angus's notes, and finally this morning's episode in Woolworth's.

Sarah had taken it hardest. Or at least had said most. Jack had been frostily silent. Which Lucy knew meant he was deeply upset. Douglas was fuming, but restraining himself from saying too much because of the company he was in.

'I knew there was something wrong,' Sarah was saying, not for the first time that afternoon. 'These last few days you haven't been at all yourself. I wish you'd told me, Lucy.'

Lucy, weary, stared at her hands clasped in her lap and kept quiet.

'You can't tell,' Angus said, answering for her.

'Usually she tells me everything.' Sarah sounded hurt.

'Not this. Only makes it worse,' Angus mumbled.

Douglas laughed ruefully. 'O, aye,' he said, 'so this isn't bad enough?'

Jack spoke his first words for more than half an hour. 'I know what Angus means. It was the same when we were kids. But something will have to be done.'

'You're telling me!' Douglas said. 'What those young devils are up to isn't just a bit of bullying. We've all had some of that. It's an organized protection racket. If I had my way, they'd be given a present they'd never forget.'

A heavy silence settled on the room.

Then Jack's anger boiled over. 'It isn't just presents that wretched girl is taking from them. Not just *things*. It's *now*. The present moment. All they've got, damn it! Taking that is the real crime.'

He stood up, unable to sit still any longer, paced to the window, looking blindly out, turned, saw four pained faces gazing back at him, and could bear it no more.

'I'm going to make some tea,' he said, and left the room.

Half an hour later they were all sitting together again, just as they had been earlier, but calmer now, refreshed by Jack's tea.

Finally Jack hitched himself forward in his chair, put his cup down on the floor, and said in his shop manager's voice, 'We can't sit here all day. We'd better decide what's to be done.'

Douglas said, 'Doesn't that depend a bit on Wool-worth's?'

'The manager agreed to wait and see what we can do,' Jack said. 'Nothing was actually stolen and the kids owned up to what was going on.'

'That's a help anyway.'

'I suppose I'd better go and see Mr Hunt,' Jack said.

Which brought Lucy back to life, protesting loudly. 'No, Daddy, no! You'll only make it worse.'

Angus too: 'He's hopeless! Other parents have tried, honest.'

Douglas said, irritably, 'Don't be stupid, Angus. He'll have to do something. He'll have to have a go at that Prosser girl for a start.'

'He sees her,' Angus said, 'but she always gets off. There's never any proof.'

Sarah burst out: 'Well, there's proof this time. There's the two of you. You both know what happened. It isn't just one person's word against another's.'

'She'll get out of it somehow,' Lucy said.

'I didn't see her take anything,' Angus said desperately. 'I only stopped them leaving the shop. By then she'd slipped the cassette to Lucy. So that's no proof, is it?'

'You see?' Lucy wailed. 'You'll go and see Mr Hunt, he'll make a fuss, but nothing will happen. Except Prosser will pick on me worse than before.'

'No she won't,' Sarah said. 'It might even scare her off.'

'It won't! It won't!' Lucy shouted, despairing now, and tears welling up. 'You don't understand. It isn't like you think. She gets worse if anybody tells. Like it was a competition between her and the grownups.' And the tears flowed. 'O, I just wish you'd *listen*. I just wish you'd leave me alone.'

She jumped up, fumbling for her handkerchief and, not finding it, ran sobbing from the room.

Sarah stood up to go and comfort her. But Jack said, 'Leave her. She'll be better by herself for a minute.' Sarah sighed, decided Jack was right, and sat down again.

An awkward silence. They all stared hard at anything except each other.

Then, her turn to lose patience, Sarah erupted: 'We can't just sit here while that – that little thug abuses our daughter. Nobody is going to make my daughter's life a misery and turn her into a thief. Not if I can do anything about it. So we've got to do something. I mean it, Jack. I don't care what Lucy says.'

Jack leaned towards her, speaking quietly. 'But we've got to be careful. Maybe the kids are right. We might make things a lot worse instead of better. In a day or two the Prosser girl will get tired of Lucy and that'll be the end of it.'

Sarah was furious by now. 'She'll leave Lucy alone and turn her obscene attentions on to some other poor child instead. Is that what you mean? It isn't only Lucy, is it? She's obviously torturing one girl

after another. Well, that's not good enough for me,
Jack.'

Jack sat back, giving in. He glanced at Angus who
was slumped unhappily on the sofa beside Sarah, and
thought there was no use in him being put through
a row among the adults.

'Angus,' Jack said, trying to smile, 'why not go
up and see how Lucy is?'

Angus, keen to but hesitant, looked at his father,
who nodded.

'I don't know where she is.'

'In her room, I expect,' Jack said. 'Up the stairs,
top floor, first door.'

With Angus gone, the adults relaxed.

Douglas said, 'It's the parents I blame. Don't they
know what their daughter is up to?'

Sarah said, 'Douglas is right, Jack. If they don't
know they ought to. And if they do know, it's time
they put a stop to it.'

'Maybe,' Jack said. 'But – '

'Never mind the buts,' Sarah insisted. 'At least if
I can't do anything about the school I can do something about the parents. I can go and talk to them.
Tell them what's happening. Ask what they're going
to do about it.'

Jack pulled a doubtful face. 'Maybe they know.
Maybe there are some parents who couldn't care less
what their children get up to. What then?'

But Sarah, adamant, said, 'Then they'll just have

to be persuaded. At least they should be faced with
the problem.'

The discussion raged on for another quarter of
an hour. But Sarah was stubborn; whatever Jack said,
she remained convinced she was right. And with
Douglas and Sarah agreeing, Jack had at last to give
in.

'I'll telephone and fix to see them tomorrow,'
Sarah said, feeling much better now there was some-
thing to be done, rather than just talked about.
'Don't tell the children, it would only worry them.
Jack, why don't you take them for a visit to Slim-
bridge tomorrow while I'm seeing the Prossers? It'll
get them out of the way, and they'll enjoy the birds.
Take their minds off all this.'

Against his better judgement, Jack agreed.

Angus stood outside Lucy's bedroom door and called
uncertainly, 'Lucy?'

No reply.

'Your dad told me to come up.'

Stirrings on a bed. Then Lucy's voice: 'Okay,
come in if you want.'

The room was flooded in late afternoon sun.
Lucy was perched uneasily on the edge of her bed,
the coverlet rumpled where she had been lying. Her
eyes were weepy-red.

Not knowing quite where to put himself, Angus
stood awkwardly at the foot of the bed, as if he
were visiting someone sick in hospital. But his eyes
wandered, curious about Lucy's private things. Her

row of big dolls – Paddington Bear, Snoopy, Gonzo Muppet – sitting in a small armchair. Her bookcase with, he guessed, twice as many books as he owned. Her bedside cabinet with its digital clock-lamp on top. Her posters on the wall above the bed, some of animals (a snarling tiger face filled one) and a couple of TV actors to whom Angus took an instant dislike. Her blue wall unit of drawers and clothes cupboard. A long mirror, reflecting himself, ungainly, looking round, and Lucy, watching him from her bed. The whole room neat and trim and bright.

'Better not go into my room,' he said, as much for something to say as for any other reason.

'Why?' Lucy asked without enthusiasm, Angus's room not being the most important topic on her mind just then.

'Bit messy.' He hitched his jeans.

'I'm made to clear mine up,' Lucy said.

'My rabbit's the real trouble,' Angus went on.

'Your rabbit?'

Angus nodded. 'Clive.'

'Clive?'

'He sleeps under my bed.'

'You keep your rabbit in your bedroom?'

'Best place. Safe and warm.'

'I don't think I'd like that.'

Angus shrugged. 'He doesn't seem to mind.'

Lucy thought it best to change the subject. And there was something else nagging at her she wanted to ask before they went any further. She had to be sure.

'Did you really go with Prosser just to find out
what she was going to do to me?'

'I told you.'

'But with everybody there. The manager and our
parents – Didn't know whether to believe you.'

Angus sat cautiously on the corner of the bed.
'Look,' he said. 'I was waiting for you by the tree.
She came up. Started wittering on, showing off,
boasting. She showed me your ten pounds, and said
about the pictures. I thought I'd go with her. To
find out why she goes on like she does. When we
were in the pictures she started hinting about today.
I thought if I could find out I could warn you. But
when I got back home and was going to ring you,
my dad was all worked up and wouldn't let me. And
this morning I didn't wake up and you'd gone to
the shop and I had to belt off into town to find you.'
Angus took a breath before adding, 'That's all there
was.'

Lucy observed him closely, making sure before
saying, 'And you're not friends with her?'

Angus looked at her, aghast. 'With her! Yikes,
no! I told you, she's sick.'

Lucy smiled inside herself. 'Still want to be
friends with me?'

''Course.' Shyness overtook him again. He looked
away. 'Why did I write them notes?'

'Boys do that.'

'I don't. Least, not that sort.'

'Do you still like me even though Prosser made

358

me look stupid?' Thinking of the scene in the playground still made Lucy feel tearful.

'Got nothing to do with it.'

'Just thought it might have – well, put you off.'

'Well, it hasn't,' Angus said, leaning elbows on
sharp knees and regarding his feet. His short blond
hair made his blushes seem all the brighter.

'If you want then,' Lucy said quietly, 'you can go
with me.'

Angus nodded.

Lucy waited for some other reply. But as none
came, she leaned forward and kissed him quickly,
lightly, on the cheek, then sat hurriedly, cross-legged
against the wall.

The red of Angus's blushes deepened, his toes
tapped on the floor in a brief little tattoo, he coughed
to clear his throat, and nodded again.

Hoping to cover their confusion, Lucy said, 'I
was glad you turned up in Woolies when you did.'

Angus shrugged. 'She'll be waiting on Monday,'
he said. 'And she'll be raving mad.'

Lucy sighed. 'I don't care now,' she said, speaking
aloud her new determination for the first time, and
trembling a little at the sound of her courage. 'She's
got to be stopped, that's all.' Her courage faded a
little in the face of itself, and she had to add, 'Not
that I know how though.'

Angus stretched his pencil length across the bed,
supporting himself on an elbow. 'I've got a sort of
idea.'

Lucy laughed, as much because of him, as what he was saying. 'Not another of your plans, Angus!'

He smiled and shook his head. 'Got it off Clare Tonks.'

'Clare Tonks? Why were you talking to her?' Lucy's nervousness for Angus and herself put an edge on her voice.

Angus, knowing, grinned. 'She's not that bad when you get to know her,' he said.

Lucy recovered herself, wagging a finger at him. 'Angus Burns, you just watch it!'

'I meant to talk to, that's all.' They laughed together. 'Anyway,' Angus went on, 'it was her talked to me, really. She said you were the nicest person in our class, and she wanted to help, only you wouldn't let her. She said how if everybody who hated Prosser because of what she'd done to them got together and made a fool of her like she makes fools of them, she would stop picking on other people.'

'Did she really say that?'

'Yeah.'

'About me, I mean?'

'Yeah. Well, you are really, aren't you? I mean, you're not pushy or anything, like Mary, and you look all right.'

'O, thanks!'

'And like Clare said, you're always good at thinking things up.'

'Did she say that as well?'

'Yeah.'

'Honest?'

'Hope to die.'

Lucy indulged in a secret glow of pleasure, but said, 'Well, she's wrong about me knowing what to do, isn't she, because I don't.'

'But she's right about you having ideas. In drama and when we write stories and that, you're always pretty good.'

The secret glow warmed up even more.

Angus sat up, his mind on plans. 'You were right. The other day, I mean. About fighting Prosser.'

'What about it?' She was always having to jump about in her mind to keep track of him.

'She would. She and her lot.'

'Would what?'

'Pulverize you if you tried to fight her.'

'So?'

'Even if you did beat her up, I was thinking – that would be just as bad as her beating you up, wouldn't it? It would be you bullying her instead of her bullying you. Right?'

'Right.' Had she said that? She couldn't remember now. But it didn't matter; Angus was obviously following some track. 'Go on, then.'

'Well, that means you have to find a way of showing her up, something she hates, but that isn't bad, like beating her up.'

'*I* have to?'

'Yeah. Like Clare says, you're good at that sort of thing.'

'And what are you going to do?'

'I'll help.'

'Thanks!'

'We all will.'

'All?'

'Clare and Olly, and Sam and some others. You can do it, Lucy, honest.'

Lucy looked at him, his eyes blazing, and laughing. 'Talk about Prosser!' she said. 'You're even worse.'

From downstairs came a shout from Jack. 'Angus, your dad's going.'

'Rats!' Angus said.

'You can't go now,' Lucy wailed.

'I'll have to.'

'But we're just getting started.'

'I know.'

They stared at each other, wishing. But another shout, this time from Douglas, proved they weren't going to be left alone any longer.

Angus opened the door and shouted back, 'Coming.' Turning, he whispered to Lucy, 'You'll think of something. Give us a ring if you do before Monday.'

'Okay,' Lucy said from her bed, sulky at Angus having to leave.

But when he had closed the door and she heard him clattering down the stairs, she found herself grinning, and hugging herself in a new kind of pleasure.

CHAPTER ELEVEN

Cynthia Prosser showed Sarah Hall into a sitting room furnished with black vinyl easy chairs and wall units made of chromium steel tubes and smoky glass. All very sharp and bright and Sunday colour-magazine modern. Or at least, Sarah thought, modern as modern had been about ten years ago.

She was not invited to sit down.

'Well,' Cynthia Prosser said in a no-nonsense voice, 'what about our Melanie?'

Sarah put herself out to be extra polite. 'I hope you don't mind me asking, Mrs Prosser, but are you worried about Melanie at all?'

Cynthia flushed. 'Worried? Why should I be?'

'She hasn't been in any trouble lately?'

'Trouble?' There was a warning in Cynthia's tone. 'What kind of trouble?'

'There's been some bullying at school.'

Cynthia went dangerously still, like an animal, Sarah thought, before it strikes.

'My daughter, Lucy, has been a victim of it.'

'Has she?'

'Along with a number of other girls, I gather.'

Sarah struggled to keep her temper. 'I wondered whether you had heard anything about it?'

'Can't say I have.' Cynthia was straining to sound offhand. 'If anybody's been bullying our Melanie, I'm sure she'd have told me.'

Sarah knew now there was no hope of a reasonable conversation. 'I'm sorry,' she said, 'but Melanie seems to be the one responsible.'

Cynthia Prosser's chin trembled, her lips tightened, a little muscle under one of her eyes flickered. 'Just you be careful what you're saying,' she said, tight-mouthed, tight-voiced.

Sarah thought: What a hard, hurt woman. And wondered what kind of life was lived in this house. Was it buckled and steely, all glossy surface but hollow inside, like the furniture?

'Melanie and two of her friends have been forcing other girls to bring them presents,' Sarah said. 'In my daughter's case, Melanie took money as well. And yesterday they went to Woolworth's, where Melanie tried to make Lucy steal a music cassette.'

'Rubbish.'

'I beg your pardon?'

'Rubbish.'

'Are you saying I'm lying?'

'Somebody is. Who did you get all this from?'

'My daughter.'

'There you are then.'

'Mrs Prosser, are you saying my daughter is lying?'

'Are you saying mine is?'

'Well — '

'Yes, you might well say well! Coming here, accusing our Melanie.'

'I've told you, my daughter – '

'Your daughter! She gets caught pinching from Woolies and makes up this cock-and-bull story about Melanie to try and get out of it.'

'That's not true!'

'Isn't it? If it's not true, why are you here and not the police? And why hasn't Woolworth's been on to me? Have they been on to you?'

'Of course, that's how it all came out.'

'There you are then. Caught red-handed was your daughter, wasn't she, and you believed her pack of lies because you're afraid your prissy reputation might get tarnished. You stuckup, self-righteous prig!'

'Now just a minute, Mrs Prosser – '

'Get out of my house, d'you hear!' Cynthia Prosser was shouting now. 'How dare you come here bad-mouthing my daughter. Put your own child in order first before you preach to other people about theirs. Hypocrite! Go on – scat!'

Sarah, shouted into silence, retreated with as much dignity as her upset emotions would allow.

The Prossers' door slammed behind her.

From upstairs, sitting on the landing outside her room, Melanie heard everything, and smiled with satisfaction.

Her mother's angry face appeared at the bottom of the stairs. 'Don't you ever drop me in it like that again. You hear, you stupid cow? And this time I'm telling your father about it.'

When Lucy and Jack arrived back from their afternoon at Slimbridge having dropped Angus off at his house, Sarah was still so distraught that she could not help telling them about her visit to Cynthia Prosser.

Lucy was appalled. Melanie really had, like a disease, infected her own home, the one place she had felt was safe, a refuge. Now nowhere was safe any more.

The whole lovely afternoon, the fun she had had with Angus and her father, evaporated, might never have been. The awfulness of the past week flooded back to take its place. And her mother's unconcealed distress became a new oppression.

She sat in the kitchen listening and watching as Jack tried to comfort and reassure Sarah. And even this seemed like another theft, another unwilling present Lucy had to give at Melanie's command.

She was jealous. Jealous of her father for giving such attention to her mother, when it was she, Lucy, who would suffer the consequences of Sarah's foolishness. Why couldn't her father see that? Why didn't he say it?

In the end, Lucy could bear it no longer. With deliberate quietness she got up and went slowly to her room, secretly hoping all the time that her father would call after her, bring her back, console her as he was consoling Sarah.

But he did not; and she closed her bedroom door on the murmur of her parents' voices from the kitchen below.

An hour later, Sarah came into Lucy's room, bearing a tray with beans on toast, a glass of Coke, and three Tango biscuits.

Lucy was huddled in bed, as if from winter cold. Sarah waited for her to sit up and take the peace offering, but she remained determinedly still.

Sarah put the tray down on the bedside cabinet and paused for a moment, hoping her daughter might say the first words. But no. Sarah would have to.

Drawing in her breath, she said, 'I've bodged it, haven't I?'

Lucy gave a hint of a nod.

'I'm sorry, sweetheart.'

For Lucy to have replied in any way would have meant a deluge of tears. She froze herself against it.

Sarah stood by the bed another moment looking down at her unhappy daughter, then said, with resignation, 'Try to eat something,' bent, kissed Lucy's cheek, and went back downstairs.

Two hours later Jack came in. By then, feeling hungry, Lucy had eaten the biscuits and drunk the Coke with a rebellious kind of pleasure.

Now she was sitting up reading *Carrie's War* and finding consolation in it, as well as fellow-feeling.

Carrie, the girl in the story, sometimes felt embattled too.

Her father sat by her side on the bed and, smiling, took her hand. 'Okay?' he asked.

Lucy nodded.

'Good book?'

'Not bad.'

'Want me to read it to you?'

She shook her head.

'Want me to go away?'

She shook her head again. Managed a faint smile.

'Better,' Jack said, leaning forward and kissing her brow.

They sat in silence. Outside, dusk was falling. Framed in the window, the sun's last rays haloed the valley top. The room glowed in reflected light.

After a while, Jack said, 'It'll pass, you know. It's bad now, but it'll pass.'

'But it won't be gone by tomorrow,' Lucy said.

'No,' Jack sighed. 'Can't promise that.' After a pause, he added, 'Want to stay home for a day or two? Let things blow over.'

'No,' Lucy said. 'I've got to go.'

Jack nodded.

Lucy said, 'Why are people so awful?'

'Are they? All of them, all of the time?'

'Melanie is.'

'Maybe you only see her at her worst.'

'Why do you always take other people's side?'

'Do I?'

'You're always saying *maybe*. Maybe they didn't

368

mean it. Maybe they couldn't help it. Maybe they weren't feeling well.'

'I take your side too.'

'But you always do say maybe.'

Jack chuckled. 'Maybe because I don't believe anybody is bad all the time.'

'Not even Melanie?'

'Not even Melanie, hard enough though it is to believe.'

Lucy was rueful. 'She could have fooled me.'

'I know. Especially when you're on the receiving end. And I'm not excusing what Melanie has done, you know.'

'What are you doing then?'

'Trying to explain. Trying to understand.'

'She's rotten, that's all. Angus says she's sick.'

'Maybe.'

'There!'

They laughed.

'But maybe,' Jack said, 'well – maybe she's taking out on you something that other people have done to her.'

'Like her mother, you mean?'

'Sounds a bit like it from what your mum says.'

'Then why doesn't her dad do something? You would if Mum was horrible to me, wouldn't you?'

'Course.'

'Well, then.'

'Maybe – sorry! – but maybe her dad's as bad.'

'Or worse.'

'Think of that.'

'Yuk! I'd rather not.'

'We just don't know. That's what I mean, you see? No one ever really knows why someone is bad.'

'Not even the person herself?'

'Least of all sometimes.'

Lucy thought for a moment. 'Still doesn't make it any better.'

'No. Not for you this minute. But later maybe.'

'Maybe!'

'Two things you do know though,' Jack said.

'What?'

'Stealing won't help.'

Glum again, Lucy shook her head. 'I won't. I didn't.'

'No, I know. But I'm just saying. For the record, eh?'

'What's the second thing?'

Jack smiled. 'Something Mum learned the hard way.'

Lucy said, 'That you and she can't do much to help?'

'Right. Not at present anyway. If there's a solution – '

'I have to find it myself.'

'Afraid so.'

'I decided that yesterday.'

'Told you you knew already.'

'Apart from sticking it out till Melanie gets fed up, you mean?'

'Yes. And that's the hard thing I'm having to learn.'

'What?'

'That there comes a moment when parents can't always help their children to sort out their lives.'

'But you do try,' Lucy said with mock generosity.

Jack bowed, smiling. 'Thanks, O Queen.'

They laughed again.

'Though mind you,' Jack said, 'talking about it to Mum and me might help. A bit anyway. And we like to know what you're thinking and what's happening to you. Not to pry, but just because we love you.'

Lucy looked away, through the window at the fading sky.

'Maybe,' she said, 'I'll just get up for a while and watch TV, if that's okay.'

Jack, matter-of-fact, said, 'Good idea. Make you sleepy for the night after lazing in bed all evening.'

CHAPTER TWELVE

On Monday morning Jack drove Lucy up to the school gate as near to starting time as he could manage.

Angus was leaning against the railings as if he had been there all night.

'Sure you don't want me to come in?' Jack said.

'No thanks,' Lucy said, kissing him goodbye.

She got out and joined Angus, and they both waved as Jack drove off.

But Lucy's eyes were already searching for Melanie.

'Hasn't turned up yet,' Angus said. 'Least, I haven't seen her, and I've been here for ages.'

'Probably one of her stupid tricks,' Lucy said. Having nerved herself for a confrontation, she was on tenterhooks again, once more being made to wait and wonder while Melanie chose the moment.

The bell went.

'I was just ready for her,' Angus said, quite disgruntled.

'Me too.'

They grinned at each other.

Melanie was not in class registration either. Sally-Ann and Vicky were there, but subdued without Melanie to direct them. No one knew why she was absent – or rather, no one admitted knowing. But from the way Sally-Ann kept her head down when Mrs Harris asked, Lucy and Angus both decided she did know but was too scared to tell.

With registration over, Mrs Harris set about the day's work. She suggested that as the end of term this summer was not just the end of the term but the end of their time in this school, they might like to make a wall newspaper. It would be about their lives here – the things they remembered, some of the funnier ones, and some of the sadder ones too perhaps, though Mrs Harris hoped there hadn't been too many sad times. There could be poems, and real-life stories, and drawings. They might even like to bring photographs and include those.

'In fact, it would be the autobiography of your last five years.'

'Auto-what, miss?' Brian Webster said, to be awkward.

'*Auto* means self, Brian, as you well know, and *biography* means – ?'

'An account of a person's life,' they all called back, except Brian, of course, who was determined to appear as stupid as possible this morning, being Monday, because he knew it tried Mrs Harris's patience.

'Can we do jokes?' Roland Oliver shouted.

'Yes, Roland,' Mrs Harris said. 'I suppose you can do jokes. Though yours I can usually do without.'

General agreement on that score gave Roland considerable pleasure and his friends a chance to cheer.

'What about puzzles and quizzes and that?' Gordon Sims wanted to know.

'The puzzles and quizzes are all right,' Mrs Harris said. 'I'm not so sure about the *and that*.'

'We'll need an editor, miss,' Mary said (expecting the job for herself, Lucy thought).

'We will,' Mrs Harris said. 'But I'll deal with that high office when you've all done your author and artist work.'

Mary subsided with as much apparent enthusiasm as she could muster.

'All right, get busy,' Mrs Harris said.

There was a general stirring and a lot of chatter at first, while they sorted themselves out, and discussed ideas, and while some of them had a quiet moan at such a soppy idea. But gradually they all got started and even began to enjoy the hard work of writing and drawing rough drafts.

It was during playtime, out in the yard, that Angus brought Clare Tonks over to Lucy.

'Tell her what you just said to me,' Angus said to Clare.

Talking to Lucy but looking at Angus, Clare said, 'I was wondering what you were doing for the newspaper.'

Lucy thought, as she waited for Clare to go on: Why do I always feel she's going to roll over and flatten me to death?

'Because – ' Angus prompted.

'Because you might be writing about Prosser.'

'Prosser!' Lucy said. 'Not likely! I don't even want to talk about her, thanks very much. Why should I write about her?'

Clare said into her chest, 'So other people would know.'

'Know what?'

'What it's like.'

Lucy said, 'Write about it yourself then. You know more about what it's like than I do.'

Clare stood stock still staring at her feet.

Unable to keep quiet any longer, Angus said, 'She will if you will, that's what she wanted to say, and so will I.'

Lucy looked at them both, and pretended to laugh this off as a silly idea. But she said to Angus, 'Whatever could you write?'

'I could do the biography of a bully, like Mrs Harris said.'

'She said do *auto*biography.'

'Forget the auto,' Angus said dramatically.

'But if you wrote about her, she'd really start on you, wouldn't she? We want to stop her, not make her worse.'

'But you don't see what Clare means,' Angus said, irritated. 'Tell her, Clare.'

Clare never said anything much, in class or out,

and was plainly not keen to have a try now. She took a deep breath and let it out loudly. 'It's what I tried to tell you before, Lucy. About making fools of people. It's not the nipping and the spitting or that Vicky. Well, they hurt. But they don't matter, not really. It's making fun of you, calling you awful names, and what they say about your mother, and everybody laughing at you. That's the worst – '

She ran out of words; gave Angus a sideways look, appealing for help.

'About laughing at her,' Angus said, smiling and nodding encouragement.

Clare even smiled back. 'I just thought, if she was made to look a fool, if people laughed at her, she would know what it was like, and that might stop her.'

Lucy said nothing. Clare couldn't go on.

Angus said, 'She thought you might write something that would make people laugh at Prosser. She says you could do that, but she couldn't.'

They looked at each other. Now he had said it briefly like that, the idea no longer sounded convincing. Angus shrugged. 'Sorry, Clare. Forget it.' And he was turning away to run off and join his friends kicking a football around the field when Lucy said, 'No, Angus, wait.'

It wasn't so much that Lucy saw now exactly what to do or how to do it, but only that, as Clare and Angus were talking, everything she had worried about and suffered over the last few days, and all her thoughts about how to deal with Melanie, seemed to fall into place. Like a jigsaw puzzle you've stared at for ages that suddenly makes sense, and you realize how the pieces fit together.

For Lucy the important piece that made all the other pieces fit was Angus's notes. Of all that Melanie had done, her threat to display the notes was the worst. Lucy had given money, ashamed of doing so though she had been, just to avoid this happening. And she would have gone on giving presents to stop it, if Melanie hadn't got rid of the notes on Saturday.

Angus's notes would have been on view for everyone to see and laugh at day after day. Everyone would have known; that was the point. Things put in writing for everybody to see were different from things that were only spoken.

'Clare's right,' Lucy said. Clare blinked in surprise. 'But it isn't just making them laugh. And it can't be just me. Not just the three of us. That won't stop Prosser. It has to be everybody.'

'Everybody!' Angus said, knowing how hopeless that would be to manage.

'Well, not *everybody*, but enough of us who Prosser has bullied to write about what she's done. What she is. And put it all in the newspaper. Then everybody will know.'

'They know already,' Angus said.

'But not that way. She picks on us one at a time, doesn't she? And no one ever tells, not to us all at once. And we don't ever do anything about her all at once.'

'But how is writing about it any different?' Angus said.

'Because nobody has to take her on in a fight that way. It isn't bullying – like you said on Saturday. It's not bullying to write down what happened to you, is it? Writing it down, I mean, so that everybody can read it. But Prosser would hate it, I just know she would. I would if I was her.'

'Me as well,' Clare said. She was getting so excited she was weaving back and forth.

Angus said, catching on, 'And if Olly did some of his jokes, and Gordon did some of his puzzles, and we get kids from other classes to come and look, Prosser wouldn't hear the last of it, would she?'

'That's what I mean, that's what I meant!' Clare said, and, unable to bear the excitement any longer, had to rush off to the toilet.

The bell went for end of playtime.

'Trouble is,' Lucy said as she and Angus walked into school, 'none of the others will listen to me.'

Angus said, 'They'll listen to Mary though.'

Lucy nodded and sighed; a problem already.

'We'll just have to get her to join in,' Angus said.

Lucy shook her head. 'Don't think she would, just for me.' And she added a little regretfully, 'She might if you asked her with me though.'

Angus grinned at her with a glance that betrayed a hint of triumph. 'Okay,' he said. 'We'll grab her in a minute.'

They cornered Mary as soon as everyone was settled to work again.

'If it's about Mrs Harris's present,' Mary said, 'I've got money from nearly everybody now. You could buy it this weekend, I expect.'

'It's something else,' Angus said, acting as go-between a little too keenly, Lucy felt. 'We've got this idea.'

'About Melanie,' Lucy said, jumping in before Angus could blurt everything out.

'She was rotten to you the other day,' Mary said.

'We think she should be stopped,' Angus said.

'What he means is,' Lucy said quickly, 'that it isn't fair what she does. Making fun of people and taking things from kids, and – and – ' She could not bring herself to say the word.

'Shoplifting,' Angus said straightly.

Mary glanced up to see if Mrs Harris had heard. But she was over at the other side of the room helping Colin Langport who was always needing help.

'What's your idea?' she asked cautiously.

Between them Lucy and Angus explained. 'Really show Prosser up,' Angus said when they had done.

Mary shook her head. 'Don't like it. Naming her, I mean. It would be like telling.'

'But why not?' Angus said, indignant. 'Why should she get away with it? Look what she's done to stacks of kids this year. And it wouldn't be telling, just describing. That's different.'

'If you want to do it, go on, do it,' Mary said. 'But I won't.' She looked at Lucy. 'It's a great idea, Lucy, but sorry.'

'It won't work without you,' Angus said.

'Well, I won't join in if you put names.'

'Well, we can't do it without saying who it is, can we?'

Lucy said, 'Yes, we can.' She had been thinking hard. 'It can be a game. We all write about Melanie *without* saying who we mean, but so anybody who thinks about it knows who it must be.'

'Puzzles?' Angus said. 'Mysteries? Guess-who jokes?'

Lucy nodded.

'Would you go along with that?' Angus said to Mary.

Mary thought for a moment, then, smiling, said, 'Sure. That would be fun.'

By the end of the morning Angus had – without too much difficulty – recruited Roland and Gordon. Lucy had started on her 'Guess Who?' biography and had managed to persuade Samantha Ling and Hyacinth Johnson to write something as well because they were friends of hers.

Mary had quietly gone round some of the others who had been on the receiving end of Melanie's attentions and talked them into doing something. She had even had a chat with Mrs Harris and convinced her that part of the newspaper should be what Mary called a 'Feature Special' on bullying.

'Sounds depressing to me,' Mrs Harris said. 'And we don't get much of it here, do we?'

'Not much,' Mary said. 'But sometimes. And a few of us thought there should be something about it, because it is part of school life, isn't it? Just like in that book you read us last term.'

'I remember,' Mrs Harris said. 'But that was quite funny, wasn't it?'

'Well, we'll be having jokes and puzzles,' Mary said, 'so it won't be terrible or anything.'

'I should think that would be all right then,' Mrs Harris said. 'Nothing unpleasant though, and you can be editor of that section, seeing it's your idea.'

At the end of the day Mrs Harris said, 'We're getting on very well. All sorts of surprises in store. Finish what you're doing for homework, and we'll put the newspaper up tomorrow.'

That evening Angus came to Lucy's house after tea and they worked together on their contributions.

They told Sarah and Jack this was secret homework, and that they would show the results later in the week.

Happy that Lucy was more like her old self again, Sarah left them to get on uninterrupted.

There was certainly plenty of laughter coming from the dining room, where they were working. Which, had any of them known it, would be an odd contrast with events at school next day.

CHAPTER THIRTEEN

Extracts from a wall newspaper by Class 4H

??? GUESS WHO ???

She has a habit of biting her finger nails, kicking, pinching, blackmailing & pulling hair. *Mary Gardiner.*

?

SHE HAS A GANG. THIS GANG HAS 2 IN IT AS WELL AS HERSELF (= 3). THE OTHER 2 ARE VERY FUNNY (U DON'T SAY!!!) AND SILLY-AND-SOPPY (IF U KNOW WHAT I MEAN). *Angus Burns.*

?

She bullies people by making them do her homework and makes you bring presents for her every day and she likes to make you cry. Her hobbies are pulling hair, taking people's things, demanding presents, telling rude lies. She has long dark hair she sometimes chews when she is working. She is clever and good at maths and soon will be twelve and is five feet tall. Lucy Hall.

?

Her hobbies with me are pulling my earings and smashing my glasses. Priscilla Moulton.

?

She comes to school very early and creeps into class and leaves nasty things in other children's boxes, like spiders and slugs and many other horrible things. She also takes posseshions from other children. *Samantha Ling.*

?

She called me bootpolish and made her gang try to wash me off in the toilet and made some others write stuff on the walls about me which said Go Home. But this is where I live. Hyacinth Johnson.

?

She is tall and I watched her saunter through the playground in her skin tight jeans with her frilly blouse with gold sequins and her wine colour swade boots. Her long brown hair was frizzed (it isn't any more) and she had eye shadow on (which Mr Hunt banned – hate hate). I saw the dominating figure coming towards me. I felt a tug pull me backwards. Her friend had hold of my hair. (I wish my mum wouldn't put ribbons in then maybe she wouldn't notice me.) 'Your gonna do my classroom duties, arn't ya.' 'Yes' I said and with that her friend twisted my arm and all three of them stalked off like chuffed lions. *Maxine Blair.*

?

SHE RUNS AWFULLY FAST AND ITS IMPOSSIBLE TO GET AWAY FROM HER. SHE IS A PERFECT NUSANCE. SHE HAS GREEN EYES A BIG MOUTH AND SHE IS AWFULLY TALL FOR HER AGE. SOMETIMES SHE WEARS A MINISKIRT AND A T SHIRT AND A JACKET AND SOME OF THE LADS WHISTLE AT HER (BUT NOT ME!!) *Gordon Sims.*

?

Joke (By Roland Oliver, the World's Greatest Comedian)
Q: What did one bully say to the other bully?
A: I get a kick out of you.

?

FATE
A Puzzle Poem
by Clare Tonks

Many a time I've come to school
Eager for the day ahead. But there,
Leaning on the gate, a bully waits
Alone with her two friends.
No one can ever escape them,
I know that for sure. Then,
Eagerness, like mist, soon vanishes,
Puffed away by fear, when,
Round behind the cycle shed,
Orders are given for your fate:
    'See you've prezzies for us tomorrow,
    See they are just like new,
    Else we'll give you something really nasty.
    Remember, we've got our claws in you.'

CHAPTER FOURTEEN

'I said no names!' Mary was brittle with anger.

Angus said, grinning, 'It's not names. It's a puzzle.'

'Rubbish,' Mary said. 'Everybody can see. Even Mrs Harris will.'

'Tell Clare,' Lucy said. 'It's her poem. She must have stuck it up after we'd all gone out.'

'Anyway,' Angus said, 'I think it's a terrific poem. Wish I could do something as good.'

'Didn't know she had it in her,' Lucy said.

Mary was haughty. 'She better look out when Prosser sees it, that's all.'

'*If* she sees it,' Angus said. 'She's not back yet.'

'Won't work if she doesn't,' Lucy said. 'Then we'll have wasted all that effort.'

Mary, knowing everything, could not help saying, 'She fell off her bike. Sally-Ann told me. They kept her home to make sure she's okay.'

'Serves her right,' Angus said and left them to join his friends who were giggling and pointing at the 'Special Feature' in the newspaper, which had a title made by Angus in large letters at the top:

BULLIES

'Fell off her bike?' Lucy said. She had to sit down; a sudden terrible guilt made her feel weak.

Please, God, she prayed, you didn't did you? I'll never, ever pray for anyone to fall off anything again, if you'll only make Melanie all right.

She felt dizzy at the prospect that God might actually have been listening all the time. She wondered what else He might have heard that she would rather He hadn't.

Half an hour later Melanie arrived.

'Good heavens, Melanie, what have you done to yourself?' Mrs Harris exclaimed.

Melanie had a fierce black-and-blue bruise circling one eye and a large dressing plastered over her forehead.

She handed Mrs Harris a letter.

The wall newspaper lost its interest at once, of course; all eyes were fixed on Melanie. There were surreptitious mutterings at the sight of her.

Meanwhile, Mrs Harris shook her head sorrowfully as she read, and then announced briskly: 'Melanie met with an accident. But apparently her wounds are only superficial.' She inspected Melanie at close quarters. 'Though I must say, you do look dreadful, dear.'

'I'm all right!' Melanie said sharply enough to make Mrs Harris bridle.

'Are you sure?'

Melanie nodded sheepishly, and, looking away, caught sight of the newspaper, picking out at once,

Lucy noticed, Angus's headline: BULLIES. But she turned away pretending not to have seen.

Mrs Harris said, 'Very well. But perhaps we'd better let you take things quietly today.'

As soon as Melanie was settled in her place, Sally-Ann, perking up, whispered, 'Have you seen what they've done?'

'Your name and all,' Vicky said. 'Need sorting, they do. A few throat chops.'

'Wait till you read it,' Sally-Ann said with smug satisfaction. 'You'll just die.'

Melanie ignored them, giving such a good performance of being relaxed, offhand, unaware, that everyone could see she was acting.

'There!' Lucy called to Angus as they sped into the playground after lunch. 'Making straight for Clare. Told you!'

They ran and caught up just as Melanie said, 'You put them up to this, didn't you, fatso!'

'No!' Clare said with a new defiance.

'Liar. And it's your poem, isn't it, and it has my name in.'

'Leave her alone,' Lucy said, pushing between them.

At the same time, Angus was shouting, 'Olly, Gordon, Sam, Hyacinth!' and waving them over.

Sally-Ann and Vicky let go of Clare to deal with Lucy. But she struggled, and slipped, and found herself sitting down with a bump. The other two, empty-handed, didn't know what to do, so turned their attentions back to Clare. Which made Lucy realize what an advantage it was being on the ground.

'Sit!' she shouted at Clare, who only stared back, not comprehending. 'Sit!' Lucy yelled, sounding as bad as the awful woman on television who barked at dogs.

Obediently, unthinking, Clare sat, plonk, as if her legs had been knocked from under her. Sally-Ann and Vicky fumbled, trying to force her up; but Clare was dead weight, even for Vicky.

'Get up!' Melanie bellowed.

But by now Angus and the others were crowding round, distracting her. She surveyed them in a rapid turn, and forced a grin. 'Ganging up, is it,' she said.

Angus, seeing what Lucy was up to (or down to) said, 'We're not ganging up on anybody, Prosser,' and he jack-knifed, sitting cross-legged on the ground. 'I'm just watching the show.' He looked up at Roland and Sam and the others.

'Yeah,' they said catching on, 'yeah, we're just sitting here to watch what you're doing.' And they joined Lucy and Angus, sitting on the ground in a circle round Melanie.

Lucy leaned back on her hands, feeling exhilarated at the turn of events: Melanie was not at all comfortable with what was going on. 'What were you saying, Melanie dear?' she said.

'Terrific poem, eh?' Angus said. 'Clare's I mean.'

Sally-Ann screeched, 'Go and crawl back down your hole, Burns!'

'Shut it!' Melanie said. 'Can't you see what they're trying to do?'

Sally-Ann apparently couldn't; her brow furrowed.

Lucy said, '*We're* not doing anything. You're the one who's doing things.'

It was an odd sight: Melanie, Sally-Ann and Vicky standing in a triangle, almost back to back, surrounded by a circle of five or six lounging on the ground. Other kids, curious, came wandering across. 'What's on?' they asked. 'Another of Mel's shows?' So a second larger crowd was very soon standing round the first. But everyone was unaccustomedly quiet. Nothing seemed to be happening, yet plainly something was. Or was going to.

For a start, no one could mistake that Melanie was seething with fury. Not just angry. But raging. And all her rage was churning inside her like steam locked inside a boiler. The bruise round her eye had turned a vivid, glowing purple; her mouth became a tight, lipless line across her face.

Lucy, sitting in range of Melanie's feet, wondered if she might lose her temper and lash out.

'I'll get you, Tonks!' Melanie said. 'Pukey and Burns won't be with you all the time.'

'Maybe not, Prosser,' Lucy said, 'but every time you do anything to one of us, we're going to put something up about it on the wall. We'll keep *notes* about your bullying, and let *everybody* read them.'

'Yeah,' Angus added, 'even if it's just the names of kids you pick on.'

390

After which, to everyone's surprise, Clare said, 'And we'll list the presents you take.'

'That's right,' Lucy said. 'A list of names, a list of things you do, and a list of things you *steal*.'

'Where everybody can read them,' Angus said.

A silence hung in the air. Melanie looked from one to the next.

Then her rage exploded: the boiler burst, and she screamed with a force that made them all flinch: 'You dare! You just dare!'

Her body was rigid, her fists, clenched, beat against her thighs.

Only Angus managed to reply. 'Why?' he shouted back. 'What'll you do? Take us all on? Make us all shoplift? Not all of us at once, you can't. And we'll be watching. And whatever you do, we'll still write the lists.'

Melanie glared at him with deep loathing. 'I'll show you if I care about your stupid notes!' she said hissing at him like a cornered animal. 'I'll show you what I think of her poem, and your pukey newspaper.' She turned, taking them all in. 'I'll show you what I think of all you CREEPS!'

And she set off, like a runner from starting blocks, scattering bodies out of her way, sprinting through the crowd and across the playground towards the school door.

Lucy and Angus scrambled to their feet, Clare struggling up after them.

'She's making for our room,' Lucy said.

Others had thought of this too and were already

racing, first after Melanie, then, realizing they might get stopped inside, swinging towards the windows of 4H's classroom, whose blank eyes were open against the heat.

Lucy and Angus chased after, Clare pounding along behind.

Sally-Ann and Vicky could not at once decide what to do: follow Melanie, stay where they were, or follow the crowd. But finding themselves alone, hesitated no longer and dashed off after the others.

Lucy, Angus and Clare reached the windows as Melanie came panting into the room. From outside, they watched as she crashed through chairs and against tables, scattering belongings and half-finished work and interrupted books. She made straight for the wall newspaper, reaching out as she got to it, and clawing at Angus's bold headline. She tore at it. BULLIES came ripping down in a streamer of wounded letters. Melanie tore it again and again and again, shredding it into confetti that she scattered around her feet.

Then she reached up again and again in a fever of passion so violent it quite took Lucy's breath away. She ripped and tore and shredded: the Guess Who descriptions, the jokes and puzzles and finally Clare's poem.

Clare's poem sent her into the climax of fury. She ripped it into smaller and smaller pieces, panting, crying, grunting as she did so.

And then, coming to the window, she tossed the

pieces out at Lucy and Angus and Clare on whose heads they fell like ragged snowflakes.

'That's what I care!' she tried to shout, but had no breath for it. 'That's what I care!'

And Lucy and Angus and Clare, the rest of the school crowding round, watched with silent, saddened faces.

CHAPTER FIFTEEN

No one saw Melanie again that term. She had been taken for an early holiday, Mrs Harris said; but Sally-Ann babbled about Melanie being sent to a foster home because of trouble with her dad.

'He do poke her in the eye again,' Vicky said, laughing.

'Serves her right,' Angus said, but felt ashamed.

The Saturday before end of term Lucy and Angus met Mary in town and they chose Mrs Harris's present. Lucy already knew what she wanted to buy but guessed that Mary would like to be consulted.

'What about a set of felt tips for marking?' Lucy said.

'Uses gallons of red on me every day,' Angus said.

At the stationer's they picked out three: a red, a green and a black, each with a new kind of tip. They were so cheap there was money left for something else.

'Have you a tray for keeping the pens, please?' Lucy asked.

'How about this?' the assistant said. 'There's a

place for paper clips, and for an eraser, and the pens rest here.'

Lucy and Angus exchanged startled looks.

'That'll be just right,' Mary said, taking charge again.

There was a party on the last day. Mrs Harris was delighted with her present. 'You've been a pleasure to teach,' she said, sniffling.

No one even mentioned Melanie, but Lucy couldn't help remembering. To cheer herself up she looked again at the note clutched in her hand. She had found it a few minutes ago stuck to an ice-cream Angus had brought her.

W8 4 U RLY XING 1630 A xxx

The Adventure Series by Willard Price

Read these exciting stories about Hal and Roger Hunt and their search for wild animals. Out now in paperback from Red Fox at £3.50

Amazon Adventure

Hal and Roger find themselves
abandoned and alone in the
Amazon Jungle when a mission
to explore unchartered territory
of the Pastaza River goes off course...
0 09 918221 1

Volcano Adventure

A scientific study of the volcanoes
of the Pacific with world famous
volcanologist, Dr Dan Adams,
erupts into an adventure of a
lifetime for Hal and Roger....
0 09 918241 6

Underwater Adventure

The intrepid Hunts have joined forces
with the Oceanographic Institute to
study sea life, collect specimens and
follow a sunken treasure ship trail...
0 09 918231 9

South Sea Adventure

Hal and Roger can't resist the offer
of a trip to the South Seas in search
of a creature known as the
Nightmare of the Pacific...
0 09 918251 3

Arctic Adventure

Olrik the eskimo and his bear,
Nanook, join Hal and Roger on
their trek towards the polar ice cap.
And with Zeb the hunter hot on
their trail the temperature soon turns
from cold to murderously chilling...
0 09 918321 8

Safari Adventure

Tsavo national park has become
a death trap. Can Hal and Roger
succeed in their mission of liberating
it from the clutches of a Blackbeard's
deadly gang of poachers?...
0 09 918341 2

African Adventure

On safari in African big-game
country, Hal and Roger coolly tackle
their brief to round up a mysterious
man-eating beast. Meanwhile, a
merciless band of killers follow in
their wake...
0 09 918371 4

Elephant Adventure

Danger levels soar with the
temperature for Hal and Roger as they
embark upon a journey to the equator,
charged with the task of finding an
extremely rare white elephant...
0 09 918331 5

It's wild! It's dangerous! And it's out there!

Other great reads  *from* **Red Fox**

Top new fiction

LETTERS OF A LOVESTRUCK TEENAGER
Claire Robertson

'I'm Gilly Freeborn and I'm nearly fourteen and I've got problems . . .' Her chest is as flat as a pancake, her sister's a mean, selfish man-eating piranha, her best friend's turned traitor and – *argh!* – she's fallen in love with The Vision. What's a girl to do? Turn to Alexa Deehart of course, agony aunt of *The Bizz* magazine . . .

0 09 94252 1   £3.99

SWITCHERS
Kate Thompson

Tess is a Switcher – she can change shape to become any animal she chooses. She always thought she was unique, but not any more. Tess meets another Switcher, Kevin, and together they have powers they never dreamed of . . .

0 09 925612 6   £3.99

MIDNIGHT'S CHOICE
Kate Thompson

With Kevin gone, Tess is feeling ever more lonely and isolated from everyone around her. Then she senses a call to which she has no resistance, and finds herself in the middle of a dilemma. For now she has found a new friend, and has a very difficult decision to make – a choice to change her life forever.

0 09 925613 4   £3.99

CHILD OF THE MAY
Theresa Tomlinson

No one is ever going to crush fiery Magda's independent streak. She yearns for the thrill of adventure and when her chance comes . . . she's going to take it. This stirring sequel to The Forest Wife continues Theresa Thomlinson's compelling account of life amongst the outlaws in Robin Hood's Sherwood Forest.

0 09 969231 7   £3.99

THE BORDERLANDS SEQUENCE

ANN COBURN

*B*e *warned: where the edges of past and present merge and the borders of time blur... expect the unexpected.*

Four very different buddies: Alice, Frankie, David and Michael, have one thing in common - photography. But their passion for cameras is developing into a very dangerous hobby...

1 WORM SONGS   ISBN 0 09 964311 1   £2.99

2 WEB WEAVER   ISBN 0 09 964321 9   £3.50

3 DARK WATER   ISBN 0 09 964331 6   £3.50

THE BORDERLANDS SEQUENCE by Ann Coburn
Out now in paperback from Red Fox